Dreaming in Egypt

The Story of Asenath and Joseph

Maria Isabel Pita

ISBN: 978-1537145150

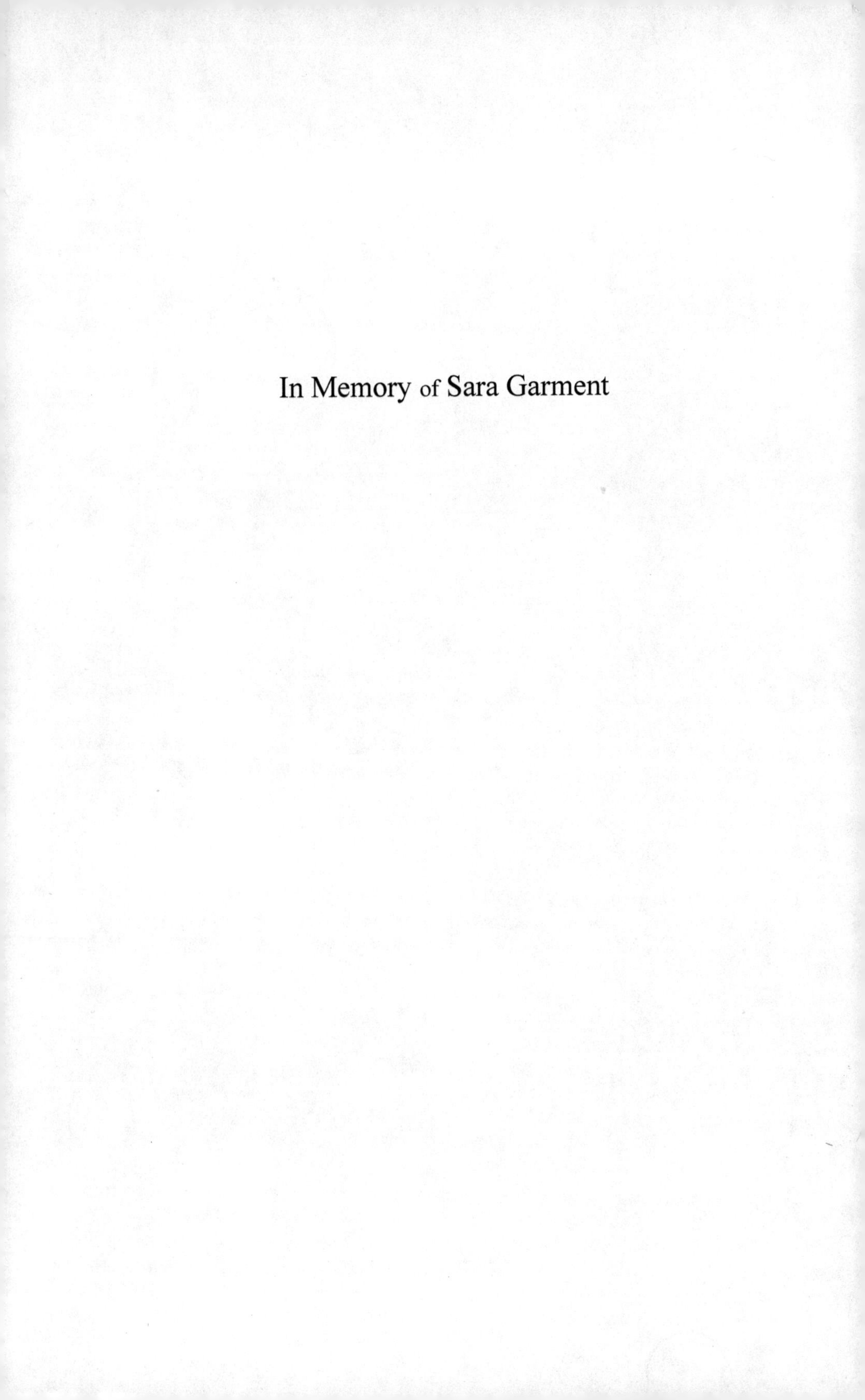

In Memory of Sara Garment

Biblical: On, Egypt

Ancient Egyptian: Iuno, Kemet

c. 1897 B.C.

Chapter 1

Asenath stood looking up at the sky with both hands shielding her eyes. Almost directly above her, a large falcon was hovering high up, just beneath the blinding sun. She was wondering what it could possibly be doing all the way up there so far away from where all its prey was. Maybe it was no ordinary falcon but the god himself looking down at her? There was no doubt he could see her—for he could see all the world below him—but was it possible he knew who she was and actually cared about her? Then, as though catching a divine wind she could not feel on the ground, the great bird began gliding swiftly across the sky away from her. Wistfully, she followed its effortless flight until the power of her vision reached its limit.

Disappointed, she lowered her hands. She felt strangely bereft, as if the god had caught her heart as easily as a falcon catches a mouse. Or had she only imagined the mysterious communion between them? The thrilling magic of the moment was already fading, giving way to the echo of Nanny's most recent outburst that morning, "By Re's secret name, Asenath, what are you thinking about? You look like a vulture brooding over the eggs of your dreams, and you're barely seven harvests old!" But Nanny's affection was usually as sweet and clingy as a honey cake, and although sometimes her reproaches were unpleasantly hot, Asenath knew they burned with love—a love she could not imagine life without. If the gods decided to take her nurse away, she feared the emptiness inside her would feel much worse than hunger. Because what could she possibly eat that would fill her heart the way Nanny's love did?

"Asenath!?" Her name suddenly soared across the garden on the invisible wings of her nurse's voice. "Your mother's brother has crossed the threshold! Do not keep him waiting!"

"I'm coming!" she cried. "Swift as a gazelle!"

"Be careful! You do not wish to break a leg!"

Sprinting fearlessly along the stone path, she ignored the warning. When a twisted finger of green light flashed across the path in front of her and disappeared beneath a bush, she ran even faster. By the time the house came into view, her heart was beating against the inside of her chest so furiously, she had to stop to let it calm down. She walked the rest of the way to the colorfully painted hieroglyph of walls, lintels and doorways spelling life, love, and safety.

Nanny breathed, "Hathor help me!" as she clutched her wrist and pulled her into the house.

Normally, Asenath welcomed the refreshing shade of the entrance foyer, but her heart still felt cold from coming so perilously close to a snake, and this intangible discomfort, combined with the sharp sensation of Nanny's grip, prompted her to cry, "You're hurting me!" as she pulled her arm free.

"There you are!" A man's voice declared cheerfully. "Ready

to go, duckling?"

"Yes!" she cried, embracing all she could of her uncle's thick waist.

"Then let's give a road to our feet. It's not every day you get to meet a new Herald of Re."

☼

Asenath was so proud of her father, she tended to lose her voice whenever they neared the temple where he reigned as the high priest of Re. Her tongue hid behind her closed lips like a mouse as the two seated massive stone lions guarding the entrance to the Mansion of Atum-Re came into view—golden beasts with the heads of smiling men. Peering awestruck between the curtains of their litter, it always came as a relief to her when they turned away from the giant paws, between which two obelisks rose up into the sky like solid shafts of light as their gold plated surfaces reflected the sun's power.

Their litter was set down before the temple's private entrance, where attendants greeted them in a chilly dark foyer that felt almost magically invigorating after the mundane heat outside. She invariably got goosebumps when water was poured over her bare feet and hands, which were then dried with clean linen towels.

As soon as they were properly purified, her uncle took her hand, and she walked beside him down a short passage into her father's private apartments. Letting go of her in order to raise both his hands with palms facing outward toward the high priest, Potifer Setka said in his most resonant voice, "Life, health and strength to you, Potiphera Meketre."

Nodding silently, the high priest said formally, "Please refresh yourselves." Then he grinned down at his daughter, who already stood beside a table on which rested a large platter of pastries artfully stacked in the form of a step pyramid. Another table was crowded with slender jugs she knew held water and wine, beer and fruit juices.

Entertained by the game of not toppling the pyramid as she sniffed out the pastries she liked best, Asenath listened to the conversation between the two men, savoring it in a different way. Words had no substance, yet they satisfied a different kind of hunger inside her.

"Finally!" her uncle sighed, pouring himself a cup of wine. "It took long enough."

"Yes. An utterly black coat, with no markings whatsoever. He is physically magnificent and also intelligent. He will make a good oracle."

Popping a whole pastry into his mouth, Setka chewed as he spoke, "All... of... Kemet... rejoices!" He raised his wine cup. "To the late Nubkaure's Golden Souls, and to his son, Senwosret Khakheperre, the Soul of Re Come into Being, and to Men-Wer, the Ba of Re! Has he met his wives yet?"

"No."

Asenath looked at her uncle. "His wives?"

"Hathor and Iusaas," he grinned at her. "Two fat beautiful cows worthy of embodying the goddesses!"

She had only eaten seven pastries before the servant of the god assigned to escort them into the presence of Men-Wer arrived, and her father sent them on their way. This was normal. She could not remember a time when he did not always have other people to meet with. Unlike the solar disc, Re's high priest was not always free to greet his wife and daughter in the morning, or to say goodnight to them in the evening. As they left his presence now, Asenath understood abruptly that she was always missing her father. She almost welcomed the blow of the afternoon heat outside that, for the moments it took her to get used to it, made it difficult to think, and by then she and her uncle were leaning against the fence overlooking the pasture belonging to the great bull of Iuno.

Potifer Setka said proudly, "Behold the embodiment of Re, Asenath."

The sacred bull had spotted them approaching and stood looking directly at them from a short distance away. Its sleek coat was intensely black, and as she stared at it, the animal began looking strangely unreal to her, almost like a bull-shaped cutout in the green, brown and blue fabric of pasture, desert and sky. Curiously, she stopped herself from blinking, and as her eyes watered from the strain, the great black bull of Re became a portal opening onto a night sky empty of stars.

If Re had not risen and filled the darkness with light, there would be nothing. She thought. *And yet how can everything come from nothing?*

The bull snorted, nodded vigorously three times while pawing the ground with its right front paw, and charged toward them.

Her uncle quickly caught her up in his arms and backed away from the fence as a circle of young men seemed to sprout up from the ground and surrounded the animal. Two carried coils of thick white rope while the others held long cattle prods. Mer-Wer, however, had already come to a stop and, lowering his head, begun munching placidly on the grass.

Feeling the tension in her uncle's body ease as he set her down, Asenath understood he had been afraid of the bull. She too had been afraid for an instant, but mainly she felt thrilled that the Herald of Re had apparently let her know he was aware of her thoughts by nodding his head three times before running straight toward her. If he had really meant to hurt her, he would not have stopped before he reached them. She knew he had not been angry with her, and she could see now that he was feeling quite content. Even the lazy swish of his tail keeping flies away looked pleased.

"It's all right, duckling, he couldn't have hurt you," her uncle assured her. "The servants of the god allow Men-Wer his freedom, but he is always under their supervision and control."

She looked up at him in surprise. "Then how can he be god?"

As though wondering how best to reply, Setka gazed over at

the bull.

Becoming aware of a dull ache, Asenath looked down at her right hand. There was blood on the tip of her index finger. She must have scraped it on the fence when her uncle yanked her away from it. Oddly fascinated, she watched curiously as a fresh drop of blood welled up from within her like a darkly shining gem the color of the River when it overflowed its banks.

"You've cut yourself," her uncle observed. "I'll take you home now."

Chapter 2

As the moon waxed and waned—the luminous Eye of Horus opening to its fullest in the night sky before slowly beginning to close again—Asenath kept remembering the day of the bull and the snake.

She had never really paid attention to the small bowls of fresh milk servants placed in out of the way corners throughout the house, but every time she entered a room now that was the first thing she saw.

"Not all serpents are evil," Nanny explained to her. "Some snakes help the household cats kill the mice that would otherwise eat our grain, so we offer them milk in gratitude, and to encourage them to remain with us."

Asenath said nothing. The fact remained—she no longer felt quite as carefree in the garden. She had even begun checking the sun dappled depths of the pool before diving in. So far, she had spotted only frogs sitting on the blue tiles painted with white lotus flowers, and there was no reason to be afraid of frogs. Yet she was uncomfortably aware of having lost something she once possessed in pure abundance.

When she attempted to tell her mother how she was feeling, Sadeh said, "You have seen the golden scales of Maat on the temple walls and how they are always perfectly level with each other. You are simply becoming more like Re's daughter,

Asenath, learning to balance pleasure with caution, fear with courage. This is a good thing. Now run along and enjoy yourself and stop worrying about snakes."

Her mother's encouragement was like a balm applied to her invisible wound. She soon stopped being afraid that every sudden glimmer of motion was a snake in disguise. What she began feeling more strongly was how much her heart longed to grow in strength and wisdom, even if the process was not entirely pleasant.

☼

"Psssst!"

The hissing sound had come from somewhere behind a row of water jugs lining one side of the inner courtyard. Smiling, Asenath propped her wooden doll against a column and walked toward it.

"There are slave traders out by the cattle pens!" Kyky whispered from her hiding place, staring eagerly up at her with the intense little brown eyes that had earned her the nickname Monkey. "The Mistress is there with Potifer Setka's wife! Do you want to come outside and watch with me? I know the perfect place to hide!"

Asenath suddenly felt uncomfortable, perhaps because she knew Nanny disapproved of her fondness for Kyky. "Not really," she murmured.

"Oh please! It will be fun to try and guess which slaves the gods will favor by uniting them with your great house!"

Kyky's primary task was to gather dung from the cattle fields and shape it into patties for the cooking fires. If she was content with her lot, surely the rest of the staff must be even happier. Her heart warmed by the compliment to her family, Asenath smiled down at the earnest little face. "Very well!"

They were soon crouching side by side on the roof of a storage building. Running along the edges, a knee-high wall of whitewashed mud brick, still warm from the sun, helped to conceal them. Far away across the River, the sun was sinking toward the desert mountains, and overhead the sky was growing pale.

Through one side of a pavilion erected not far below them, they had a good view of the Lady Tarset sitting in a gilded wooden chair. The hard edges of her profile were somewhat softened by the lush wig she favored, its two long black plates, composed of hundreds of fine braids, hanging down over her floral collar. Her thin lips were painted a bright red, and although the quantity of kohl framing her brown eyes lightened them to the color of honey, there was nothing sweet about their expression. Asenath had never thought much about her uncle's wife, who she saw only on formal occasions, but this evening she decided that she did not much like this woman and her cold little smile.

The Lady Tarset blocked their view of the Mistress of the House, whose much finer beauty Asenath was wonderfully familiar with. She had once overheard her father making fun of harpists who compared beautiful women to lotus flowers as he told his wife that her skin was much softer, and her presence an infinitely more sublime perfume filling his heart with the divine fragrance of love itself. Wholeheartedly agreeing that her mother was the most beautiful woman in Kemet, Asenath focused on the tall figure of Nebt, their domestic administrator. She was standing behind her mistress' chair, and as she bent over to whisper something in Sadeh's ear, a breeze wafted the sweet scent of perfumed oils and bees' wax up to their rooftop.

The open pavilion was flanked at all four corners by young men of the house guard who stood perfectly still with their arms at their sides. The white shendyts wrapped around their hips fell to mid thigh, and were held up by two white sashes crisscrossing their bare chests and backs. Two old scribes, sitting cross legged on a mat near her mother's feet, recorded the transactions.

Abruptly, a stronger gust of wind brought with it the unpleasant odor of unclean human flesh. Reluctantly, Asenath looked away from the beautiful order of the pavilion, her eyes following Nebt as she approached the foreign merchants. The three men wore coarsely woven ankle length robes the color of sand decorated with dark-green bands of color at the hem, and at the edges of the long loose sleeves. A great quantity of fabric was also wrapped around their heads. Noticing that the skin around their mouths was noticeably lighter than the rest of their sun-browned faces, Asenath realized they had been obliged to shave off their dirty beards before being allowed into the presence of noble women.

Huddled sullenly together behind their masters—like a flock of human fowl caught in an invisible net—were a handful of women. A single man stood a little apart from the group, and as she stared at him, Asenath suffered the impression he was even farther away from her than the solar disc as it prepared for its journey through the darkness. He wore a threadbare robe of no definable color that was too small for him, tight across the chest and barely falling to his knees. The garment clearly did not belong to him, and she found herself wondering how he had lost his own robe. It must have been taken away from him by the slave traders. But why?

A crow flying by seemed to angrily echo her question, "Why! Why! Why!" and as the male slave looked up at the bird sacred to Neith—the goddess for whom she was named—Asenath realized with a shock that he was just as aware of everything as she was. Watching his eyes follow the bird's flight, an emotion seized her that was so large and heavy she could not fit it into her thoughts. The feeling was mysteriously forced down into her heart, and she gasped at the sudden pressure in her chest. She had to look away from him. But when her eyes fell on Potifer Setka's wife instead, the sight brought her no relief because Tarset was also staring at the male slave. It was impossible then not to look back at him, and now she noticed the gentle wave in his black hair, which was long enough to rest on his shoulders.

Kyky's whisper was barely audible, “I'm guessing the Lady Tarset will buy the man!”

Even though she felt there were much more important questions, Asenath heard herself asking, “How old do you think he is?”

“Well... his beard is still trying hard to grow... his arms and legs are too thin for his shoulders... I'm guessing he's a few years shy of twenty.”

Kyky was so small and thin, it was easy for Asenath to forget she was three years older. Maybe that was why she seemed to know a great deal more than she herself did about subjects not covered in the Wisdom Texts. “Monkey... what do you think he did wrong?”

“What makes you think he did anything wrong? Fate is fate... See, I was right!”

Asenath looked back down at Tarset. The lady was holding her right thumb erect, and her female attendant responded to the signal by bending over her. After listening for a moment, her aunt's domestic administrator approached the slave traders, passing Nebt on her way back to the pavilion.

Kyky murmured, “I'm guessing the one with the strong arms will be the new grinding girl. The tall pretty one will be the new housemaid.”

One of the traders was separating two of the women from the

group while his companions negotiated with Lady Tarset's administrator. Asenath studied the two female slaves who would soon belong to her family. All these people had suffered the misfortune of being born beyond the Paths of Horus, in the barbaric lands where people did not worship Maat, who personally protected all of Re's children. Yet as she focused again on the male slave, she thought that maybe Re's daughter, while traveling with her father across the sky, had caught sight of this young man and—for some reason known only to her divine mind—chosen to spread her protective wings over him, delivering him safely to Kemet and a position in Potifer Setka's household. The young man's body obediently faced the pavilion but his head was turned away from it. Because she had watched his eyes as they followed the crow's flight, she knew he was looking at something invisible to her now. He stood so still, she was reminded of the wooden doll she had left propped up against a column. Before running outside with Kyky, she had been engrossed in one of her favorite games, the one in which she was grown up and being admired by everyone at Pharaoh's court. It had seemed so real and exciting while she was playing, but now it felt less substantial than a dream as she stared at the slave's arms hanging limp at his sides, powerless as a doll's. What did it feel like to be standing there so far away from home, dirty, smelling, and wearing some other person's old robe? He was all alone and being sold as a slave, but he could not simply set his life aside as she had her doll. He could not stop being part of this game he obviously did not want to play, even though the story of his life had become no fun at all.

"Yesss!" Kyky hissed triumphantly. "I was right. The Lady Tarset has bought him."

In a single heartbeat, Asenath felt both glad and angry. She could not explain the anger, but it was easy to understand why she was happy—because she did not doubt that in Potifer Setka's household slaves were as well treated and cared for as they were in her own. This male slave was now her uncle's property, a fact that left her free to wonder if she would see him again.

As her Nurse secured the mosquito netting around her bed that night, Asenath stared up at the woman she loved so much, wondering why she suddenly looked like a stranger. She had suckled those heavy breasts from birth and—for a time that already felt like forever—she had believed Aneski was her own flesh and blood. When she was eventually old enough to realize they were not related, her heart had seemed to stop for an instant. But she had immediately dismissed this hard fact, spitting it out like a grain of sand baked into the warm and wonderful bread of her life. Tonight, however, she felt in danger of cracking the invisible teeth of her thoughts on the knowledge. She had never known a life before Nanny, but she could no longer pretend the same was true for this woman with the strong handsome features and somberly hooded eyes.

When her nurse bent over to blow out the first lamp, Asenath sat up in bed and spoke the question burning in her mind, "Nanny, where did you live before here?"

Straightening, Aneski was silent for a long moment before replying, "I lived with my husband."

"You were married?!"

"Yes, naturally I was married, and I had my own house, and a small but fruitful garden in which I grew cabbages and lettuce, cucumbers and radishes... Well, it does not matter now."

"Oh go on, please!"

Obligingly, her nurse sat down on her chair beside the bed. "My husband was a scribe and a teacher at one of the Houses of Instruction run by the temple. I myself could read and write a little, enough to manage our little household. My mother taught me. She worked as a supervisor at the Guild of Weavers and was especially skilled with dyes, so that my sister and I never lacked for anything, not even after our father died when I was twelve. I was so proud of my father, the brave soldier!"

"He died in battle?"

"No, Asenath, he merely served in the palace guard. It was an evil spell, cast by one of the many demons of the Inundation, that slipped into his barracks one night and swiftly took him away from us."

"Your father served under my uncle?"

"Yes, he was one of Potifer Setka's men. Then, as now, your

uncle's men had little to do. Pharaoh moors in Kemet's greatest city only when he has business here, for Iuno will always be the administrative center of the Two Lands. But as soon as he is able, he returns to his provincial new capital, where he thinks only of his fancy new irrigation systems and his pyramid, which he began building as soon as Nebkaure made him co-regent."

Questions crowded Asenath's mind, but the simplest one reached her mouth first, "What was your father's name?"

"Our child was but seven months old," Aneski went on as if she had not heard her. "A fine boy was my little Henenu..."

Asenath felt uncomfortable when she noticed her nurse's cheeks were suddenly shining like a funeral mask in the lamplight. "Nanny, please don't cry!"

Rising abruptly, Aneski announced, "It is time to sleep!" and blew out the bedside lamp.

"But you haven't finished your story! What happened to your husband? And where is Henenu now? I won't be able to sleep if you don't tell me!"

"My husband died." With a deep sigh, she extinguished a second lamp. "Our son followed him three months later. The Seven Hathors had been busy weaving our fates together, Asenath, for it was at precisely during the most terrible time of my life that you were born. Your mother was unable to nurse you, and so Potifer Setka—who genuinely cares for his men and their families—brought me here with all haste before grief could dry up my milk. So all the love brimming within me for my son went to you instead, and you became the daughter of my heart. I have lost everything I can call my own, but through you, my dear, the gods are kind to me. Sleep safely."

After her nurse had blown out the final lamp and silently left the room, Asenath lay on her back feeling much as she did whenever she ate too much food too quickly, except that the uncomfortable pressure was located higher up, in her chest. She did not like knowing she had stolen another baby's milk. She felt as though the infant's ghost was in the room with her now, still starved for the milk of life she had greedily drunk all by herself, without even once tasting the bitterness of her nurse's grief.

She loved her bed, but tonight she could not get comfortable in it. It seemed she would never fall asleep. At one point, she ended up on her back, and that was when she noticed the roughly circular opening directly above her, through which shone a faint blue-white light, as if the sun had already risen. She could not decide which was more impossible—that all the long hours of the night had already passed or that there was a hole in the ceiling. Staring up in bewilderment through this new window in her bedroom, she saw the far away silhouette of a vulture flying across the sky.

Comprehending that the hole was much farther away than it could possibly be, her confusion sharpened into fear. She tried to sit up, only to discover she could not move. She wanted to cry, “Nanny!” but her voice was trapped in her throat. Despite the intense effort she made to yell for her nurse, all she could manage was a moan. Then a knowledge as mysterious as a night flowering lotus welled up from within her, and she was able to speak as she realized out loud, “I'm dreaming!” The incredible fact instantly dissolved her anxiety as it flooded her with energy. It was no effort at all now to stand up as she prepared to fly out of this dark hole in the earth. She stretched her arms out on either side of her, and there they were—the colorful wings of a goddess.

It was by the magical light of her dream wings that Asenath suddenly saw a man standing a body's length away from her. He was staring up at the distant sky, his lips forming words she could not hear. Recognizing her uncle's new slave, she experienced another surge of joy, for she knew now what his real clothes had looked like. He wore a bright white robe with long sleeves, and as she gazed in wonder at the luminous material, her wings flew away from her. Landing lightly on his back between his shoulder blades, the wings came together before suddenly dissolving into blood or wine, she could not tell which, and it did not matter, because in drenching the pure white fabric, the darkly shining liquid dyed it a dazzling array of brilliant and beautiful colors, some of which she was sure she had never seen before.

Asenath abruptly became aware of lying on her bed, and seeing only darkness when she opened her eyes, the intensity of her disappointment made her groan. She quickly closed her eyes again and made an effort to step back into the dream. But all she had left was its memory. Stubbornly, reasoning that the door to this mysterious place—where being in a dream was as real as being awake yet much more exciting—had to be somewhere in the space behind her eyelids, she lay awake focusing on the faintly luminous swirling currents of darkness searching for it.

When she woke again to the light of the sun, all her other dreams immediately slipped out of her mind like fish from a torn net.

Chapter 3

As the River rose—transforming Kemet into a reflection of heaven by flooding canals and inundating the land—Asenath prayed to Neith to help her rise above the dark depths of sleep into a conscious dream. The goddess was listening. On several occasions, usually in the early hours of the morning, she became aware of being in a dream. But she always woke up.

When the seeds were being sown in the freshly nourished black earth, Asenath began copying the endless advice given by Pharaoh Merikare to his son, along with the even more numerous maxims of Ptah-Hotep. By the time she finally completed this exercise, the first crops were being harvested. Months of uninterrupted tedium for three long hours every morning had not made her feel much wiser, but she could finally ask her teacher the question that had been smoldering impatiently inside her, "Harkhaf, have you ever woken up and still been in a dream?"

The old man lifted his eyes from the papyrus spread open across his lap, and Asenath thought she detected a surprised glint in his keen black eyes as he replied, "Why do you ask?"

Eagerly, she described her special dream to him, but only up until the moment she opened her arms and saw that they had become the wings of a goddess. "I knew I could easily fly out of the pit I was in and up into the sky!" She then explained how, ever since that night, she had been searching for a door in the darkness behind her closed eyelids through which she might enter another conscious dream.

"Stop looking for an actual door, Asenath."

His prompt and apparently knowledgeable response made her heart skip with excitement.

Harkhaf's large black eyes were set just a little lower and farther apart than normal between a fine hooked nose that overshadowed his thin mouth. These distinctively unattractive features, sculpted in wrinkled leathery skin beneath the white stubble covering his shaved skull, gave him the appearance of a human eagle. In the four years he had been her teacher, he had failed to inspire within her any feelings of affection for him, yet now that he seemed prepared to educate her on the science of dreaming, she felt there was a chance she might come to like him, at least a little. But the index finger of his left hand still marking the spot on the papyrus he had been reading, all he said was, "The gods sometimes choose to communicate with us in our dreams."

"I wish you would tell my nurse that! Aneski thinks dreams are dangerous. She says demons try to fool us and attack us while we're dreaming. She says bad things can happen to me in my dreams and that I need to be careful and stop thinking about them so much."

"It is true that not every god has our well being at heart. But we will discuss dreams some other time. Right now..."

"But Master Harkhaf, you have not answered my question yet! Have you ever woken up and still been in a dream?"

He stared at her for a moment as though considering whether or not to reprimand her for interrupting him. "Yes, a handful of times," he admitted, "when I was younger and did not sleep as deeply as I do now. But since you are so interested in the subject, I will arrange for a scribe in the temple's House of Life to begin copying a papyrus that should answer at least some of your questions. It will be yours to own and study at your leisure."

Asenath impatiently awaited the arrival of the Dream Papyrus as the River, rising again, reflected her growing excitement. But when the River reached its full height and the Papyrus still had not arrived, she felt her life was standing as still as the water. She began suffering from bouts of feverish impatience and ill temper. It did not help that the house had temporarily lost its heart. The high priest and his wife were away at Pharaoh's court enjoying themselves in unimaginably splendid ways that made her own existence seem even more dull and lonely by comparison. Yet there was one benefit to her parents' absence. It served to relax Nanny's vigilance, and the night Aneski got together with other high ranking household servants to celebrate the feast of Hathor's birthday, she and Kyky spied on them.

Asenath was intrigued by how subtly different her nurse's face looked when she was not aware the daughter of her heart was watching her. Aneski wore an expression of placid contentment, until slaves appeared to replace half empty platters of food with fresh ones and to refill everyone's wine cups, then her handsome features hardened with an emotion Asenath recognized as a blend of pride and resentment.

One of the slaves attending the servants was the foreign woman who had been purchased the evening they had spied on the slave traders, and Asenath once more found herself thinking about the male slave she had seen in her conscious dream. She had told her mother and Harkhaf only the first part of her dream. Her pride had shied away from describing how her wings had flown away from her to a foreign slave. She had felt that her truest self was expressed by those wings, yet she could not deny that, in the dream, she had been happy when they suddenly flew away from her to him. While she was awake, it was impossible for her to understand why her dream self had reacted that way. But now—observing the blood-red wine being carefully poured into cups by a woman who had arrived in Kemet with the man from her dream—she allowed herself to remember how her wings had poured over the man's luminous white robe, and how instead of dismay she had experienced an awestruck joy. The cow-shaped candles illuminating Hathor's birthday feast dimmed in her eyes as she saw again the resplendent colors that had magically woven themselves around a foreign slave.

“Monkey, what do you know about the slave pouring the wine?”

“Her name is Asher, and she is a proud one! One of the chosen people, she says.”

“Certainly chosen to serve as slaves in Kemet. Can you tell me more about her?”

“Well, I just happened to overhear her talking to Chef one night. I remember he said to her, 'I want to know all the ingredients of your life, Asher. But then you must discard them and season your days with the new ones you have been given, for there must be no bitterness in your service here'. Then Asher told him that her husband had set her aside because she was barren. Although she said she didn't blame him. She insisted it was her own fault for failing in her most important duty as his wife and one of the chosen people. But when Chef asked her what she meant by that, she didn't answer.”

“Did she say what gods her people worship?”

“They believe in only one god. I forgot his name.”

“Think, Kyky.”

“It begins with an E... Ey... no... Ely... no... Elohim!” she cried triumphantly.

Walking past their hiding place at that precise moment, the slave they had been discussing dropped the platter she was holding with a gasp.

The last thing Asenath saw before she turned to run back to

her room was Kyky happily snatching up some of the scattered pastries.

☼

The long anticipated Dream Papyrus finally arrived. Asenath read it eagerly. But when she reached the end, and there was no longer any hope of coming upon a passage describing a reliable method for inducing conscious dreams, she became angry with Harkhaf for failing to teach her about the one subject she truly cared about. She promptly complained to her mother, who must have spoken to her husband that evening, because the following morning, the high priest summoned Asenath to his private garden.

She was in a sullen mood and unable to fully appreciate the rare pleasure of being alone with her father. But as they sat together on one side of his pool, their legs partially in the water, the mildness of the day—combined with the jubilant singing of birds harmonizing with the sonorous chants of frogs—quickly cast a spell of well being over her heart in which hope sparkled and glimmered like sunlight on the water.

"Regarding dreams, Asenath," her father said quietly, "I cannot tell you much more than Harkhaf. Can you tell me what you learned from the Papyrus?"

"A lot," she admitted reluctantly, "but not enough. Not what I wanted to learn."

He looked over at her, and for a long moment they smiled at

each other. When he gazed back down into the pool she did the same, and she found herself thinking that reflections were like the dreams she had on most nights, vague and fluid and nearly impossible to catch hold of when she woke up.

"Tell me something you did learn," he prompted.

"There are supposedly three kinds of dreams. Dreams in which the gods speak to us, either to help us or to demand something from us. Dreams that foretell the future. And dreams that reveal information. That's what the Papyrus says. But I know there's another kind of dream, the kind of dream in which you know you're dreaming."

"Go on," he urged.

"The papyrus says that if we're sick, and the physician can do no more for us, we should seek a cure in our dreams." She sighed. "But how are we supposed to do that if we don't even know we're dreaming?"

"Good point!"

Becoming aware of a quiet rumbling sound at the same moment she felt its vibration in her lower back, Asenath could almost believe the purring was emanating from her soul in response to the warm approval in her father's voice. Turning slightly to caress one of her parents' many cats, she concluded, "The book says that if someone or something keeps chasing us in our dreams, we should stop and ask what it wants because the answer may surprise us."

She did not mention the Papyrus also said that if you saw

yourself looking down a well, you would be be sentenced to be jailed. Did that mean the reverse was true? If you saw yourself looking up from the bottom of a well, would you be freed from captivity? If so, did that mean the male slave from her dream would one day be freed?

"I forbid you to become a slave to your dreams, Asenath." Meketre ended their time together with this gentle command. "Dreams are meant to enrich the joys of life, not eclipse them."

☼

Asenath's tenth birthday was a major event. The kitchen was constantly busy baking all of her favorite sweet and savory pastries, and the delectable aromas rising from behind the house made Asenath feel almost wild with impatience for the special day to arrive. The house was decorated with even more freshly picked flowers than usual. Dozens of lamps and candles were placed all throughout the gardens, where pavilions were erected for both adults and children, and every pool was drained, cleaned and filled with fresh water.

Also contributing to Asenath's pleasure at being the center of everyone's activities was how intensely satisfied Nanny looked as she supervised every facet of the preparations, exercising the authority granted to her as the woman who had played a vital part in making this joyful occasion possible. Her nurse's temporary power over the other servants was a way of honoring her contribution to the happiness of the high priest's household by seeing to it that his beloved daughter survived the dangers of infancy and continued to thrive.

It seemed a dream coming true when the sun finally rose on the day of her birthday. She knew that the houses and apartments inside the enclosure of Re's temple were already filled with some of the invited guests who had traveled to Iuno to attend the celebration. But it was not until covered litters and carrying chairs began arriving in the welcoming coolness of early morning that she suddenly felt nervous, for she had little experience interacting with girls her own age. Yet it turned out she barely had time to catch her breath, much less worry about anything, as she fell naturally into her position as the mind of a flock flying tirelessly from one activity to another shrieking with laughter, and settling down only for as long as it took to clarify the rules of the game they had decided to play next.

They spent the hottest part of the day in her pool, where they divided into two teams and hit a ball back and forth between them. When they eventually tired of all the competitive jumping and splashing, they dove beneath the surface and played underwater tag, until hunger sank its sharp teeth into their bellies. Then they rested beneath a pavilion devouring platters of pastries, washing down the delectably sticky crumbs with a variety of fruit juices. The adults were nowhere to be seen. It was as though the whole world belonged to them and she, Asenath, was its undisputed queen.

All to soon, the sun began to set and all her new friends were rounded up by their respective nannies so they could return to their lodgings before nightfall. With a sharp sense of loss, Asenath watched them go. When the last of the gilded conveyances vanished beyond the reach of the torches burning in the entrance courtyard, a warm arm slipped gently around her shoulders.

"I hope you're not sick of presents yet," her uncle said, "for I have yet to give you mine!"

She replied, "Of course I'm not sick of presents!" But the truth was she was too tired to feel excited.

"I'm glad to hear it, duckling, because I think you will like my gift very much! Unfortunately, it isn't quite... ready yet. You may have to wait until tomorrow."

"Uncle!" Turning to face him, she jerked free of his heavy arm. "I don't want to wait for my present! My birthday is today! Give me my present now!"

Emerging from the house, her mother said sternly, "You are cawing like an angry crow, Asenath. Please show your uncle the proper respect."

He laughed. "Oh no, I deserved it, sister! I should know better than to provoke a tired child."

"Come, daughter." Her golden bracelets shining in the torchlight, Sadeh took her hand. "Sit with me for a moment before you retire for the night. You too, brother. You have already enjoyed too much wine and the night has not even begun."

"Indeed!"

As she followed her mother into the house, Asenath wondered what exactly her uncle was agreeing with his sister about. About drinking too much? But if that was the case, he should not sound so happy, for her mother's tone had been disapproving. Why then was he pleased the party was only just beginning if he had already drunk more than he should? Sinking into a chair, it struck her that the laws adults lived by must be like the rules of a game, which had to be obeyed in order for it to be truly enjoyable to play.

Silently, a house maid entered the room, her head lowered and her back gently bowed as both her hands grasped the opposite shoulder. "Does the Mistress desire anything?" she inquired.

"No thank you, Asher."

Before the woman could leave, Setka commanded genially, "Wait a moment!" and then asked his sister, "Is this not one of the slaves you purchased the day my wife bought Joseph?"

In the midst of her pleasant physical lethargy, Asenath felt her mind grow perfectly alert. The experience reminded her of what it felt like to wake up in a dream.

"Yes, it is," Sadeh replied. "We are well pleased with Asher."

The slave was still staring humbly down at her feet, so it was impossible to tell what she thought of this compliment.

"Well, Asher," Setka's voice brimmed with approval, "it might make you happy to know that your fellow countryman, the one with whom you arrived in Kemet, is excelling in my service."

Asher did not react.

"You have my permission to speak, woman."

"Most honorable Potifer," Asher murmured, still not looking up, "I did not really know Joseph."

"Oh... Well, it is clear to me that your god favors him. The first thing Joseph did, the very night he arrived at my house, was save the life of my prize bitch. I learned he had been a shepherd, and having observed firsthand his skill with animals, I assigned him to assist my Overseer of the Cattle. Joseph excelled in this position, so I awarded him more responsibilities. All his overseers found him invaluable, and were quite impressed by how quickly he mastered understanding and speaking our language. I myself was very gratified by the growth of my herds, so I had a scribe teach him how to read and write. Joseph succeeds in everything he does, and he is such an agreeable young man that, three months ago, I decided to make him my personal attendant. It was a wise decision. Ever since I put Joseph in charge of my household and property, my affairs run even more smoothly and my crops and livestock continue to flourish. I don't have to worry about anything. All I have to think about is what I want to eat every day!"

With a thrill, Asenath thought, *My dream has come true*! And out loud she asked hopefully, "Then he is no longer your slave?"

"What?" Her uncle's grin dimmed to a confused little smile as he looked over at her. "Of course he is still my slave. Have I not just been saying that Joseph is the best slave I have ever owned?"

Her mother said quietly, "You are dismissed, Asher."

"And at this very moment," Setka's complacent smile returned, "my Joseph is supervising the... um.. the delivery of your birthday present."

Asenath did not reply as she thought, *The best present would be knowing dreams can come true*.

"Brother, can you not see that my daughter's soul is lying in her hand? The poor girl is half asleep. Stop teasing her and tell her what your gift is so that she can go to bed."

"My darling niece, you will soon be-"

"No, uncle!" She leaped to her feet. "Please don't tell me! I want to see it for myself! It will ruin the surprise if you tell me!"

He glanced at his sister.

Sadeh rose. "Because it is still your birthday, Asenath, I will indulge you. In the morning, you may go and see your present. Will it be ready by tomorrow, brother?"

"Yes," he replied without hesitation. "Joseph assured me it would be, and he always speaks the truth."

Walking through the garden just before sunrise, Asenath saw Kyky waiting for her beside the pool. It surprised her how absolutely lovely the slave looked. She must have been permitted to dress up for the party. Her trim figure seemed taller in a dress of the finest mist linen, and her floral collar was such a bright white, it erased the usual shadows beneath her eyes.

"Monkey, you look beautiful!" she said, suddenly feeling guilty that she had not even thought about her all day yesterday during her birthday celebration.

Yet Kyky was clearly not upset. In fact, her smile was radiant as she turned and, walking lightly over to the pool, dove gracefully into the water.

Following her, Asenath stood on the edge watching the slave swimming deeper and deeper through a golden shaft of light penetrating the clear water, until her figure was so far away it resembled a fish. She would have liked to follow her but had no idea how to. If there was such a large hole in the tiles, why wasn't the water draining out of the pool? And how could she hold her breath for so long? Where was Kyky going?

All her questions were answered as she said to herself, "This is a dream! I'm dreaming!"

With an exquisite joy, she dove into the pool, only to discover that all the tiles were intact. There was a dark crack running the entire length of the pool's bottom, yet it was far too narrow for her to swim through. Then she realized what she was seeing was a huge serpent as it began rising toward her, its mouth open to strike. She watched in mounting horror as its jaws dislocated and its fangs lengthened into columns, so that she was suddenly staring at the threshold into a fiery realm, from out of which a forked tongue of flame slithered toward her.

Asenath commanded herself, “Wake Up! Wake Up!” and the burning red maw dissolved in a shower of sparks as, opening her eyes, she found herself safe in bed.

Chapter 4

Asenath did not recognize the man who strode into her uncle's receiving room until their eyes met, then the evening she had crouched with Kyky on a rooftop came back to her with the swiftness of a pigeon carrying important news to the temple of her heart. However, she did not have time to fully open and read the message delivered by the fluttering wings of her pulse, for Aneski was announcing in a cold voice, "We are here to see Potifer Setka."

Grasping his left shoulder with his right hand, Joseph replied, "Yes, Lady, the housemaid so informed me. Unfortunately, my Master is still sleeping. The festivities last night so greatly pleased him, he did not return home until just before sunrise. However, if you wish for me to wake him..."

Asenath spoke quickly, "No, please let my uncle sleep. He had too much wine. I just came to see my present."

Without looking at her, Joseph replied, "And it will be my honor to take you to it" keeping his full attention on Aneski. This enabled her to study his eyes, and notice that their dark brown irises were strikingly outlined by a fine ring of shining green. His black hair was cut short, and his face was freshly shaved. He wore a pristine white linen shendyt—held closed by a large scarab pin—that fell to just above his knees, and his muscular arms now matched his broad shoulders.

“Take her to it?” Aneski sounded almost breathless with indignation. “You will bring it here to us.”

“Lady, it would be best if-”

“It would be best,” Aneski interrupted him sternly, “if you did as I said this instant.”

Joseph's features remained passive, but the intense emotion in his eyes made them even more striking. Asenath longed to know what he was thinking as the tense silence in the room seemed to shout at her to say something.

“Dear nurse, I am going now with uncle's personal attendant to see my present. You can wait here.”

“Asenath!” Her name emerged as a shocked gasp from Aneski's throat.

She experienced a thrill of excitement as her feet moved toward the slave. She was taking her first flight away from the comfortable nest of Nanny's authority, and it felt a little like waking up from a dream she had been having all her life. She had never disobeyed her nurse in front of others, and it frightened her a little, yet it was also stimulating to assert her own will.

In her dream of him, Joseph had not seen her, but his eyes were focused on her now, and this time she could hear what he was saying, “Follow me, my Lady.”

Aneski's furious silence was like a sandstorm brewing behind her, and she was glad to escape the room. She would endure her nurse's stinging reprimands later.

Out in the neutral territory of the corridor, there was an awkward moment when Joseph, who had led her out of the room, suddenly stopped and, half turning to face her, stood waiting for her to precede him. She did so until they reached an intersection, where she was obliged to stop, having no idea which way to go. He was following so close behind her, she could smell his unique scent mingled with familiar oils. She had never been alone with a man who was not of her own blood, except for Harkhaf, of course, but he was old, and Joseph was young and handsome...

"Perhaps, Lady, it would be easier if we walked side by side?" he suggested. "It is still a ways to the... to your present."

"Yes, please," she said, relieved not to have to continue enduring the sensation of his eyes on her back. She wanted to be able to see his face, which might give her some clue as to what he thought of her, if anything. But they did not look at each other as they walked through the great house. He kept pace with her in such a way that he gave no impression she was slowing him down. She was very glad her uncle was still sleeping, and that her aunt was away at court. Tarset had been gone for a long time now. Her mother, who was a handmaiden of the queen, was supposedly quite sickly and relied on her daughter's assistance. Asenath could not quite imagine her aunt in the role of nurse, but it was very good to know there was no chance of running into her.

She was surprised when they left the house and headed in the direction of the animal pens. Until that moment, she had not even though to wonder what her present was, a surprising fact that forced her to acknowledge just how much more curious she was about Joseph, the man she had seen in her first conscious dream. Last night she had had her second such dream, but it had turned into a nightmare and spoiled the joy of it.

By the time they turned toward a low building shaded by palm trees that was obviously the dog kennel—for from it rose the constant sound of yapping and barking—Asenath was burning with questions, the answers to which felt as vital as water in the empty desert of her ignorance. Harkhaf, the Dream Papyrus, and even her father had all failed to satisfy her on the subject of dreams, and she was growing almost painfully parched for more knowledge. But much as she wanted to bring the subject up now, she could not find a reasonable excuse to do so.

Joseph smiled at her. "Your gift is within," he said, and walking ahead of her into the kennel, led her over to a quiet corner. At first she could scarcely see anything in the shadowy interior as his smile lingered before her vision just as the sun did whenever she chanced to look directly at it. He crouched beside a white bitch resting peacefully on her side while her newborn puppies struggled to secure and defend one of her precious teats. It was a delightful skirmish to witness.

Her uncle's gift was a dog!

Forgetting the difference in their stations, she crouched

beside Joseph, but he was not Kyky, and at once she regretted putting herself so close to him as her body became acutely aware of his.

She asked, “Which one is mine?” distracting herself with the delightful energy of the blind little creatures that did not much resemble dogs yet.

“You may have whichever one you like, Lady.”

She was relieved he did not look at her because his face was so close she was a little afraid of meeting his eyes. At the same time she worried that any moment now he would move away.

“My name is Asenath,” she informed him, a little jealous that his smile was directed exclusively at the puppies. But then she felt like a fool because obviously he already knew her name. A bit desperately, she sank to her knees, and dipped her hands into the warm wave of life before them. When one of the puppies licked her fingertips curiously, she declared, “This one! I want this one, please!”

“A fine choice, Asenath. She was the first to emerge from her mother.”

She felt inordinately pleased by his praise.

“Naturally you cannot take her with you today,” he told her as he gently cradled the puppy in both hands. “You must wait two full moons.”

She turned to take the puppy from him, but it wriggled so energetically, he was obliged to assist her by placing one of his hands over hers for a long moment, until her grip on the animal was both gentle and secure.

"There!" he whispered. "Now hold her against you so she can feel your warmth, and listen to your heartbeat."

She did as he instructed, and nothing had ever felt quite so wonderful as having a puppy resting against her heart. "Thank you, Joseph. This is the nicest present I have ever received!"

He replied quietly, "Thank God."

"Thank you, Elohim."

He stood abruptly.

Quickly setting the puppy down amidst its siblings, she followed him up.

"I will escort you back to the house now, Lady. We do not wish your nurse to grow overly anxious."

How chilled the spot over her heart suddenly felt, combined with the change in his tone of voice, struck her as intolerable. "I do not want to go back yet, Joseph."

"Why?"

Her breath caught. Was a slave daring to argue with her? But that was not the reason she was upset. She noticed the puppies' mother was sitting up now, and staring at her.

"Is your god's name not Elohim?" she asked respectfully, and when the dog turned her liquid black eyes on Joseph, she felt free to do the same. "I'm sorry if I got it wrong. Our housemaid, Asher, told our Chef that Elohim is the name of her god. So I thought, when you asked me to thank god, that you meant I should thank Elohim."

He was silent for a breath before he spoke in a tight voice, "Forgive me, Asenath. This slave is still far from conquering the sin of pride. I feared you were mocking me when, in truth, you were showing me respect."

He stood almost as stiffly as he had the evening she first saw him, but it was worse. He was not gazing into some inner distance, he was staring down at his feet the way Asher had last night, as all slaves did. The situation had become unbearable. She had to say something...

But before she could speak, he raised his head and, staring past her, said, "We call Him Elohim even though He has no name, for He is the Creator of all things, the One who has always been and will always be. In the beginning, Elohim created the heavens and the earth."

Remembering the bull of Re, Asenath spoke out loud the question she had silently asked herself then, "How can everything come out of nothing?"

"There is no such thing as nothing." Joseph met her eyes. "There is only God."

This made perfect sense to her, and desiring to show him that she respected him and his god enough to put him on the same level as hers, she said, "In Kemet, we call Elohim Atum-Re. Atum is the darkness of the primordial waters from which the sun rose at the beginning of time."

"The primordial waters are already something," he informed her neutrally, not looking at her. "Even darkness is already something. God existed before anything."

Suddenly, she could wait no longer to ask him, "Do you dream, Joseph?"

He flinched as though she had picked up a stone and flung it at him. He turned half away from her, and now the tone of his voice when he replied echoed his defensive posture, "Do all the little girls in Kemet go around asking men if they dream? What a fascinating country I find myself in!"

"Yes, and since Elohim created everything, he created Kemet as well, and he must find it pleasing since you are here... My uncle is convinced your god favors you."

"Asenath, your nurse is waiting..."

"Let her wait! It will do her good. I am ten years old now and no longer a child to be ordered around." She resisted the urge to stomp her foot impatiently. "And I am tired of waiting for an answer to my question."

He turned to face her again. "Yes, I dream. It is because of my dreams—and how proudly I spoke of what God had revealed to me through them—that I came to be a slave in Kemet. Now please answer my question, Asenath. Why do you ask me this?"

She was about to confess, "Because I dreamed of you!" when a boy ran into the kennel yelling, "Joseph?! Joseph, Merit sent me to look for you! She says the lady in the receiving room is threatening to wake the master if you do not return at once with the high priest's daughter!"

“Run back and tell Merit to explain to our guest that the Lady Asenath had a difficult time deciding which puppy she liked best, but that I am escorting her back to the house now.”

“Yes, Joseph!”

A moment later, she was alone again with her uncle's treasured slave, but like a dream cut short, their conversation was impossible to continue.

“My Lady Asenath, when your puppy is ready to leave her mother, I will personally bring her to you... That is, if Potifer Setka gives me permission to do so.”

The sadness threatening to possess her vanished in the unexpected light of his promise. “Thank you, Joseph. I look forward to that day, and will make sure my uncle understands there is much you have to teach me... about caring for my dog. I will also tell him that I made you promise me you would come.”

☼

Nanny did not speak to her on the journey home. Asenath made no effort to engage her in conversation, smoldering as she was herself with emotions she could scarcely find words for. Besides, her nurse would not wish to hear about dreams, or about Elohim, or even about her puppy, which she had already complained would generate messes she had no intention of cleaning up. As they left Potifer Setka's house, Aneski had warned her, “The animal will be entirely your responsibility!”

Asenath had scarcely heard her, but now she found herself embracing the idea that the dog would belong exclusively to her. She would be responsible for its well being, and between them they would share an affection all their own. The only other person who would understand their relationship was Joseph, who had brought them together the moment he laid the helpless little creature against her heart. She would need to keep the house cats away from her puppy, who she hoped would have eyes like her mother's, dark-rimmed, slanted and oval, lovely as the eyes of a goddess. But unlike a statue's, they would be dangerously vulnerable to cat's claws.

As one day led to another, Asenath daydreamed about Joseph bringing her their puppy. Awareness that her pet was swiftly growing strong enough to leave her mother reflected her own feelings of growing away from her nurse. Something had changed between them. Aneski no longer kept such close watch over her. This was agreeable, yet it also made her a little sad. Her nurse did not seem to love her as much anymore. Or was she less worried about Asenath because she realized the daughter of her heart was growing up? An entire cycle of the moon was a long time, even for Aneski, to nurture a resentment because of the way Asenath had treated her in front of a Hebrew slave.

The next time her uncle came to visit, Asenath was exceptionally attentive toward him, even going so far as to pour his wine for him after the housemaid brought in the jug. Setka watched her with an odd little smile, one side of his mouth turned slightly downward. It also seemed to her that his dark-brown eyes shone a little too brightly.

Accepting the cup from her, he observed wistfully, "You are growing up, my dear."

"Uncle, I just want to tell you how much I love my birthday present!"

"Your present? Oh, yes, the dog. I'm so glad you like it."

"Uncle, I made Joseph promise me he would bring me the puppy himself. He has much to teach me about how to care for her properly. He said he would come, but only with your permission, of course. You will let Joseph come, won't you?"

At these repeated mentions of Joseph, Potifer visibly relaxed in his chair. "Of course, my dear. Just do whatever Joseph says and your puppy will thrive!"

When her mother entered the room and Setka rose to greet and embrace his sister, Asenath slipped away and ran outside to her garden pavilion. There she sat with her arms around her knees, once again reliving the moment when Joseph had promised he would bring her the puppy himself. Mysteriously, the more time passed, the more vividly she recalled the sound of his voice, firm yet also hesitant, uncertain. Because he had been worried she might reject his offer? Or had he been reluctant to make the promise and done so primarily for the puppy's sake?

Roused from her reverie by a gentle plopping sound, she

looked over at her pool, where the afternoon sunlight was glinting off delicate ripples created by the frog that had just leaped into the water. And just as abruptly, a question leaped into her mind: *Where is Monkey*?

Rising, she walked over to the pool, and the exact spot where she had stood in her dream watching Kyky swimming deeper and deeper into the reflected sky through a ray of sunshine akin to a celestial current, until she was no bigger than a fish. She could not remember reading anything in the Dream Papyrus about bottomless pools, or about people who dove into them turning into fish. Maybe her dream didn't mean anything except that Kyky fervently wished for a pool of her own. Did her uncle permit Joseph to swim in one of his many pools? Surely his prized personal attendant would at least occasionally be allowed to cool off after a long day of work. Suppressing the urge to run back into the house and ask him, she remained staring pensively down into the water.

Joseph had told her that god had revealed things to him in his dreams, and that his dreams were the reason he was here in Kemet. Had his god revealed to him that he would one day be a slave? And had her own gods revealed something terrible to her about her future—that she would one day be bitten by a huge snake?

There! She had finally dared to ask herself the awful question which had kept her from wanting to think about this dream. But could not the images of a dream be read and interpreted like hieroglyphs? Before she had learned to read, hieroglyphs had seemed to be only random pictures of people, animals, places and objects. But she had learned that when arranged in specific patterns, these pictures conveyed a meaning beyond themselves. If so, there was no more reason to be afraid of a dream serpent than there was to fear the hieroglyph of a snake.

Elated by this reassuring thought, Asenath slipped off her dress and, diving fearlessly into the pool, enjoyed a vigorous swim. Afterward, pleasantly anticipating dinner, she returned to her room, where she came upon a young slave girl sweeping natron water across the floor.

Asenath asked her casually, “Have you seen Monkey today?”

After a surprised glance, the girl lowered her eyes and said quietly, “Kyky died.”

“Oh no! When?! Why didn't someone tell me?!”

“Her Ba bird flew away about a week after your birthday feast,” the girl replied, but then fell silent, apparently having no idea how to answer the second question.

Suddenly feeling very cold, Asenath hurried over to a chest, and pulled out a towel she wrapped tightly around herself. “How...? What...?”

“She died of a fever, miss. Chef thinks it was caused by all the extra dung she had to collect for the extra cooking fires. In the end, poor Monkey was as hot as a fire herself.”

Chapter 5

A suspicion slithered into Asenath's thoughts like an invisible snake. Had her nurse known about Kyky's death and deliberately not told her about it? Did this explain her relaxed vigilance—the fact that Aneski knew she no longer needed to worry about her noble charge secretly consorting with a dung slave? But the moment these questions began working in her like venom, she felt it was worse than that—she felt Aneski might actually have taken a sinister satisfaction in believing the longer Asenath remained ignorant of her secret friend's death, the more it would serve to prove she had never truly cared for Monkey but primarily used her to annoy her nurse. And it only made her feel worse knowing she could tell no one about her dream without revealing just how fond she genuinely had been of Kyky.

Then she began wondering if there might be something a little wrong with her. Why had the two most vivid dreams of her life—dreams in which she knew herself to be asleep yet also mysteriously awake—centered around two slaves? At least Kyky had been born in Kemet, a poor orphan, kin to one of the servants, kindly taken in by the high priest's household when she was still too young to do anything besides collect dung in the pastures. But why had she never been promoted to a less menial position? The pain in Asenath's heart when she asked herself this question was so great, she attempted to run from it, and so ended up in her garden pavilion, where there was less chance of Nanny showing up and, catching her crying, guess the reason.

She felt better outside in her favorite place in the world. She was facing the exact spot where Kyky had stood in her dream looking so lovely and happy. On the night she had that dream, her friend had still been alive. Maybe Kyky's Ba, knowing it would soon be flying away into the land beyond the sunset, had first flown into her dream to tell her she was not afraid. The tension in her heart eased somewhat at the thought. Still, she missed Kyky, and regretted how little she had thought about her when they were not together.

The longer she sat there, the more she felt her thoughts and emotions becoming hypnotically absorbed into the swelling and ebbing music of the cicadas. The taut, vibrating sound climaxed like a passionate discussion abruptly cut off before, after a mysterious intermission, resuming with a slight, almost indicernable variation on the theme. Were they sharing secrets about the garden they lived in? If so, they found it endlessly fascinating for they always had information to broadcast and exult in. If it was true Kyky's Ba had flown into her dream, had her own soul mysteriously flown into Joseph's dream? But why had the wings of Neith flown away from her to him, a Hebrew who believed in only one god?

Coming from the direction of the house, a man's voice

yelled, “My Dream!”

Surging to her feet, she ran to the garden path, down which she suddenly saw a white puppy sprinting toward her. She couched down to greet it, but instead of stopping, the animal dove straight into her arms. The delightful impact knocked Asenath over onto her side, where she lay giggling helplessly as she was energetically sniffed and licked.

Joseph remarked, “And here I thought she was more a sight than a scent hound” and rescued her from the onslaught of canine adoration.

Standing, Asenath quickly smoothed down her dress, grateful the red and blue garment was made of wool and not of easily wrinkled linen, which would have made it impossible to salvage some of her dignity. “You named her My Dream!”

“Yes.” He quickly slipped a leash around the puppy's neck and offered it to her. “I hope you don't mind.”

“Of course not! It's the perfect name. Thank you, Joseph!”

“She ran off before I reached the door,” he explained, glancing over his shoulder in the direction of the house. “I had best...”

“Don't worry about it!” She interrupted him. “I know you're here.”

His eyes did not look convinced.

“Would you please join me in my private pavilion, Joseph? I'm eager to learn whatever you have to teach me... about training my new puppy.” Turning, she began walking away, and was delighted by how My Dream trotted obediently along beside her. Joseph would simply have to follow them.

The first thing she learned about her new pet was that sitting obediently was not yet an option. My Dream was too intrigued by her new surroundings to patiently tolerate being confined to the pavilion while her mistress was instructed on how to handle her. Asenath surrendered the leash to Joseph, who actively illustrated many of his instructions. "This breed lives to pursue, which is why it is so valued by your people," he told her. "I have already taught her how to play a game of chase. All you have to do is attach a stuffed animal to one end of a rope, and run away from her dragging it behind you. This is a good way to reward her for coming when you call her, because as you've already witnessed, she will most certainly run away from you if she catches sight of anything interesting. But don't go chasing after her yourself, just stay where you are and keep calling her, waving your arms and moving around a little if you're out in an open field. She'll return to you eventually. When she does, reward her with approval and affection. You want her to know that being with you is the best place in the world. Train her just before each meal, but only for a short time, to keep her focused. This breed loves to work, so another fun game would be to hide her favorite treats around the garden and let her enjoy hunting them down. And of course, she loves to play ball. Throw it as far as you can and let her fetch it for you. Dogs learn quickly and live to please their owner."

By the time he stopped talking, Asenath was seriously contemplating asking her mother to tell Nebt that they needed a new slave to take care of the new dog, but all she said was, "Thank you, Joseph, I will do my best" as she averted her eyes, worried he might see in them how overwhelmed she was feeling by this immense new responsibility. She already loved My Dream, but the mere idea of structuring her whole day around her was exhausting. She had never before had to think about anyone except herself.

"I know that sounds like a lot of work, Asenath, but you will enjoy it as much as she will, trust me." He paused, then added more quietly, almost as if he was telling her a secret, "I know you can do this."

"Will you promise to come back to make sure I'm doing everything properly, Joseph? My Dream already loves you and will miss you terribly if she does not see you again."

He looked away. "I'm not sure that will be possible."

"Why not?" She asked desperately. "I'm sure my uncle won't mind."

Gazing up at the sky, he said, "I am your servant." Then lowering his eyes to her face, he promised, "I will do my best."

When several seasons passed and Joseph still had not returned, Asenath accompanied her mother one day when she went to visit her brother. Sadeh permitted her to bring My Dream with them.

Sitting obediently beside her mistress, the dog returned Setka's admiring gaze with her usual quivering alertness. Except for a soft golden mask around her left eye, My Dream was entirely white.

“She is a true beauty!” he declared. “As are you, my dear, Asenath. What a pair you make. You are keeping her well exercised?”

“Yes, uncle.”

“She has help with that,” Sadeh remarked with a touch of impatience. “The entire household is besotted with the dog.”

“Well, you have to admit, sister, that exercising My Dream is having a very nice effect on your daughter's figure. She is swiftly leaving behind the skinny child and growing into a slender young woman.”

Asenath's primary reason for coming to visit her uncle had been to try and see Joseph again, but she suddenly found it impossible to ask about the slave, much less request he be allowed time off his duties to play with her and her dog. Only a child would make such a request expecting it to be indulged. A young noble woman would never dream of desiring a slave's company, no matter how exalted his position was.

“She is not a woman yet, brother.”

“Well, it won't be long now. Just think what an entrance she and My Dream will make at court!”

Looking shyly away from Setka's appraising smile, Asenath studied the blue collar around her dog's neck. It came to her then—more clearly than she had ever thought about it before—that once she began her monthly bleeding, she would no longer be free as a puppy. Literally overnight, she would become a woman in need of training for her future roles of wife and mother. A man would become her master, and beside him she would walk, obeying his commands, for the rest of her life.

A low whine of distress confirmed Asenath's feeling that My Dream was a mysterious extension of her own heart when the dog seemed to give a voice to her anxiety as, for the first time, she faced her future head on.

☼

Potifer Setka left for the capital to join his wife, whose sickly mother had finally gone to her Ka. He would remain at court until after the burial, then bring his wife home. On their way back to Iuno, they would be traveling with Pharaoh and his court, who every year came to worship Atum-Re in his temple.

Asenath received the news of her uncle's departure with mixed feelings. She had no reason now to visit his estate, which meant there was no chance of seeing Joseph again. But why should she even want to see Joseph? The answer was always the same, and yet different. If she asked herself this question while sitting and petting their dog, the answer was simple—because she liked Joseph just as she had liked Kyky, whose immortal Ba had appeared to her in a dream as lovely and noble in essence as any lady's. She wanted to see Joseph again because she liked how she felt in his company, and because he was the only person she had seen more than once in a dream in which she knew she was dreaming. The only other living creature who could claim this honor was the dog he had given her. The hound had been her uncle's gift, but it was Joseph who had placed My Dream against her heart. The gesture had opened some mysterious door inside her through which the dog was able to enter her dreams, and in so doing alert her to the fact that she was dreaming. Almost as soon as the puppy became part of her waking life, she had also found her way into Asenath's dreams, and begun training her human mistress to become more aware in them. Asenath's sleeping mind now regularly pounced as joyfully as a hound catching its prey on the triumphant thought—I'm dreaming!

She fervently wished there was someone she could share her nocturnal adventures with. How many other people had conscious dreams? It seemed to her that after the sun set was when life had the potential to become truly magical. It pleased her to imagine that the dead sleeping in their tombs in the western desert possessed the power to consciously dream forever. Could it be true that the Ba's of the Justified flew away from their burial chambers every night, and did whatever they pleased in the next world? Until the sun rose and forced them to return to their linen-wrapped mummies, just as she woke up surrounded by mosquito netting every morning?

Asenath never tired of recalling her conscious dreams. They were like gold, never fading, always luminous and beautiful no matter how often she fingered them with her thoughts, or how many days passed after the nights her soul mysteriously mined them from the dark depths of sleep.

By the time news reached them that Pharaoh—accompanied by most of his family and closest friends—was making his leisurely way up to Iuno, Asenath had become a woman. The widening distance between her and Aneski was bridged in a heartbeat as she cried out for her nurse in mingled fear and excitement. The household women celebrated by bringing their young mistress whatever special treats she craved during her confinement. At first it was nice being the center of attention, but she soon missed being able to go swimming, and the initial but persistent ache low in her belly was no fun either. Not to mention how strange and inconvenient it was that every month now for years to come she would be losing so much of her blood. Where did it all come from? Obviously her physical body was not like a jar, the finite contents of which would soon have been exhausted. It was clear that her life-giving blood flowed into the tributaries of her veins from a divine source which was never exhausted.

Perhaps it was the pent up energy from her enforced idleness that made her feel reckless enough, after her confinement ended, to conceive the idea of ordering the young slave boy in charge of exercising My Dream to accompany them both out into the fields early one morning, before Nanny was awake. This same slave often ran messages to and from her uncle's estate, so he knew the best and quickest way to get there. My Dream was delighted with the group outing, and though she kept running away, she returned almost immediately, as if she sensed her mistress was on an important mission and had no time to waste. They arrived at Potifer-Setka's house when the sun was still low in the sky. She told the boy to go seek refreshment in the kitchen, clipped on My Dream's leash, and announced herself.

The housemaid looked very surprised to be greeting a visitor so early in the day. "I'm terribly sorry mistress, but Potifer Seka is away."

"Yes, I know." Asenath made an effort not to sound impatient. "I'm actually here to see his personal attendant. I have a question for him regarding my dog. My uncle told me that Joseph knows everything there is to know about animals. My Dream was a gift from my uncle, and Joseph helped train her. I need to speak to him now about something. That is, if he's not too busy. If he is, I'll wait out in the garden beside the pool... but I can't wait too long..."

"Yes, my Lady, I will fetch him for you."

"No you will not! I mean... please, just *ask* him if he can spare some time. I have a few important questions to ask him about my dreams... I mean about my dog, that's her name, My Dream."

Looking sleepy, the woman replied, "I will do that, Lady.

Once they were alone, she let My Dream off her leash, poured some water out for her, and then drank a cup herself as the dog wandered curiously around the room. She had pictured Joseph out in the kennels, or somewhere else on her uncle's large estate, but only moments had passed before My Dream barked happily.

"Asenath?"

Turning, she saw that Joseph had already entered the room. They were separated only by the dog, who was standing on her hind legs, with her front paws braced on his broad shoulders, her joyfully wagging tail threatening to lash her mistress painfully across the belly.

Grinning, Joseph commanded, "Down girl!" and was reluctantly obeyed.

With their palms facing outward, Asenath raised her hands until they were level with her heart. "Life, health and strength to you, Joseph."

Reflecting her gesture, he echoed her greeting, "Life, health and strength to you, Lady Asenath."

Seating herself in a chair, she forced her hands to remain relaxed around the carved lion's paws as, pulling up a stool, Joseph sat down facing her.

"It's good to see you again, Asenath," he said warmly as the hound lay on her belly between them with a contented sigh, her head resting on her front paws as she kept watch on the open doorway.

"And it's good to see you again, Joseph," she replied, resisting the urge to ask him why he had not come to visit them. She doubted the house maid would disturb them, but she did not know how long she could endure the breathtaking pressure of feeling so happy in the presence of someone so far below her station she should never even have noticed him, much less sought his company. The only relief was to tell him the truth, and it felt like finally letting out a breath she had been holding for years. "I had a dream with you, Joseph."

Lowering his head, he slowly caressed the dog's sleek back. "Did you?"

"I was wondering if... if you would like to hear it, and maybe tell me what you think it might mean."

"Interpreting dreams is God's business." Sitting up again, he rested both hands formally on his knees. "But go ahead and tell me your dream."

And so she did, avoiding his eyes until she was finished speaking.

"When did you dream this, Asenath?"

"The evening of the afternoon my uncle's wife bought you from the slave traders." She had hoped he would not ask her that. "I was secretly watching from a rooftop."

"I see."

"It was the first time I realized I was dreaming."

Leaning forward and resting his elbows on his knees, he clasped his hands between them and stared down at the dog as he asked, "Does that happen to you often?"

"Once or twice a moon now. At first it happened rarely." She paused. "Joseph, the Dream Papyrus says that if you find yourself looking down into a well, it means you will be imprisoned. Well, shouldn't that mean the opposite is true? If you find yourself looking up out of a well, you will soon be freed..."

He appeared deep in thought, for he neither looked up or replied.

"I believe, Joseph, that you must have been talking to god in my dream. I wonder what you were saying to him."

"Yes." He sat up again. "I'm sure I was asking God to forgive me for being such a proud young fool."

"But what did you do that was so foolish, Joseph?"

He smiled suddenly. "I told everyone my dreams."

She was shocked. "You're not making fun of me, are you?"

"No, Asenath, I'm not, believe me. It is only that a slave must be able to laugh at himself if he wishes to be free."

"So you think that's what my dream means?" she said eagerly. "That you will one day no longer be a slave?"

"I can certainly hope so! Because I believe my dreams are from God, I trust in them. I have faith in what my dreams reveal to me, even when it seems impossible they can ever become reality."

"My tutor, who is a very wise old scribe, told me that not every god has our well being at heart."

"Asenath," he leaned toward her so their eyes were on the same level, "trust me when I tell you there is only one God."

"Then you're not afraid of demons who try to trick us and hurt us through our dreams?"

"No, the Lord is our Protector. And one meaning of your dream, Asenath, is clear to me. Elohim wants me to tell you about Him." Slowly, so she could see what he was about to do, he laid his right hand over hers. "God wants you to know that He sees you."

She gasped.

He promptly withdrew his hand.

"I believe you, Joseph!"

Rising abruptly, My Dream shook herself happily.

"Then pray to Elohim for us both, Asenath. And tell no one."

Chapter 6

For the festival celebrating the opening of the new year, Asenath was permitted to wear select items from a collection of jewelry that had been in her mother's family for generations. Although she scarcely dared admit it to herself, she was inclined to agree with Nanny that the delicate ancient pieces would look rather provincial compared with the heavier, and more colorful modern arrangements Pharaoh's wife and daughters would be wearing. Priceless heirloom or not, she did not really like the scarab beetle necklace her mother chose for her. Even when made of gold, beetles disgusted her. But this particular beetle was sacred to the goddess Neith, and placed the wearer of the necklace under her special protection. At least she very much liked, and was able to admire, the two silver bracelets inlaid with carnelian, lapis lazuli and turquoise butterflies.

She submitted patiently while her nurse perfumed and dressed her, applied her make-up, fastened the jewelry around her neck and wrists, and finally set about the lengthy task of weaving dozens of fine braids with her thick shoulder-length black hair. My Dream had been banished from the room, and entrusted to the young slave boy she relied on to exercise the endlessly energetic dog when she was otherwise occupied, or simply not in the mood herself.

“You are no great beauty like your mother,” Aneski observed as she stepped back to admire her handiwork, “but I dare say you are lovely enough.”

“Do you really think so?” She was nearly of a height with her nurse, but she suddenly felt like a baby about to take her first steps. She was afraid of literally tripping in front of the king or otherwise disgracing herself.

“I do.” Aneski began carefully putting away the little bottles of ground minerals with which she had painted the young woman sitting tense and straight backed as a statue behind her. “Yet I dare say your parents indulge you too much. They have not prepared you as they should have for your future.”

Asenath said nothing. She was growing all too familiar with Aneski's falsely casual tone of voice, flung out like a fishing line in the hope she would bite by asking, “What do you mean?” She was learning not to.

Pharaoh's daughters were indeed wearing much more contemporary jewelry. The oldest princess smiled condescendingly down at Asenath's beetle necklace as she whispered something to one of her sisters, after which they both laughed. However, in the temple of Re her father was the equal of Pharaoh, and her mother's beauty far exceeded any of the queens'. She walked behind her mother near the head of the procession, and because Pharaoh only had three daughters, the youngest princess fell into place beside Asenath with a friendly smile she gladly returned. They were the same height, but she knew the princess was a year older. Led by Pharaoh and the high priest of Re, no one spoke as they ascended a ramp into the inner temple. The formal introductions would occur later at the banquet, but what Asenath had already seen of Pharaoh had calmed her nerves considerably. Senwosret looked like a kind man, older than she had expected, with a sagging chest that made the large pectoral resting against it look even harder than it was, the imperishable gold and precious stones in striking contrast to his aging flesh. The necklace matched the circlet he wore set with a cobra that reared from his forehead. The lovely little snake was made of gold inlaid with red carnelian and green feldspar, and its garnet eyes were also rimmed in gold—Pharaoh's personal deity that spit fire into the eyes of his enemies.

Asenath proudly watched her father standing beside the king. Both men faced a conical stone altar—representing the primordial dirt mound of creation—from which rose a miniature obelisk symbolizing the first ray of light at the beginning of time. The stone mound had looked much bigger to her when she was little, and today it completely failed to fill her with awe as she wondered what Joseph would think of it. But watching the two most powerful men in Kemet pouring water and wine over the stone, she already knew what Joseph would say—that a mound of dirt, primordial or otherwise, was already something, and that it was Elohim who had created the dirt in the first place, and even the darkness he filled with light. She knew Joseph personally talked to his god, but how did he and his people formally worship Elohim?

The inner courtyard grew increasingly warmer as the sun rose in the sky outside the temple. At the height of the ceremony, a shaft of light thrust through a hole in the ceiling straight down over the golden obelisk, which for a few breathtaking moments shone like the divine procreative light it symbolized. It was a splendid climax to the sacred rite, but it quickly passed, and suddenly all Asenath cared about was how thirsty she was. Glancing beside her at Sithathoriunet, she caught the girl staring at her. The princess' cheeks were soft and plump, and her large dark eyes were made even more prominent by the liberal amounts of black kohl and green malachite framing them. Asenath felt the subtle challenging pressure of the person inhabiting the liquid depths studying her with an avid interest she found herself naturally returning. When they turned to begin making their way out of the inner temple, the princess' shoulder brushed hers as she whispered, "You will be sitting at my table."

Months after her first royal banquet, Asenath enjoyed feasting on its memory. She had since learned that Sithathoriunet, Daughter of Hathor of Iunet, was Pharaoh's most beloved daughter. People said it was because she was the youngest, but Aseanth thought it was because she was by far the most interesting of the three princesses.

"You feel that way simply because Sithathor was nice to you," Aneski told her. "After all, you did not really speak to the other princesses. Did you?"

"No, and I did not need to!" she replied hotly. "I could tell just by looking at their faces, and by listening to them laugh with each other like hyenas. They kept secretly making fun of people for their own selfish amusement!"

Whining softly, My Dream thrust her head beneath Asenath's right hand.

Rlaxing as she stroked her dog, she mused out loud, "I wish people had tails, then they could never lie. Their tails would always give away what they were really feeling and thinking!"

Aneski stared at her a moment, and then, obviously against her will, let out a bark-like laugh.

☼

Some time in the night, Asenath flung off her linen sheet, parted the mosquito netting, and quickly slipping into a white tunic, left the room. The tiled floor was cool and hard beneath her bare feet, and the high ceiling above her was lost in darkness. Here and there along one wall, small oil lamps burned on wooden tables with three legs. Along the opposite wall, between columns carved and painted to evoke papyrus plants, the barred windows were dark and the night outside utterly silent. Passing the staircase leading up to the roof, she entered the part of the house where the administrative office was located, beyond which slept the higher ranking servants. No lamps burned here, but the first door on the left was open, and from it poured a golden light by which she was able to see some of the different types of fish decorating the floor of the corridor. Normally they were painted to look as if they were swimming up and down the hallway, but the illuminated fish—their colorful scales glimmering like precious gems—were all facing the door through which the light emanated. In her heart, she had known he would be here, but suddenly she was afraid. Most men found her beautiful, but would he? She was completely unadorned, her hair tangled with sleep, and her face naked of flattering paint. He would see her just as she truly was. The thought was so appalling, she came to a stop a few feet from the light, unable to take another step. Yet she found her feet wading silently through the dry river of the floor toward the open door, where she paused and, holding her breath, peered into the room.

Joseph was bent over a table covered with papyrus scrolls, concentrating on the one spread open before him. She was not surprised he could read hieroglyphs. Nothing seemed impossible for him. Everything went smoothly, life grew more rich and pleasurable by the day, with him in charge. Whenever she was concerned about something, she put the matter in his hands and he took care of it for her. She knew all she had to do was trust him, and she would never again want for anything.

Already, she had all she needed in the form of a happiness she had never known before—a joy that just kept growing and intensifying, until it bordered on a pain that only went away when she looked at him. Still scarcely daring to breathe, she watched as he gently rolled up the scroll. Heating a stick of wax in the heart of a flame, he carefully let three hot red drops fall, one over the other, onto the papyrus, and then firmly impressed them with his seal ring.

Before he could look up, she quickly turned and ran. Fleeing was the only way she could resist stepping into the room. She longed to caress his firm chest, slip her arms possessively around his neck, and kiss him until the painful hunger he aroused in her was satisfied. Instead, she hurried back to her bedroom. There was no doubt, however, that she would seek him out again. The days were growing too long, and the nights almost unbearable. Her desire for him was becoming terrible. Like the lioness goddess Sekhmet, she hungered to sink her nails into his flesh and devour him—a foreigner more uniquely delicious in her eyes than any other man, a Hebrew slave who did not even believe in the divinity of her ferocious passion.

Joseph!

Much as she wanted to cry out his name, no sound emerged from her mouth as, striding over to her dressing table, she picked up the mirror resting on it. The silver disc had been recently polished, and shone like the moon as it rose before her. Another woman's eyes met hers—her aunt Tarset's eyes. A scream trapped in her throat, she dropped the mirror, and stumbled against furniture that should not have been there as she hurried out into the corridor. Crouching with her back against a wall, she wrapped her arms around her knees and whimpered, “Nanny!” Immediately, her nurse was there, and Asenath told her what had happened. “I looked in a mirror and saw myself as another woman! If it had happened in a dream, it would have been scary enough, but I was awake!”

Murmuring reassurances, Aneski urged her to get up and return to her room.

“No! I really don't want to go in there!”

But her nurse insisted, and the next thing Asneath knew, she was lying in bed.

The air around her was so absolutely still, she could tell Aneski had not just left her. She had been sure she was awake, but in truth she had been dreaming. It had felt so real being in her uncle's house, she found it hard to believe she had not actually come from there. Her Ba must have flown through the darkness to Setka's estate, where she had seen Joseph working late into the night. It seemed her soul had somehow temporarily nested in Tarset's heart as she dream walked through the strange but familiar house. Was that really how her aunt felt about Joseph? Was it how she herself felt about the Hebrew man? Or was it because they both felt this way about him that a mysterious link had been forged between them? Yet how could this be possible? Apart from being a married woman, Tarset was much too proud to ever desire a slave. It was all too confusing to think about while still reeling from the shock of seeing another woman's reflection in the mirror instead of her own. She was certain of only one thing—there had been something extraordinarily wonderful about the golden light emanating from the Seal Room, and she already knew there was something special about the man she had seen standing in the magical light.

☼

The days passed swiftly as she spent a great part of each one reliving her dream. After the excitement of Pharaoh's visit, life had returned to normal, until she had this dream she could not stop thinking about. Although the dream had possessed no flesh and blood to begin with, it remained intensely satisfying to mull over again and again—much as her dog relished chewing on a big cow's bone—as she recalled the enticing new feelings she had briefly tasted in it.

What this meant was that she could not stop thinking about Joseph. That golden light emanating from the Seal Room, and the sight of him standing within it, was as irresistible to her soul as a honey cake was to her tongue. Had she really seen and felt everything through Tarset's eyes? Whenever she let herself dwell on how strongly she had desired to caress and embrace and kiss Joseph, she experienced a very real sensation of warmth deep in her belly which left her feeling uncomfortably restless. She could not think of it as just her dream, or even as only a dream. The experience felt like something which had truly happened to her soul while her body was asleep. When the sun was up, it was impossible to enter another person's heart and mind, but once darkness fell, it seemed all manner of things might be possible.

There were moments when Asenath succeeded in convincing herself the dream meant nothing, and had simply been a creation of her own imagination. But these rare moments evaporated as swiftly as drops of water on sun heated stone. All too vividly, she recalled the sensation of cool tiles beneath her bare feet as she moved silently and purposefully through her uncle's familiar house straight toward the Seal Room, like a lioness hunting her prey—Joseph. What mysterious power did this Hebrew man possess that made women dream of him and long to be with him? Nanny had told her about sorcerers who misused the power of the gods for their own evil ends, but she already knew, in her heart, that there had been nothing evil in the golden light she had seen in her dream. It was that light she remembered most of all, and which calmed her whenever she relived the shock of seeing another woman's face in the mirror instead of her own. In that golden light the wax Joseph melted onto the scroll had been such a deep and luminous red, whenever and wherever she saw that particular color now in the waking world, it always looked dull to her by comparison.

My Dream benefited from her owner's restlessness. Nearly

every morning, just after sunrise, Asenath took her dog for a long outing. Together they alternately ran and walked along the edges of the flax and barley fields, until her human legs tired, then she sat in the shade of date palms as her hound sprinted away, eventually returning with a dead animal dangling from her triumphantly grinning jaws.

It was after one such outing—while Asenath was hungrily perfuming her mouth with bread lavishly slathered with butter and pomegranate preserves—that Aneski came to tell her, an excited glint in her eyes, "Your parents wish to see us."

"Both of us?"

"Yes. Clean yourself up, quickly."

Her mother and father were in their garden pavilion seated side by side on wooden stools, a cat curled contentedly on each of their laps. Four sets of eyes watched them approach, two with cool indifference. Her parents' eyes were warm, yet the feelings in them were faceted with a complexity that suddenly made Aseanth nervous. She seated herself on a papyrus mat at their feet while her nurse stood to one side.

As her mother smiled, her father said, "My daughter, it is time to discuss your future. A messenger bird arrived from Shedet yesterday bearing a message for you from Princess Sithathoriunet."

"Really?" she replied stupidly, her heart fluttering with excited dread as if this same bird had abruptly flown into her chest.

"The princess sends her most affectionate greetings, and lets it be known that she very much hopes you will consider going to live at the palace as one of her handmaidens."

Aneski made a small sound that might have been one of triumphant pride, yet it also bore an uncanny relationship to the sound made by the small creature she had watched her dog catch that morning—the sound it made the instant it lost its life.

Her parents regarded her patiently. They did not need to tell her this was a great honor and that they were proud of her, or that the messenger bird had merely fulfilled their expectations. "For how long?" she asked bluntly.

Her mother replied, "Until it is time for you to marry."

She felt her life running away from her even faster than her dog, vanishing beyond some unknown horizon, and stealing her heart away with it even as her body remained behind on the papyrus mat, small and helpless as a rabbit caught in the implacable jaws of her future.

Her father asked abruptly, "What are you thinking, daughter?"

"I'm not sure... I'm thinking my future feels more like a dream than my dreams do."

Her mother almost sounded anxious, "Have you had a dream about your future? If so, you must tell us."

Looking down at her clenched hands, she recalled what Joseph had said to her, "Then pray to Elohim for us both, Asenath. And tell no one." *For us both... tell no one...* "No, mother. As far as I know, I have not dreamed of my future."

Her father said, "Then how do you wish to respond to the princess' request?"

"Please tell Sithathor I would be honored to serve her... and that I will be there as soon as I can."

"My sweetheart!" Sadeh sounded both amused and a little worried. "No one likes to wait for what they desire, especially a princess!"

"I know, and yet I feel... I feel I need until after the next harvest to properly prepare myself for life at court, so that I may serve Sithathoriunet with all the skill she expects from a highborn daughter of Re."

After a moment's silence, her father replied, "Very well. I will grant you this time to use wisely."

"No one is more experienced in the subtle etiquette of court life than my brother's wife," Sadeh pointed out. "I will ask Tarset to teach you all she knows."

"Yes, mother, thank you!" Conflicting emotions battled within her, but it was excitement—at the possibility of seeing Joseph again—that swiftly emerged victorious. Then she suddenly remembered something of vital importance. "Oh, and father, please tell Sithathor I'm bringing my dog with me!"

Aneski accompanied her back to her room, where Asenath finally found the courage to ask, "Will you be coming with me to court, Nanny? All handmaidens are entitled to their own personal attendants..."

"No, my dear." Sitting down in her chair, Aneski smiled up at her. "I will remain here. In Iuno, I mean, not here in this house."

"But where will you go?" Sinking to her knees beside her, Asenath grasped her nurse's hands and stared earnestly up at the familiar face which wore a confusing, almost excited, little smile. "Surly you know that wherever I am will always be your home?"

"So you say now, but we both knew this day would come, my dear. Now get up off the floor. You must begin, this very moment, to stop behaving like a child. A lady does not kneel before a servant."

Asenath stood obediently.

My Dream suddenly ran into the room. Rising onto her hind legs, she gave her mistress a hug and several passionate kisses, as if they had not seen each other in years.

"I doubt Sithathor will let you bring your dog, Asenath. How many times have I told you not to let her lick you on the lips like that? Her mouth is constantly full of dead animals! You will not last one day at court if you continue to behave in such a childish, even disgusting, fashion."

Sinking to her knees again, Asenath slipped both arms around her dog and hugged her for comfort.

Aneski sighed, and when she spoke again, her voice was

more gentle, almost lazy with satisfaction, "Your father promised me, when I became your wet nurse, that should you live to become a woman, I would be rewarded with a little house of my own. And your mother, Hathor bless her, has since told me that she will also give me a slave to tend my garden and clean the house... in which I will not be living alone."

Asenath learned a great deal that morning, including that her nurse's life had, for some time now, not revolved exclusivly around her, as she had assumed. And if Aneski had a secret life, it was entirely possible that all the servants and slaves around her nurtured hopes and dreams completely invisible to her, but which she suddenly felt permeating the house like a strong, cloying incense demanding some recognition from her in exchange. Rising reverently toward heaven, sacred incense created a channel through which the gods could make good things happen because people believed in and revered them. And as if it had only been yesterday, she remembered what her father had once said to her—that a person who does not believe in the gods is a person who can never be fully and truly happy, a person at the mercy of blind natural forces which will inevitably destroy them. "Maat is the eternal beauty and justice of Re," he had told her, "and as long as Maat flows through your heart, informing all your actions, your life will bloom and flourish."

She had not really understood what he meant then, but she suspected her father had deliberately planted this concept in her heart when all she had the power to do was accept it. And now, years later—listening to Aneski confessing her secret joy—she experienced an odd sensation, both painful and sweet, as she realized the love they felt for each other, which at first had flowed so strongly, was a divine water that would never evaporate. The love between them had become placid as a canal, defined primarily by external circumstances, and even those were soon to be diverted into the gardens of two entirely different futures. Yet she knew the water—the love—would forever remain to rise to the surface whenever they saw each other again.

Aneski stopped talking, and with a hint of exasperation said, "Were you listening to me, Aseath? You have that look..."

"Yes, of course I was listening! I was just thinking how happy I am for you, and how much I look forward to coming to visit you in your new home and meeting your husband, who sounds wonderful!"

Aneski looked away. "He became a slave only through the fault of his father, who could not pay his debts. But he worked hard and well for many years, and when his master died, his master's children—who had grown up with Kuhy and loved him dearly—at once offered him his freedom, along with a generous sum of money, two goats and a pig. He would have spent most of his money renting a house in town, but by the grace of Hathor, we had already met, and I asked him to wait. I told him that one day I would own a house of my own. I dared to be so bold because from the moment our eyes met, I felt our hearts beating as one."

"Really? You loved him from the moment you saw him?"

"Yes, I believe I did," Aneski replied thoughtfully. "Even more powerful than the smell of the dyes he was delivering—as he did regularly when he was still a slave—the perfume of the Lady of Love pervaded the courtyard when he rode in on his master's cart, and I went out to meet him in place of Nebt, who on that day was lying sick in bed, Hathor be praised!"

Asenath found herself thinking, with a wonder laced with regret, that just when she was preparing to leave the comfortable bed of her home, was when she was beginning to wake up to the secret dreams of people she had always taken for granted as mere characters in her own.

Chapter 7

One afternoon a week, Asenath traveled respectably by covered litter to her uncle's house, where she met with Tarset for lessons on court etiquette. Potifer Setka's wife did not favor pets of any kind, and refused to let My Dream anywhere near her spacious bedchamber, which also served as a sitting room opening onto the garden.

After less time than it took a rug woven of sunlight and shadow to move the length of a step across the floor, Asenath was bored. The days were growing shorter, but to her they felt longer than ever. Glancing only occasionally at her aunt, she studied the fine latticework screens overlooking the garden. Her lessons consisted primarily of court gossip.

"Listen up, little niece," Tarset demanded every now and then when she sensed her student's attention wandering. "These are all things you should know about the illustrious individuals you will soon be living around. It will be well for you if you pay attention. Such fine details may seem inconsequential to you now, but I assure you that there is no better way to win a person's affection than by sharing their opinions and tastes."

Despite the fact that all she did was sit on a stool and listen, such statements made Asenath feel not only bored but indescribably weary. She had learned not to challenge her aunt's views and opinions on their first afternoon together when she had dared to observe, "But when I was Sithathor's table companion, the princess did not seem to-" and Tarset had immediately interrupted her with the statement, "She was performing. Everyone at court is always acting. The trick is to understand what they are really thinking."

Asenath did not believe her, she could not. It was impossible to imagine people who worshiped Maat rarely speaking and behaving truthfully.

The first time she had seen this bedchamber was in a dream. It had been at once frightening and exciting when, upon entering it, she had known exactly where to look for the dressing table. The mirror had been lying at a different angle, and was not as luminous as it had appeared in her dream, but it was still right where she had expected it to be.

"I don't suppose, Asenath, that your dusty old tutor has exposed you to the latest love poems?"

"Love poems?" She had just been wondering where Joseph was.

"By the lost phallus of Osiris!" Tarset laughed. "What a dull household you have grown up in! Do your parents never hire musicians and dancers to entertain their guests? Love songs are becoming quite popular at court, and especially pleasing to the oldest princesses are the duets in which a handsome young harpist sings the part of the pining lover, and a female singer the part of the woman he desires more than life itself. The royal women employ their own musicians, and spend countless hours dreaming of young noblemen, all of whom are more handsome and desirable than their own husbands."

"Sithathor does not join them?" Asenath said hopefully.

"No. That one still behaves like a child. I can see why she took to you at once. Oh please, there's no need to be offended. I wasn't insulting you. I simply meant to say that you and Sithathor are still free to do as you please because your parents love and indulge you. You are both rather immature for your ages, I think. Do you realize that I was only fourteen when Setka made me his wife?"

"No..." The thought made her feel a little sick.

Tarset smiled. "Don't look so worried. A great deal of pleasure awaits you as a woman, for I seriously doubt your parents will force you to wed a man you don't desire. They love you too much. However, should Pharaoh decide to honor some powerful Nomarch by offering him the daughter of the high priest of Re as his wife, well, that is another matter entirely."

After waking up in the dead of night and lying sleepless for a long time, Asenath found the courage to whisper a prayer which she felt—and almost truly believed—might be both heard and answered, "Elohim, please help me become fully conscious in my dreams!"

Joseph had told her to "pray for us both" and this seemed one way to do so, for it was probably only in a dream she would be able to see him again in order to bid him farewell before she left for the capital.

Attempting to fall asleep consciously, she lay on her left side imagining, in as much detail as possible, her ship sailing away from Iuno, her beloved home, gradually growing smaller and smaller, until it vanished behind a bend in the River as her awareness remained behind hovering over the dark water, for the sun was setting on her childhood... Abruptly, she experienced the sensation of dry stone beneath her bare feet, and becoming aware of walking through her garden at night, she realized she had succeeded in consciously entering a dream.

Elohim had answered her prayer!

In the darkness, she came upon something resembling a curtain made not of cloth, but of living vines, from each of which grew three rows of silvery-green oval leaves. The vines all hung from the branches of an enormous tree. She could see only this living curtain of vines, and she distinctly felt one of them inviting her to interact with it. But when she tried to raise her hand to touch it, she became aware of someone clinging to her—a faceless shadow preventing her from moving forward.

She commanded, "Let go of me" and after a brief struggle was able to separate her dream body from the shadow, which fell gently to the ground at her feet. She was now able to glide up to the vine, and lightly touch some of its small yet sturdy leaves with her fingertips. Up close, the vines also resembled rows of columns, and as she drifted deeper among them, touching one here and another one there, she began feeling, as well as hearing, a high vibrating sensation humming through the infinite depths of the dream night.

She said softly, "Joseph?" and then more boldly, "Joseph!"

Suddenly, between several rows of vines, she perceived the beginning of a staircase made of luminous white stone curving gently upward. This temple of vines seemed to hold the secret to reaching Joseph, for she could feel his presence...

Slowly, she woke up.

☼

The following day, Asenath was late for her weekly appointment with Tarset. Engaged in writing down some of her dreams, beginning with the most recent one, she lost track of time. It had occurred to her that she was in the position to do something about Kemet's need for another dream papyrus, this one specializing in conscious dreams, and all their unique qualities and possibilities. She did not mention Joseph by name in her written account but referred to him simply as "my friend." To her surprise, she had discovered that the exercise of writing was almost pleasurable when she was not merely copying what someone else had said.

She was daring to hope that, from now on, she would become conscious in her dreams more often, for clearly Elohim had heard and answered her prayer. She absolutely had to tell Joseph. It was imperative she find a way to see him again before she left. He had to know she had prayed to Elohim and that his god had heard her.

It was not until her wrist began to ache that she realized how late it was, and her positive mood soured with every jolt of the litter carrying her to her uncle's estate. The bearers were practically running, for she had urged them to hurry, yet she still had too much time to think and worry. Would Atum-Re be angry with her for praying to a foreign god? She fervently hoped not, because at night, Re seemed too busy fighting and defeating the evil serpent Apep to bother with helping people wake up in their dreams.

When a housemaid confirmed that the Lady Tarset was in her bedchamber, Asenath ran all the way there, only to stop dead on the threshold when a scene as unexpected as one in a dream rose before her eyes. Joseph and Tarset were sitting across from each other playing the ancient board game Mehen. Personally, she had never liked this game, made for two players, because the upper surface of the circular stone board was in the form of a coiled serpent, into which had been carved regular scale-like slots. Tarset's board was made of limestone, and the seven coils of the snake—which even from a distance she could see contained hundreds of slots—were black with yellow stripes. Beginning at the tip of the tail, the two players raced each other around the serpent, working inward toward the head. Asenath had come upon the scene just as her aunt was casting the sticks. Laughing triumphantly, Tarset moved her piece, a seated ivory lioness still far behind her opponent's ivory lion.

Although Asenth stood motionless on the threshold, Joseph sensed her presence, and looked up at her. Tarset followed his gaze, and a fierce displeasure tightened her mouth for an instant, before she smiled and spoke with false sweetness, “You are late, my dear... No, go ahead and throw, Joseph, I have no intention of interrupting our game... In fact, you're so late, Asenath, that I thought you weren't coming today.”

She stepped into the room as Joseph cast his sticks across the table with a little too much force, because two of them rolled off onto the floor.

Tarset cried cheerfully, “You lose your turn!”

His back visibly tense, Joseph said nothing.

Asenath wondered if he had been resigned to playing the game all the way through to the end before she arrived, or if he had actually, in some sense, been enjoying himself, but now felt awkward with her as an audience. His mistress had commanded him to ignore Asenath and continue playing, putting him in the uncomfortable position of behaving rudely to another lady.

Suddenly, her dislike of Tarset burned so hot, for a breathtaking moment it flared into hatred. Moving to stand on one side of the gaming table, she observed with undisguised satisfaction, “You are losing, aunt.”

Tarset ignored her as she moved her lioness, but then abruptly stood up. “I can't possibly enjoy myself with you hovering over us like that, Asenath. Since you are here now, we will proceed with the entertainment I had arranged for you, a taste of what you can expect at court. No, Joseph, you are not dismissed. You work so hard for us, you deserve some time off. After my husband, of course, you are the most important man on the entire estate. It scarcely matters anymore that you're a slave, and it is not becoming to your exalted position that you don't seem to appreciate that. Your excellent work entitles you to more pleasures than you seem to realize are at your disposal."

For the first time in her life, Asenath found herself wholeheartedly agreeing with her aunt, which worried her.

Striding to the door, Tarset yelled for a servant, and one immediately came running. "Find my new harpist and tell him to meet me at the green and white pavilion by the fountain. I also desire some light refreshments. Joseph, if you please."

He strode to the double doors leading out into the garden, and opened them for her.

Following her aunt, Asenath looked up at him, but he avoided her eyes.

It would have been very pleasant out in this especially cool and shady area of Potifer Setka's lavish Pleasure House, Asenath thought, if only she and Joseph had been alone there. In the gathering dusk—before servants arrived and began lighting lamps hanging from various branches—the leaves of the trees had vividly evoked last night's dream. She had felt very close to Joseph in her dream, but unable to communicate with him, and the same thing was happening now, for although he was sitting on a mat on the other side of Tarset, they were not free to speak to each other. She longed to share with him the idea that had just bloomed in her mind, "Dreams are mysteriously nourishing fruits growing in the darkness of sleep" but she could not.

A handsome young harpist sat quietly tuning his strings as attendants set a platter of fresh fruit before them, and filled their wine cups. Meanwhile, Asenath grew increasingly restless listening to Tarset whisper in private asides to Joseph, pointedly ignoring her. She guessed her aunt was deliberately being rude to punish her, not so much for being late, but for having come at all, and spoiled her private time with Joseph. There was no doubt in her heart now that she had dreamed true the night she found herself seeing through Tarset's eyes.

When the harpist ran slender fingers across the strings of his instrument, an accompanying silence descended over the garden as even frogs and crickets seemed to pay momentary homage to the richly promising sound by falling silent.

As Tarset leaned toward the artful arrangement of bite-size pieces of watermelon, red grapes and mulberries, Asenath glanced over at Joseph, and was thrilled to see that he had also taken advantage of the moment to look over at her, the lamp hanging just behind her reflected in his dark eyes. But then Tarset's haughty profile rose between them again as the harpist began to sing:

Your love has penetrated all within me
like honey plunged into water.
Your love is like the advance of flames in straw,
its longing like the downward swoop of a hawk.
I am a wild goose, a hunted one, my gaze on your hair
a blue-black bait concealing a trap that is to catch me.
The voice of the wild goose cries out as she seizes her prey.
I shall not set the snares today for your love has caught me.

His hands hovering over the vibrating strings as they grew silent and still, the harpist reverently lowered his head.

Tarset inquired lightly, “Well, Asenath, what did you think of the song?” even as she turned toward Joseph and, pressing a plump red grape against his lips, forced them to part and accept it onto his tongue.

Asenath answered sharply, “I can't really admire a woman who makes a man feel like a goose.”

Flashing her an almost approving smile, Taset reached for a slice of watermelon. “And what would you know about that, child?”

Speaking in the politely indifferent tone of voice her aunt had instructed her to use at formal court gatherings, she replied, “Even a baby knows that real love is not cruel.”

The harpist raised his head. Maybe he was getting a crook in his neck.

"My innocent little niece. How sweet that you still believe desire and love will always hold hands. Eventually, you will learn otherwise." She raised her voice. "Another song, please!"

This time the music made by the strings, caressed with one forceful stroke, sounded more ominous than lovely to Asenath, and despite the soothing depth and resonance of the singer's voice, her body tensed listening to his words:

> "She is unique; there is no one like her.
> She is more beautiful than any other.
> Look, she is like a star goddess arising
> at the beginning of a happy new year;
> brilliantly white, bright skinned;
> with beautiful eyes for looking,
> with sweet lips for speaking;
> she has not one phrase too many.
> With a long neck and white breast,
> her hair of genuine lapis lazuli;
> her arms more brilliant than gold;
> her fingers soft as lotus petals,
> her thighs offer beauty and capture
> my heart in a night that belongs to us!

"ASENATH, WAKE UP."

She opened her eyes.

Listening to a lone bird singing, she slowly realized it was not mist but mosquito netting surrounding her bed. Someone had just spoken to her... She must have dreamed the voice. But whose voice had it been? Who had addressed her dreaming soul with such forceful yet calm authority, fully expecting to be obeyed? The answer that occurred to her was both infinitely exciting and terrifying.

Had it been Elohim commanding her to wake up in a dream? Yet she could not remember being in a dream at all, and the Voice lingered like a presence in the room even now that her eyes were open. Never had she heard such a Voice. Its tone had been male, yet at the same time she could not really think of it as having come from a mere man. Although there was a supreme masculine authority in the Voice, it was tempered with the understanding gentleness of a mother's love.

She lay there thinking about this mysterious Voice as the room grew light around her, until the increasingly loud chatter of birds began feeling urgently directed at her. The Voice had told her to wake up, yet here she was still lying in bed, postponing for as long as possible the beginning of her last full day at home. Tomorrow her ship sailed for Iuno. Her uncle would be accompanying her. Setka was looking forward to showing her the sites, and had already arranged for them to overnight in the homes of some of his friends and acquaintances along the way.

Sitting up, she fought a brief skirmish with her mosquito netting as she struggled with a fact that abruptly stung her. It was probably Joseph who had arranged for his master's accommodations during the journey. This meant he knew she was leaving Iuno, and when. It was old news for him. Why then was she so surprised, even hurt, to realize he was aware she was leaving? Because he had not sought an opportunity to bid her farewell? But how could he?

Quietly entering the room, Aneski avoided her eyes as she washed, oiled and dressed the daughter of her heart in a brightly colored wool dress, around which she wrapped a warm red wool cloak. It was the coldest month of the year, when the River had receded, but the fields were still too wet to securely accommodate the seeds of new life. They were grieved to be saying goodbye to each other yet also excited by their respective futures. As a result, their daily rituals had become tense, silent affairs. Though outwardly they continued behaving as child and nurse, in truth they were already two women soon to be living very different lives.

"Chef is preparing a great feast," Aneski informed her. "Potifer Setka is at the dock inspecting the boats, but naturally he will be here before the first cup of wine is poured."

"Naturally."

It was a tired old joke at which neither one of them even smiled.

When Asenath felt her eyes growing hot, she announced,

"I'm not hungry. I think I'll take My Dream for a long walk on this lovely cold morning!"

"As you wish." The fact that Aneski did not object to her skipping breakfast testified to the strangeness of the day. For Asenath, it was like hearing the sound of the tomb door closing on their old dead relationship, and in her heart she knew they would never again be able to resurrect anything but a pale ghost of their former intimacy.

Escaping the room, she found My Dream with her young handler, and the three of them set off together. It was not long before Asenath realized what her true intention was, at which point she separated from her companions as she took the path leading to her uncle's house. It was very early, and she was confident Tarset was still asleep. One reason she had visited her aunt in the afternoons was because the lady was known to stay in bed until Re was high in the sky. Aneski had told her that Setka was at the dock, so it was possible she might be able to see Joseph alone, if only for a few moments, which was far better than not seeing him at all. It would not take long to tell him that she had begun praying to Elohim every night.

When she arrived at her uncle's estate, she did not announce herself. Instead, she entered the grounds through one of the garden gates, and followed the paths that led to the wing where the Seal Room was located, fervently hoping Joseph would be there reading scrolls and setting his seal to them as she had seen him doing in her dream. She passed a handful of gardeners, none of whom looked up from their work. She seemed invisible to them, as though she was in her dream body. But as she approached the windows of the Seal Room, she heard no sound of movement from within, and when she peered through one of the screens, she was profoundly disappointed by the stillness and emptiness of the interior space. Refusing to accept it, she simply stood there waiting and hoping. When only a few heartbeats later Joseph walked into the room, she could scarcely believe it. He was alone, and he got quickly to work. There were numerous scrolls piled on the desk, almost as if he had not been free to attend to them for some time. All she had to do now was slip into the house through the back door, and from there it was a short walk to...

Tarset's angry voice intruded on her thoughts, “Did you really think you could sneak past me?”

Asenath glanced wildly around her, but she was obviously alone in the garden. Looking quickly back into the room, she saw her aunt standing in the doorway. Through the latticework screen, the older woman's face appeared shattered by some great inner torment. Then she realized Tarset's expression was not an optical illusion, for she could see Joseph's face clearly.

“Come with me!” Tarset commanded as she turned her back on him. “I have a much more important task for you!”

Asenath sensed Kyky's silent ghost standing beside her when, returning her eyes to Joseph, she was transported back to the day she had first seen him. As he looked slowly around him, the expression on his face was very much as she remembered it —strained and tired, yet mysteriously calm and resolute. Then he followed Tarset out of the room without looking back.

Turning, Asenath sprinted down the path that would take her to the other side of the house, and one of the windows looking into her aunt's bedchamber. She made it there just in time to hear Tarset, who was perched on the edge of her bed, demand, "Come and sleep with me!"

"No," Joseph replied firmly from where he stood just inside the open doorway. "My master trusts me with everything in his entire household. No one here has more authority than I do. He has held back nothing from me except you, because you are his wife. How could I do such a wicked thing? It would be a great sin against God."

Rising and striding toward him, Tarset cried, a shrill note of desperation in her voice, "Oh come on! Sleep with me!" and grabbed his cloak.

Tearing himself away from her, Joseph ran from the room.

For a long moment, Tarset stared down at his cloak, still clutched in her hand. Then she screamed.

Feeling caught in her aunt's nightmare, Asenath desperately wished she had the power to wake them both up, but it was too late. Every servant within earshot had already come running.

"Look!" Tarset told them. "My husband has brought this Hebrew slave here to make fools of us! He came into my room to rape me, but I screamed. When he heard me scream, he ran outside and got away, but he left his cloak behind with me!"

At once, the male servants turned on their heels to chase after Joseph, while the women stood staring at the robe in their mistress' hand with unconcealed dismay.

Taking a shaky breath, Tarset declared, "I will keep the cloak with me until my husband comes home! Then I will tell him what happened, that the Hebrew slave he brought into our house tried to come in and fool around with me!"

Asenath turned away from the window, but the nightmare failed to dissolve around her. What would her uncle do to Joseph when he heard this lie about him spoken as the truth? Fortunately, she knew for a fact that he would not be home for hours. She was walking swiftly, almost running, but inside she felt weak and sick thinking about her uncle happily eating and drinking with no idea what awaited him when he returned home. He would believe Tarset, he had to, she was his wife, the mistress of his house, and Joseph was only a slave.

The situation remained a nightmare, but Asenath was fully conscious of what she had to do.

Chapter 8

The way home felt endless. As she walked alongside the empty fields, Asenath marveled at how easy it had been for Tarset to sow the seed of a lie in the minds of her household. Whether or not the lie germinated in their hearts and they actually believed her did not matter—if enough people cultivated a falsehood it could appear to be the truth.

By the time she crossed the threshold, she was breathless more with anxiety than from the exertion. By the time she crossed the threshold, she was breathless more with anxiety than from the exertion. But her uncle had sent a message indicating he would be delayed because of an issue with the transport boat, her mother had gone to the temple with her husband, the servants and slaves were busy as usual, and Nanny was also conspicuous by her absence. It was Asenath's last day living at home, yet it was as though nothing momentous was due to happen the next time the sun rose. Her room suddenly felt like a prison, but it was too chilly outside to go for a swim. Only My Dream's affectionate warmth kept her from screaming in frustration. All her chests were packed, there was nothing to do except wait, and wait, and wait...

When the solar disc came to rest on top of the desert mountains, and there was still no sign of her uncle, she went for another long walk with her dog feeling it was high time somebody wondered where she was, and had to wait for her! She did not know which hurt more—the thought that her parents seemed to be avoiding her, or the possibility that, for them, this day was no more remarkable than any other. The official last day of her childhood was heavy and important as a great foundation stone in the pyramid of her life, but apparently for everyone else it was not much weightier than a pebble. Her departure tomorrow would make a small ripple in their lives, which would be quickly absorbed into the smoothly placid routine of daily existence.

Stars were slowly beginning to appear overhead, faint and far away and completely indifferent to all the feelings burning in her heart. Yet whenever she looked up, a star seemed to manifest in response to one of her emotions, until there were too many to keep track of. Unable to remember ever being this cold, she clutched her wool cloak more tightly around her. Her life in Iuno was ending and so was Joseph's. She was leaving her parents' house and he was leaving her uncle's house. As My Dream ran ahead of her along the familiar paths, she almost felt Joseph walking beside her in the falling darkness. It was easy to imagine him gazing up at the stars, the same stars she was looking at now, as he prayed to his god, and with a thrill of intimacy—as if her thoughts were magical fingertips touching his naked soul—she dared to add her prayer to his, "Elohim, please help us!"

As the lights of her home came into view, Asenath finally

understood why in her first conscious dream her goddess' wings had flown over to Joseph. The wings belonged not only to Neith but to Maat, the goddess of truth. This part of her dream was being fulfilled, for she was on her way now to tell her uncle the truth of what had happened between his wife and Joseph. Tarset would demand the slave's life, for that was the law, but she would not get it. Joseph's fate could not possibly rest in that terrible woman's hands. She, Asenath, would tell the true story and, somehow, all would be well.

The aroma of roasting meats drifting toward her from the kitchens roused impatient growls from her empty stomach, but she could not possibly eat anything until the battle was over and she had proved victorious. Only after her hunger for justice was satisfied could she take any pleasure in gratifying her physical appetite. The one consolation she had taken from this awful day was knowing that it must have felt equally endless to Tarset as she sat clutching Joseph's robe, and nursing the lie she would spit like venom in her husband's face the moment he got home.

"There you are!" Aneski declared. "Your uncle finally arrived, and he and your parents have been waiting for you in the dining room! Come, I will quickly help you change into the dress..."

"No!" She literally ran from another intolerable delay, and before the servant could even think of announcing her, barged into the dining room.

"There she is!" Her mother smiled indulgently up at her.

Sadeh sat across from her husband at a table on which were arranged a variety of bite size delicacies intended to stimulate the appetite before the main courses.

"Before we eat, the truth must be served!" she declared breathlessly. "I have come to Cut Maat!"

Her father asked sharply, "What is this about, daughter?"

"It is about the truth, father! I am going to tell you the truth and you must believe me!"

Pushing her chair back, Sadeh hurried over to her. "My dear! What has happened?"

Her mother's loving concern had no power to soothe her now, a distressing fact that intensified her already nearly unbearable tension. Backing away from her, she begged, "Please, sit down mother! I must speak!"

Her hands poised uncertainly in the empty air where her daughter had just been, Sadeh hesitated a moment, then obeyed her.

Asenath held her father's eyes. She needed his support, for the high priest had Re's ear and Maat was the daughter of Re. She felt she could not begin speaking until the importance of the situation was in some way acknowledged by him. His eyes were unreadable as he nodded, just a slight inclination of his head, but to her the world seemed to shift back into its proper place. She was able to take a deep, steadying breath. In order to make the truth's power fully felt by her audience, she would need to condense time with one small lie that would hurt no one.

"I had a dream last night," she began, looking away from her audience at the lamp closest to her. "It was a true dream. I am experienced enough to know that not all dreams are journeys, but some are, and last night my Ba bird flew out of my body and traveled to Potifer Setka's house. In my dream, I walked down the familiar corridors with a mysterious purpose I could not define, and soon found myself in the passage leading to the Seal Room. A beautiful light shone from within it, and when I looked inside, I saw Joseph hard at work. As I watched him in secret, I saw him set the Potifer's seal on a scroll. The wax looked red as blood. But then I abruptly ran away, and found myself in Lady Tarset's bedchamber. It was very strange... I was experiencing feelings unfamiliar to me, emotions and desires that all centered around Joseph. He looked so handsome to me, I could not stop thinking about him. I longed to... to caress his chest... to slip my arms around his neck... to kiss him..."

Her mother gasped.

Ignoring the sound, she began speaking more quickly. "Instead, I walked over to the dresser, and picked up the silver mirror lying there, which shone bright as the moon. But when I held the mirror up before me, it was not my own face I saw reflected in it. I saw Tarset's eyes staring straight into mine. The shock was so great, it woke me up. Feeling the gods had sent me a message, and it was important I go visit my aunt, I left even before perfuming my mouth. It was not until I arrived at the house that I remembered how early it was. So, not wishing to wake her, I walked through the gardens. When I came to the windows of the Seal Room, I couldn't resist looking in, and there was Joseph working at the table just as I had seen him in my dream. Then suddenly Tarset appeared on the threshold, and commanded him to follow her. She sounded angry when she told him she had a much more important task for him. As he followed her obediently, I ran around the house to a window looking into my aunt's bedchamber, for I knew, from my dream, that was where she was going."

When she paused, the silence in the room was so intense, the subtle sputtering of wicks in hot oil sounded unnaturally loud. She did not take her eyes off the flame she was focusing on. She herself felt like a living wick through which the painful fire of the truth was burning.

"As I watched in secret," she continued more slowly and firmly, "I saw Tarset sitting on the edge of her bed as she commanded, 'Come and sleep with me!' But Joseph refused her, and Maat has helped me remember his words just as he spoke them. He said, 'No. My master trusts me with everything in his entire household. No one here has more authority than I do. He has held back nothing from me except you, because you are his wife. How could I do such a wicked thing? It would be a great sin against God'. But Tarset did not listen. She walked over to him and cried, 'Come on, sleep with me!' and grabbed his cloak. Joseph tore himself away from her and ran from the room, leaving only his cloak in her hand. And when Tarset realized he had fled, but she was still holding his cloak, she screamed. All the men came running, and she told them, 'Look! My husband has brought this Hebrew slave here to make fools of us! He came into my room to rape me, but I screamed. When he heard me scream, he ran outside and got away, but he left his cloak behind with me! I will keep the cloak with me until my husband comes home! Then I will tell him what happened, that the Hebrew slave he brought into our house tried to come in and fool around with me!' I heard everything she said, and all day she has been waiting for you to get home, uncle, so she can tell you this lie."

She had been staring directly at the flame for so long that when she looked away from it, the faces of the three adults were overshadowed in her eyes, and she could not discern their expressions. However, the silence emanating from them was reassuring—it seemed to say that they believed her. And well they should, for she had invoked both the power of dreams to foretell the future, and the law of Maat, which demanded the truth from all of Re's children. It was the rule of Maat on which the beautiful order and prosperity of the Two Lands depended, for more than anywhere else in the world, in Kemet truth and justice ruled supreme. Then the soothing shadow cleared from her eyes, and she felt her heart crash into the room like a bird plummeting from heaven as her vision seemed to collide with tables and chairs, before coming anxiously to rest on the faces of the three people sitting before her.

Clenched hands resting on his table, his expression haggard, Setka was the first to speak in a listless voice, “If a male slave is even suspected of sexually assaulting a noble woman, the penalty is death.”

“But uncle, I told you-”

Her father cut in sharply, “Let him speak.”

“If the entire household did not already know about this, I would have the power to deal more fairly with Joseph, but as it is, I cannot accuse my wife of lying, or of desiring to commit adultery against me. Tarset is a highborn lady and Joseph is a slave. I cannot possibly honor his word above hers. The Mistress of my house would lose the respect of all our staff. Inevitably, she would demand I send them all away and hire new servants. But by then the tale would have spread, and there would be no foreseeable end to her shame or her fury.” His mouth twisted with a disturbing hybrid of anger and pain. “Joseph has served me well. The blame must fall on him... but I will not have him killed.”

His tone neutral, the high priest said, “A woman loses all her legal rights if it can be proven she was unfaithful to her husband, who may then do with her as he wills.”

It was Sadeh's turn to speak. “Tarset was unfaithful to her husband only in her heart and the laws of men have no authority over our hearts.”

Like a man waking from a nightmare, Setka vigorously

rubbed his face with both hands as he sat up. "Whether he was, in fact, guilty of sleeping with my wife or not, if Joseph was a free man, I could demand financial compensation from him or command him to work off his offense. But Joseph is a slave. All I can do is spare his life, and send him to the Place of Confinement."

Asenath glanced desperately at her father, Maat's living representative, but he was looking at his brother-in-law. "What is the Place of Confinement?" she demanded.

"It is where Pharaoh's prisoners are held," her uncle replied, still avoiding her eyes. "It is run by the Captain of the Guard, my counterpart in the palace at Shedet. I cannot tell him the truth, but I will make Joseph's special talents known to him, and personally see to it he is given a comfortable cell of his own."

Her mother said, "Maat has been well served by you today, Asenath, but now it is time for my brother to go home, where he will undoubtedly meet with a rage worthy of Sekhmet when he dares to deny Tarset Joseph's blood."

"But Maat is *not* being well served, mother, not if a man who is innocent must go to prison!"

Her father spoke. "It is impossible to discern from your dream, Asenath, or from what you later saw with your waking eyes, whether or not Joseph's behavior in any way encouraged Tarset's lust. It is justice enough that this slave is being allowed to live."

She was forced to seal all her protests in her mouth as in a tomb. The tone of the high priest's voice had made it clear there was nothing more she could say to help further Joseph's cause, while the haunted look in her uncle's eyes revealed how much he was dreading the scene awaiting him at home. Not only that, he was also losing his favorite slave, the slave who had helped make him even more wealthy. She could not help feeling sorry for him, and perhaps—once they were both far away from Iuno and Tarset—she might be able to persuade him to set a date for Joseph's release.

When Asenath opened her eyes the next morning, she could not remember any of her dreams, and as the first day of her new life unfolded, she began to feel as though she had not completely woken up. Colors looked deeper in a sunlight that flowed more richly into rooms, like a divine honey reminding her of how long ago—at the very beginning of memory—her father had told her bees were sacred to Re, and a symbol of kingship, because they always knew where they were in relation to the sun.

When the household lined up in the front courtyard to see her off, she saw every individual face with a dream-like clarity, almost as if for the first time, and she suffered the impression that, until that moment, she had been sleepwalking through life. She was glad Kyky was not among them. Her secret childhood friend lived in her heart now, and was coming with her in the form of the smiling young woman she had last seen in a dream.

"We will embrace again soon, my love!" Her mother whispered in her ear as she held her close. "Your father and I will be traveling to court just as we always do. Be good, and enjoy yourself!"

"I will!"

"But please, my love, keep your dreams to yourself. If you must talk about them, do so only with Sithathor. Through her you will have Pharaoh's ear and protection. Trust no one else."

"Yes, mother." She had not wanted to believe Tarset's cynical view of life at court, but her mother had just made it clear that Maat was not as revered in the new royal capital as she was here in the ancient city of Iuno.

Eight men of the house guard accompanied her covered litter to the dock, four bearing her on their strong shoulders, one walking ahead, one behind her, and two beside her. She was glad of the cool weather, for her emotions remained uncomfortably hot, and the more of an effort she made to fan them with pleasant, idle thoughts, the worse she felt. She was surrounded by linen dyed a sky blue that seemed to seduce the sun into lingering in its soft folds, yet even as her eyes rested on the lovely color, she saw the darkness behind it—not the darkness of the night sky jeweled with stars but the depressing darkness of the prison Joseph would soon be confined to. And the harder she tried not to think about it, the more impossible it became.

It was a relief when the litter was set down. The curtain parted, and her uncle stepped forward to help her dismount. His hand was reassuringly firm and familiar, the very sensation of love and safety, yet this morning she resented how much she depended on it.

"Where is my dog?" she asked. "Mother assured me My Dream had already been brought to the dock."

"Indeed!" Gratitude flashed in his eyes that she had asked him a question he could answer in a way that would please her. He pointed in the direction of one of the smaller vessels docked behind the ship looming before them. "She is safe and sound on the transport boat with her handler. That other one is the kitchen boat."

The River was a brilliant blue and men were moving busily around them, but she did not look away from the transport boat. When her uncle turned to speak to one of the sailors, she shaded her eyes with both hands, intently searching for a glimpse of her dog. She thought she could just make out the front of her crate behind a large wooden chest, but she could not be sure. She continued scanning the boat, and when she came to the ramp leading up to the deck, she saw two of her uncle's house guards boarding on either side of a man walking between them whose hands were bound behind his back. Joseph! Joseph was being loaded onto the transport boat with the luggage! It came as a shock, yet also a relief that My Dream would be with him, and at least she knew now where they both were.

Lowering her hands, she did her best to emulate the affectionately stern voice she had heard her mother use with her brother countless times, "My darling uncle!"

Immediately turning toward her, he said solicitously, "Yes, my dear?"

"I just saw Joseph escorted onto the transport boat. His hands were tied behind his back. I'm assuming once we set sail it will no longer be necessary to restrain him. My dog loves him and he loves her. I'm very glad they will be together during the journey. And also, I just want you to know that I'm very proud of you for Cutting Maat."

"My dear..."

Pretending not to notice that his eyes had watered, she grasped one of his hands with both of hers. "And I'm very glad you're coming with me!"

"Sweet Asenath!" Blinking furiously, he stared down at her hands a moment, then gazing fixedly out at the River, he spoke in a confidential undertone, "Your love and respect are a balm for my heart, and because Maat is the health of our heart, I will confess to you, as I have to no one else, even my sister, although I suspect she knows... I confess that marrying Tarset was the biggest mistake of my life. My happiest years were when she was away at court with her sick mother. I should have divorced her long ago."

"Why didn't you?"

"I was too proud to let everyone know I had been a fool to marry her." Gently, he extricated his hand from her sympathetic grasp. "It was easier to pretend all was well between us."

"Did she... did she want you to kill Joseph?"

"Yes, of course she did, and I hope it will torment her to know that he still lives, forever out of her reach. But she has a wildcat's heart, that one. As soon as she's done licking her pride, she'll forget all about the man who injured it."

Asenath thought it best not to tell him she was certain it would be a very long time before his wife forgot about Joseph. She had seen through her aunt's mind and felt through her heart and knew perfectly well that Tarset had not only lusted after Joseph, she had been in love with him.

Asenath dreamed that she and Joseph and their dog were all together on a boat sailing upriver to the palace, where Pharaoh was waiting to receive them. Waking abruptly in an unfamiliar room felt stranger than her dream. It was a moment before she remembered they were in Itjtawy, honored guests of the Mistress of the House Senebtisy, a distant relation of her mother's family and a very wealthy woman. Last night over dinner, she had told them all about the tomb she was building very near the pyramid of Pharaoh Amenemhet.

Wishing she could return to her dream, Asenath closed her eyes again, but she saw only what she saw every day—the great

River bordered by fields being prepared for sowing. But when the land rose and she could see more from the boat, she was visibly reminded of how life ended suddenly—yet also mysteriously continued—as fertile land gave away to desert, from which sprouted the imperishable crop of great shining pyramids. Every Mansion of Eternity filled her with awe as she imagined the dead king sleeping deep inside the stone, yet never returning to his mummy, for his Ba bird had flown away long ago into the magical realm of a conscious dream that would last forever. But when her eyes tired of a pyramid's brilliant certainty—and she rested them on the soothing vision of moist fields waiting to be impregnated with new life—Asenath felt that eternity itself was a dream from which she would always wake to the simple miracle of each moment, as completely full of life as each blade of grass being savored by cattle oblivious to the unmoving monuments rising above them on the horizon.

Though the days of travel were long and monotonous, she did not tire of them. There was something wonderful about never having to stay in one place for too long. She also relished the intense relief and excitement she experienced every evening when, as darkness began swiftly and inexorably swallowing the world, the sight of welcoming torches being lit along the shore thrilled her heart. They always arrived at their scheduled mooring place just in time to avoid her childish fear of the ship running into a hidden sandbank, from which crocodiles could slip on board and devour them. Instead, she could now safely look forward to her own dinner.

She spent a good part of the day in the ship's cabin, occasionally accompanied by her uncle, but he seemed to prefer being on deck with the captain. The cabin was made of a light wooden framework covered by heavy linen hangings decorated with bright yellow and green squares. During the day, the cloth was rolled up to let the breeze in through windows set on both sides, and it was gazing out between their thin vertical slats that she spent most of her time watching land giving way to land as her thoughts, obeying deep hidden currents, flowed behind her eyes as tirelessly as the River.

Occasionally, a lookout standing in the front of the boat used a weighted line to determine the depth of the water, while at the stern a helmsman controlled the rudder's long paddle. They were traveling south, so the wind was with them and the rowers were often idle. They took to the oars when there were sandbanks to avoid, to increase their speed if necessary, and when the ship turned toward a pleasant location along the shore for the midday meal, the highlight of the day.

Whenever they relaxed together in the cabin, Setka took great pleasure in describing all the work happening on the kitchen boat. She happily indulged him in his detailed descriptions, aware that it helped him avoid thoughts of his wife and former slave. He had spoken to her only once of Joseph—when he informed her that he had been released from his bonds for the duration of the journey, and was helping row the transport boat. She had always thought of her uncle as a man heartily content with life, but she was beginning to suspect that what drove him toward food and drink was not merely a desire for pleasure. She knew he had never really been as happy as she had always believed him to be—he had confessed as much to her—but she found herself wondering if his less than fulfilling marriage was not so much responsible for his discontent as a symptom of a deeper, darker weakness. Did a cold and selfish woman live in his house because a demon lived in his heart? A demon he both bribed and stupefied with excessive amounts of delicious food, fine wine and loud laughter?

During the journey, Asenath entertained many similarly strange thoughts that made perfect sense to her. Yet in truth, she looked forward to the daily picnic as much as her uncle did. There was freshly caught roasted fowl and grilled fish, hot bread, dried fruit, and every day a different grain and vegetable soup. The beer—prepared on the kitchen boat and sweetened with the sugar of trampled dates—was as good as dessert. The daily picnic was also the only time she got to spend with My Dream, who was not her usual energetic self. This was, in a sense, a blessing, for if she had made an effort to escape her handler, she might have tried to find her way back home and been lost forever. The dog did not hesitate to wet her nose and paws in order to cool off, but it was obvious she did not relish being surrounded by water all day, every day. Asenath consoled her pet with slices of roast fowl while assuring her they would soon reach their destination. A sad intelligence glimmering in her beautiful eyes, My Dream listened intently, and it seemed to her owner that the dog could not have spoken more clearly if she had actually opened her mouth and said, “I know we've left home and everything dear to us, and there's no guarantee we'll even like where we're going.”

It was after lunch—during which she always drank at least one cup of the delicious beer—that she found it most difficult not to think about Joseph, and what awaited him when they reached Shedet. She could not bring herself to accept, much less believe, prison would be the end for him. She knew it grieved her uncle the Hebrew slave's talents would all be going to waste now instead of continuing to serve him, but when she finally dared to ask him how long Joseph would have to remain in prison, he said he heard the captain calling him, and quickly left the cabin.

She could tell they were drawing close to a city whenever the traffic on the River increased. Smaller fishing boats gave way to noble pleasure barges, and more somberly elegant funeral barges that moved straight from east to west. It was not until they drew near Shedet that the River began to feel almost crowded, and the sail was lowered so the rowers could take over. Standing with her uncle at the prow, she watched her future drawing swiftly closer—soon it would be her present.

Earlier that morning, Setka had enjoyed telling her things about Pharaoh's city her aunt had never mentioned. Tarset's stories had all revolved around life in the palace, but Setka was more interested in the innovative design and features of Kahun, the nearby worker's town built near the edge of the desert, conveniently adjoining Pharaoh's growing pyramid, Senwosret Shines. The king had lived in Kahun when work first commenced on his Mansion of Eternity, and only then had he begun construction of his earthly palace in Shedet, where he now resided.

They were in the Nome of the Southern Sycamore, in the realm of Sobek, the god with the head of a crocodile. She could just make out the brick wall surrounding the worker's town, which from a distance looked like a god child's toy. It struck Asenath again that if Princess Sithathor had not taken a fancy to her, she would have remained behind in Iuno, while Joseph traveled north unaccompanied by My Dream or her. She was powerless to help him anymore than she already had, but it felt very important to remain close to him. The fact that they had journeyed to the royal city together felt like a strange dream full of some impossible, mysterious promise. Joseph was not aware that Potifer Setka knew he was innocent of the crime he was accused of, nor did he know about the part she had played in saving his life. She hoped to be able to tell him one day, not because she desired his gratitude, but because she wanted him to know she cared about him. Once, she had been ashamed to feel this way about Kyky, a lowly dung slave, but she was learning that the laws of waking life could be wonderfully broken by dreams.

Chapter 9

Disembarking on the west instead of the east bank of the River confirmed Asenath's impression that her old life was dead, and a new one beginning which would challenge her in ways she could not imagine. Once they docked, a messenger was sent to the palace to announce their arrival. Her uncle accompanied her in the litter that entered Shedet through the eastern gate and proceeded down a long avenue. Until then, they had left the curtain slightly parted, but now he pulled it closed. Deprived of her sight—for the sun was low in the sky and it was quite dark in the litter—she was better able to distinguish individual voices conversing on the rooftops of houses. The gentle, almost musical droning sound of numerous conversations was regularly punctuated by laughter that helped her relax, gradually making her feel more excited than anxious. The contentment of so many people was akin to the purring of a pyramid-sized cat curled comfortably up within the bed of the city's enclosure walls.

Setka announced in a tired voice, "We will be there soon. Are you excited?"

"Yes, a little."

"Just a little? I thought all young women dreamed of coming to live in a palace as the handmaiden of a princess."

When after a moment she did not reply, he cleared his throat and said, “There are not many windows in the palace, I'm afraid, but it's ingeniously ventilated, and each member of the royal family has his own private wing. There are over one-hundred bedrooms, and dozens of bathrooms with state of the art drainage systems. Joseph was looking into having a similar system installed in-” He stepped talking abruptly.

On impulse, Asenath laid one of her hands over his and gave it an affectionate squeeze. “I'm very sorry you've lost Joseph,” she told him, and was astonished to realize that she was feeling more pity for her uncle than she was for the the Hebrew slave he was about to throw into prison. In fact, she felt no pity for Joseph at all, only indignation on his behalf, and hope—a hope her reason could not defend, but which her heart had a stubborn, absolute faith in.

From the moment Sithathor took her hand in hers and eagerly led her to her private apartments, Asenath's soul gratefully relaxed across the soft bed of the princess' smiling mouth. Pharaoh's daughter did not need to say anything to make Asenath feel she was now free to dream whatever she wanted to. She scarcely noticed the dreaded moment of parting from her uncle, her last link to home, as Pharaoh's favorite daughter whisked her eagerly—some might say rudely—away from him, and up a complicated series of narrow staircases to a spacious inner courtyard, flanked on all four sides by brilliantly painted columns. Visible behind and between the columns were wooden doors exquisitely decorated with a variety of flora and fauna. In the center of the courtyard, red granite steps led down to a magnificent blue pool made entirely of lapis lazuli. The pool was comfortably surrounded by thick papyrus mats, and gilded wooden stools with animal skin seats.

"I was hoping you would arrive before sunset, dear Asenath, so we could enjoy the view from my rooftop, but we can have that pleasure tomorrow!" Sithathor hugged her again warmly and, reclaiming her hand, led her down to the pool and a pair of leopard skin stools, the legs of which terminated in goose heads clutching the wooden support frames in their beaks. "I dismissed all my other handmaidens for the evening so we could be alone together!"

"I was wondering where they all were," Asenath admitted. "But I'm honored and happy that it's just you and me this evening, princess."

Sithathor's large intelligent eyes gazed directly into hers as she said softly, gratefully, "Thank you for coming."

"It is my great pleasure to be here, prin-"

"No, please! I am Sithathor to you now. It can be very tiring being a princess, you know. When we're alone together, I want you to feel perfectly relaxed. Promise you will simply be yourself with me."

"I understand, and I promise."

"I knew you would! I'll show you your room soon, it's right

next to mine. Placing you so close to me before the customary probational period caused quite a stir, I'm afraid. If any of my handmaidens say anything nasty to you, or do anything to distress you in any way, you must tell me about it at once. But now I'm sure you must be starving."

Sithathor, who had already eaten, appeared to delight in watching her new handmaiden enjoy all the delectable dishes she had had prepared for her first dinner at the palace. On the table were boiled quail eggs, a variety of smoked fishes with creamed cheeses, thick slices of breaded fried eggplant, a chickpea and yogurt salad sprinkled with toasted cumin seeds and chopped scallions, bite size morsels of lamb fried in olive oil seasoned with garlic and rosemary, and for dessert there were little barley almond cookies lightly drizzled with honey.

Once her stomach was full, Asenath inquired about the food necessary to sustain her heart. "Sweet princess, is there a House of Life in the palace?"

"Of course. It adjoins the temple. Why do you ask?"

"Because I... I wish to learn more about certain subjects. Whenever I have the time, that is."

"It's my favorite place." Sithathor grinned. "You may go there as often as you desire, whether I accompany you or not. I brought you here to be my friend, Aseanth, not another silly boring handmaiden. That's your official title, yes, but I want you to be free as the others can never be. I felt, the moment our eyes met in the temple of Re, that you and I could be sisters, and it seemed to me that you felt the same way."

"I did!"

The reflections of a lamp flame flickered in the dark pools of Sithathor's eyes, which never ceased to shimmer with the inscrutable currents of her thoughts and feelings. Like sailors at the prows of their respective ships using a weighted line to determine the depth of the River, Asenath felt that in those moments they plumbed each others depths, and judged them deep enough to be both reassuring and exciting.

After they had talked for a long time, the princess said, "Before I let you go to bed, I should tell you a little about my family, although you've probably been told all this before. Queen Nofret, the Beautiful One, is my mother. Her titles are King's Daughter, Great of Scepter and Lady of the Two Lands. She is one of father's sisters and his great royal wife. He loves her so much he's building her a small pyramid next to his. She is also the mother of my brother Sonbe, who died when he was three. Khenemetneferhedjet was father's first wife, but she is second in his heart. You will know her by the short old-fashioned wigs she favors. She is the mother of my sisters Itakayt and Neferet, and of my older brother, the Crown Prince. I wish my sisters were as kind and as serious as their mother, but they are more like my father's other consorts, Itaweret and Khnemet, vain and stupid."

She paused for a sip of wine before continuing with obvious pleasure at having come to the most important member of her family, not only to Kemet but to herself as well. "Because my father was born before his own father became pharaoh, he was no longer a young man by the time he became king, so he had to begin work on his eternal home right away. He actually began construction a year before Nubkaure finally went to his golden Ka. We're all here in Shedet, instead of in Waset, so work on the pyramid can proceed as quickly and efficiently as possible. Father designed the entire complex himself. Nothing is more important to him." Smiling slightly, she gazed expectantly, almost challengingly, at her new handmaiden.

"Well, since this life soon ends but eternity lasts forever," Asenath said carefully but truthfully, "I think Pharaoh is being imminently sensible."

Smiling broadly, the princess clapped her hands and, looking past her, declared triumphantly, "I told you!"

Glancing over her own shoulder, Asenath immediately slipped off the stool and prostrated herself.

"Oh, honey, get up, please! It's only daddy."

"Yes, please rise, Asenath, daughter of Potiphera Meketre, high priest of Re. Your face is too lovely to squash against the floor."

Breathlessly, she resumed her seat.

"I was informed you had arrived." Pulling up a stool, Pharaoh sat down beside his daughter. "I hope you will be happy here, Asenath. I am confident you will be, for Sithathor's company is by far the most interesting in the entire city. With her, as with me whenever we are alone, you may speak freely."

The princess was obviously enjoying Asenath's nervous discomfiture. There was a friendly warning in her voice as, reaching for a date, she declared, "Just because father is divine doesn't mean he's a prig, and should be treated like one." Popping the fruit into her mouth, she grinned as she chewed.

Senwostret smiled fondly at his daughter, but when he looked back at Asenath, she saw that his eyes were even more sober than his voice as he said, "Watch over her for me, please, daughter of Re."

Sithathoriunet had no pets of her own but she welcomed My Dream with open arms. The dog immediately became a favorite of all the handmaidens, though they soon learned not too indulge her with too many treats, which had unpleasant consequences. Asenath also sensed the princess grew a little jealous of the animal if she lavished too much attention on her, so My Dream spent a good part of the day outside the city walls with her handler, while her mistress remained in the palace. Asenath did not feel too confined, however, for the view from the rooftop was splendid. It was on her own private section of the roof that the princess often held court in the cool hours of the morning, and later in the afternoon when the sun was at its kindest. When the nights grew warmer, lamps were lit, and they often did not return inside until Asenath was sure everyone else in the palace was asleep.

Asenath did not miss her mother as much as she did her solitude. She did little more than sleep in her tiny bedroom, for possessing no window, it was dark even when the sun was up. Her days were filled with the chatter of young women, combined with the even shriller exchanges of their pet monkeys. At least while on the roof she could occasionally detach herself from the company, and stand gazing east toward the River.

Her favorite times were when she and Sithathor were alone in the House of Life, relishing the peaceful silence that reigned amid the papyrus scrolls, both ancient and new. The more precious papyri rested in their own slots in the honeycomb walls, while the less important ones were piled on top of each other on shelves. The priest in charge of the collection always greeted them with a friendly smile, then found work to do at a distant table. He genuinely regretted not being able to locate for Asenath any papyri devoted exclusively to dreams and dreaming.

Naturally, Sithathor had wanted to know why she was so interested in dreams. The response had taken much longer than the question, one reason being that she had to be careful to edit out any mention of a Hebrew slave.

"So you actually know you're dreaming while you're dreaming?" The princess was seriously intrigued. "You remember that your body is lying on the bed, and that you've left it behind?"

"Yes."

"Oh Asenath, I would love it if we could meet each other in a dream! What can I do to acquire this mysterious ability?"

"Well..." She dared not tell her that praying to Elohim had proved more effective than anything else she had tried, so she said, "Lying in bed at night with your eyes closed, take a few slow breaths, inhaling and exhaling slowly. This will relax you, and help you focus on the darkness swirling with subtle lights behind your eyelids. Don't let your eyeballs wander around aimlessly, but instead anchor your inner vision, focusing only on any shapes or images that appear directly before and beyond you. This will help keep your mind awake even as your body begins falling asleep. The darkness flows like an endless River around our awareness, which is like a boat. If we manage to stay awake long enough, distinct and detailed landscapes and places will rise up before us, and sometimes we are able to consciously step into one. But this is difficult to do. Normally, I'm already in a dream before something prompts me to ask myself if I'm dreaming."

"Fascinating!" Sithathor whispered. "We must try and meet in a dream!"

☼

"The earth trembled as you passed by,
turning everything sacred as you walked.

And you set your eyes upon me for the first time,
speaking at me with the depth of the night
like a nightingale who doesn't need its wings to fly.
What a blessing it is to be worthy of your look.
I have seen rain on the desert,
and all impossible things coming true.
All of my prayers carry your name.
I wish to be pure so that I can desire you.
Take me as you will.
Your slave."

Lowering his head, the old blind harpist slowly let his hands fall from the strings onto his lap.

Your slave! Your slave! Your slave!

The words echoing in Asenath's head made her heart feel hollow, empty as a tomb from which her happiness would never rise, because there was no reason for its existence.

Your slave! Your slave! Your slave!

How could she have forgotten about Joseph?

The gentle notes of the harp lingering in the cool night air rang in her heart as loudly as the hammering of men working on the eternal homes of Pharaoh and his family did during the day. That morning, the princess had proudly shown her the spot where her tomb would be built, very close to her father's pyramid, so that its shadow would fall over it like a great wing sheltering his beloved little chick. Now Sithathor, sitting beside her on the lamp lit rooftop, murmured in her ear, “More wine, my dear?”

“No, thank you!”

“Another whiff of the blue lotus?”

Asenath closed her eyes and attempted to take a deep breath. Her heart was beating so hard, all the air in her lungs seemed to be gathering beneath its invisible wings as it struggled to fly out of her body. Then she suddenly felt a novel sensation that made her picture a mysteriously warm flower, moist with dew, opening against her mouth, and gently thrusting its thick stamen between her lips. The experience was strange yet sweet. She welcomed the distraction from her racing pulse, until she realized what was happening—Sithathor was kissing her! But just as suddenly, the princess pulled back when her harpist began singing again. This time, he performed a merry tune that felt so wrong to Asenath, she stood up with the intention of running down the steps to her room. The choppy misery of her emotions was like water unable to mingle with the rich oil of drunken laughter surrounding her. But when the floor of the rooftop abruptly tilted beneath her like the deck of a ship, she sat down again.

“Asenath, what's wrong, honey? I didn't mean to upset you...”

“It's not you... I just feel very strange...”

“Well of course you do!” Sithathor giggled. “Isn't it wonderful? Enjoy it! I suspect it's nearly midnight, but until then it's still Hathor's birthday, and Bes insists we celebrate with abandon, mischievous little dwarf that he is! Oh, look! Can't you see him there?! He's leering up at Sennuwy from where he's hiding just behind her stool! Oh, no... he's gone now... Where did he go? Can you see where he went?"

Asenath groaned.

"Come!" Pulling her to her feet, the princess led her to the edge of the roof, protected by a waist high wall. There she turned her profile toward her and, standing rigid as a wall painting, held her head high.

"Oh!" Asenath exclaimed in awe. Below them, the moon shone on the black River so that it glimmered like a giant snake with starry scales.

"I'm going to swallow the moon!" Sithathor declared, and opening her mouth wide, very slowly closed it again as she leaned forward slightly. "Did I do it?"

"Yes! You swallowed the moon!" She was feeling better suddenly. In fact, she was feeling quite wonderful, almost as if she had fallen asleep and slipped into her dream body. Throwing her head back, she gazed up at the stars while walking away from the princess, who continued swallowing the moon for the entertainment of her handmaidens.

Standing by herself in a dark corner, well away from the lamplight, Asenath recalled an ancient painting she had once seen—on the rear wall of a small chapel deep in the section of Re's temple dedicated to the goddess—in which the sky was portrayed as a woman bent over the world so that only her fingertips and toes touched the earth. Every night, the goddess Nut swallowed the sun, which she gave birth to again at dawn. But no sooner had this image flashed in her mind's eye than she heard Joseph's voice as clearly as if he was standing beside her, "There is only God" and on the wings of her heartbeat, her Ba immediately flew back to that morning when he had first spoken to her of Elohim, the Creator of heaven and earth. Elohim, who actually seemed to hear and answer her prayers. She had always enjoyed imagining that the stars were lamps burning in the palaces of the gods, but if Joseph was right, there was only one unimaginably vast and splendid palace and only one almighty God. And suddenly, with their inescapably brilliant and infinite voices, the stars all began singing his name down at her, "Elohim! Elohim! Elohim!"

☼

The following morning, a bird flew into the royal coops with a letter from Iuno. It bore Potifer Setka's seal and was addressed to the Lady Asenath. The message read:

> The prison warden has put Joseph in charge of all the other prisoners and over everything that happens in the prison. His god is with Joseph and causing everything he does to succeed.

"I forbid you to look so cheerful today, Asenath," Sithathor mumbled. "Not while I'm feeling as if a stone from my father's pyramid just fell on my head! All my other handmaidens look equally crushed, so why are you feeling so fabulous? You drank just as much wine and inhaled as much of the blue lotus as we all did."

"A pigeon brought me good news."

"Oh? Do tell!"

Joseph remained a prisoner, but at least he had found favor with the warden, and surely his important position now entitled him to many of the same privileges as his master. He was standing on a threshold, one foot in the darkness of confinement, the other foot in the light of freedom, and God was with him. She could now truly dare to hope he would not be in prison forever.

"Asenath? You aren't leaving me and going back home, are you?"

When her attention turned outward again, she was shocked by how haggard Sithathor's face looked, her plump cheeks sunken so that her mouth seemed too big. "Oh, no princess, I'm staying right here with you. How could I look so happy if I was leaving you?"

"Thank you, honey," she murmured, and did not ask again what news the pigeon had brought from Iuno.

Three nights later, there was a great royal banquet. Asenath's table companion was Nomarch Djer. His father having died recently, he was fulfilling his obligation to live at court for a while so that Pharaoh could get to know the man who was now in possession of the lands held in trust for him. Senwosret got on well with the rulers of Kemet's many Nomes, for as long as they paid him their full tribute, he essentially allowed them to govern themselves.

Nomarch Djer was considered a highly desirable young man in every sense, and it was Princess Sithathoriunet who had arranged to have her favorite handmaiden seated at his table. She wanted Asenath to marry a powerful Nomarch, ideally one whose lands adjoined the royal capital, which helped guarantee his wife's regular attendance at court.

Nomarch Djer smiled at her a great deal and she smiled shyly back at him, but it was not until he had drunk several cups of beer that he began telling her all about the fine herds of cattle he owned, and the two grand villas between which he divided his time. After a while, she stopped listening, preferring to concentrate on enjoying the music. Dancing girls shook sistrums and made a sweet tinkling music with their hips in rhythm with the beating of a large drum, above which the sublime notes of a flute soared like a bird escaping the percussive net.

In a lull between songs, Djer remarked, “I see Pharaoh has found himself a new Cup Bearer.”

Looking over at the dais, she noticed that Hepsefa—who had been Senwosret's Cup Bearer ever since she had arrived in

Shedet and long before that—was indeed missing, and another nobleman was pouring the king's wine. "Perhaps Lord Hepsefa is not feeling well tonight," she suggested.

"You are right about that, Lady! Tonight, Lord Hepsefa is sleeping in the Place of Confinement in the company of Lord Ikudidy, the Chief Baker."

Intensely interested in the conversation now, Asenath leaned over the table toward him. "Is the royal prison a very awful place?" she asked with unconcealed dread.

"I have no idea what it's like, and I have no desire to find out." Djer drained his cup, and a passing female servant immediately refilled it.

She was obliged to wait until after the banquet to learn from the princess that Hepsefa and Ikudidy were both suspected of heading a conspiracy against the king. This was more than sufficient cause to have them thrown into prison, where they would remain indefinitely while the matter was investigated.

"Personally, I don't believe Hepsefa is guilty," Sithathor confided in her. "He has an open, honest laugh, and is much too fond of concubines to waste precious time in bed with conspirators. But Ikudidy has eyes like little black beetles, beneath which his smile appears too swiftly. The evidence indicates one of these two men tried to have my father poisoned, the question is, which one."

Several months later, the high priest of Re, accompanied by his beautiful wife, arrived in Shedet just in time for Pharaoh's great birthday banquet. It was always a joyful occasion for Asenath to share a table with her beloved parents. It was also a happy day for Pharaoh's Chief Cup Bearer and Chief Baker, who had been surprisingly released from their prison cells, and were sitting together near their master on the dais. Before the feasting and the music began, a hush fell over the hall as everyone gave their full attention to the royal dais. Before the eyes of all assembled, Pharaoh restored the Chief Cup Bearer Hepsefa to his former position, so he could again hand him his cup. Asenath was delighted for the man but also a little jealous of him. Joseph would have been assigned to look after Hepsefa, as he did all the other prisoners, which meant Hepsefa had seen Joseph, spoken to Joseph, been in Joseph's presence. Her jealously was mounting when she was distracted by Pharaoh who, in an entirely different tone of voice, officially condemned the Chief Baker for conspiring against him, and ordered the traitor be immediately impaled just outside the city gates, where all could see what happened to enemies of the king. Meanwhile, inside the banquet hall, the treacherous Ikudidy's ghastly fate only seemed to increase everyone's appetite for life's honest pleasures.

Chapter 10

"Hiding in here again?" Sithathor whispered conspiratorially as she closed the door of Asenath's bedroom behind her. "Writing down another dream?"

Asenath resisted the temptation to lie and avoid further questions. "Not this time." She set aside her pallet. She had almost run out of black ink anyway.

"Really? Then what were you writing?" The princess made herself comfortable in the room's only chair—placed there for her benefit—and there was undisguised hope in her next question, "A love poem?"

"It is a poem," she confessed, carefully laying the unrolled papyrus on top of a chest at the opposite end of the room. "But it's not a love poem to Nomarch Djer, in case you were wondering."

"I was!" Sithathor slumped in the chair. "More than wondering. I was hoping."

Asenath sat down again on the edge of her bed. She could not determine if her friend was performing or if she was genuinely upset, which meant the truth balanced somewhere between the two.

"In your conscious dreams, you do indeed seem to be stepping over a threshold into some new sort of awareness," Sithathor waved an ostrich feather fan before her face. "I'm glad you're keeping a record of them, and I hope that, one day, you will permit my scribes to make copies of your papyri. I would like to have them placed in my tomb to remind me of you, as well as to give me some ideas about what to do when all of eternity stretches before me!"

Asenath laughed.

Sithathor grinned, but then her hand and the fan it held dropped heavily into her lap. Looking down at them, she said, "Understanding the brevity of our time is one of the great challenges of this human life. Each time we draw a bit closer to that understanding, often through the passage of time or some deep loss, our grasp loosens its too-tight hold a bit more and, if we're lucky, we understand still greater freedom lies ahead... I'm hoping to learn what that means one day!"

"So am I."

Sithathor straightened in her chair. "But not today!"

"No, not today! Or tomorrow. Or the next day. Or the day after that. Many years from now."

"Yes, far too many to count! I think I will hide in here with you this afternoon, sweet Asenath. My handmaidens weary me. Let's play a game. I'm rather in the mood for the new version of Men. Are you familiar with it?"

"Yes." It was a relief her friend did not want to play Mehen, the game she had seen Joseph and Tarset engaged in. "My uncle gave me one for my thirteenth birthday and I brought it with me."

"Excellent! I'll play as the jackal, for I'm sure you want to be the dog. Where is your lovely pet this morning?"

"Out running with her handler, as always." Asenath set a small table between them, then fetched the game from one of her chests.

The princess sighed. "I wish I could also run as swiftly as my shadow. I think I would enjoy that even more than flying, for I would still be able to feel the ground beneath my bare feet, and smell the soil and the flowers while sights and sounds rushed toward me in waves of delight through the power of my own strength and grace!"

"You possess a different kind of strength and grace, princess." As she spoke, she placed the five long jackal-head pegs in their starting holes, and then arranged her five shorter dog-head pegs in their respective slots. "Flying swift as falcons, your thoughts pounce upon the most delightful observations and ideas, which help nourish the hearts of all those fortunate enough to listen to you speak."

"Now I am ashamed of myself. Nomarch Djer is not remotely worthy of you, Asenath. I'm being selfish trying to marry you to him so you'll always be nearby, and able to spend most of the year at court while he is away inspecting all his considerable holdings. Yes, he is handsome and kind, but he thinks of nothing but crops, cattle and hunting. Father and I will find you someone more worthy of you, I promise."

"Thank you, princess, but I have nothing against crops, cattle and hunting, for if I did, I would also have to dislike eating and, by extension, being alive."

Sithathor sighed dramatically. "He is boring! Admit it."

"A little." Her relief lasted only a moment, however, before she began wondering, and worrying, at whose table her royal masters would place her next, like a living peg on the great board of the banquet hall. Her father would, of course, need to approve the match, but she doubted he would go against Pharaoh's recommendation. The topic of her future marriage made her uncomfortable, but putting it out of her mind required more and more of an effort. "You go first, princess."

The Men board was of the finest quality—her uncle's gifts to her always were—although none could match her dog, who had also mysteriously come with Joseph.

While Sithathor rolled and moved her pegs, Asenath wondered again if the Hebrew slave meant so much to her because she had seen him in her first conscious dream, and therefore found it impossible to think of these special dreams without also thinking about him. Yet she really had to stop thinking about him. He was nothing but a foreign slave destined to spend the rest of his life as a prison steward. He was the property of the warden now, who found him as invaluable as her uncle had. It was beyond foolish for her to continue thinking about Joseph as if he could possibly have anything whatsoever to do with her future. He was literally beneath her, in the palace prison. She was only dreaming with her eyes open whenever she thought and felt that he was still part of her life.

"Your turn," Sithathor prompted.

Asenath made an effort to concentrate on the ivory, ebony and sycamore board which stood on four little ivory bull's legs. It was carved in the form of a shield from two smooth ivory sheets, in which there were sixty small holes, thirty for each player. At the top and center of the board was one shared central hole, larger than all the others, in the form of the hieroglyph for Eternity written as a circle over a line—the sun resting on the horizon. Nineteen holes ran down along both outer edges of the board, with ten holes leading up the center on both sides of a large palm tree painted beneath the Eternity hieroglyph, where the game both began and ended. Lines connecting holes number six and number twenty, as well as holes eight and ten, provided short cuts and diversions, while the hieroglyphs for Goodness and Beauty provided safe havens. The first to place all five of their pegs in the end holes on either side of the Eternity sign, won the game.

They played silently for a while, and Asenath could not help it—her thoughts returned to Joseph as she wondered if he had ever played this particular game with Tarset. Thinking about her aunt always made her angry. Yet despite how intensely she disliked the woman, she could not find it in her heart to hate her. It seemed that once you dreamed so intimately of someone —actually feeling what they did as your soul mysteriously nested in their heart—it was impossible to hate them or even wish them ill. The truth was that she felt sorry for her aunt, and that they had something in common—Joseph. Did Tarset think of him as often as she did? It disturbed her to think Tarset had simply forgotten all about Joseph, but she found this hard to believe after having personally experienced the intensity of the woman's longing for him. Then she remembered how her aunt had made fun of her innocent assumption that love and desire always walked hand in hand. It frightened her to think that her innocence was some kind of weakness she had to overcome. Fortunately, her parents were living proof that love and desire could indeed always walk hand in hand. But thinking of her father only led her to wonder what the high priest of Atum-Re would have to say if he ever found out his beloved daughter prayed not to the sun god, but to the one God of the Hebrews. She still honored Maat, and Neith—her own patron goddess—was closest to her heart whenever she contemplated her future as a woman and a wife, but Elohim was the God of dreams, and she could not imagine life without her dreams.

"Asenath, if you do not tell me this instant what you are thinking," Sithathor said lightheartedly as she thrust one of her jackal-head pegs into a hole beside the sign for Beauty, "I'm going to scream, which means the palace guard will come running, and then what well I tell them? That my handmaiden is confounding me by not sharing her secrets with me? Naturally, they will become suspicious. They may even wonder if you are conspiring against my father, and throw you into prison until your innocence can be proven."

Asenath felt as though the princess had thrust her jackal-head playing peg straight into her heart. She felt mysteriously wounded as feelings rushed through her with a frightening lack of control, like gushing blood.

Her eyes fixed on the board, Sithathor said quietly, "Forgive me. You have a right to your private thoughts. It's just that... "

"I was thinking of my future."

"Well, seeing as it's your turn, your immediate future is casting the knuckle bones. In my defense, I will say that Men is rather boring unless we are talking of other things while we play."

"Really?" Asenath cast the bones and began moving her pegs. "I feel Men is a lot like living. We all begin in the same place—in the solar disc that gives us life—and from there we proceed in our own directions, apart from each other yet on the same board, which represents the world. But on the way, we grow closer together as we climb the tree in the center, which is given life and fruit by the eternal sun above it. And no matter who gets all his pegs in first, in the end we both stand beside the sun."

After taking her own turn, Sithathor replied, "That was a lovely way to avoid sharing your real thoughts with me." Her voice was subdued, as though she was hurt but did not want to admit it.

Asenath silently moved her pegs, for she could not admit that she had been thinking about herself and Joseph and how their lives, even when traveling in totally opposite directions, mysteriously continued to parallel each other. They had both left Iuno on the same day and were now both living in the royal capital. But it seemed Joseph had run out of throws and would remain buried beneath the palm tree, while she moved inexorably toward the slots of marriage and childbirth.

"I suddenly tire of Men," Saithathor announced as she sat back in her chair. "I would like you to read me what you were writing when I walked in. I simply must know. My curiosity will keep me awake, and I will become ill from lack of sleep, and you will be forced to tear you hair out and scratch your chest until you bleed when I fly away to my Ka out of sheer frustration! I promise you I will tell no one your secrets. If it was not Djer, to whom were you writing a poem when I walked in?"

"I was writing a poem to God."

"A poem to Re?"

"Yes." She had been thinking of Elohim but had been careful to write "Re" on the papyrus.

"Well, I'm glad. I was afraid you might have a secret lover I knew nothing about, which was silly of me, of course, since he would have to be invisible for me not to know about him!"

Asenath busied herself putting away the game board.

"Will you read your poem to me? I would love to hear it."

"I would be honored, princess."

"Oh stop that! It's me, Sithathor. You know how much I enjoy songs and poems. I even once memorized part of a hymn to Re. Let's see... 'Be praised, Oh Re, in your rising! Atum-Horakhty! Let your perfection be worshiped with my eyes, and let your sunlight come to be within my breast!'... There's a lot more, but I only remember the first lines."

"'The unwearying stars give praise to you,'" Asenath recited. "'The indestructible stars adore you—you who go to rest in the horizon of the Western Mountains, beautiful as the Sun each day, beautiful, enduring, as my Lord'."

Sithathor took up her fan waving again as Asenath retrieved her papyrus. "Perhaps I will have my harpist set your poem to music. Would that please you? We can have him perform it at a banquet the next time your parents visit. Imagine how proud they will be."

"You have not even heard it yet," Asenath protested. "It's much too short to be a song, and not really appropriate for a banquet."

"Then perhaps I will have it buried with me, inscribed on my heart scarab amulet. That way you will always be close to my heart, dear sister!"

Asenath smiled to herself. She loved how extravagant Sithathor was with her feelings and ideas, even though it was not entirely clear how many of them she remembered after expressing them, or how many she took seriously. She felt shy about sharing her poem, but it was also exciting to be able to do so, especially if she imagined that Joseph was also listening.. With a thrill, she remembered again how he had looked in the dream where she saw him standing in her uncle's Seal Room, and imagined that the scroll he had been reading so intently was the one she was holding in her hands now—the one containing all her dreams. He had told her that interpreting dreams was God's business, which in her heart translated to dreams being his, Joseph's, business.

After clearing her throat, she read:

> Watching My Dream running
> down the sun dappled path, I thought:
> We are all Light and Love.
> My dog is a spark
> flown straight from Re
> into my heart and arms.
> Gone is the confusion of gods
> in my head, just the One remains.

The princess' eyes were closed as she said, "Quite lovely, but you're right, not suitable for a banquet, except in Iuno, of course."

"I've also written a love poem to a man," Asenath heard herself confess. "Not any man in particular... I was just dreaming..."

"Go on!"

"I mean, it's a love poem inspired by a dream." Since Joseph was a Hebrew slave he was, in a sense, only a dream figure she could never really have anything to do with in waking life. Yet because he knew about dreams—and because she had seen him in her first conscious dream—he had become confused in her mind and heart with how much she loved dreams, and how they could come true. Or so she desperately reasoned before reciting slowly and quietly:

While my soul journeyed with Re
    through the darkness
I dreamed with you, and the sun rose
    in the form of my heart
when I woke to your words of love,
    sweeter to my ears
than any sistrum, lute, harp or drum,
    for they issued from the lips
of my beautiful brother, beloved of Re
    for millions of years and beyond!

She quickly got up and returned the papyrus to the chest at the opposite end of the room.

"Thank you, Asenath." Sithathor opened her eyes. "Both those poems are something special. I mean it. I was teasing when I said that about inscribing one of your poems on my heart scarab, but I would consider it an honor if, when the time comes, you will make a copy of all your most special dreams, and your poems too, so I can have them buried with me. I'll let my hemu Ka know you'll be providing these items for my burial."

"Please stop talking like that, princess. Life, health, and strength will be yours for many years to come. I know this in my heart. Besides, I haven't dreamed of you dying."

"You've had dreams that come true?"

"Sometimes," Asenath admitted, and told her about the dream she had had with Kyky a few days before the slave went to her Ka. It felt good to tell her new friend about her old friend without concealing how fond she had been of her. But being fond of a female slave of your own race, and close to your own age, was very different from being fond of a Hebrew slave who was a grown man. She longed to share her thoughts of Joseph with someone but she simply could not. She herself scarcely knew what to think about him, for she could do nothing more to help him. He was in the Place of Confinement now, and so he also had to remain confined in her heart.

Asenath was delighted to be walking along the River's edge, her bare feet partially submerged in the clear warm water. At first she seemed to recognize one of the locations where her uncle's boats had moored during their journey to the royal capital, but as she looked around her, she realized two things in swift succession—she had never actually been here, and she could not be here now. For nearly three years, Princess Sithathor and her handmaidens had always been nearby, so why was she completely alone? And why were there no boats anywhere in sight? Where were all the fishermen?

To all these questions there could be only one answer: "I'm dreaming!"

At once she understood why she felt so wonderful, free from all worries and concerns as her heart expanded like wings, tempting her to launch herself into the sky and go flying. But it was so lovely here that she simply decided to continue walking. Looking down again, she observed that her feet appeared just as they really did, except for the fact that the paint on her toenails was a deeper and much more beautiful red color.

Pausing, she looked around her again, knowing that she risked waking up if she focused on one thing for too long. She could see everything distinctly in a light that cast no shadows. The water stretched a long peaceful distance to the opposite shore, where a low line of greenery fronted gently undulating blue mountains such as she had never seen before. The River was the same vibrant blue as the sky and just as still. There was no sound, no wind, no movement at all. Then she saw a figure standing on the opposite shore—a man wearing a white robe. She raised both hands before her to help stabilize the dream, and quickly lowering them again, she saw that the man had begun walking toward her. She wondered if he had interpreted her gesture as a greeting. In a sense it had been, for it was his presence that had made her feel it was imperative she not wake up yet.

Out loud she observed, “He's walking on water” and already he was close enough for her to discern his black shoulder-length hair.

She cried, “Joseph!” and would have plunged into the water to swim toward him if he had not stopped her by raising his right hand, and in the next instant, he was standing so close to her she had to look up to see his face. Although he resembled Joseph, she could see now that he was someone else entirely. Yet she was not disappointed, instead she felt intensely happy because he was smiling at her. When he spoke, she actually felt a gentle breath of wind against her dream body as he said, “I am coming soon.” Then his Voice followed her into the darkness of her bedroom with the command, “BE READY.”

☼

Queen Nofret's birthday was a cause for great rejoicing and everyone who was anyone was invited to her party. As soon as Pharaoh and his great royal wife, accompanied by their children, had made private offerings to the gods, the public festivities began and lasted until well after sunset. They commenced with wrestling matches between young men. The competitors wore only loin cloths, held up by heavy belts their opponent struggled to get hold of, for their bodies were so slick with oil they shone like living copper statues in the sunlit courtyard. It seemed to Asenath that many of the women enjoyed this sport as much as the men, but for a different reason. This observation made her uncomfortable every time she glimpsed the athletes' private parts, which looked painfully vulnerable. Although it was rather thrilling when one of the wrestlers managed to throw his opponent, the different holds and techniques they practiced were much easier to see when drawn on a papyrus. In reality, everything happened so fast, it was difficult to appreciate that this sport was considered an art form.

Personally, she preferred the controlled elegance of stick fighting, for it was much more like a dance. But when it came time for the boxing, she found an excuse to retire to the princess' apartments, avoiding the often bloody violence everyone seemed to take so much pleasure in. How, she wondered, could anyone enjoy watching two men—some mere boys—inflict painful blows on each other that could do real damage?

The area around the lapis lazuli pool was deserted and blissfully quiet. She was able to enjoy sitting alone with her calves and feet in the cool water. On such long and loud days at court, she desperately missed the peace and solitude of her private garden and pool. She also missed being able to run free with her dog. Two of the bracelets the princess had given her were heavy on her wrists, and her skin was perspiring beneath the thirty-seven rows of carnelian and turquoise beads, strung on threads held together at intervals by six gold space-bars. The gold cowrie shell girdle—another gift from Sithathor, who owned an identical girdle—made her awkwardly conscious of her hips as the tiny silver pellets contained in each hollow shell made a delicate tinkling sound that drew the attention of young men when she walked, just as it was intended to. The problem was that older men, both single and married, also stared at her, and the expression she had glimpsed in many of their eyes was less than kind. She also wished she could remove her heavy wig for a while, but doing so would ruin the lotus flower pinned to it so that it rested against her forehead. She suspected it was sadly wilted by now.

She enjoyed her break from the queen's birthday celebration both physically and in her heart, for in the peace and quiet of the empty courtyard—where only a faint roar of unbridled enjoyment reached her ears—she was again free to think about the dream in which a man who could have been Joseph's brother had told her, "I am coming soon." She had no idea who he was, so why had he appeared to her in a dream to tell her he was coming soon? Was he perhaps one of Joseph's brothers? Did Joseph even have any brothers? She knew nothing about Joseph's life before he became a slave in her uncle's house, a fact she was becoming ashamed of. If only she could tell him about this inexplicably wonderful dream. Would he possibly know who the man was and be able to explain the dream to her?

She could find no answer to these questions, and yet she never tired of asking them. It was impossible to forget the joy she had felt in that dream, which had been much more intense than the happy elation she always experienced whenever she became conscious in her sleep. The dream had ended, but even after many weeks, the feeling the dream had left her with—that some unimaginably wonderful promise was soon to be fulfilled—had not faded. The man who resembled Joseph had commanded her to be ready. Ready for Joseph to be released from prison?

Only when she was sure the boxing matches had ended did she return to the celebrations. She enjoyed the dancers and acrobats, who were both male and female but never performed together. At the banquet, she was able to relax because she was sharing a table not with Nomarch Djer but with Nit, one of her fellow handmaidens, who completely ignored her as she strove to catch the eye of all the handsome available men sitting nearby. So it came as quite a surprise when Nit suddenly leaned toward her and whispered excitedly, "The prince is staring at you!"

Asneath did not dare look up at the dais. She did not want it to be true. She was afraid of the prince, not because of anything he had ever said or done to her, but because she would be powerless to turn him down if he asked her to become one of his wives or concubines. Would Sithathor be pleased? If her brother fancied her favorite handmaiden, it meant Asenath would remain at court the rest of her life. Yet she did not think the princess would welcome the arrangement, for she would lose all claim to Asenath's time and attention despite their physical proximity. This gave her hope, as did the fact that Pharaoh doted on his youngest daughter, so much so that she might be able to persuade him to tell his son to forget about Asenath and find some other young lady for his bed.

☼

Three days after Queen Nofret's birthday celebrations, Sithathor dismissed all her handmaidens from the courtyard, except for Asenath, to whom she confessed, “Father is feeling very disturbed by two dreams he had last night.”

“Really?” Anything to do with dreams immediately sparked her curiosity and interest. “Did he share them with you?”

“No, but we will hear them soon enough, for he has ordered all the magicians and wise men of Kemet to the palace. He hopes they will be able to tell him what the dreams mean. So many messages flew out today, both up and down the River, the pigeon coops are nearly empty. I'm sure this means you will soon be treated with a visit from your parents, for the high priest of Re is one of the wisest men in the Two Lands, and he never travels without your gorgeous mother. I thought of telling daddy about your dreaming skills, but was afraid too. I didn't want to put you in the position of disappointing him if you couldn't understand what his dreams meant. Yet I'm worried. He's never been troubled by bad dreams before. I hope they don't have anything to do with him... or with me."

"Don't be afraid," Asenath said firmly. "I haven't dreamed of him or of you. I'm sure all is well, but I think... I think Pharaoh's dreams might possibly have something to do with the River."

"Truly?" Sithathor visibly relaxed. "You have dreamed of the River recently?"

"Yes."

"Oh thank you, honey! You have set my mind at ease! And it makes sense. If father is so worried, it must be because his dreams have to do with the well being of his people, and he understands this much, at least. I can't wait to hear what the wisest men in Kemet have to say about them."

Chapter 11

On the morning all the wisest men in Kemet were scheduled to meet with Pharaoh and attempt to interpret his disturbing dreams, Re rose adorned with a celestial collar composed of horizontal alternating rows of blue and red blended with a bright white light to make the loveliest of colors, which stretched for almost as far as Asenath could see from where she stood on the roof of the palace. The River was smooth and white as milk flowing straight from Hathor's divine teats, the points of which she could just make out glimmering in the last two stars to fade from the sky. The flax fields were in bloom, so even the land appeared to have donned its finest gown that morning woven of luminous green linen embroidered with tiny blue flowers.

Asenath had spent the evening with her father and mother and would see them again every day before they left. Yet for the first time in her life their company—though she treasured it—had not soothed the restlessness possessing her. She was increasingly anxious about her future. She could not avoid the thought of marriage much longer. In her parents' eyes she saw now not only how much they loved her, but also how much they desired to love her children. Yet it was not only the troubling thought of marriage that had driven her out of bed, and up to the rooftop when only servants were awake. She had been impatient to hear Pharaoh's dreams ever since Sithathor had told her about them. She was irresistibly attracted to the mystery of dreams so intense and provocative, they had the power to disrupt the normal course of events. Like moths drawn to a bright light surrounded by darkness, the wisest and most powerful men in Kemet had traveled to Shedet for the sole purpose of hearing and interpreting two dreams. She found this fascinating and exciting and entirely proper, for she had known since she was very young how important dreams could be.

However, weeks had been a long time to wait and find out what Pharaoh had dreamed, so one night she had intended, when she went to bed, to try and enter the king's dreaming soul as she had her aunt's. Perhaps she would be able to find in his mind, as in a treasure room, the gems of these two special dreams. But all she got for her misguided effort was a headache from lying awake most of the night. The insomnia she suffered was a most effective punishment for her evil intention, because if she could not sleep, she could not dream, and that thought did not bear thinking of.

But today the suspense would finally end, and the morning was so fresh and lovely, Asenath felt forgiven for attempting to break into another person's soul, sealed by divine powers just as Pharaoh and his nobles sealed their tombs to protect them from robbers. It was with a light step that she returned to her room, where a servant was waiting to help her dress.

In honor of her father's illustrious guests, Princess

Sithathoriunet was wearing her most magnificent crown—an imitation of the boatman's circlet worn by sailors except that instead of being made of white linen it was forged of gold, and inlaid with carnelian, lapis-lazuli and green faience in the form of stylized flower buds. A serpent similar to her father's, but smaller and more delicately carved, reared from her forehead. In the crown, the excess strip of cloth that hung down one side when the circlet was tied around the sailor's forehead was represented by a straight fine band of solid gold. Asenath thought the crown the most beautiful she had ever seen, and also a very clever way of proclaiming to all who saw it that Princess Sithathoriunet's name was spoken and revered all up and down the River.

The throne room was empty when they entered it through the door concealed at the rear of the dais. She walked behind the princess, who was the last in the line of royals and their attendants. Pharaoh seated himself on his solid gold throne, inlaid with precious stones, which occupied the front and center of the wooden dais, decorated on all three of its visible sides with golden ankh signs. Pharaoh sat straight backed, his hands crossed against his bare chest gripping the crook and flail. Just behind him and to his left sat Queen Nofret, and parallel to her sat the crown prince. The backs of both their wooden chairs were carved in the form of the kneeling god who embodied Eternity. Sithathor's chair was set at the far right of the dais behind the others. The royal family's personal attendants stood at the very back of the raised platform, except for Asenath, who stood directly to the left of Sithathor's chair simply because there was no room behind it. Shaped like lotus chalices, eight alabaster lamps set on tall stone bases cast a bright steady light over the royal family.

From her position, Asenath had an unobstructed view of the great room. Two rows of colorful columns, their tops lost in shadow, rose alongside both walls, lamps burning between them. The prince sat close to her and she had a good view of his partial profile. He was not handsome in the traditional sense, but her eyes were drawn toward him in grudging admiration of the way his feelings were openly carved on his features. This did not mean, however, that it was possible to know what he was thinking, for you could never really see into anther person's mind and heart. Yet it was also true that some people were more like pools than the River, their depths more quickly and easily plumbed. This was true of many of Sithathor's handmaidens but definitely not of the prince, something she could not help but admire about him despite the fact that he made her feel helpless as a gazelle in the presence of a hungry young lion. Sithathor was obliged to love and admire her brother from afar, for he showed absolutely no interest in her. Asenath was secretly of the opinion that her brother felt Sithathor received more than enough attention and affection from their father. But it was no secret the prince intended to rule differently when he became king. Life at court was much like journeying on the River—

many courtiers drifted contentedly on the currents of the present administration, while more restive and energetic people welcomed the prince's ideas slowly being raised like sails to catch wind of the future. The prince was in charge of the king's militia and was gradually growing the army in preparation for the day when a soldier would once again wear the Double Crown.

Just before the doors were opened and the royal herald began announcing Pharaoh's honored guests, the prince—who had seemed to be staring fixedly at his own thoughts—abruptly turned his head in her direction. He did not smile, and she scarcely dared to breathe feeling she had been spotted by a crocodile only a few feet away. The prince's cool black stare was alarming because she could not tell—as she usually could with other men—if he was feeling hungry for her body. If he was, there was no hope of escape.

"Potiphera Meketre, High Priest of Re, Greatest of Seers!" proclaimed the herald, and the prince looked away from her toward the man striding into the throne room. She felt her father's title had been flung like a shining lance, just in time, at the predator prince threatening to devour her life by honoring her with a place in his harem, which in her opinion would be akin to ending up in the dark belly of a beast where her heart would perish, leaving behind only the gilded bones of her jewels.

The next two men to enter the throne room were the high

priest of Ptah, and the first prophet of Amun, who wore a leopard's skin draped over his left shoulder. All the priests the herald announced were entrusted with keeping the Divine fire burning in the heart of every temple. When the herald at last fell silent, the great throne room was full of Kemet's most important men.

The chief cup bearer carefully placed a golden goblet to Pharaoh's lips so he could take a sip of water before addressing the assembled company. Asenath listened intently as the king recounted his dreams, in both of which he had been standing on the bank of the River. The dreams were different yet similar, and though at first they sounded disappointingly ordinary, she soon realized they were actually quite disturbing, for both dreams centered around living things devouring other living things.

When Pharaoh had finished speaking, she looked over at her father, but was unable to read his expression, and when the high priest of Ptah cleared his throat, everyone focused on him expectantly. Apparently, however, his throat was simply dry, for he remained silent.

Pharaoh did not raise his voice as he demanded, "Well?" but Asenath saw his hands tighten around the crook and flail. "Before me are all the wisest men in the Two Lands. Cannot one of you tell me what my dreams mean?"

An official, whose names and titles Asenath could not recall, spoke up, "Majesty, may I ask what color the cows were?"

"What color were the cows?!" The king's rising frustration threatened to spill over into anger. "What does it matter what color they were? They were cows! And the grain was grain!"

Once again, a profoundly uncomfortable silence fell over the throne room.

She stared hopefully, and a little desperately, down at her father, praying he would be the first to say something, but he turned his face away from the dais, almost as if he felt the pressure of her eyes on him.

There was a murmur of voices as the wisest men in Kemet gathered in small groups to discuss the dreams, giving up on the possibility of individual glory.

Sithathor touched her wrist, and when Asenath bent toward her solicitously, whispered, "Do you have any idea what the dreams mean?"

"No," she admitted. "They are truly strange dreams."

After what felt like a very long time, the high priest of Ptah separated himself from the others and announced, "Majesty, we are all at a loss. No one here can tell you what your dreams mean."

Abruptly, his voice surprisingly pitched to carry, the Chief Cup Bearer spoke. "Today I have been reminded of my failure," he confessed to Pharaoh, and bowed his head over the golden cup he held in his hands.

Like everyone else, Asenath stared at him in surprise.

"Some time ago," Hepsefa went on, "you were angry with

the Chief Baker and me, and you imprisoned us in the palace of the captain of the guard. One night the Chief Baker and I each had a dream, and each dream had its own meaning. There was a young Hebrew man with us in the prison who was a slave of the captain of the guard. We told Joseph our dreams, and Joseph told us what each of our dreams meant. And everything happened just as he had predicted. I was restored to my position as cup bearer, and the chief baker was executed and impaled on a pole."

"Asenath, what's wrong?" Sithathor whispered urgently. "Why are you trembling?"

She felt incapable of speech watching Pharaoh extend his right arm, his hand held vertically so that his thumb was on top—the gesture of summoning.

A herald immediately approached the throne and, beating his chest over his heart with his right fist, awaited instructions.

"Bring me this Hebrew prisoner named Joseph!"

The herald hurried to obey him.

Asenath understood in that moment why her dog's entire body quivered when she saw something no one else could see, and longed to chase after, as for the first time in her life, she felt exactly the same way—she longed to run after the herald and straight to Joseph. Suddenly, it felt impossible to wait even one more heartbeat before finally seeing him again after all these years he had been so close to her yet impossibly far away. Scarcely able to believe what was happening, she refused to ask herself if she was dreaming. This was another first in her life—she did not want to be dreaming. Thank God she was awake and this was really happening. Today she would see Joseph again! There was no need to fear she would wake up before he arrived. She was definitely awake, and her dream was coming true. At long last her dream was coming true! Joseph was being released from the dark pit of prison! She could not think beyond this seemingly impossible fact as she concentrated on containing the blazing fire of her impatience.

Feeling the princess glance at her again, it finally occurred to her to wonder what everyone else was thinking. How would the wisest men in the Two Lands feel if a Hebrew slave was able to do what they could not? What about her father? He knew who Joseph was and why he had been imprisoned. Was Meketre glad the slave was being offered a chance at freedom, for surely Pharaoh would not just throw him back into prison if he proved himself the wisest man in the room. She hoped her father was feeling generous toward Joseph. But beneath her rising excitement was an undertow of fear that Joseph would not be able to interpret Pharaoh's dreams.

After a brief eternity, the double doors finally opened again and the herald announced, "The Hebrew slave, Joseph!"

She saw now why it had taken almost longer than she could endure for Joseph to arrive—he had had to be washed and shaved first. In order not to keep Pharaoh waiting any longer than necessary, the grooming had been performed hastily, and the thin trail of blood gleaming on his left cheek in the lamplight struck her as the most arresting sight she had ever beheld. He had lost weight in prison, but more than ever before, she could appreciate what a remarkably handsome man he was. The white linen shendyt they had wrapped around his lean hips was of the finest quality, and he approached Pharaoh with his hands unbound. He stared straight ahead of him, not down at the floor, and when he reached the foot of the dais, he did not prostrate himself, but simply rested both hands on his knees as he bowed slightly.

The regal impatience in his voice tempered by hope, Pharaoh said to Joseph, "I had a dream, and no one here can tell me what it means. But I have heard that when you hear about a dream you can interpret it."

Looking up and grasping his left shoulder with his right hand, Joseph dared to meet Pharaoh's eyes as he replied, "It is beyond my power to do this, but God can tell you what it means and set you at ease."

Asenath felt her body relax, for there was no doubt in her heart now that Joseph would succeed where all the wisest men in Kemet had failed.

"In my dream," Pharaoh began, "I was standing on the bank of the River, and I saw seven fat, healthy cows come up out of the River and begin grazing in the marsh grass. But then I saw seven sick-looking cows, scrawny and thin, come up after them. I've never seen such sorry-looking animals in all the land of

Kemet. These thin, scrawny cows ate the seven fat cows. But afterward you wouldn't have known it, for they were still as thin and scrawny as before! Then I woke up.

"In my dream I also saw seven heads of grain, full and beautiful, growing on a single stalk. Then seven more heads of grain appeared, but these were blighted, shriveled, and withered by the east wind. And the shriveled heads swallowed the seven healthy heads. I told these dreams to my priests, but no one could tell me what they mean."

Asenath felt the suspenseful silence last only three heartbeats before Joseph said, "Both of Pharaoh's dreams mean the same thing. God is telling Pharaoh in advance what he is about to do. The seven healthy cows and the seven healthy heads of grain both represent seven years of prosperity. The seven thin, scrawny cows that came up later and the seven thin heads of grain, withered by the east wind, represent seven years of famine.

"This will happen just as I have described it, for God has revealed to Pharaoh in advance what he is about to do. The next seven years will be a period of great prosperity throughout the land of Kemet. But afterward there will be seven years of famine so great that all the prosperity will be forgotten. Famine will destroy the land, and this famine will be so severe that even the memory of the good years will be erased. As for having two similar dreams, it means that these events have been decreed by God, and he will soon make them happen.

"Therefore, Pharaoh should find an intelligent and wise man and put him in charge of the entire land of Kemet. Then Pharaoh should appoint supervisors over the land and let them collect one-fifth of all the crops during the seven good years. Have them gather all the food produced in the good years that are ahead and bring it to Pharaoh's storehouses. Store it away, and guard it so there will be food in the cities. That way there will be enough to eat when the seven years of famine come to the Two Lands. Otherwise this famine will destroy the land."

Taking her eyes off Joseph only long enough to glance quickly down at her father, she saw the high priest staring up at her with a subtle but distinctly proud smile on his lips. Her joy in that instant was so great, if she had been dreaming she would immediately have woken up. And when she returned all her attention to Joseph, she slipped deeper into this most marvelous of dreams as he looked in her direction. The emotions that flashed in his eyes when he saw her were more beautiful to her than the brightest stars. She was very glad then of the fine jewelry the princess had given her, and that her wig had been freshly polished with beeswax that morning until it shone a rich blue-black over a mist linen dress the pale blue of the sky at sunrise. Although his eyes rested on her only for a moment, she mysteriously felt him see all of her. She felt nothing about her had escaped his notice as, beneath his regard, she seemed to understand everything her life could mean.

Becoming aware of murmuring voices filling the room as

they grew louder, she reluctantly looked away from Joseph, who was now staring steadily straight ahead of him, seemingly at nothing in particular, but she felt he was gazing inwardly at Elohim, who had sent Pharaoh these dreams and made it possible for his servant Joseph to interpret them. Kemet's priests had formed a circle, in the center of which stood the high priest of Re next to his long time friend, the high priest of Ptah. The conference was a brief one. Almost at once, the men made way for her father who, stepping forward to face Pharaoh, grasped both his bare shoulders, and crossing his arms over his chest inclined his head. He then returned to his original position in the assembly.

Standing, the king addressed the room. "Can we find anyone else like this man so obviously filled with the spirit of God?" he demanded.

When no one spoke, Pharaoh looked down at Joseph and said, "Since God has revealed the meaning of the dreams to you, clearly no one else is as intelligent or wise as you are. You will be in charge of my court, and all my people will take orders from you. Only I, sitting on my throne, will have a rank higher than yours."

Asenath saw the prince grip the ends of his chair with fists that suddenly looked carved of granite, and the last thing she heard was Sithathor's small cry of surprise before a thrumming silence flooded the space between her ears, as if the air had transformed into water. The invisible power flooding the throne room almost made her feel weightless, and it seemed a long moment before Pharaoh's voice reached her as if from a great distance, “I hereby put you in charge of the entire land of Kemet.” Removing his signet ring from his hand, Pharaoh descended the dais, and transferred the ring onto one of Joseph’s fingers.

Queen Nofret stood up, the prince followed her example, and Asenath felt Sithathor grip her arm. But the sensation of her friend's touch also registered as if from far away in another world. She seemed to be in her dream body in the midst of God's power flowing around her and through her as a ringing began in her ears that grew louder and louder. She felt a pressure building up in her chest she did not think she could endure much longer... Then abruptly, she could hear and breathe normally again, as though she had leaped straight out of the River and onto dry land again.

“Walk!” Sithathor commanded in an undertone. “We're leaving!”

For a moment the prince's rigid back blocked her view of Joseph, but then she saw him again. He was walking just behind Pharaoh and his queen as they turned away from the throne room, where all the priests stood with their arms held up in praise. The royal persons and their attendants retired through the small door behind the dais, only now there was one more member in the party—the former slave, Joseph.

☼

“Lady Asenath.”

“Yes?”

“Come with me, please.”

The royal herald turned his body so that he was in profile to her where he stood on the threshold of her room, leaving her just enough space to slip past him into the corridor. His expression told her nothing. One of the first things a royal herald learned to do was school his face to a perfect neutrality, and in those moments she found it as frightening as the calm surface of the River beneath which she imagined she glimpsed all sorts of dangers lurking. She could not forget how the prince had looked at her that morning in the throne room. But surely the young Senwosret had a more pressing matter to think about now than adding to his harem, namely the shocking promotion of a Hebrew slave to Vizier of all Kemet. The crown prince could not be happy about having been demoted to third most powerful man in the Two Lands. She had spent the whole day since the momentous event imagining Joseph giving orders to princes and nobles, awestruck by how easy it was for her to do so. She had never even dreamed of such a possibility, yet it was now a reality.

Silently she prayed, “Protect me, please, Elohim” as she walked past the herald, then waited for him to precede her. He measured his stride so she was able to walk behind him with dignity as he led her out of Princess Sithathor's apartments, along corridors and cramped stairways until she had no idea where she was. She regretted telling Sithathor everything. It had been a mistake to confide in a royal princess even if she was your dearest friend. But she had wanted, needed, longed to speak openly of Joseph and her dreams of him, and of how he had come to be in prison, and of her great joy at finally seeing him freed, for he had committed no crime. On and on she had talked. She could scarcely remember now all she had said as a load lifted off her heart that told her the scales of Maat were now properly balanced.

At last the herald stopped, and knocked four times on a plain wooden door. "The Lady Asenath," he announced in a low voice.

From within the room a man replied, "Enter, your name is pronounced."

The herald opened the door for her.

Bracing herself with another silent prayer, "Protect me, Elohim! " she crossed the threshold.

Facing the door, two men sat on gilded wooden chairs set on either side of a small table, on which rested two translucent alabaster cups half full of what appeared to be red grape wine. Pharaoh and the high priest of Re both smiled up at her when she entered, and the herald closed the door behind her. She was so relieved not to see the prince she could scarcely think, which almost made her feel like a little girl again simply waiting for her beloved father to tell her what to do.

“I understand,” Senwosret nodded at the stool in front of him, “that Kemet has you to thank for saving Joseph's life, Asenath.”

“I did no such thing, majesty,” she replied as she perched on the stool before him, her back straight and her hands resting on her thighs. “God saved Joseph. I was merely one of his instruments.”

“I believe my daughter's dreams are sent to her by Re,” the high priest pronounced. “Since childhood, she has possessed the gift of dreaming consciously.”

“Your father has told me, Asenath, why Joseph was imprisoned, and how your dream helped save his life. He has also told me how much your uncle treasured Joseph, and when I spoke to the prison warden this morning, he had nothing but praise for this Hebrew. It was obvious he was reluctant to part with him. But Joseph is a slave no longer. Tonight he sleeps not in a cell but in a room befitting his new station, and a well guarded one, for not everyone is happy with his promotion.” He smiled ruefully. “Even Sithathor is upset with me, although not for the same reason.”

“I told the princess everything about Joseph,” she admitted. “I love her!”

“And my daughter loves you, very much.” He sighed. “That's the problem.”

“Prepare yourself, Asenath,” her father said firmly. “You will be leaving Shedet soon.”

“What?!” She felt as though he had struck her. “Why? Are you sending me back to Iuno?”

“All will be revealed to you in three days time.”

“I cannot wait that long!”

“Have patience and trust in your elders,” her father commanded gently. “These are essential virtues.”

“But when can I see Joseph?” she asked, too desperate for an answer to conceal how much she desired to know.

“You will see my vizier,” Pharaoh replied, reaching for his wine cup, “along with all my other lords and ladies, at his investiture ceremony tomorrow.”

“Now off to bed,” her father said.

Senwosret did not quite succeed in hiding a smile behind his cup.

She wanted to stomp her foot and yell, “I'm not five years old anymore!” but respect and pride prevented her from doing so. She had no choice but to follow the herald all the way back to her bedroom, afraid it would be impossible for her to sleep. She was right.

Chapter 12

Sleep, the best friend she had ever known, abandoned her, driving home the truth that her future was not a dream, and whether she wanted it to come true or not, she could not escape it. She felt like a small branch caught in the River's currents, cut off from the secure roots of her past with no knowledge of where she would end up. But since she was not a mindless piece of flotsam, she kept imagining possibilities that all made her breathless with anxiety. Pharaoh had bestowed a great honor upon her by acknowledging her service to Kemet, making her father even more proud of her, and she clung to this centering happiness which rose above her other turbulent emotions.

The darkness of her bedroom was utterly indifferent to her inner turmoil, and at one timeless moment in the night, unable to bear the stillness and silence any longer, she whispered, “Elohim!” as she remembered the way Joseph had looked at her in the throne room. No one had ever looked at her that way. Joseph's regard had been the exact opposite of the prince's stare. The latter made her feel helpless as prey, and important only insofar as she roused his sensual appetites.

Again she prayed softly, “Elohim!” and felt a measure of relief from the growing pressure in her heart. Even though Joseph was a Hebrew who did not believe in Re, her father had told Pharaoh he believed it was Re who had sent her the dream which helped save Joseph's life. There could be no doubt all three men respected God's power, and in the midst of her uncertainty, she felt profoundly reassured and protected by this fact. The face of her future remained hidden from her, but in the long hours of darkness, Joseph's eyes, and how they had looked at her, was better than lamplight as she felt that his perception of her was who she truly was—who she could be.

She sighed, "Joseph!" and not long afterward finally fell asleep.

Asenath stood beside her mother in the front row of spectators filling the throne room on either side of a central walkway. Up on the royal dais everything looked as it had the day before, except that Sithathorinunet was not present. Asenath was certain the princess' sudden indisposition had something to do with her, and it grieved her there was nothing she could do to make her friend feel better. She did not even know how she would soon be feeling herself. And it was impossible for her to think about anything except the man who had just been announced, and toward which all heads turned.

Staring up at some point just above Pharaoh's throne, Joseph walked with complete confidence along the path of honor. Lamplight and shadows lapped over his face and body as he passed between the living banks of Kemet's nobility, so at first she was not sure if she was only imagining the smile on his lips, until he drew nearer, then she was thrilled to see that he truly was smiling.

A disturbing hissing sound slithered through the large room as people began whispering among themselves. The giant serpent Apep, enemy of Re, almost seemed to become visible coiled around the columns, its scales glimmering in the gold and precious gems of the men and women staring coldly at Joseph. Asenath could sense what they were thinking, that a Hebrew slave was no more important than a mouse, and this slave was even worse—a rat that had sneaked all the way into the throne room from the dark bowels of the palace prison. Yet instead of crushing the foreign pest, Pharaoh had made the dirty creature not just his prize pet but his near equal. She felt surrounded by angry frustrated cats with human faces.

Sadeh whispered in her ear, "He does not look as I expected."

"What did you expect, mother?"

"I feared your father had exaggerated in order to make the best of Pharaoh's disastrous impulse, but now I see it is true what he said about Joseph, that every god is in him." She sighed, "Re be praised! Now I no longer have to be angry with my husband!"

The high priest of Re stood at the foot of the dais facing the assembly. When the new vizier stopped before him, Meketre dipped the two principle fingers of his right hand into one of the dishes of sacred oil—resting on a tray held by a temple servant—and anointed Joseph's forehead. Asenath stood at the foot of the dais, so Joseph was in perfect profile to her, and she seemed to feel her father's touch on her own body. Dipping his fingertips into a different sacred oil each time, the priest anointed the base of Joseph's throat, the center of his chest, his navel—exposed by the knee length shendyt he wore—and finally his genitals. As he did so, the sharp sensation of warmth she experienced between her own legs attested to the ritual's power.

When the temple servant departed with the tray of sacred oils, the high priest stood to one side as Pharaoh rose and, handing his flail to one attendant and his crook to another, waited for Joseph to ascend the eight steps and stand before him. Senwosret then spoke in a voice pitched to carry as he hung a gold chain around Joseph's neck, "I am Pharaoh, but no one will lift a hand or foot in the entire land of Kemet without your approval." He then placed his hands on the younger man's shoulders and, turning him to face the room, commanded all assembled to, "Kneel down!"

Asenath turned to help her mother to her knees before quickly kneeling herself as Joseph, preceded by Pharaoh—and followed by the high priest of Re, the prince, the queen and all their various attendants—began filing out of the throne room, but not through the private door behind the dais. Today the royal procession made its way between the spectators. As soon as the last member had walked by, Asenath regained her feet, helped her mother up, and together they fell into step behind the royal line. The silent wave of shocked and angry incredulity coursing through the throne room washed harmlessly over her. Joseph was now the second most powerful man in the Two Lands!

Outside in the great festival court, no stick fighting or boxing matches were planned for the day. Only one man was on display—Joseph, the gold around his neck and forearms catching the sunlight, and reflecting the glowing satisfaction Asenath experienced watching him ride in the chariot reserved for Pharaoh's second in command. Royal heralds—positioned strategically around the courtyard—once again commanded all the noble spectators to "Kneel down!" as Joseph passed.

When the ringing of the horses' hooves ceased, and the whisper of the wheels died away as the chariot came to a stop, the new vizier dismounted, sank to one knee before Pharaoh, and beating his chest with his right fist three times, extended his arm with the palm held up and open.

Senwosret then gave Joseph his new name, proclaiming it for all to hear, "Zaphenath-paneah: The God Speaks and He Lives!"

And so Pharaoh put Joseph in charge of the entire land of Kemet.

The hours after the investiture ceremony and before the celebratory banquet felt endless to Asenath, who found herself the center of attention in Sithathoriunet's private courtyard. The princess was not present, but her handmaidens had gotten wind of the fact that Lady Asenath would soon be leaving their company. Most of them looked pleased. They would not miss her anymore than she would miss them, but they were still curious to know where she was going.

"Oh come on, you can tell us!" Lady Nit exclaimed. "Has Nomarch Djer finally won your heart? Have you agreed to be the mistress of his house?"

"No," Asenath replied shortly, thinking, *I want to be the mistress of Joseph's house!* She could scarcely believe Joseph would soon actually possess his own home, and more. The vizier of the Two Lands was entitled to apartments in the palace, to a personal fleet of ships, and to land of his own, where he was free to build as many homes as he wished.

Lady Nefer asked, a note of nervous awe in her voice, "Is it the prince?"

A hush fell over the group of women. One of their pet monkeys grabbed a grape, but instead of eating it, the mischievous creature tossed it into the pool. Asenath watched the red fruit floating on the water as if it was her own heart, cut off from the vine of her family and easily consumed by a powerful man's appetites. She felt forced to consider the dreadful possibility that Pharaoh had decided to honor her in a more public way—by giving her to his son.

"Well?" Nefer prodded.

"No," she said firmly, willing her response to be true. The intelligence of her heart told her it was. She really did not think marriage to the prince was what Pharaoh or her father had planned for her. Her mother had been of no help whatsoever. "Do you not trust your father, Asenath, to do what is best for you?" she had demanded gently. Of course she did, she was simply not sure if what her father considered best for her was also what would make her happy. Yet could there be a difference? How could she ever truly be happy if she was not doing what was best for her?

My Dream, who had been sitting beside her, abruptly stood up and began chasing her tail around and around, distracting the handmaidens from her mistress by making them laugh. The conversation then inevitably returned to the unprecedented promotion of a Hebrew slave to vizier of Kemet. Sithathor's handmaidens had all seen Joseph for the first time that morning. He had been so utterly unlike the unflattering picture they had painted of him yesterday, it was as though, believing it to be only a dirty old lamp, they had accidentally looked straight at the sun. Immediately, they seemed to forget all the nasty things they had said about Joseph before. The unanimous opinion now was that Zaphenath-paneah was a handsome and obviously virile man in need of at least one wife.

It was a relief when it came time to retire to her room, where a servant was waiting to undress and bathe her, oil and massage her, apply her make-up, and dress her again. A long wig was secured to her head, then anklets, a girdle, matching bracelets, a necklace and earrings were variously clasped, tied, hung and pinned to her body. She had deliberately chosen not to wear her loveliest dress or jewelry, holding them in reserve for the all-important third day when she would finally learn her fate.

Her parents were waiting for her outside the banquet hall, and the quality of their regard as she approached them made Asenath feel self conscious, for she suffered the impression they did not see her as completely as Joseph did. Telling herself she was imagining how he had looked at her in the throne room did not diminish the very real effect the memory of his gaze had on her.

She had dined on the royal dais on several occasions, either sharing Sithathor's table or her parents'. This evening, Pharaoh himself was the new vizier's table companion, and when the high priest of Re arrived with his family, Senwosret surprisingly smiled at her, prompting Joseph to look her way. Asenath managed not to trip as she sat down, and when her eyes met his, the soaring notes of a reed flute perfectly expressed the perversely joyful flight of her heart when Joseph failed to smile at her. All men smiled at her. Smiling was easy and meant nothing. The serious cast of Joseph's features showed her infinitely more respect and, mysteriously, seemed to promise her everything. Or so she felt in the brief timeless moment during which she floated in the heaven of his regard, before he looked at her father and mother and respectfully inclined his head.

She felt at once bereft and relieved when Joseph returned his full attention to Pharaoh, who obviously had much to say to his new vizier. The prince, to her immense relief, was not present. He was not required to attend every banquet held by his father, but that his absence tonight was intended as a direct insult to Joseph no one could doubt. This was not the first time a commoner had been elevated to a position of power, but this was definitely the first time a Hebrew had been so honored, and so swiftly, all because of two dreams. She wondered what Joseph thought of his new position as he listened earnestly to the king. How could he possibly find time to think about her? Was her proximity distracting him at least a little? Would he look over at her again? Was there a reason she was the closest person to him apart from the king? Everyone looking up at the dais would see both her and Joseph in the same glance.

"Lady Nofret sounds like a hyena," her mother remarked as a woman's loud shrieking laughter rang across the hall.

"Asenath," her father spoke her name soberly, but there was a mischievous glint in his eyes, "the food before us is not a sacred offering. Feel free to eat it."

"Do not tease her," Sadeh reprimanded him lightly. "There is nothing wrong with her appetite, she is simply starved for answers. Secrecy and intrigue can be delectable spices in very small doses, otherwise they ruin every dish."

Smiling appreciatively, Meketre reached for his wife's hand, turned it so her palm was facing up, and raising it to his mouth kissed her wrist, pressing his lips directly against the dark-blue river of a vein rising up against her delicate skin.

Suddenly, Asenath saw sitting before her a man and a woman separate from herself even though they had given her own body life. She looked around her in almost frightened wonder feeling like a baby bird poking its head from the egg of her breaking heart. Only one day remained to her in the nest of her family, then never again would her mother's warmth and her father's strength protect and nourish her well being as intimately as they always had. All too soon she would be taking flight into her own future.

Grape wine tasted better than ever to her as the evening progressed—too good, she realized, when, with a curt gesture, her father dismissed the servant who was about to refill her cup again, and commanded her to eat something.

She had just bitten into a slice of bread when Joseph finally looked her way again. The piece of bread remained resting on her tongue as she stared back at him. His hair was cut short, his face shaved, and there was black kohl around his eyes, but she still saw him as he had looked all those years ago, the shadow of a beard around his mouth, his dark hair waving gently down to his shoulders. And as they stared into each others eyes, something happened—she perceived him not as he had been, or as he looked now, but as he would one day appear. The vision filled a single beat of her heart, after which she realized it was the face of the man who had walked on water in her dream she had just seen. Then time, momentarily suspended, rushed forward again as Joseph returned his attention to Pharaoh, and she swallowed the piece of bread in her mouth. She was taking a sip of red wine to wash the bread down with when Joseph unexpectedly turned toward her once more, and leaning forward in his chair said, "How are you, Lady Asenath? And how is My Dream?"

"We are well, Joseph," she replied, and dared to add, "but she misses you terribly."

"I look forward to seeing her again very soon," he replied, and held her eyes a moment longer before turning away again.

For the remainder of the banquet, Pharaoh and his new vizier remained deep in conversation, ignoring most of the entertainment provided by musicians, dancers and acrobats. Meanwhile, feeling utterly fullfilled by Joseph's promise, Asenath recovered her appetite.

Asenath was surprised when, hearing a soft whisper of cloth behind her on the rooftop, she glanced over her shoulder and saw not another of Sithathor's handmaidens but her own mother. She turned quickly away from her contemplation of the sunrise, but her mind remained full of the scene of royal ships on the River being prepared and equipped for a journey.

"Asenath, my dear!" With a hesitant smile, her eyes troubled, Sadeh reached up and stroked her daughter's cheek. "I could not sleep thinking of you lying alone in the dark completely ignorant of what awaits you. I don't care what your father says, I've come to tell you-"

"No, mother, please, don't! I trust my faith in father will not lead me astray. My heart already knows the direction in which it is beating, and no matter what, my feet will follow it."

Intently studying her daughter's face, Sadeh pulled her shawl more closely around her shoulders. Her mouth, slightly pinched at the corners, revealed that she was not entirely happy. She did not like being caught off guard. Her eyes remained troubled as she strove to discern what she had missed, wondering why she had not seen it before.

Asenath perceived all this in her mother's beautiful face with an almost painful clarity. "I love you, mommy," she declared, slipping her arms around her and hugging her gently, acutely aware that Kemet's legendary beauty was not so much slender and supple anymore as thin and delicate.

"And I love you, Asenath, but it is chilly up here. Have you perfumed your mouth yet?"

"No."

"Then let us go down to your room and have a servant bring us some bread and fruit."

Though she would have preferred to remain on the roof, she

obediently followed the woman who had blessed her childhood with so much attentive grace, she had not even realized how fortunate she was until she came to live at the palace, where she quickly learned that not everyone had parents as wise and loving as hers.

It was warmer in her bedroom, which felt smaller with every passing moment—not much bigger than a chest—for she was leaving the life she had led in it behind like a dress. When they entered, My Dream's tail made a loud thumping sound on the mat she was curled up on. Her eyes followed them but she did not get up.

"I will be adding another chest to your luggage," Sadeh informed Asenath, sitting in the chair reserved for the princess while her daughter perched on the stool. "I believe you will take great pleasure in all the special things I have filled it with."

"Thank you!" Secretly, she hoped the necklace of golden beetles was not one of the items.

"But tell me, my dear, where is your heart running to with such brave confidence? I would hate for you to be disappointed..."

Standing restlessly, and considering how best to answer her mother's question, she went and knelt beside her dog, whose tail beat a leisurely thump-thump-thump of pleasure as her mistress gently stroked her. "When I put a collar around My Dream," she said, "and tie a leash to it, she trusts me not to lead her anywhere she herself does not wish to go. And when the time is right, and I remove the leash so she can run free, she always comes back because she is happy with me and we love each other. In the same way, I trust and obey father, for in my heart I know that where he wants me to go is where I also wish to be. My heart is a lot like a teshem hound, for I understand now that it caught sight of its desire from the great distance of many years ago when my Ba was no more than a puppy. For long stretches of time, my heart lost sight of its prey, but it was always there, as all my growing senses continued chasing after it. Now my heart's desire has come clearly into view and is so very close, there is no stopping me from attaining it. The instant I am off my leash, I will run to him no matter what father or anyone else says. I am only hoping he is where father wishes me to go."

Sighing, My Dream lowered her head onto her paws and closed her eyes.

Sadeh confessed softly, "I felt the same way about your father."

"But you're both cat people!" She laughed. "No one would have dared slip a leash around either of your necks even when you were children!"

There was a respectful knock at the door.

Asenath gave the servant permission to enter.

As the girl set a platter of food on the table, My Dream finally got up and stretched luxuriously.

After the servant left, Sadeh spread a modest amount of

butter on a slice of bread, still warm from the oven, as she said, "You have the makings of a poet, Asenath, but your words are also a riddle I am unable to solve. Who could you possibly have loved since childhood I don't know about?"

Asenath felt a gentle shock as for the first time she plainly admitted to herself—I love Joseph! She had been going around and around the truth without grabbing hold of it just like her dog chased her tail. Feeling as though she was taking deep exultant breaths, she thought—I love Joseph! I love Joseph!

"Asenath, your dog is licking the butter off your bread!"

Laughing, she obligingly tossed the slice of bread onto the floor as a special treat.

"Asenath, I fear you won't be happy with the choice Pharaoh has made for you, and to which your father readily agreed without even consulting me. I should tell you-"

There was a firm knock on the door—the knock of a royal herald.

Surging to her feet, she cried, "Come in!"

"Lady Asenath," the man beat his chest with one fist, "Princess Sithathoriunet desires that you to attend her immediately, although she told me to make sure I said 'please'."

"Thank you. I will be there at once."

The moment the herald closed the door behind him, Sadeh said, "Before you go, Asenath, I should tell you-"

"I'm in love with Joseph!"

Her mother's expression became unreadable, and it was a

long moment before she asked quietly, "Because of the dream you had in which you saw him through Tarset's eyes?"

"No, even though though it was through my aunt's eyes that I first began waking up to certain... feelings."

"I still don't understand, and we have no time to discuss it now, the princess is waiting for you. But you will tell me later the full story of how my child, a daughter of Re, came to love a Hebrew slave!"

The moment Asenath's name was pronounced, Sithathor dismissed her attendant, and from where she reclined on a couch, summoned her handmaiden to her by opening her arms in a pleading fashion.

Asenath gladly ran to the princess and, perching on the edge of the couch, embraced her. At the same time she thought how nice it would be to once again own a spacious bedroom like this one, with windows that let in the north wind and sunlight.

Sithathor hugged her fiercely. "Even though I knew it meant losing you, honey, I could not keep the truth to myself! I told father that you love Joseph because I want you to be happy. I know this means we will spend long months apart, but it also guarantees that you will always return to the palace. My brother is not pleased, but that is good for you."

"How can that be good for me?" she asked nervously.

"It is good for you because my brother is suddenly too busy

being furious with father and despising the new vizier to even think about you. I know you do not like him and that-"

"I never said I-"

"Be quiet and let me finish." It was the princess speaking now. "My brother did not want you to marry Nomarch Djer because your father is one of the most powerful men in Kemet and it is his intention, once he is crowned Pharaoh, to diminish the power of the Nomarchs. To that end, he was seriously considering forging an alliance with the temple of Re by making you one of his wives. I was sure this arrangement would not make you happy, and after you told me how you felt about Joseph, I knew there was no doubt it would make you miserable."

Asenath suddenly understood all the secrecy. Pharaoh and her father had not been so closemouthed merely to test her trust and obedience, but also to prevent the prince finding out about what else Pharaoh intended to give Joseph—Asenath, daughter of the high priest of Iuno.

Chapter 13

Asenath was up before the sun. Her night had been one long dream, from which she kept waking only to slip back into it again. Staring into the darkness of the room in which she would never sleep again, it seemed to her that her soul had been caught like a fish on the mysterious thread of this dream, which she had been unable to escape no matter how restlessly she tossed and turned on the shore of her bed.

In the dream, she was an old woman peacefully waiting to die, for this was the only way to return to the future where she could at last be with the man she had glimpsed here in the past —the man she desired to be with more than anything. And suddenly, she was a young woman again, sitting at a table with this man, who smiled as he explained that he had ransomed her past and thereby saved their love. He told her this had been the plan all along. Then she was in a bedroom she knew to be part of her home even though she had never seen it before. The room was filled with a gentle white light. The only shadow was the man she loved approaching her wearing a long black robe, a fishing pole propped against his right shoulder. She wanted him to know she was there, yet some part of her feared it was too soon for them to meet. Yet he had already seen her, and without hesitating, he opened the door, stepped into her personal space, and sitting down on the bed beside her, blessed her with a beautiful, unclouded smile. All her reservations immediately vanished. Their love was all that mattered. She was wondering if anyone else in her house was aware of his presence in her heart when she woke from this dream for the last time.

She lay in bed waiting for the dream to dissolve like a reflection in water, but it did not. The details blurred slightly, but the man, and the timeless love they shared, remained vivid in her mind. It was very strange to be thinking about another man this morning, because before she went to sleep, all her thoughts had been of Joseph. The silent shadowy room felt a little too much like a tomb, from which her Ba would fly away today toward a life so splendid, she could not even imagine it.

Her heart beating with mingled excitement and dread, she struggled briefly with the mosquito mesh around her bed which seemed to embody the plans woven around her she could not so easily escape. She could only hope she would end up in Joseph's hands. Her own hands were trembling sightly as she lit a fresh floating wick from the one she had left burning all night, and the stronger light helped steady her nerves somewhat. In Kemet, she reminded herself, women were permitted to choose their husbands. She knew her parents desired her happiness, and that she had an ally in Princess Sithathor. Pharaoh was also clearly predisposed to giving Joseph everything befitting his position, and the daughter of the high priest of Re was certainly a worthy prize for the new vizier. If she had too, she would let it be known that Joseph was the man she wanted, and no other.

Yet there was another anxiety germinating in some deep dark place inside her like a poisoned seed.

Her instincts told her that if she hurried, she would be able to watch the sunrise from the roof, an experience which never failed to lift her spirits. But nearly all her possessions had already been packed, and by the light of a single lamp she found it difficult to navigate the unfamiliar bulky shadows. When she stubbed her toe on a chest, the pain stabbed straight into the doubt bruising her soul, and as she cried out loud, she silently asked herself: Can I really be happy with a Hebrew?

Sitting back down on the bed cradling her offended foot in both hands, her throbbing toe abruptly struck her as a gift. The chest she had stubbed it against was real, but the awful question she had just lashed her soul with was only a shadow cast by popular opinion, not by her own heart.

Sleepily raising her head, My Dream regarded her silently.

"We are leaving here today," Asenath told her. "And I pray to God it is with Joseph!"

The dog lay her head lazily on her paws again, but her eyes continued to watch her.

Asenath slipped into a linen shift, and wrapping a light shawl over her shoulders commanded, "Let's go!"

My Dream leaped to her feet and eagerly followed her out of the room, then up the steps to the roof, promptly heading to the corner where she was permitted to do her business in the sand box made just for her.

Meanwhile, Asenath went and stood in her favorite spot at the edge of the roof. Clutching her shawl around her against the predawn chill, she gazed hopefully east. Below her, the blooming flax fields were laid out like the rich dark cloak of the earth god, not yet woven by his wife, the sky, with the colors of life. On the other side of the River's broad gray ribbon, grazing pastures bordered by groves of sycamore figs and date palms were not yet visible, but here and there she could just make out tiny white houses belonging to a handful of small villages where lived some of Pharaoh's farmers, herders and fishermen. Beyond them stretched the eternal sands, and on the brink of this fateful day, the undulating desert mountains resembled the sensual silhouette of bare shoulders and hips, as if she was looking at a god-sized man lying on his side facing away from her, still sleeping, but about to wake and turn his face toward her as the sun rose.

Before the solar disc came into view, its light slowly began suffusing the world, and by its growing illumination she saw the royal ship dominating the crowded harbor. There was no mistaking that long silhouette with its distinct papyrus shape, its straight bow post, its curved stern fitted with a tall mast, and its two great steering oars. She knew, as did the rest of the court, that Pharaoh was not planning a journey. Nor was the prince. This could mean only one thing—all the ships she could see were being furnished for the vizier.

"Joseph is leaving the city today," she said out loud, "and so am I!”

Absolute certainty dawned on her with the day, and by the sun's infinitely generous light, she spotted two great falcons perched side by side on one of the ship's black masts. She took an exultant breath as the sail was raised, and the birds flew away on the wind of her exhalation. She discerned the figures of sailors busy at work, white circlets tied around their foreheads. She counted twenty-five ships, at least four of which would be filled by the soldiers she now saw marching down the road leading from the palace to the River. She knew that soon they would be followed by scribes, personal attendants, a chef and his many assistants, a handful of priests and numerous officials and, of course, musicians. Then finally the vizier would board his yacht, and the royal fleet would set sail for all ports south. This very day, Joseph would begin taking charge of the entire land of Kemet. He was leaving the capital to initiate preparations for the famine God had revealed would strike in seven years time. He would begin piling up huge amounts of grain like sand on the seashore... He would store up so much grain that finally he would stop keeping records because there would be too much to measure...

My Dream barked three times.

Looking down, Asenath saw that her dog was grinning up at her, her mouth open and her tongue lolling out one side. Her tail wagging happily, she glanced in the direction of the steps leading down into the palace, and then expectantly back up at her mistress. She could not have spoken more clearly. “It's time! It's time!” She was saying. “Come on! What are you waiting for?! Let's go!”

☼

Three of Princess Sithathoriunet's handmaidens were standing outside Asenath's bedroom door. Two of them held small wooden chests, and the third cradled a bundle of neatly folded garments. Asenath stopped short when she saw them waiting there, but My Dream ran on, eager to receive their admiring caresses. On this particular morning, however, the dog was disappointed, for the young women did not even look at her.

Sennuwy, Nit and Ashait stood staring at her in a way that made Asenath feel like a prize cow they had been instructed to decorate before it was led away to the temple, where its throat would be slit as a sacrifice to the gods.

“What are you doing here?” she demanded.

“The princess ordered us to attend you this morning,” Sennuwy replied as they all finally remembered to bow their heads respectfully. “She commanded us to make you as beautiful as possible, and she wishes you to accept these gifts from her.”

The women followed her into the room, where Asenath saw that breakfast was waiting for her.

“The princess also said,” Sennuwy began slowly, reluctantly, "that you may take two of us with you to serve as your handmaidens, until you set up your household and are at leisure to personally select your attendants."

"Please tell the princess how much I appreciate all her beautiful gifts," Asenath said quickly, "but that I cannot accept the offer of her handmaidens, who mean so much to her. The two servants who have attended me in the palace will do for now."

She was too excited to feel hungry, but since she did not wish her stomach to greet Joseph with a hungry growl, she sat down and perfumed her mouth with two small rolls of emmer bread flavored with nuts, a handful of figs, and a cup of cow's milk sweetened with honey. Meanwhile, two of the women unpacked the chests of jewels and precious oils as the third laid out the dress and a matching shawl. Once she had finished eating, Asenath rinsed her face and mouth with water, then seating herself in the room's only chair, silently submitted herself to being made beautiful.

The handmaidens had nearly finished their work when the wife of the high priest of Re entered the room without knocking. Walking straight over to Asenath, who was standing now, she rested a cool hand on her cheek and smiling up at her said, "Now you look like my daughter."

"Thank you..." She had no idea what Sadeh meant by this cryptic compliment, for they could not be said to resemble each other physically, but any praise was welcome from her. "And now will you finally please tell me, mother, who is to be receiving the gift of my beauty?"

Glancing at Sithathor's handmaidens as though she would have preferred to dismiss them before replying, Sadeh was silent a moment before she said proudly, "Only the vizier of all Kemet, Zaphenath-paneah, The God Speaks and He Lives, would be worthy of you, Asenath. Pharaoh is giving you to Joseph, of course."

Nit gasped, while Sennuwy and Ashait both suddenly looked like cats who had caught a mouse, and could scarcely wait to begin dropping it in everyone's lap.

☼

No sooner had Asenath and her mother stepped out of the room than servants arrived for the luggage in the company of My Dream's handler, who had grown into a tall, slender young man. He had come to take the dog to the transport boat.

It was a relief when she and her mother took a different stairway than Sithathor's handmaidens, and she imagined them breaking into a run the moment they were out of sight. Soon the whole palace would be buzzing like a hive with the news Pharaoh—He of the Sedge and the Bee—had desired to keep a secret for as long as possible.

Expecting to end up in a small, secret room similar to the one she had been led to the other night, Asenath was surprised to suddenly find herself in the broad corridor leading out to the festival court.

The sun had not yet risen above the enclosure walls, but already the air was warm for it was the end of the ninth month of Shemu, during which the days grew longer and hotter as the level of the River sank lower and lower. Yet it was also the joyful season of harvest, and stepping outside—walking beside instead of behind her mother as she always had—Asenath felt that in those moments, all the years of her childhood were reaped. What lay in store for her now was the supremely rich mystery her heart had been hungering for. As a trumpet sounded an imperious note, she glanced behind her into the dark bowels of the palace, preparing to make way for an important official, perhaps even Pharaoh himself, but she saw no one exiting into the crowded courtyard.

Grasping her hand, her mother gave it a reassuring squeeze. "You are the one being announced, my love. Go now, and be happy. We will see you again soon." Releasing her hand, she stepped back.

Asenath realized then that the king was already in the festival court, and beside him on the dais stood Joseph. Both faced the palace door from which she had just emerged. Behind them, four attendants slowly waved great ostrich feather fans to help keep them cool and the flies away. The trumpet sounded again even more loudly, commanding her to keep moving as effectively as an invisible hand shoving her forward. All the people staring at her were indistinct as figures in an ordinary dream for she saw only Joseph—God Speaks and He Lives. If she had not been so awkwardly conscious of the sandals Sithathor had given her to wear—she was accustomed to walking barefoot even on formal occasions—she might truly have been afraid she was dreaming, but the small sound of a courtier coughing, closely followed by one of the horses attached to the chariot snorting impatiently, also reassured her that she was in no danger of waking up.

She was only half way to the dais when Joseph quickly descended the steps, and sinking to one knee before her, lowered his head as he crossed both wrists over his heart.

Gazing down at his head, so close to her body, awoke a sensation between her legs as warm as honey, and as sharp as the knife used to cut the dry honeycomb. Suddenly tasting something of what her aunt had felt when she was close to Joseph, she was flooded with compassion headily mixed with triumph. Not caring if it was the proper ritual gesture or not, when Joseph rose to his full height before her again, she simply offered him her left hand so he could take it in his right hand, and looking up into his eyes, she saw that he understood she had just put her life—and all her dreams—in his keeping. She also sensed that he received this gift of her trust very seriously.

"Come, Asenath," he said gently. "Our ship is waiting."

He led her over to the chariot, and before she knew it, she was gripping the edge of the leather compartment. But even if she let go of it, she would be safe, for Joseph's left arm was around her waist, and pressing her firmly against his side as he gripped the reigns with both hands. She felt every downward thrust of his arms and every subtle twist of his wrists as he spurred the horses into motion, driving them rapidly through the city's eastern gate, and along the paved road leading to the River.

Now that they had left the spectators and witnesses to their official union behind, she felt free to exclaim over the exhilarating thunder of the horse's hooves, “I feel like we're flying in a dream, Joseph!”

“Yes, Asenath! Elohim be praised!”

As they neared the River, he slowed the pace of the horses as the chariot cut effortlessly through the organized chaos of servants, sailors and baggage handlers—like a golden shaft of light penetrating murky brown waters. She loved feeling it in her body every time he tugged on the reigns, and she could scarcely distinguish the exultant beating of her heart from the drumming of the horse's hooves on the wooden dock. The noise around them rang in her ears like music composed of a single resplendent, powerfully vibrating note on which it seemed their souls were soaring together as she felt more alive than ever before.

When the shadow of the vizier's ship fell across them, Joseph gave a final pull on the reigns, and the horses obediently came to a stop. As his arm slipped from around her waist, she looked up at his face, and his expression almost frightened her, for the smile on his mouth failed to illuminate his eyes. But perhaps it was only the ship's sail blocking the sun. Already she missed his strong arm holding her possessively against him.

He stepped off the chariot, grasped her slender waist with both hands, and lifted her down beside him. "I must play my part now, Asenath," he said, studying the scene with that same penetrating look in his eyes. Spotting some significant detail in all the activity around them, he extended his right arm in the summoning gesture. How naturally he exercised the authority so recently bestowed upon him amazed her. After enduring the darkness of prison for three years, he had stepped directly into full sunlight, yet he did not stumble or appear in the least bit overwhelmed by its power.

Accompanied by four soldiers, the two young female servants who had attended her in the palace materialized beside her on the dock as if by magic, and as the sun crested the ship's sails, the polished tips of their bodyguards' spears shone with almost painful splendor.

"Escort my lady to our cabin, and see to it she has everything she needs," Joseph instructed the women, then bent and whispered in her ear, "I will be with you soon, Asenath!"

"Please!" she breathed, and forced herself not to stare longingly after him as he strode away. How very different this day was from that one three years ago—when she had watched him, his hands bound behind his back, walk up onto her uncle's transport boat. Now it was she who walked up the much broader ramp of Joseph's own ship.

Her ladies led her to the small cabin in the center of the vessel. It was already uncomfortably warm inside, but the wooden walls were high, and all four sides boasted fine window screens that would let in River breezes, and which could also be closed for privacy. She instructed her attendants to open them all so she could look out, and secretly watch for Joseph's return.

After obeying her, Ana and Ipy waited silently on their knees by the door, their eyes on the sky-blue papyrus mat softening the hard wooden planks of the floor.

"Is there somewhere else you can go and embrace the shade?" she asked them bluntly.

"Yes, my lady," Ana replied. "There is an awning behind the cabin, within earshot should you need us or require more refreshments."

"Very well, you are dismissed until I call for you." Suddenly, Asenath wished she was commencing her married life in a spacious villa rather than on a crowded ship. But she immediately quelled the discontent, for to change one detail, no matter how small, was to change everything, and each thread in the web of circumstances she found herself in now was precious.

Despite the sounds of activity around her, she felt much too alone with her thoughts as she moved restlessly back and forth between the east and west windows of the cabin, through the former enjoying a glimmering expanse of water and a view of the opposite shore, and through the latter watching to see if she could catch sight of Joseph boarding the ship. And, at last, there he was!

Wiping the corners of her eyes clean of any kohl that might have smudged, she nervously smoothed the dress over her hips and stood facing the door. She would not pretend to have been doing anything besides waiting for the man who was already officially her husband. It seemed to take him forever to reach their cabin, but finally the door opened, and he quickly closed it behind him. The next thing she knew, his arms were around her and her cheek was resting against his chest, or rather against the heavy pectoral necklace he was wearing. The jeweled falcon pin holding up his shendyt also pressed into her belly, yet despite these minor discomforts, the pleasure of embracing him as he held her against him, of feeling more of his body than she ever had before, was more marvelous than anything she had ever experienced.

Slipping his arms from around her, he whispered, "Sweet Asenath!" and raised his hands to her head.

Expecting him to turn her face up toward his for their first kiss, she was surprised to feel him gently pulling off her wig instead. The sensation of cooler air against her warm skull was a welcome relief, yet also mortifying, for beneath the sleek blue-black braids her own hair was gathered up in a tight bun at the nape of her neck, so that she suddenly felt plain as a vulture.

“I told Pharaoh I would do all he asked,” Joseph said as he tossed the wig onto a nearby chest, “except wear one of these. As my wife, Asenath, I hope you will let your hair grow out as long as it wants to, for one of a woman's glories is her hair.”

“But my natural hair is very unruly,” she protested, trying not to resent him for ruining her perfect beauty.

“As long as it is also generous and soft, that is the best kind of hair.” Gripping her hands, he slipped her arms around his neck again, then reaching up behind her, began unpinning the knot at the nape of her neck. “Or so I have always enjoyed imagining, for I have never lain with a woman. We have much to learn about each other, Asenath.”

“Yes, Joseph...” The feel of him was making it hard for her to think, and then her thoughts all seemed to dissolve as he began running his fingers through her hair's silky depths.

His right hand lightly caressing her left arm, his left hand found her chin and tilted her face up toward his as he said, “Today we will talk. Tonight, when we have reached a mooring place and are alone in our chambers, then we will begin to know each others hearts without words.”

Her response welled up from her deepest self, “It will always be as you say, Joseph!”

“And as you dream it.” He did not smile. “Your father, whose wisdom is great, told me about the dream he believes Re sent you; the dream in which you saw, and felt, through your aunt's eyes; the dream that led you to Potipher Setka's house that fateful morning. He told me how you bore witness to the truth, and then urged your uncle to follow the promptings of his heart and spare my life."

"And now my dream of the well has come true, Joseph. You are free. More than free! You are the second most powerful man in the Two Lands!"

"I am only as powerful as Elohim wishes me to be, Asenath. And there is more to your dream of the well than you realize." Taking one of her hands, he led her away from the door to the center of the papyrus mat. Keeping hold of her hand, he knelt and reclined on his side as she followed his example, so that they lay facing each other. She found herself thinking it was true that a man could be beautiful. His features were slightly larger and firmer than any woman's, but that only made their tenderness more exquisitely appealing. And his eyes struck her as darkly luminous celestial orbs bringing to life the landscape of his face. Daring to imagine his lips touching different parts of her body would have been hopelessly distracting if she had not been so fascinated by what he was telling her. She was seeing and hearing him now as she never had before, and the more her eyes and ears feasted on him, the more she knew he would always exceed the sum of her perceptions.

"Throughout the years, I often remembered, Asenath, how you asked me that morning we first met if I dreamed. You reminded me, and helped me hold to my faith that God had a plan for me, even though I felt lost and abandoned. I want you to understand, I never doubted God in my mind, but my heart was not so strong. You were a sweet reminder to me that God's intentions are always bearing fruit, even if too slowly for our comfort. Your earnest, innocent question, 'Do you dream?' surprised me out of my gloom. It was like suddenly catching sight of a white lotus blooming from a dung heap as in your child's voice, I both heard and felt the grace of God. Although I remained a slave for many years afterward, I also remained free in both mind and heart, for no one and nothing can truly control a man who knows God created him. God has been watching over me with you. God loves you, Asenath, and so do I."

"And I love you, Joseph! If it was not so hot in here, I would be sure we were dreaming together!"

"Are you uncomfortable? Would you like to step out on deck?"

"Oh no! I wish to be alone with you as much as possible! This pleasure has been too long in coming! Please, will you not tell me of your life before... before you came to Kemet?"

"Yes, I will tell you, briefly, about my former life, but then I do not wish to speak of it again. My father was... is Jacob, for perhaps he still lives, I do not know. My mother is Rachel, the younger sister of my father's first wife, Leah. I was the youngest of Jacob's many sons, born to him in his old age, after he had settled again in the land of Canaan, where his own father had lived as a foreigner. When I was seventeen years old, I often helped tend to his flocks. I worked for my half brothers, the sons of my father's secondary wives Bilhah and Zilpah. Unfortunately, my brothers were not the most honest and industrious of men, and I was obliged to report to my father some of the bad things they were doing. When I was seventeen my father also gave me a special gift—a beautiful robe of many colors. My brothers hated me because our father loved me more than the rest of them and they couldn't say a kind word to me.

"Then one night, I had a dream, and when I told my brothers about it, they hated me more than ever. 'Listen to this dream,' I said to them. 'We were out in the field, tying up bundles of grain, when suddenly my bundle stood up, and your bundles all gathered around and bowed low before mine!' To which my brothers responded, 'So you think you will be our king, do you? Do you actually think you will reign over us?' And they hated me all the more because of my dream and the way I talked about it."

"Your dream came true, Joseph! You are a king now, nearly as powerful as Pharaoh! But please forgive me, I did not mean to interrupt you..."

Staring down at their clasped hands, he continued quietly, "Soon I had another dream, and again I told my brothers about it. 'Listen, I have had another dream,' I said. 'The sun, moon, and eleven stars bowed low before me!' This time I told the dream to my father as well as to my brothers, but my father scolded me. 'What kind of dream is that?' he asked. 'Will your mother and I and your brothers actually come and bow to the ground before you?' But while my brothers were jealous of me, I know my father wondered what the dreams meant.

"Soon after this, my brothers went to pasture our father's flocks at Shechem. When they had been gone for some time, Jacob said to me, 'Your brothers are pasturing the sheep at Shechem. Get ready, and I will send you to them.' When I told him I was ready to go, he said, 'Go and see how your brothers and the flocks are getting along. Then come back and bring me a report.' So I traveled to Shechem from our home in the valley of Hebron. When I arrived there, a man from the area noticed me wandering around the countryside. 'What are you looking for?' he asked, and I replied I was looking for my brothers, and asked him if he knew where they were pasturing their sheep. 'Yes,' the man told me. 'They have moved on from here, but I heard them say, 'Let's go on to Dothan.' So I followed my brothers to Dothan and found them there.

"When my brothers saw me coming, they must have recognized me in the distance, and made their plans, for when I arrived they ripped off the robe I was wearing, the one my father had given me. Then they grabbed me and threw me into an empty cistern. I couldn't see them, but I could hear them, and as they were sitting down to eat, they looked up and saw what I soon learned was a caravan of camels heading toward them. It was a group of Ishmaelite traders taking a load of gum, balm, and aromatic resin from Gilead down to Kemet.

"Then Judah said to his brothers, 'What will we gain by

killing our brother? We'd have to cover up the crime. Instead of hurting him, let's sell him to those Ishmaelite traders. After all, he is our brother—our own flesh and blood!' And all my brothers agreed. So when the Ishmaelites, who were Midianite traders, came by, they pulled me out of the cistern and sold me to them for twenty pieces of silver. You know the rest. The traders brought me here to Kemet. And to you, Asenath."

Chapter 14

When the new day was come, it dawned on Asenath that her waking life was now a dream. The excitement and pleasure of the journey was merely a reflection of how she felt when Joseph's arms embraced her at night. Their hearts traveling as one on the current of their lovemaking, they never failed to reach a place that felt like the divine shore of all feelings and sensations. Their bed linens a sail, their mingled breaths the wind, they reveled in the adventure of exploring their bodies together. During the day, they used words to express themselves, but at night it was their eyes and lips and hands that spoke with an eloquence no scribe would ever be able to copy with reed and ink.

Much better able now to appreciate the mysteries of the goddess Hathor, the Lady of Love, Asenath never failed to make an offering in her chapel everywhere they stopped. She invariably had time to herself while Re was journeying through the sky and Joseph was busy attending to his duties as vizier. Traveling with the man second in power only to Pharaoh was even more luxurious than traveling with her uncle had been, yet also more demanding, for uniting with their final destination was secondary to enforcing the king's will.

In every sense, Asenath was going places she had never been before. The land of her birth unfolded around her like the living hieroglyph of her own soul growing mysteriously richer with every sunrise. Her eyes feasted daily on scenes of harvest on both sides of the River. The ships' passengers were presented with moving paintings of people—men, women and children of all ages—reaping what had been sown. Sickles flashed tirelessly beneath the sun—a life giving weapon gradually conquering great fields of emmer and barley. She was utterly at peace watching the harvest from the cooler vantage point of the River in Joseph's company. They stood side by side beneath a small pavilion erected near the front of the ship, her two attendants fanning them, while along the shores young men felled ripe ears of grain with flint edged wooden sickles. Often led by children, cattle trampled the grain, and women following behind them gathered the fallen ears, removing the grain, and then tossing it up in the air so the useless chaff would blow away.

On one particular afternoon, she was filled with an especially lazy contentment watching the rhythmic motion of the field hands, hypnotic as a ceremonial dance granting Kemet and her people continued life, health and strength in the year to come.

Joseph observed quietly, "That is hard work."

Abruptly, the illusion of a living painting vanished, and suddenly she could distinctly imagine the crushing heat and thirst, strain and exhaustion composing a silent music the laborers moved in time with. They had no protection from the sun, and certainly no attendants to fan them and keep flies and other insects away from their eyes and skin. Yet as the laborers took a break from their work to watch the royal ships pass, even from this distance she seemed to discern on their faces the same grateful contentment she was experiencing from her more exalted and comfortable position.

"Yes," she agreed. "But they are happy."

Grasping her hand, he whispered in her ear, "Are you happy?"

"Yes!"

He asked her every day, at least once, if she was happy, which naturally contributed to her happiness.

Some of the fields they passed were not yet ready to be harvested, and here the activity was more quiet yet just as vital, for at this stage the crops needed to be watered more often. Kept full by reservoirs, irrigation canals cut straight lines through the land, and it was a different sort of pleasure to watch men—whose shoulders and arms were broader and thicker than the rest of their bodies—lifting water from a canal with a long large pole balanced on a crossbeam. A rope and a bucket hung from one end of the pole and a heavy counter weight from the other. When the men pulled on the rope, the large bucket was lowered into the canal, then brought back up again as they pulled down on the weight and, swinging the pole around, emptied its contents onto the field.

But above all, she loved gazing at Joseph's face whenever he was too intent on observing the scenes unfolding around them to notice her studying him. For her, his presence was the fine grape wine accompanying the visual feast of their journey upriver, intoxicating to her body, mind and heart. Reflected in his eyes, the world was even more fascinating. When he was concentrating, his eyes were sharp and focused as a falcon's, but deep and dark and warm with his human soul.

He had told her scarcely anything about his time in Pharaoh's prison, and she had no intention of asking him to. She did not like to think about it, and she especially disliked wondering if everyone around them was thinking about it, and remembering that the man they all bowed to now, and whose orders they all hurried to obey, had until recently been a slave and a criminal locked away in the Place of Confinement. That some of the officials traveling with them—thankfully on their own ships—never forgot their new vizier's origins was painfully apparent. Outwardly, their behavior was beyond reproach, but ritual gestures and phrases of respect could not hide the expression in their eyes. And she had only to glance at Joseph to know he saw it too.

She was increasingly proud of how nothing seemed to escape the fine strong net of her husband's perceptions. She was not surprised, for she well remembered how swiftly he had risen in the ranks of her uncle's household, and how quickly he had become invaluable to the prison warden. But during the long days when she was alone with her attendants, she had time to marvel at the power and agility of Joseph's mind which, like a great falcon, could catch hold of, master and assimilate whatever he needed to in order to thrive in the land of his captivity. In just three days—from the time he interpreted Pharaoh's dreams to the moment he set sail as vizier—he had learned enough of what he needed to know to begin doing what Pharaoh required of him, which was to implement his own plan for saving Kemet from the ravages of famine.

The officials ordered to accompany the new vizier had undoubtedly expected him to rely more on them and on their advice than he was actually doing. In fact, he essentially ignored them, spending most of his time with his scribes, as well as with the scribes who served the headmen, mayors and Nomarchs he met with. On more than one night, she had woken to the dream-like vision of Joseph intently bent over an open papyrus scroll, its contents illuminated by a single lamp. She knew he had not lit another lamp for her sake, and she was equally reluctant to disturb him as he concentrated. Deliciously tired from a long day on the ship, and by the breathless way their bodies rocked together whenever they were alone in their new bedroom, she had watched him contentedly for a while before slipping back into a restful, dreamless sleep.

Her first days and nights with Joseph were strung together like gold and onyx beads. Superficially, they were all the same, but in truth each one was uniquely special. After the sun sank below the desert mountains every evening, she experienced a sensual thrill as their ship made contact with the landing site, and her husband personally helped her up the steps to the platform, where a carrying litter awaited them. They never disembarked until all had been made ready for them by the persons in charge of welcoming them. Torches seemed to burn the fuel of her own excitement, which in those first moments in an unknown town flickered beneath a gust of anxiety as she worried they might not be as well received here, so far away from the pharaoh who had promoted a Hebrew to the second highest office in the land. However, her fears had proved groundless, and she grew more relaxed every day.

Though they sometimes varied dramatically in size, the provincial palaces were generally well equipped to receive them. Most owned their own farmland and served as regional grain storage centers. Messenger birds were sent ahead of them, so that in addition to the stored grain and produce, the staff had time to hunt for additional meat, and to catch fresh fish. Once they were in residence, the officials accompanying Joseph also enjoyed stocking the larder by spending mornings out in the desert hunting antelope, while their vizier went straight to work meeting with local headmen.

Torchlight flickering on its closed curtains, their litter was carried along a road that led straight from the dock to an enclosure wall with two large gates marking the entrance to royal grounds. The service buildings and quarters were located just inside the gate, providing even more privacy between the road and the palace itself. In the royal entrance court, they were met by the Sole Companion and Superior Custodian of the Domain of Pharaoh, who saw to it that the palace was kept in excellent condition, and the surrounding walls intact. It was gratifying, but also a bit boring listening to him describe, in minute detail, the excellent condition everything was in, and exactly how much wood and feed, fish and fresh beer, bread and wine, and so forth, was on hand for their enjoyment.

One night, her head resting on Joseph's chest where they lay in bed together in a mooring place of Pharaoh, she found the courage to tell him, "I see God everywhere, and yet, at the same time, he is nowhere except in you, Joseph."

He replied, "I am not God, Asenath." His voice was pitched deeper than normal, which she already knew meant he felt very strongly about what he was telling her.

"I know you are not God... but I imagine you must at least resemble God, for you are so beautiful and wise, Joseph."

This time he responded by rolling over onto his side, and taking her in his arms in a way that made it hard for words to come between them, and soon they were communicating exceptionally well without them.

They remained for several days in the city of Djeba, capital of the Nome of the Throne of Horus. Built near the River, the city was raised above the broad valley, safe from the inundation. While their ships were moored there, Asenath rarely saw Joseph until after sunset. During the day she was not idle, however, for as wife of the vizier and daughter of the high priest of Re, she was much sought after by the governor's wife and her lady friends. She spent a handful of boring afternoons in the shade of Nefermut's Pleasure House, feeling surrounded by smiling vultures prodding her for gossip from the royal capital. She was obliged to satisfy their appetite as best she could, which inevitably meant describing how her husband had come to be made vizier. Some ladies did not bother to mask their disbelief and disgust, others behaved more politely, while those who had already seen Joseph—and instantly been seduced by his physical charms, wealth and power—simply smiled. But it was only when a lady looked at her with condescending pity that Asenath became so furious, it was all she could do not to empty the wine cup she was holding in the foolish woman's face.

A much more pleasant duty was presenting offerings at the temple of the falcon god, where she never failed to visit the beautifully decorated little chapel of Hathor, whose local title, Mistress of the Red Cloth, put her in mind of the blood that had stained the white linen sheets of the bed where she and Joseph first kissed and caressed and knew each other. Each time she gave gifts to the wife of Horus, she mysteriously felt that she herself was the goddess and Joseph the god, so that as the statue smiled benevolently over her head, she seemed to be offering herself the nourishment and pleasure of bread and wine, milk and flowers. Hathor's image did not respond in any way to the gifts laid at her painted stone feet, most of which would end up with the temple servants. Human mouths would eat the bread and drink the milk and wine. If she had offered prayers to the goddess as well, where would they have gone? Again, Asenath felt she would only have been talking to herself. Although outwardly she worshiped Hathor, it was Elohim she was thinking of—caught between a comforting ritual, and the frightening yet also exhilarating possibility the gods she had grown up with were only some of Elohim's offspring. Children could intercede with their father on behalf of someone they loved, so perhaps it was not a waste of time to make offerings at all the temples she had the opportunity to visit. At the very least, it gave her something to do while her husband was busy all day being vizier.

When they were finally alone together, Joseph often told her about his day as she listened attentively, vaguely surprised that she actually found what he was talking about interesting. When her old teacher had instructed her on administrative matters, her mind had inevitably wandered, for in his hands the subject had been dull as a rock. Joseph, on the other hand, could transform any subject that interested him into a gem able to catch and engage her attention as he threw light on its many different facets.

She learned that the administrative buildings, and the large mud-brick silos in the center of the city, were the busily pumping heart of Djeba and, to a certain extent, of all the towns and cities they had already visited. Joseph was very impressed by the hall of records adjoining the governor's palace—a mud-brick building boasting no less than sixteen wooden columns—where scribes performed accounting and answered all official correspondence.

"Every man I've met so far responds to Pharaoh's decrees as if he really is their god," Joseph said while thoughtfully stroking My Dream's head. The dog sat beside his chair looking regal as a statue, her eyes fixed on the closed door of their private dining room, as though she fully intended to pounce on anyone who dared intrude on the little time she was able to enjoy being with both her master and mistress. The quivering joy with which the animal had approached Joseph when they were reunited had made Asenath cry, and her eyes still watered whenever she remembered the event. A dog's heart was truly faithful.

Abruptly, Joseph stood. Leaning over the remains of their meal, he braced one hand on the table, clutched a fistful of Asenath's hair with the other, and kissed her mouth with a rough hunger.

She gladly parted her lips for his tongue, savoring its special taste more than the flavor of the red wine and spices they had both just enjoyed. His kisses were feasts she would never get her fill of.

When My Dream whined jealously, Joseph sat down again,

and resumed where he had left off as he stroked the animal's head and neck, "That doesn't mean, of course, that they all jump to obey Pharaoh's command, for it will cost them dearly in manpower and resources. But whether sloppily or efficiently according to their nature, they will do as they are told, which makes my job a lot easier."

His kiss having distracted her, it was with difficulty Asenath made an effort to concentrate on a subject much less interesting to her.

"The River is mother and wet nurse to everyone, no matter what Nome you're born and live in," he mused as My Dream closed her eyes with pleasure beneath his firm caresses. "The River is a great bitch overflowing with nourishing milk, the Nomes are her teats, and there is not enough room between the water and the desert—between life and death—to compete for more. But there is also no need, for she gives generously to all her children."

Suddenly, Asenath very much wanted to ask him what life was like where he came from, but he had told her he did not wish to speak anymore of his past, so she kept silent. She knew only that he had tended his father's flocks, and that his brothers had been murderously jealous of him. What despicable men his older brothers must be! It would give her immense satisfaction, she thought, to throw all of them into the lake of Sobek's temple as food for the sacred crocodiles!

"Asenath, what are you thinking?"

She started guiltily. "Nothing!"

"You seem to be feeling quite strongly about nothing."

"I was thinking that Elohim must be very angry with your brothers for how they treated you, and yet it was God who sent you the dreams that made your brothers and your father so angry with you... which means it was God's will you be brought here to Kemet... Do you believe, Joseph, that your dreams will come true, and that one day your family will bow down to you?"

He looked away. "I can no longer pretend to understand the meaning of those dreams. At the time, I didn't even think about how my family would interpret them. I was intoxicated by the power and beauty of the dreams, which were like no other dreams I had ever had. Those dreams were more vividly real than being awake, the light was brighter yet also somehow softer, and the colors more vivid and beautiful, but it was how I felt that I shall never forget—I felt nothing was truly separate from me. I woke up feeling as though I had drunk the most magnificent wine from a golden cup, a wine made not of crushed grapes but of shining stars. I was filled with energy, and my mind felt bright and clear as a cloudless night when the moon is full and at its zenith. No doubts or fears darkened my heart or my thoughts. I had to share my dreams, for not to speak of them would have meant containing this joy in myself, which was impossible. What I failed to understand was that anyone listening to me describe my dreams would not be able to feel what I had felt in them. They would see only pictures in their heads which, read like hieroglyphs, would not deliver a message pleasing to them. At the time, I did not realize that having such dreams did not make me more special than anyone else, for they were gifts from God, not of my own making. I had to learn that the hard way."

Rising, Asenath walked around the table as My Dream, with canine intuition and obedience, ceded her place beside their mutual master. Kneeling, she wrapped her right arm around her husband's left leg, rested her left hand on his knee, and looking up at him said, "I love you, my brother."

Returning to the room, Joseph's gaze fell onto her upturned face, and for some time, neither of them spoke.

The silence was broken when My Dream growled.

A moment later, a servant slipped into the room bowing low, hands on her knees. "My lord, my lady, is there anything else you desire?" she asked.

"Yes," Joseph replied, "I desire to go to bed, and sleep untroubled by dreams."

They left Dejeba a week after the Opening of the Year. The current was with them, for they were heading north now. The season of Shemu was drawing lazily to a close as the River very slowly began rising. Asenath suffered a thrill when she noticed that the bottom landing step in now familiar ports was already wet. They were returning to the royal capital, where they would be staying for a few weeks before embarking on the second leg of their journey, during which Joseph would meet with headmen and Nomarchs of the Red Crown, just as he had met with those of the White Crown in the name of Pharaoh, Lord of the Two Lands.

Although she was eager to see Princess Sithathor again, and share some of her happiness with her, Asenath was of two minds about returning to Shedet. Like the River, her joy grew subtly deeper every day, and she knew she would be able to capture only a tiny fraction of her happiness in the vessels of conversations. Already she was looking forward to when she and Joseph would be alone again on the River, far away from the crowded royal court. Once they rowed past Iuno, all would be new for her again. They would be staying in the north longer than in the south, for the land there was rich with emmer and barley, and Joseph would have much work to do. Many additional silos would have to be built along the River's various tributaries, which meant first establishing the infrastructure that would be in charge of storing and protecting a greater portion of every coming harvest. In the south, it had been from younger officials Joseph had encountered the most resistance, for they could not remember a time when the River had failed to flood, and so it seemed foolish to them—even if they refrained from actually saying so—to invest so much time and resources preparing for a famine that would probably never happen. But like everyone else, they obeyed Pharaoh, and set into motion the plans his vizier outlined for them.

Asenath was also of two minds about returning to her childhood home. She was naturally looking forward to seeing her parents again, and she wanted to visit Nanny in her new house, but she was not really looking forward to seeing her uncle, fond as she was of him. And the thought of seeing Tarset was intolerable. Fortunately, there was no reason to think about all that now, for any possible reunions were still months away, and the present was so rich, it was as though the seed and the flower magically existed in every moment—she had all she desired even while anticipating more.

Whenever she was alone—which was not often on the journey back to the royal capital—Asenath dreamed of the house she and Joseph would one day live in together. She enjoyed wondering where it would be located, and what it would look like, and when—not if—she would have her first child. It was inconceivable she should not give Joseph strong and beautiful children, none of whom would be lonely as she had often been with no siblings to play with. Which thought led her to reminiscing about Kyky, a bittersweet pleasure spoiled by the question she was forced to ask herself as she thought about Nanny: Will I also discourage my children from befriending the household slaves? Unsettling as this question was, it bred an even more disturbing one: Would Joseph, who had once been a slave, own slaves himself? Certainly he would never purchase any of his fellow countrymen. The only answer was simply not to own any slaves. Everyone who worked for them would be a paid servant. The vizier of Kemet could afford as many servants as he wanted, and in his own home could live however he pleased.

Joseph spent just enough time in each city they had previously visited to remind the officials, by his presence, of the work they had agreed to undertake, and to check on how much progress had been made in preparing to initiate construction of the grain silos during the time of the flood, when manpower would be most readily available. The mooring palaces of Pharaoh, having known to expect them back, were even more luxuriously equipped than before. Yet she did not think it was her imagination that, as they drew closer to Shedet, Joseph grew more reserved. His caresses seemed less ardent, and the night before they reached the royal harbor, all he did was hold her in his arms. She could only imagine what he was thinking about, but she wondered if he was fearing what she did—that the prince, during their absence, had managed to make his father regret his hasty promotion of a Hebrew slave to the second highest office in the land. She knew this fear was not rational, for Pharaoh had officially sent Joseph out as his Mouth and Ears, yet it succeeded in eating away at the edges of her happiness like a persistent little mouse. It was after Joseph had fallen asleep beside her that she felt most vulnerable. She was not proud of herself for being such a coward in the dark, but she dreaded being forced to wake up from the dream of happiness in which they had lived together for so many splendid months.

Come sunrise, however, her anxiety evaporated like mist over the River. It was with a confident step that she disembarked in Shedet, where she proudly took her place beside Joseph on his chariot. She had already seen from the ship that not only had her fears been unwarranted, they were the exact opposite of reality. The avenue leading from the harbor to the palace was lined with people who all knelt and cheered, their arms extended in praise, as the vizier's chariot sped past them. Adulation followed them all the way to the palace's festival court, where Pharaoh himself met them, his entire family arranged around him. Asenath's heart leaped in her chest when Sithathoriunet, ignoring propriety, waved eagerly, quickly descended the steps of the dais, and began running toward the chariot, forcing Joseph to pull fiercely on the horses' reigns so they would not trample the princess, who simply could not wait to embrace her most beloved handmaiden.

The night of their arrival, Asenath sat at the same table with Joseph in Pharaoh's banquet hall for the first time. She was no stranger to sitting on the royal dais, but now she was no longer a maiden in the company of her illustrious parents—she was the wife of Kemet's vizier, and the attention they drew from the other guests was of a different, more penetrating quality. She could not be sure if it was a trick of the lamplight, or if some officials and Nomarchs actually dared to wear expressions of disgust whenever they looked up at Joseph. She wanted to blame her oversensitive imagination. After three years at court, she was no longer so innocent, but it was still hard for her to believe how many people failed to see the intelligent and handsome man who had—when all others had failed to do so—interpreted Pharaoh's dreams, thereby saving Kemet and all her people from future starvation. Joseph was now publicly Zaphenath-paneah, the God Speaks and He Lives, but some still saw only a dirty Hebrew, a man of the despised People of the Donkey who had not only been a slave but a criminal as well.

As the weeks passed, Asenath was obliged to reconcile herself to the fact that there was nothing she could do about such people, nothing Joseph could do, and nothing even Pharaoh could do. It made her furious for Joseph's sake and, she had to admit, for herself as well. She knew for a fact—because she had heard it from Sithathor's own lips—that some people felt sorry for her, the lovely daughter of the high priest of Re, forced to marry not only a foreigner, which was bad enough, but also a former slave who before that had been a shepherd, the lowest of vocations. She would never be able to communicate to them—or to anyone else for that matter—how fine her husband was, in every sense, how sensitive to her expressions, to the tone of her voice, to the slightest glance of her eyes, and how generously he responded to them, wholeheartedly applying himself to the pleasurable task of making her the happiest woman in the Two Lands, for so she felt herself to be.

That did not mean, however, that Joseph spoiled her, on the contrary. She felt rather like a field he was tending, his words—watered by his love—sinking into her mind and heart like seeds that were bearing mysterious fruits pleasing to both their souls. He never spoke loudly, but when he was displeased, his voice was pitched lower than normal and seemed to slip beneath her skin, so that she experienced his unhappiness in a visceral way that drove his meaning even more deeply into her consciousness.

On their first night back in the capital—when they were at last alone in the large bedchamber connecting their two smaller private bedrooms—he said to her, "Women in Kemet drink as much as their men, sometimes even more."

Abruptly, she recalled how frequently she had held her wine cup out to be refilled during the banquet in his honor, and knew he was not simply making a general observation.

His manservant had divested him of his jewels and clothing, providing him with clean water for washing, and a paste for brushing his teeth. Feeling tense, she silently watched him perform his ablutions, after which he walked over to her and, tossing the towel away, grasped her forearms with both hands. "Good night, my wife," he said, and kissing her lightly on the forehead, left her standing there alone as he retired to his own room, closing the door behind him.

"Nothing is more subtle or more terrible than Joseph's displeasure," she confided to Sithathor the next day. "If he had scolded me for drinking too much, I could have tried to make excuses, but instead he just left me alone with his disapproval, which remained with me all night, and completely sobered me up despite all the wine had drunk."

"Hmm."

"Hmm? Is that all you have to say?"

The princess shrugged. "What's wrong with having too much wine now and then? And Joseph should know by now that in Kemet women may do as they please, except cheat on their husband with another man, of course. That's why it's so much more pleasurable to be single. Oh don't look so shocked, honey. You know I've often wished I wasn't a king's daughter. It would be so much easier to be a poor farmer or fisherman's daughter, for then I would be free to sleep with as many handsome young men as I pleased, just like in the love songs. Ah, to lay daydreaming beneath date palms, then stroll along the River feeling the cool mud between my bare toes, serenaded by the lovely music of the wild goose calling honk! Honk. Honk!"

Asenath laughed.

"Honk!" Thrusting her neck out unnaturally, the princess leaped to her feet and began running around the room flapping her arms. "Honk! Honk! Honk!"

The amused grin on Asenath's face dimmed as she sensed

something of desperation in her friend's humor which had not been there before, or at least had not been so apparent. Sithathor's mother and brother were both urging her to marry, and very soon they would begin insisting, but until Pharaoh added his voice to their cause, his favorite daughter was at liberty to remain single. "I begin to regret confiding in you," she said loudly when the princess kept pretending to fly around the room like a goose desperately trying to escape a hunter's net.

Instantly sobering, Sithathor came and sat beside her on the couch, and taking her hands murmured, "Honey, you know I'm only teasing you, perhaps even challenging you a little, like Joseph, who everyone can see adores you. Every lady in the palace envies you, even the ones who, when their husbands are watching, look down their noses at the new vizier. But among themselves, they talk of nothing except his broad shoulders and narrow hips and-"

Asenath interrupted her, "Stop it, please!" freeing her hands.

"Stop what?" Sithathor smiled innocently. "Singing your husband's praises? I thought that would please you, for you know everything I say is true. I'm not making fun of your feelings for him. I would never do that."

Asenath felt a little like a goose herself now caught in the net of her friend's clever way of weaving fact with fiction, honesty with sarcasm, praise with criticism, so that the truth could never fully spread its wings without being wounded. When a bird was caught in a hunter's net it was for a purpose, to serve as nourishment for him and his family, but she could see no life-giving purpose to this verbal sport the princess was so very good at.

In most respects, however, their stay in the capital was quite pleasurable, for as the heat grew less fierce, Pharaoh and his court escaped the confines of the palace more often. Led by the Prince, the men enjoyed harpooning fish and crocodiles in the lake or hunting in the desert, and whole families went fowling together in the marshes. Whenever she could, Asenath accompanied her husband on these outings. Joseph always distinguished himself with the throwing stick, bringing down several ducks that My Dream delighted in fetching for him, unless they landed in the water, of course, then she was happy to let servants dive in after them.

As the River rose, rushing into canals and slowly swallowing the land, Asenath experienced the inundation in a way she never had before—as an inexorable swelling, a subtle but profound rerouting of life-giving fluids in her own body. When the crescent moon rose in the sky, and she was not confined along with Sithathor and many of her handmaidens during their monthly purification, she began to hope, and to pray to Elohim every day. She felt him answering her prayers with every drop of blood that remained in her body nourishing the seed of new life inside her. She was increasingly certain she was with child, but only when there could be no doubt whatsoever would she tell Joseph the good news, and together they would share it with the world.

Chapter 15

Northward bound, the vizier's yacht rowed majestically away on the current. Holding the gilded staff of his office in his right hand, his right foot extended in front of the left foot in a statuesque striding pose, Joseph stood at the front of the boat staring straight ahead of him, ostensibly toward the work he would be performing in Pharaoh's name throughout the provinces of Lower Kemet. Asenath stood behind him, but slightly to his left, so that she too could see the way ahead. Held in her right hand, a fresh lotus flower rested over her heart. They held their positions until the ship gently rounded a bend in the River, and all the people watching them from the shore could no longer see them.

It was a lovely morning in the third month of Akhet, but they did not linger on deck. Hand in hand, they retired to their private cabin, where a second breakfast was waiting for them. Kneeling on one side of the low table, Asenath was intensely relieved not to be feeling queasy this morning. She was so enjoying the pleasure of eating without unpleasant side effects, it took her a moment to notice that Joseph was simply watching her.

Smiling shyly, she asked, “What are you looking at?”

“I am looking at you, Asenath.”

“Obviously. Aren't you hungry?”

"Obviously I'm not, since I'm not eating."

His eyes were sober, and she felt the loss of their regard when he suddenly wrapped both arms around his bent knees, and looked away from her at the door of the cabin.

She cleaned her fingertips in a small bowl of water, dried them, wiped her mouth, and gave him her full attention. She could tell he was staring straight through the door to far beyond where their ship would travel. She had learned to sense when her husband's soul was flying eastward along the Horus Road all the way to his old home in Canaan. He was thirty years old, but whenever he sat hugging himself like this, she saw again the youth whose eyes—while her aunt negotiated his price with the slave traders—had followed a crow's flight somewhere the bird could never reach, for it was not only a place but a past.

She considered telling him now that she carried the priceless seed of their child in her belly, but she wanted to be absolutely certain and, she admitted to herself, she was jealous of that special moment—resplendent with future life and joy—and did not want it overshadowed by past sorrows. So once again she swallowed her delicious secret, and asked, "Joseph, what are you thinking about?"

"My father."

She waited.

"Like Jacob, I journeyed a long way, and had to labor many years before I was freed, and wed to the girl who lived in my heart."

She longed to embrace him, but his posture resembled a pyramid hiding mysteries only he had the power to reveal to her, so she neither moved or spoke, treating the treasure of his confidence with a receptive silence.

"Unlike his older twin brother, my father was a dutiful son, nursed on God's promises for him, and for all the branches of the covenant family."

When he paused, she took a breath, intending to ask him what a covenant family was, but before she could speak he continued, and from the tone of his voice now, she understood that he had decided to set his feet on the road of memories he was at last going to share with her.

"Abraham, the father of my father's father, Isaac, had many sons, but he gave all he owned to Isaac. When Isaac was forty years old, he married Rebekah, and he pleaded with the Lord on behalf of his wife, because she was unable to have children. The Lord answered Isaac's prayer, and Rebekah became pregnant with twins. But when the two children began struggling with each other in her womb, she went to ask the Lord about it. 'Why is this happening to me?' she asked. And the Lord told her, 'The sons in your womb will become two nations. From the very beginning, the two nations will be rivals. One nation will be stronger than the other; and your older son will serve your younger son'."

Asenath was thrilled. "The Lord spoke to Rebekah in a dream?"

Joseph stood up. “Come here,” he commanded, and pulling her to her feet, he led her over to the bed placed beneath one of the windows, the blinds of which were closed. He lay on his back, and as he cradled her beneath his arm, she settled into her new favorite place in the world—her head resting on his chest so that, as he spoke, the steady drumming of his heart accompanied the story he told her. It was the most exciting story she had ever heard.

“Whether you are awake or asleep, it is not a dream when God speaks to you,” Joseph told her. “When God speaks, you know it is real, for there is nothing more real. I know only what my father told me about his mother, but she must have been awake, not dreaming, when God spoke to her, for she went to the Lord to ask her question. The first twin born to her was very red at birth and covered with thick hair like a fur coat. So they named him Esau. The other twin was born with his hand grasping Esau’s heel. So they named my father Jacob. He was an obedient son, and his brother, Esau, hated him because their father gave Jacob the blessing.

“And so Esau began to scheme: 'I will soon be mourning my father’s death. Then I will kill my brother, Jacob.' But Rebekah heard about Esau’s plans. She sent for Jacob and told him, 'Esau is consoling himself by plotting to kill you. So listen carefully, my son. Get ready and flee to my brother, Laban, in Haran. Stay there with him until your brother cools off. When he calms down and forgets what you have done to him, I will send for you to come back. Why should I lose both of you in one day?' Later, Rebekah said to Isaac, 'I'm sick and tired of these local Hittite women! I would rather die than see Jacob marry one of them.'

"So Isaac called for Jacob, blessed him, and said, 'You must not marry any of these Canaanite women. Instead, go at once to Paddan-aram, to the house of your grandfather Bethuel, and marry one of your uncle Laban's daughters. May God Almighty bless you and give you many children. And may your descendants multiply and become many nations! May God pass on to you and your seed the blessings he promised to Abraham. May you own this land where you are now living as a foreigner, for God gave this land to Abraham.' So Isaac sent Jacob away to Paddan-aram to stay with his uncle Laban, his mother's brother, the son of Bethuel the Aramean.

"Jacob left Beersheba and traveled toward Haran. At sundown he arrived at a good place to set up camp and stopped there for the night. He found a stone to rest his head against and lay down to sleep. As he slept, he dreamed of a stairway that reached from the earth up to heaven. And he saw the angels of God going up and down the stairway."

Asenath wanted to ask, "What are angels?" but held the tantalizing question in reserve for later.

"At the top of the stairway stood the Lord, and he said, 'I am the Lord, the God of your grandfather Abraham, and the God of your father, Isaac. The ground you are lying on belongs to you.

I am giving it to you and your seed. Your descendants will be as numerous as the dust of the earth! They will spread out in all directions—to the west and the east, to the north and the south. And all the families of the earth will be blessed through you and your descendants. What's more, I am with you, and I will protect you wherever you go. One day I will bring you back to this land. I will not leave you until I have finished giving you everything I have promised you.' Then Jacob awoke from his sleep and said, 'Surely the Lord is in this place, and I wasn't even aware of it!' But he was also afraid and said, 'What an awesome place this is! It is none other than the house of God, the very gateway to heaven!'

"The next morning Jacob got up very early. He took the stone he had rested his head against, and set it upright as a memorial pillar. Then, pouring olive oil over the stone, he named that place Bethel, which means 'house of God', although it was previously called Luz. Then he made this vow: 'If God will indeed be with me and protect me on this journey, and if he will provide me with food and clothing, and if I return safely to my father's home, then the Lord will certainly be my God. And this memorial pillar I have set up will become a place for worshiping God, and I will present to God a tenth of everything he gives me.'

"Then Jacob hurried on, finally arriving in the land of the east. There he fell in love with my mother, Rachel. It is a long story how he was obliged to marry her sister Leah first. My mother was pregnant when my brothers threw me in the well and sold me to the slave traders. I hope she gave birth to another son my father could love as he had loved me—another son for his old age to console him for the loss of the one stolen from him by the offspring of his concubines and of Leah, his first wife."

Abruptly, Asenath was not thinking about God and dreams but about multiple wives and concubines. Would Joseph do as his father had done and take a second wife? And would he do as many wealthy men in Kemet did and bring a concubine or two into their house? It was not so much the possibility that shocked her as the fact she had never even thought of it until now. Turning desperately away from the unbearable thought, she asked, sitting up, "What are angels?"

Studying her face, he replied, "Angels are messengers of God."

She turned her back on him. "What do angels look like?"

Draping an arm over her shoulders, he whispered in her ear, "Like men!"

"You are my Angel, Joseph! Please do not oblige me to share you with other women!"

Forcing her gently down onto her back, he braced himself over her body with the strong columns of his arms as he gazed down into her eyes, smiling. "There is no room in my heart for another woman," he assured her, tenderly kissing both her cheeks.

Asenath did not think she was imagining that he savored the flavor of her love's tears as a sublime wine reserved strictly for his pleasure.

☼

They settled back into the routine of docking every night at a mooring place of pharaoh, where they remained for several days as Joseph went about his business. Meanwhile, she dutifully made offerings at the local temple while not organizing banquets. Some were large affairs attended by minor officials accompanied by their wives, older children and close relatives. Other gatherings were smaller but even more lavish, for they were held in honor of the most important men of the district and their families, usually just before they were planning to leave because they used up most of the palace's food stores.

When they were in the great and most ancient city of Inbu-Hedj, the White Walls, Asenath devoted herself to another secret activity. Their first morning there, after Joseph left for the day, she had one of her attendants fetch her a small basket of barley and emmer, and place it in a corner of her bathroom. Then, dismissing the smiling woman with an answering smile of her own, she lifted her dress, crouched over the grains, and moistened them with her urine. She repeated the process everyday, praying she would see results before it was time for them to leave. One morning, a small sound of immense joy escaped her when she saw the barley had sprouted. Running into her bedroom, where Ana and Ipy were waiting to bathe, oil and dress her for the day, she exclaimed, “The barely is growing! It is a boy!”

Ana exclaimed, “Congratulations my lady!” but Ipy, completely forgetting propriety in the joy of the moment, fervently embraced her mistress like an equal.

Rising onto her hind legs, My Dream gave a happy little jealous bark as she tried to join in the celebratory hug.

That day, Re seemed to take forever to cross the sky. She visited the temple of Isis, but in the dim coolness of the sanctuary—to which her illustrious position gave her access—her elation dimmed somewhat in the flickering lamplight. After the brilliant sunshine outside, the shadows seemed to limit the power not just of her body's vision but of her soul's as well. As soon as the temple servants deposited her offering on the table, and left her alone with the goddess, she slowly poured milk over the base of the statue remembering what Joseph had told her about his father, “He was nursed on God's promises for him and all the branches of the covenant family.”

Observing the milk trickling through special grooves, and flowing away toward invisible openings in the wall, Asenath wondered where exactly it was going. Was it collected somewhere, and used to feed the temple snakes and cats? Where did all her hopes, all the love and gratitude flowing through her heart, end up? These questions made her feel mysteriously accompanied in the silent sanctuary, but the Presence she sensed was not contained in the statue of the goddess, given only an illusion of life by the flickering flames and caressing shadows. No, the Presence had already been with her, had entered the temple with her, and was with her now as she thought about God Almighty, who actually spoke to Joseph's people, and even made them personal promises. Joseph had told her the Hebrews did not have temples. Where then had Rebekha gone when she wanted to talk to God? Could you talk to God anywhere? Yet she could not imagine talking to God in this shrine to Isis, and hearing him respond as if he was just a man standing behind the statue. Was it possible God might send one of his angels with a message for her? But if angels looked like men, how could she be sure, if she ever saw one, he really was an angel? If angels flew down from the eternal sky to do God's will, then surely they had wings?

She looked up at the face of Isis, daughter of Re, conceived by the sky and the earth when they came together at the beginning of time. The goddess was smiling contentedly...

Abruptly, Asenath was not looking up at the stone face, she was looking down at it, and suddenly she could also see her own body standing before the carved image. Both female figures were swiftly receding, growing smaller and smaller, farther and farther away from her awareness as it gazed weightlessly down at the chapel, which had no ceiling but was open on top like the model of a shrine made to be placed in a tomb...

Just as suddenly, her awareness was back behind her eyes, and everything was the same size it had been before her consciousness took flight. Except that now she knew everything she saw was much smaller, smaller than the toy of a child's toy, and tinier even than that, for if her awareness had continued ascending, the shrine would have condensed into a shimmering drop of colors, and then vanished like a flame blown out from where it trembled on the floating wick of her vision. Nothing but darkness would have remained... darkness and her sense of God's Presence.

She closed her eyes, and the silence struck her like a force more real than anything she could see as she prayed in her mind, "Elohim, please bless my child, Joseph's son!"

☼

That evening, Asenath told her husband the good news. Some part of her had worried he would begin treating her like a breakable vessel, but to her delight, the very opposite happened. He almost seemed intent on making it clear to their son that he was not, and never would be, the lord and master of the body in which he was growing so comfortably.

Joseph showed no sign of being troubled by the fact that he had not married into the covenant family. But did he secretly wonder, as she did, if God's promise to his people would include their son? Yet if Elohim was the Creator of heaven and earth, what did it matter that Joseph's seed had taken root in Kemet, which God Himself had made so fertile? Joseph was here because his brothers, and even his loving father, had been jealous of the dreams God had sent him, and she was convinced it was God who had brought Joseph straight to her birthplace, the City of the Sun.

Such thoughts occupied her mind only when she could not immediately fall asleep at night. During the day, her happiness was established by the way Joseph's eyes shone with an even deeper warmth, and by how his expressive mouth—so firm when he was engaged in the business of his high office—softened into a proud and hopeful smile whenever he looked at her.

Those same beloved lips were pressed against hers one afternoon when there was a knock at the door of their cabin on the ship, and the captain's voice announced, “My Lord, we are in sight of Iuno.”

Joseph turned his face away from hers just long enough to reply, “Thank you, Bebi!” before diving back into their kiss.

They were lying on their sides in each others arms, their bodies pressed together, so when it happened, they both felt it.

She gasped.

“Are you all right?”

“Yes! I felt our son, Joseph! He moved inside me!”

“I know! I think he was trying to kick me away!”

Shortly after that special moment, the vizier of Kemet and

his lovely wife stood like statues at the head of their ship as it pulled into the harbor, joyful smiles painted on their faces by the invisible artist of their unborn child. Feeling her womb was a magical threshold between heaven and earth, Asenath could much better appreciate now, as she watched the shining temple of Re drawing nearer, what the priests believed—that the starry universe was the divine seed of Atum, who was also Re, his son, the light and life of the world.

The vizier's retinue was lodged in the houses, buildings and servants quarters of the old palace under her uncle's command, but she and Joseph, and a handful of their personal attendants, were staying in her childhood home. Her parents had prepared the guest apartments for them, and it was a welcome change not to have anything to do when they arrived except relax before bathing and dressing for dinner. This naturally included walking through her old Pleasure House with My Dream. The trees had grown taller, and here and there the gardener was experimenting with new flower arrangements, but these were not the only reasons why the place did not feel the same—it was because she had grown and bloomed in mysterious ways since she was last here.

Coming to the spot where My Dream, having run away from Joseph, leaped into her arms, Asenath paused to relive the moment, and even the dog seemed to catch scent of the past as she happily sniffed the air. When they came to her pool, she felt like a child again as she saw her old pavilion standing where it always had. She wondered if it had been erected again for her visit, or if it had never been taken down. Vividly, she recalled sitting there after she learned that Kyky had been dead for days. She had never told Joseph about that dream, but she finally did so then, and the pain of that day, years ago, was washed away by the joy of the present. They had just enough time to linger in her old garden before the musical rattle of Hathor's sistrum coming from the house announced it was time to begin dressing for dinner.

From his position beside the high priest of Re, the new vizier received the guests in the dining room, greeting each in turn. Tanned by the sun, the gold around his throat and wrists shining in the generous lamplight, his chin-length hair tucked neatly behind his ears, Joseph was, in Asenath's eyes, more beautiful than any pharaoh had ever been or ever could be. She studied the faces of each new arrival, and was relieved when none of their expressions threatened to interfere with her appetite. Then the moment she had dreaded arrived when the herald announced, “Potipher Setka and Mistress of the House, Tarset.”

She glanced beside her at her mother, but Sadeh was bestowing an untroubled smile on her brother, and she had no choice but to do the same. It would have been a pointed insult not to invite her aunt. It would have made people talk, and that was the last thing she wanted, but it was like watching a lioness enter the room. Men had been known to walk safely right past a lioness who had just fed. Was Tarset still hungry for revenge?

Surely she would not dare to attack Pharaoh's second in command, at least not overtly. Perhaps she would take a subtle swipe at him here and there throughout the evening, so that at first no one noticed she was gradually and insidiously bleeding Joseph of more and more of his dignity and authority? Tarset was walking beside her husband, the smile on her thin mouth not reaching her golden predator's eyes, which were fixed defiantly on the vizier.

Asenath looked over at Joseph. She knew him better than anyone else, so she was aware that the muscles of his face had tightened slightly, but otherwise his expression remained open and welcoming, which helped her relax. Was that pity she glimpsed in his eyes before he inclined his head as his former mistress, coming to stand before him, did the same? But as she watched his eyes follow her aunt to the table she would share with her husband—who did not bother to pull her chair out for her—Asenath recognized the feeling in his eyes as compassion. At that point, she understood she was looking at the situation from the wrong perspective. Joseph was the lion now, and it was Tarset who had everything to fear from him. Another look at her aunt's face confirmed that behind the stiff shield of her smile, the woman was indeed afraid, and worse. There was pain in her dread, a pain that suddenly stabbed Asenath in the heart as, through the power of empathy, she too, for a terrible moment, suffered the unthinkable—loving and desiring Joseph knowing he did not love her, and she could never be with him.

“What is it?” Her mother asked. “Is the baby kicking again?”

“No. It's nothing...” Nothing, that was what Tarset possessed, for not even her husband loved her, and she had no children who might love her, and she was too old now to ever have any children. How terrible to live in that big beautiful house with no one to love, and with no one who loved her. She had seen how her aunt treated even her closest servants, too proud to ever think of them as friends. When the lady Tarset was carried to her eternal home in the desert, furnished with everything she could desire through magical paintings, would she even notice the difference between her house and her tomb? She could not have a statue of Joseph carved and placed in her burial chamber, where she would be accompanied only by her own image staring out a narrow window into her public offering chapel. But who would come to feed her Ka with bread and meat, milk and wine, honey and flowers? And when her heart was weighed in the judgment hall of Osiris against the feather of Maat, surely its emptiness would make it so heavy it would be thrown to Ammit and devoured.

Asenath was rescued from her morbid musings when Joseph, pulling her chair out for her at their table, whispered in her ear, “All is well!” After that, she was able to enjoy the banquet, during which she occasionally smiled fondly over at her uncle. His eyes, shining with pride in her, reminded her how much she loved the way his emotions were always prepared to rise to the surface and reveal themselves in his gaze, whether or not he was able to express them with words. But it was when Tarset boldly met her eyes, and waited for her reaction, that Asenath truly felt herself to have become a woman. Lifting her full wine cup, she saluted her aunt, and then waited for the other woman's cup to be filled so she could properly reflect the gesture. Then smiling at each other, they drank together. True happiness, she discovered in that moment, was indistinguishable from courage and compassion and, perhaps eventually, forgiveness.

☼

Accompanied by the twelve soldiers assigned to her by her husband, Asenath's litter stopped in front of a small two-story home at the end of a clean residential street. A narrow staircase on one side of the house led up to the front door, and from there to the roof, on which she glimpsed a variety of potted plants. Her personal guard remained behind on the street as she hurried up the steps to Aneski, who stood proudly beside her husband at the entrance to her little dream home. Her old nanny stiffened slightly when the now great Lady Asenath hugged her like a child, but she returned the embrace warmly. When they came apart, both their eyes shone with fond memories, all others forgotten like shadows at noon in the timeless light of love. Asenath felt then that the meaning of Asneski's name, She Belongs to Me, was written on both their hearts. Her husband, Kuhy, resembled a human ibis he was so tall and slender, and his thin lips never stopped smiling beneath an old-fashioned black mustache.

With her old affectionate brusqueness, Aneski commanded, "Come inside!" sniffing back tears as they entered a miniature receiving room. Although he resembled Thoth physically, Kuhy was not fond of words for he seldom spoke, and after a short time, murmuring something under his breath, he left the two women alone to catch up on everything that had happened in their lives since they were last together. The visit, however, was a short one, for Asenath could not really express to Aneski all the feelings flowing through her heart—the most important part of everything that had happened, and would ever happen to her, for plain facts were there mere bones of life. Aneski proudly showed her the two papyrus shaped alabaster lamps, and the sycamore wood dining table inlaid with ivory, the high priest and his wife had given her, before leading her outside to her vegetable plot. In addition to the female servant bestowed on her by her former employers, Aneski now owned a male slave who did all the gardening. The little boy—whose entire family had died of the coughing sickness—showed up when they were in the garden, and in a sharp voice Aneski said, "Not now!" The boy immediately ran away, and soon afterward, Asenath bid her old nurse goodbye. On the way home, she cried in the privacy of her litter thinking that the next time she and her old nurse saw each other would be on the other side of the River, in the land beyond the sunset.

Joseph had much to do in Iuno, Kemet's administrative

capital, where he established a new department in charge of overseeing the storage of additional grain supplies. Another department—of which he himself would be in charge—would handle the distribution of the grain to where and when it was needed during the years of famine. She did not admit to him that she sometimes wondered what would happen if, when the seven years of bountiful crops ended, the River continued to rise and nourish the land just as it always had. Joseph's interpretation of Pharaoh's dreams would then be proved wrong, and she had no doubt many important people were biding their time—patient as vultures—hoping this would happen so they could openly attack the vizier, and convince the king to transfer his position to one of them instead. She did not, however, allow herself to dwell on this possibility, not only for the sake of her unborn child—who would not benefit from her distress—but because she believed God truly did communicate with his chosen people in their dreams, and so to doubt such important dreams as Pharaoh's was to doubt God himself. Only then would she have reason not simply to worry, but to really and truly be afraid.

When the time drew near for Joseph to leave Iuno and travel further north toward Rowaty—The Door of the Two Roads—they had their first argument. Where the River branches out on a map like a great lotus flower, more grain grew every year than anywhere else in Kemet, and so a great many more additional storage silos needed to be built there. When he suggested she stay home because she would soon be heavy with child, and being on board a ship all day would probably make her nauseous, she responded with hurt incredulity, “You want to leave me behind?”

“That is not what I said, Asenath.”

“Well, that's exactly what you'd be doing if you left Iuno without me, you would be leaving me, and your baby, behind. You might not even have returned before your son was born!”

“There is time...”

“No, Joseph, we are coming with you! You want us to come with you, don't you?”

The argument ended when he replied, “Of course I do!” and pulled her to him.

“This,” she whispered, smiling triumphantly, “is the only harbor in the world that matters to me, and where I feel truly at home.”

So when the time came, she gladly bid farewell to her parents as they boarded the ship, from which she proudly displayed her promisingly round little belly to all those waving goodbye to them from the shore.

Asenath's waters broke in Rowaty. She was standing outside in the palace garden when a trumpeting sound from the sky announced a flock of wild geese. As she watched them flying past in the shape of a dark arrowhead, she suffered a sharp pain in her womb, and her two legs became as the banks of the River overflowing. She had known this would happen, but it still came as a shock to suddenly be standing in a puddle of life-giving water, which until that moment had been safely contained in the vessel of her body. The trumpeting of the geese sounded urgent now, as though they were winged heralds of her unborn child announcing he was on his way and would soon land in the birthing arbor, which had already been prepared for him.

Her attendants came running when she called out for them, and while Ipy went to fetch the midwife, Ana helped her over to the small pavilion surrounded by lattice-work screens admitting breezes while offering privacy.

"Ana, make sure Ipy also sends a messenger as swift as his shadow to my lord!"

"Of course she will, my lady, do not worry yourself about anything except welcoming your son into the world." She gently thrust an object into her mistress' right hand. "Here, hold this, my lady. Tawaret will protect you and give you strength."

Looking down, Asenath saw herself holding an amulet of the the hippopotamus goddess. The Great One was carved standing erect on her hind legs, with her two front paws braced on the hieroglyphs for Life and Protection.

As she stared at the amulet, unsure how to feel about it, her son kicked hard in her womb in a way that distinctly struck her as a protest. She whispered, "Elohim, help us!" and when Ana was not looking, flung the ugly little carving into a bush.

Before the wicks of the lamps burning in the arbor had to be replaced, Asenath gave birth to a strong and perfectly shaped baby boy. Waking from the hot and often blinding pain to the soft golden light of joy, the ordeal that had felt endless vanished like a nightmare. But then she lost sight of her precious child during another contraction, which frightened her as none of the others had, until the midwife reassured her it was only the afterbirth.

Her baby's first indignantly loud cry seemed to burst open her heart like an overripe pomegranate, scattering seeds of pure delight through her entire being she prayed would bear fruit in the many years to come.

Watching the midwife cut the umbilical cord with an obsidian knife, Asenath marveled at the profound connection between mother and child, only physically severed now like a divine fishing line which had served its purpose—to wrest this unique being from the depths of a bottomless mystery.

The lustful protests of her son as he was washed and swaddled filled her with such pride, she might have drifted off on a current of contentment—irresistibly merging with an undertow of exhaustion—if his cries had not been so loud, making sleep impossible. Then, at last, she was cradling him in her right arm and, very gently, stroking his infinitely soft skin with the fingertips of her left hand.

"Turn his body toward you," the midwife instructed, "so that you are heart to heart, and then touch his mouth with your nipple."

Never having held anything so precious before, Asenath very carefully obeyed. Her son, less conscious of his vulnerability, seemed to know better than she did what to do. Opening his mouth, he succeeded in demanding that she pull him onto her right breast, which she held up for him with her free hand. The birthing arbor rang with delighted laughter—Hathor's living sistrum—as the newborn boy caught hold of his mother's nipple, and did not release it until he had drunk his fill after only a few eternally precious moments, for his belly was still so small.

"Now the spirits that protect your body from disease will also protect him," the midwife promised her.

Asenath commanded quietly, "Bring his father! He must know he has a son! Quickly!"

"Lady, he has already been told," Ana informed her as the midwife, her job done, enlisted Ipy's help in cleaning up. "But a man should not-"

Asenath cut her off impatiently, "Fetch your master immediately."

Moments later, Joseph entered the lamp lit arbor, and as he seated himself on the stool placed for him beside the bed, she said, "I have never felt so rich, Joseph! I feel as though, in these moments, we are in a place that is both real and a dream. I wish we could stay here forever!"

"Sweet Asenath!" Leaning forward, he tenderly kissed their sleeping baby's cheek. "Let us pray that God may grant us this blessing, and wake us from the darkness of death to the light of eternity together."

"What name have you chosen for our son, Joseph?"

"His name will be Manasseh, which means Causing to Forget, for God has made me forget all my troubles and everyone in my father's family."

16

Even before his son was born in Rowaty, Joseph had told Asenath he was thinking of building their home here. Located along the River's easternmost branch, the town was strategically located at the starting point of the Way of Horus, the road Joseph had traveled with the slave traders. The fourteenth Nome of Lower Kemet was in grape-raising country, not far from the northern frontier, where the land ended and the River flowed into the Great Green Water.

She did not tell her husband she had no desire to live in this provincial town, so far away from the great cities. She longed to share the joy of their baby with her parents and her uncle and Sithathor, and was very glad they would soon be traveling south again. Rowaty was slowly expanding around the temple of Set, her least favorite god, whose red hair embodied the Red Land of the desert. Set had murdered his brother Osiris, who her father had explained to her long ago was the body of Re. Jealous of how much the people loved Osiris, Set tore his body into sixteen pieces, and scattered them all across the world. Isis, wife and sister of Osiris, recovered all the parts of her husband's body except for his phallus, but she still managed to conceive their son, Horus—the resurrected spirit of his father who perpetually challenges and defeats Set for eternal kingship of the world.

She knew that if they came to live in Rowaty, she would not often see her parents, much less the princess. She desired to share her misgivings with Joseph, but then she would have to ask him why he thought they should build their home here, and she was not sure she wanted to hear his reasons, which he might not, she suspected, wish to admit even to himself. So she said nothing, content for the present to know that whenever they were not traveling, they would be dividing their time between the old palace in Iuno and Pharaoh's new capital.

By the time they reached Nay-ta-hut, she had learned that traveling on a ship with an infant was not remotely as pleasurable as traveling alone with Joseph. The first two days they were on board, she did not see very much of her husband. She could scarcely blame him for keeping away. The cabin smelled awful after Manasseh made it clear, again and again, that he had no intention of growing up to be a sailor.

As the gilded obelisks of the temple of the sun drew nearer, Asenath squinted her eyes as her heart expanded with joyful anticipation. The shining splendor of the city of her birth temporarily made her forget the shadows recently cast over her unclouded happiness—one of them being that she could no longer comfortably accompany Joseph on his travels, not until Manasseh was weaned and she could safely leave him behind with his nurse and attendants. It had been her decision, and her husband had fully supported it, not to procure a wet nurse for their little boy. She believed her milk would be the most deeply nourishing to Manasseh, and not only physically. She felt her growing faith in Elohim was supernaturally mixed into her milk. She knew Ana and Ipy were surprised, and worried, their mistress set no amulets around Manasseh's crib to ward off demons who roamed the night hungry for the souls of infants. Asenath could not explain to them it was to Elohim she prayed several times a day, for she had much more faith in God Almighty's powers of protection. It was becoming quite natural for her to talk to God as if he was always listening.

On their first night back in her childhood home, Asenath found herself standing outside the house. A strong wind was blowing through the garden and making the palm leaves rattle loudly. Fearing an impending sandstorm, she was about to run back inside to protect her baby when, abruptly, everything became still and silent. A bright and mysteriously eloquent silver-white light above the trees drew her eyes up toward the sharp black peak of a man-made mountain too close to really be there. She was dreaming!

She did not need to flap her arms in order to fly swiftly out of her childhood garden, and through the silent darkness. Almost as swiftly as thought, she found herself near the top of the largest and most ancient of the great pyramids of White Wall. It had been erected generations ago by Pharaoh Khnum-Kufu, popularly known now as Khufu the Merciful. She was outside the monument, and yet she also seemed to be partially within it—in a corridor of air suffused with a reddish gold light

—drifting past colossal faces carved into a long horizontal column. Without thinking about the words first, she said out loud, “Because I believe in Elohim, I can also have my toys.” The beautiful face she was brought to by an invisible current was the height of her body, and she recognized the goddess Hathor when she distinctly saw one of the Lady's cow ears. She paused there a moment before gliding effortlessly as a fish around the goddess into a semi-enclosed space, where she was surrounded on all sides by dark wooden carvings of various deities, including the cat goddess Bast. There were also human faces carved into the fronts of massive wooden doors. Curiously, she opened the pair of doors nearest her, and discovered two colossal stone male heads sitting inside the shrine.

Closing the doors again, she continued floating around slowly, filled with wonder as she became aware of music playing in the dream space. Listening to it, she found herself wishing that, when she woke up, she could somehow replicate this sublime music flowing all around her, bottomless and boundless... Ah-om... Ah-om... Ah-om...

She thought with regret—I may never be here again in a dream—but knew she would never forget this living music with no beginning or end.

She was in the process of opening another pair of great wooden doors when she began waking up as a male Voice said, “The Lord pours forth for those who seek.”

☼

After Manasseh, filled with the energy of his mother's milk, tired of enchanting her with his every gesture, sound and expression, Asenath lay him gently back in his crib, and left him with Ana. Joseph had no sooner perfumed his mouth than he had departed to make his report to Pharaoh's son and heir. They had discovered the prince was staying in Iuno as they approached the harbor, and saw it already crowded with royal vessels. The anxiety she suffered now wondering how her husband's meeting with the prince would go was ameliorated by the lingering peace of her dream, which she very much looked forward to sharing with him later.

She spent a wonderfully lazy morning with her mother indulging in sporadic, idle conversation as they were massaged. Lying on her stomach, she nearly fell asleep more than once, half hypnotized as the heat of the day intensified and diminished with the motion of the fan bearers as cool oils were stroked into her flesh.

In the afternoon, Sadeh claimed her grandson for herself, while Asenath spent time alone with her father in his Pleasure House. As they sat side by side on the edge of his pool, she asked him, “Why is there a temple to Set in Rowaty? Why are there any temples to him at all?”

Slipping smoothly into the water, Meketre briefly submerged himself, and as he came up vigorously rubbing his face with both hands, replied, "Because people—and it seems they grow in number every year—are inclined to believe Set will listen to them more than Re will." Not bothering with the steps, he lifted his lean, fit body out of the pool, and sat beside her again.

Excited, she waited for him to say more; his expression told her he was giving her question serious thought.

"It is easier for people to believe that demons and evil spirits are closer to us than the gods. But in Set's temple, the evil that is part of the world is represented as a deity inseparable from his divine brother, Osiris. It does no good to deny that evil exists, everyone knows it does, so in making it subordinate to the lord of resurrection and eternal life, we confine its power. Osiris is our friend, a personal god who listens to everyone's prayers, so there is no need to turn to Set. Yet there will always be people who with their mouths say they honor Re and Osiris, but who in their hearts keep secret council with Set for their own selfish reasons. Set is strong enough to indulge their desire for wealth and power, or whatever it is they ask of him, but the price is high. In the end, the souls of these people wither and die like plants in the desert, Set's domain. Those who choose to worship Set are deliberately throwing their hearts to Ammit, the beast who devours them."

"Father, does Re ever speak directly to you? Do you actually ever hear Re's voice?"

He was silent a moment before answering quietly, "Through the intelligence of my heart, I do the best to discern the will of

Re."

She was working up the courage to tell him God actually spoke to some of Joseph's people, but as in some of her conscious dreams, she could not manage to get the words out. She loved and respected her father, and she worried that telling him this would, in some subtle but vital way, undermine his authority. There was also the possibility he would think she was only interested in Elohim because she loved Joseph, and Elohim was his god. She knew this was not true, yet she would never be able to prove it. So she compromised by remarking as if casually, "I believe God Almighty can speak directly to us in dreams, with a Voice and with words we can hear." And now it was her turn to slip into the water. Submerging herself in the blessed coolness, she suspended herself for several heartbeats in the space between having made this statement, and her father's response. Then the thrumming quiet was swept away by birdsong flooding her ears as she breathed again.

Meketre waited until she was seated beside him again before asking, "Have you had a conscious dream recently?"

"Yes, last night," she admitted, both disappointed and relieved he had not commented on her statement.

"Would you like to tell me about it?"

She felt a little like a cat he was indulgently stroking. Nevertheless, she took pleasure in describing her dream to him in detail. She did not pause to consider that uttering the words she had spoken in the dream, "Because I believe in Elohim, I can also have my toys" was not exactly honoring her father's authority.

"There are many names for Re," he said after she fell silent, his face turned away from hers. "The Supreme Creator, Lord of the Universe, Ruler of Eternity, King of the Gods, King of the World... I have not heard him called Elohim."

"That is what Joseph calls him."

"And we, who were born of the god's tears, call him Re."

"Father, why is it written that we were born of Re's tears? Was creating us so painful? Or did Re know, before he even dreamed of creating us, that we would displease him and cause him grief? Is that why Re never speaks to us directly, but always hides his face from us? Is that why Amun-Re means the Hidden One?"

"This brings us back to Set and his temple, Asenath. You have only to look at all the evil in the world to know Re cannot be completely happy with us. From the beginning, we caused him grief, which is why he commanded one if his daughters to destroy humanity. But before Sekhmet had time to obey him, Re changed his mind, and had mercy on us."

"Yes," she sighed. "I know. Re flooded the world with beer, and then dyed it red so Sekhmet would believe it was blood and, drinking it all up, fall asleep and miss her chance to kill us all."

Realizing the tone of her voice was revealing her impatience with this old myth—which made Re sound like a silly old man who could not even control his own daughter—she continued more mildly, "Harkhaf told me that Re grew so weary, he had his daughter Nut turn into a cow and lift him up on her back into the sky where he lives now, crossing from sunrise to sunset on his barque, always far away from us."

"That is only a story, daughter."

"A story? But you actually believe Re is the Supreme Creator, don't you?"

"The sun is the Eye of Re, but if you put out that eye, Re can still see. Re will never be blinded, for he is the eternal sky, and the stars are the shining spearheads of his infinite power. Although, of course, to put it that way is also a story, for while we live, the truth can only be as a dream to us."

"But how is it possible for the Supreme Creator to grow old and weary?" She did not add what she was thinking—that she was the one growing weary, of these stories.

Perhaps it was fortunate that at this point in their conversation, Sadeh strolled into the garden cradling her grandson, and Re silently joined them as they all devoted themselves to adoring this precious new life. Bending over the baby, witness to the creative power of God, she and her father resolved their differences more eloquently than they ever could with words.

"Joseph," she lifted her head from his chest and gazed up at his face, “when did God first speak to your people?”

He did not open his eyes. “Asenath, please blow out the lamp. It is late, and I am tired.”

“Too tired to talk about God?” she challenged him.

His body heaved beneath her as he sat up, obliging her to do the same. He sighed, “You're not going to let me sleep, are you?”

Judging the question rhetorical, she did not reply.

“God first spoke to Abraham. His name was Abram then, and he was living in Ur in the country of Chaldea. Later, God changed his name to Abraham. The people of that land worshiped idols. Abram’s father Terah did not know the true God, and neither did his son, but one day the Lord God revealed Himself to Abram and spoke with him. The Lord said to Abram, 'Leave your native country, your relatives, and your father’s family, and go to the land that I will show you. I will make you into a great nation. I will bless you and make you famous, and you will be a blessing to others. I will bless those who bless you and curse those who treat you with contempt. All the families on earth will be blessed through you'.”

She glanced toward the room where Manasseh lay sleeping. “*All* the families on earth? Is that what you meant to say?” She was afraid he had translated the Hebrew word incorrectly.

“Yes, that is what I meant to say,” he replied, and curling his tall body up like a child on the bed beside her, lay his head in her lap. Closing his eyes, he continued speaking while she gently stroked his hair. “God spoke to Abraham many more times over the years. And I have already told you that God also spoke to his son, Isaac, my father's father. When there was a famine in the land, as had happened before in Abraham’s time, Isaac moved to Gerar, where Abimelech, king of the Philistines, lived. There the Lord appeared to Isaac and told him not to come here to Kemet, but said, 'Do as I tell you. Live here as a foreigner in this land, and I will be with you and bless you. I hereby confirm that I will give all these lands to you and your descendants, just as I solemnly promised Abraham, your father'.”

Asenath said in wonder, “God not only speaks to men, he has a relationship with them, and makes them promises? God is a living Father to your people, not a story far away in the sky!”

“Stories are entertaining, and also easy,” Joseph pointed out, “for we are not obliged to obey them.”

She declared fervently, “I would gladly obey God if he spoke to me when I was awake, as he did to Rebekah. But he is still so very kind to me! I know he speaks to me in my dreams, and I have already obeyed him. I obeyed him that morning when He commanded me to 'WAKE UP.' That's why I was at my uncle's house so early in the day, just in time to witness what truly happened between you and Tarset. Even though it may take years, we both know that dreams can come true, and I believe yours will, Joseph, because God sent them to you.”

After this conversation, the two colossal stone heads she had discovered—sitting in a wooden shrine in her dream of the pyramid—became identified in her mind with Abraham and Isaac, the first men to whom God had spoken. She wanted to ask Joseph more about his father, Jacob, but Manesseh's name was a constant reminder her husband preferred to forget all his former troubles and everyone in his father's family.

After she told Joseph her dream of the pyramid, he had murmured sleepily that it sounded very interesting, but said no more. If only he could have been in the dream with her! If only he could hear that peaceful yet exciting, reassuring but also infinitely mysterious, all pervasive, all encompassing rhythmic music, like the dream's own heart beat. God's heart beat? But attempting to describe the music with words was like throwing rocks into the River in a vain effort to show someone, who had never been immersed in water, what water felt like.

These days, however, it was the prince's words her husband heard more than anyone's, and how inseparable the two men had become was not entirely pleasing to her. They went hunting together, often dined together, and even played Thirty Squares, the prince's favorite game, while discussing how best to go about the tricky business of limiting the power of the Nomarchs without overtly challenging it. Joseph's way of thinking about his duties as vizier had quickly won him the prince's favor. In their first meeting, Joseph had told the young Senwosret that in order to ensure more grain was grown and put away, it was necessary to increase and secure the king's authority. "An unassailable central authority must be firmly in place if Kemet is to survive the coming famine."

☼

Back in the royal capital, Sithathor appeared delighted by Manesseh, but Asenath suspected she was not really as fond of him personally as she was of how useful he proved for distracting and occupying her handmaidens, so the two of them could be alone together.

"I see Joseph has won my brother's full approval. They are of one mind in thinking that local officials and nobles are growing too powerful, and that the more wealthy and comfortable they become, the less receptive they are to obeying Pharaoh. Having so often insisted to father that this state of affairs can lead to the return of darkness and chaos, my brother is very pleased indeed that the new vizier agrees with him. And father, in his turn, is delighted to see them both getting along. So now you have no reason at all not to spend more time here at court with me!"

They had not been in Shedet more than a week when an elderly official, who had survived all his offspring, at last went to his eternal Ka, and Pharaoh awarded his mansion to Joseph. The vizier and his family had been staying in one of the royal apartments, and were more than happy to move out of the crowded palace.

Asenath soon discovered that owning a home of her own did a strange thing to time, which flowed along its corridors and rooms like an invisible River through canals which, in addition to containing the passing days and nights, directed them so swiftly into the future it almost immediately became the present. This smooth, unobstructed passage of time was a little frightening, but her heart was flooded with such fruitful contentment, it was easy to believe there would be no end to life's rich harvests.

No sooner was Manesseh weaned than she conceived again. She was delighted, yet also disappointed that her dream of accompanying Joseph on his regular progresses up and down the River once again had to be postponed. From the start, her second pregnancy was a trial. She could not remember a hotter summer, during which the child in her womb seemed to greedily harvest as much of his mother's strength and appetite as he possibly could without killing her, and therefore himself. She found herself welcoming Joseph's absence, for she was not very good company. He had worried about leaving her, but they both knew he had to go, and she felt it was secretly a relief for them both. Until he actually left, then his absence made the stiflingly hot house, crowded with servants and attendants, seem depressingly cold and empty. After a few days, however, the sensation passed, and she went from regretting his leaving to looking forward to his return.

The days were growing milder, and the nights cooler, when she began recovering her appetite, and feeling generally good enough to welcome the pleasure of a visit from her uncle. But even as she enjoyed preparing the menu for their private little feast, which would include two of his favorite dishes—pheasant with pomegranates, and roast pork with a honey yogurt sesame sauce—she was thinking about her family's ancestral burial plot in the ancient city of White Wall, and of the adjoining tombs her parents had built for themselves. For as long as she could remember, they had talked about the progress of their eternal homes as contentedly as they discussed an addition to the house or gardens. As she was wondering whether or not Joseph would wish to be buried beside her, the baby kicked inside her for the first time, and drove the troublesome thought out of her mind.

She received another shock, which felt like the opposite of her baby's kick when, after being announced, Potifer Setka entered her receiving room. Forcing herself to smile at him, she hoped he would not notice how much the sight of him disturbed her. He had lost so much weight, she could see the elegant bones beneath the exceedingly comfortable garment of flesh he had always worn over them as a living expression of affluence and well-being. Now she could imagine, all too vividly, the mummy he would one day be.

Grinning, Setka opened his arms wide, "My dearest duckling!"

Embracing him, she ignored the chill she suffered when she felt how much less there was of him to hug. "Uncle, you are so thin. Has your physician put you on a diet again?"

"On the contrary." Holding her at arm's length, he looked her up and down proudly. “My physician has commanded me to eat as much as I want to. I'm looking forward to my niece's first banquet in my honor!”

She was somewhat reassured by the fact that his smile, always so open and honest, was as bright as ever. It inspired her—while a servant poured wine and they sat down to enjoy the first appetizers—to reminisce. “Uncle, do you remember the time something, I can't recall what it was now, made us laugh so hard we couldn't breathe? I really thought we were both going to suffocate laughing!”

“Yes, I remember,” he chuckled, staring fixedly at something behind her. His smile lingered stubbornly, but his mouth twisted slightly from the effort of maintaining it.

Just returned from her afternoon exercise, My Dream trotted into the dining room, and Asenath sensed her uncle was as pleased by the distraction as she was. During dinner, the dog was treated to more scraps from the table than was probably good for her. She was still so sleek and beautiful, it was easy for Asenath to forget how old her beloved pet was, and for a terrible moment, she was confronted with the imminent presence of death in the form of two beings she loved dearly. But there was nothing wrong with My Dream's appetite, or with her uncle's, which gave her hope.

“She has lived a long time,” Setka observed as he tossed the dog another piece of pork. Then he asked casually, as though simply pursuing a related subject, “How is Joseph?”

Because her uncle already knew, like everyone else, that his former slave enjoyed the full approval of both Pharaoh and the crown prince, she replied, “He named our son Manesseh, because it means 'God has made me forget all my troubles and everyone in my father’s family.' He is very well, uncle.”

“His God never abandoned him,” he observed, picking out another treat for My Dream, and tossing it to her with a bit more force than was necessary. “And naturally he is well, for he is married to you, Asenath, the sweetest, loveliest young lady in the Two Lands. Iuno has not been the same since you left. I have missed you.”

This was too much for her. She was unable to dam the tears that welled up into her eyes.

“My dear, what is the matter?” He looked alarmed.

“Nothing...” She looked down at the dog, who fixed her with an expectant stare. “It's just that My Dream... well, I've been thinking that she's old now. You gave her to me for my tenth birthday, remember? I just wonder how much... how much longer she will be with me.”

“She looks perfectly fit to me,” he observed, but when she looked up at him, he met her eyes, and allowed her to see the fear and sadness he had been attempting to conceal.

“Uncle...”

“It's all right, child. I'm not in any pain, the gods be praised! And they have also not deprived me of my appetite, although I'm beginning to get an idea of how it will feel when I partake of the food and drink brought to my offering chapel." He gave her that strange twisted grin again, but this time she recognized it now for what it was—a grimace of mortal dread. "I will be able to magically enjoy the bread and meat and sweets left for me by my relatives, and by the priest in charge of feeding my Ka, but it will not make my Shade anymore solid."

"Oh uncle, please believe me when I tell you that your Ba will be mysteriously nourished, and that it will soon be strong enough to fly far away from your offering chapel! And you will not be alone, for Isis and Nepthys, the loving sisters of Osiris, lord of death and rebirth, will escort you to his eternal golden fields, where everything will be as it was here but infinitely sweeter, for in the land beyond the sunset, death casts no shadow!"

His eyes shone with a desperate hope struggling not to overflow into self pity. "Do you really think so?"

"Yes, uncle! I know God loves us, and will never let any harm come to us, for we are the children of His heart." Looking down at her womb, she gently rested both hands over it. "We should not be afraid of dying anymore than a baby fears being born. I don't know what he's thinking, but I can feel that my baby is at peace, and when the time comes, he will endure the struggle of birth because he must. Athough he may experience fear while he is being forced to leave the safety of the only kind of life he has ever known—and for a few terrible moments he will suffer the shock of breathing air instead of water—the life that awaits him in the light of the sun is far greater than the one he left behind. So I imagine dying must be like being born. It will be frightening, for we will be heading into the unknown, and it might be traumatic if we are not positioned properly, but it seems to me that childbirth is much more painful for the mother. If the mother of our souls is Isis, the other goddesses may be like midwives helping to welcome the dying soul into its new, imperishable life."

"I want to believe you." His face haggard, he avoided her eyes now. "I am a man, so it shames me to admit it, but I will do so here, just this once, for I know my secret is safe with you, Asenath. I am afraid. I am afraid that what you say is but a lovely dream, and that when I die, I will not even remember I ever lived!"

"Dreams are real, uncle, at least some of them are," she assured him. "You know I have dreamed true before. Years ago, Joseph told me there is no such thing as nothing, that there is only God, who created everything and everyone."

He sat up straighter. "And Joseph always speaks the truth."

"Yes! And now I will tell you a secret, uncle. I believe in Joseph's God. It is to Elohim I pray now."

Meeting her eyes again, he said with quiet desperation, "Will you pray to Joseph's god for me, Asenath? His god must be aware that I always treated Joseph with kindness. I know Joseph was my slave, but..."

She said firmly, "Don't worry about that now. It was God's

will all along to bring Joseph to Kemet, and to plant him safely in your household, where he could grow to fulfill his purpose. And if you were part of God's plan from the beginning, it means God always knew about you, and knew what a good man you are in your heart." She said no more, feeling as though she was watching a rare sun shower as her uncle smiled at her while at the same time tears flowed openly down his sallow cheeks.

"Thank you, my dear, for all you have said, but now let us please stop talking about death. My physician tells me he has seen this wasting illness before, and sometimes the person recovers to live many more years. It is a mystery, but there is still hope I may not go to my Ka just yet."

"There are many medical papyri in the House of Life here, uncle..."

"I am receiving the best care possible, Asenath, I assure you. There is no need for you to concern yourself about that. But, if it will make you happy, it can't hurt to consult with another doctor while I'm here."

"I will ask the princess to tell her father to send you his own personal physician!"

"She will tell Pharaoh?" He smiled. "Not ask him?"

They both willingly diverted the conversation into more pleasantly shallow topics before their private banquet ended, after which Asenath was so exhausted, she went straight to bed.

Less than four months later, her uncle was dead. Three days after receiving the news, she went into labor, and the whole time she was giving birth to her second child, she felt she was also mysteriously assisting in her uncle's rebirth. Her labor pains became confused in her mind and heart with the emotional anguish he had suffered fearing that, when he died, he would cease to exist forever. She wondered if it was proving as difficult for him to let go of his physical body as it was for her baby to separate himself from hers, and sincerely hoped not as she prayed to God for all three of them.

Joseph named his second son Ephraim, a Hebrew term that means fruitful. "For God," he said, "has made me fruitful in this land of my grief."

☼

Exhausted from efforts to nurse her son, Asenath surrendered Ephraim to a sweet but sad young woman named Yamtisey, whose husband and baby had both died from a fever which burned briefly through the capital during the season of immersion. Asenath had asked God every night to protect her and her family, and he had done so. She wished now she had remembered to specifically include My Dream in her prayers, but that would have been pointless, for it was not fever, but the inescapable ailment of old age, that robbed them of their beloved pet.

"She did not suffer, my lady," her handler assured her as he lay the dog gently down on one of her many beds. "She looked right at me before suddenly racing off, running as swiftly as she did when she was much younger, so that I soon lost sight of her. When I finally caught up with her, I thought she was just resting in the shade. Then I saw her eyes..."

"Thank you!" Asenath sounded angry because her voice collided with a sob in her throat. "She was your dog as much as mine, and I am very happy she seems to have run fearlessly to meet her death."

"Oh lady!" He turned his face away.

"You must stay with us," she said gently. "My son, Manneseh will be very distressed, and we will need to get him another dog soon. But... we will wait... a bit... until after... she has been embalmed. Then I will ask you to escort her body back to Iuno, where my father will see to it she is buried with our family."

While her beloved dog was in the hands of the priests of Anubis, Asenath commissioned a small shrine for their rooftop. As the vizier's wife, she had access to Pharaoh's own artisans, and soon a small wooden box was delivered to her house—a miniature version of the massive shrines she had seen in her dream of the pyramid. Its sole decoration was an ankh sign, covered in gold leaf, that split in half when the two doors were opened.

She placed the shrine in the intimate little pavilion which she also had built to order. Only Joseph knew there was nothing inside the shrine, no carved figure of a god or goddess, no amulet, not even an ostrich feather representing Maat. In this shrine, Asenath kept the invisible treasures of her hopes and dreams. Burning costly incense, every evening she prayed to Elohim. Sometimes she prayed silently, at other times in a whisper, but occasionally she spoke out loud, as if God was actually on the rooftop with her. She knew in her heart God could hear her however she addressed Him, it was only her own moods that varied. Joseph had told her his people did not build shrines or temples to Elohim, for He could not be contained anywhere or in anything. But her husband never disturbed her when she climbed the steps to the roof to be alone with God, and she knew her devotion pleased him.

The pavilion where she kept her shrine was narrow, but nearly twice as tall as she was, and from its slender frame hung the finest mist linen curtains, so that even when they were closed, she could see through them. Because of the position of their house, the pavilion was on the western edge of the roof, for it was there the best view was to be had. This was how she discovered that she found it mysteriously fulfilling to pray when the sun was drawing closer to the earth. At first, it was too bright to look at, but sometimes, for a few precious instants, she could gaze directly at the molten solar disc before it sank into the desert mountains.

Sometimes when she prayed to God, she felt nothing at all—the sun was just the sun in the sky—and worried she was only telling herself a different kind of story from the ones she had grown up with, a story she preferred now because she loved

Joseph, and because all her life she had longed for a God who saw her—a God who cared enough about her to speak to her personally, even if only in dreams. But remembering how Elohim had spoken to Abraham and Isaac, and to others of His chosen people, Asenath often felt her thoughts and feelings soaring while she prayed like a flock of birds silhouetted against the sun drawing slowly closer to the world. On those blessed evenings, the light did not seem to fade but rather to enjoy coming to rest in her heart. The darkness gradually falling around her was warm as an embrace, and the first star that appeared overhead felt like a kiss that filled her to overflowing with joy. Afterward, she ran down the steps into the house to kiss and embrace her own beloved children and, if he was home, Joseph, her earthly lord.

Chapter 17

For his thirty-seventh birthday, Asenath gave Joseph a silver wine cup. It looked empty but, in truth, it was full of feelings too deep for her to express with words.

Manasseh—slender as a gazelle and sweeter than water in the desert—had just turned five. Ephraim was still a baby, but growing in size and strength as swiftly as a lion cub. His mother was relieved he was the youngest, for she feared he would have terrorized his much less aggressive brother. Manasseh's constant companion was the new teshem hound his father had given him. The dog was a male, and as far as Asenath was concerned, nowhere near as beautiful and special as My Dream had been. It comforted her to know she would one day be buried close to her beloved pet in White Wall's ancient cemetery. And since Joseph had made no remark to the contrary, she chose to believe he would also rest there with them.

More and more, Asenath found herself cherishing the hope of life eternal. She trusted God Almighty would not deny His children their inheritance, which was to share his celestial residence and power. She had faith Elohim loved her as she loved her children, who she would never dream of exiling into the lifeless desert, where they would become meat for jackals and vultures, until only featureless bones remained of their once unique faces—and nothing of their eyes, which could reflect the imperishable stars as their hearts wondered at their mysterious beauty. The blood of the chosen people flowed through both Manasseh and Ephraim as it did not flow through her own body, but when this worried her, Asenath remembered what God had said to Jacob, “And all the families of the earth will be blessed through you and your descendants.”

One evening—when she finally dared to ask Joseph if God Almighty had promised Abraham a special place of honor in his Palace of the Other World—he looked at her for a long moment, as if he did not quite understand the question, before replying, “God said to Abraham, 'I will make you a great nation.' God's promises will be fulfilled here, in this world.”

“But what about the life to come?”

“What about it?” he shrugged. “Life is life, and always will be.”

“Tell that to Pharaoh!” She was aware her husband was impatient of all the funds and manpower being channeled away from the vital work of preparing for the coming famine by the king's elaborate pyramid complex. Yet although she feared the answer, she was compelled to ask, “Has Elohim not said anything about life in the world to come?”

“The world, Asenath, has already come. It is right here beneath our feet, and before our eyes, responding to the intentions of our minds, the gratitude of our hearts, and the work of our hands. The world is life, and God has promised my people that we will flourish and become a great nation in this world."

"I am happy for your people, Joseph. But I was born in a nation that is already great, except for the fact that all its citizens must die, so we prepare for the moment when our souls will fly away from the nest of our physical limbs. Pharaoh's Ba bird—soaring straight into the sun like a lance crowned by the spearhead of his pyramid—will help lead the way for all of us into an imperishable reality of which this world is only a reflection... When we're under water, we must hold our breath, but maybe when we die, and cease to breathe, we will all swim like fish in the blue waters of heaven..."

"Well, as long as you actually don't turn into a fish but continue being a beautiful woman," smiling, he drew her into his arms, "I will gladly soar through the sky with you. Your dresses will all be woven of feather-soft clouds dyed by the rising and setting sun. And at night, when the moon is full, we will toss it to our sons like a silver ball. Until it dwindles to a crescent, then we will use its shining sickle to harvest the stars, and grow endlessly drunk on their light without ever regretting it!"

She laughed, and for a while forgot all about death in her husband's arms. The following day, however, she returned to pondering—but more contentedly this time, like a dog with her favorite bone—what God had meant when he said, "And all the families of the earth will be blessed through you and your descendants." Just as the sun shone equally on both sides of the River, she believed God's blessings in this world could not be separated from his blessings in the world to come—where life would be even more splendid, like a fully lucid dream from which she would never wake.

They were currently residing in the palace of Iuno. To her delight, Joseph was spending more of his time in the City of the Sun, making use of the administrative infrastructure that had been in place there since the first pharaohs. He employed its army of messengers, heralds and pigeons to communicate with cities up and down the River, enforcing his will in the name of the king without needing to make more than one royal progress a year.

Then one morning, dark news flew into the temple coop. The Horus of Fine Gold, Khakheperre Senwosret, had gone to his Ka. It came as a shock to Asenath, for Sithathor's most recent letter had been lighthearted, giving no indication whatsoever her father was not well. A royal herald arrived not long after the messenger bird, and from him they learned the king had died unexpectedly in his sleep one night.

As though grieved by Pharaoh's passing, that year the River failed to rise to its full height.

The oarsmen rowing south as swiftly as they could to Shedet, she was alone with Joseph in their shipboard cabin when he warned her quietly, "It is beginning."

She had been thinking of Sithathor, who was undoubtedly

devastated by grief, but she knew at once what Joseph meant, and a perverse elation lightened her heavy heart. During the last harvest, measurements had been taken at all the usual landing stations which indicated the level of the River was much lower than normal. So it had come as no surprise that, when the River rose, less than half the cultivatable land was inundated. Even in the face of a coming famine that would last seven long years, this evidence of her husband's close relationship with God through the power of dreams filled her with joy.

For the next few weeks—in that mysteriously barren stretch before the burial of the old king and the coronation of the new Horus of Fine Gold—Asenath saw little of Joseph, and nothing of her children, who had remained behind in Iuno in the care of their attendants and devoted grandparents. Most of her time was spent attempting to console Sithathor, whose father's body was with the embalmers.

"You should think of your father's Ba now as an infant being swaddled," Asenath suggested one afternoon when they were alone together in the princess' living room. They were curled up on their sides across from each other on gilded, and exquisitely painted wooden bed-couches, the fronts of which had been carved in the form of lovely cows with their slender legs placed tightly together, and their heads crowned by gently curved horns cradling the solar disc. The couches were positioned to catch the breeze that occasionally caressed the women as it slipped, silent as a secret lover, through the lattice work windows which kept all but the tiniest of insects out of the room.

In response, Sithathor raised a painted eyebrow and said flatly, "Are you calling Pharaoh a baby?"

"You know what I mean." Asenath made an effort not to sound impatient. "The priests of Anubis are preparing him to be born into his new life."

Her mouth twisting oddly, Sithathor stared lethargically down into the wine cup cradled in one of her hands. "Countless dead babies have had their brains dissolved and pulled out through their nostrils, but my father was a man."

"You are right, that was not the best analogy," Asenath admitted, and thought longingly again of her little boys. Yet, strangely enough, the more despondent her friend became, the more confident she grew that such apparently inconsolable sorrow was more selfish than realistic, a conviction that prompted her to say firmly, "But I seriously don't think your father would appreciate you feeling so sorry for him, princess, as if you didn't really believe in his eternal Ka."

The silence which followed her words was broken only by the angry buzzing of a bee that, apparently having confused the window screen with a great honeycomb, was now stuck in one of the openings.

"That's a really stupid bee!" Sithathor declared darkly. "He's all alone now, far away from his hive and his queen, and there's nothing on this side of the partition except you and me, two giant goddesses ready to squash him!"

Inwardly, Asenath winced, but when her friend looked up at her, she felt herself smiling, and then she could not stop herself from giggling.

Sithathor's eyes widened in surprise, but there was a hopeful glint in them now, and an answering smile resurrected the dimples that had for too long been banished from her cheeks.

The princess had recovered some of her positive good humor by the time of the funeral. It was impossible for Asenath not to believe in Senwosret's eternal Ka as the procession moved slowly along the ceremonial walkway leading to the gateway in the enclosure wall, behind which rose the blindingly bright slopes of his Mansion of Millions of Years, coming together far above them in a golden cap stone impossible to look at directly. Pharaoh's hope and faith, so beautifully and forcefully expressed, was visible to everyone as his Ka rose invisibly into the eternal sky on the wings of Horus, son of Osiris. She knew they could not see it happen, could not actually watch his soul flying away—for this mystery was beyond the ability of mortal eyes to perceive—yet she could not stop herself from trying to catch a glimpse of the king's Ba bird. The closer they drew to the pyramid, the more impressively it loomed over them like solid shafts of divine light. Its godlike immensity, so precisely erected by human minds and hands, filled her with reverent awe. She longed to be able to look all the way up at its burning golden apex and see not Senwosret's Ba making its way heavenward, but God's infinitely brilliant gaze meeting hers. She almost felt that if she was willing to sacrifice her eyesight, she just might be able to glimpse Elohim gazing down at her. But naturally she could not make this sacrifice, for then she would never again be able to see Joseph and her children. And in her own reticense to go to such unhealthy extremes, she heard God telling her something—that when she looked at everyone she loved, she was already glimpsing Him.

The entrance to Senwosret Shines was hidden in the pavement on the south side, and only the young nobles entrusted with the honor of carrying the Master of Life in which the king's mummy rested were permitted to enter. Asenath was hot and thirsty, and already a little tired, but she still longed to take home with her, and preserve, the transcendent feelings overflowing her ability to express them. The only truly sad moment for her came when Sithathor, who was standing in front of her, let out a strangled scream as her father's gilded wooden profile disappeared from view. Then, on their way out of the burial complex, she suffered a chill as they passed the small tomb in which her beloved friend would one day be buried with her jewels and cosmetics and all her other favorite worldly possessions. The priests devoted to the service of Pharaoh's eternal Ka would also serve and protect the souls of his beloved family.

The prince had not waited until after his father's burial, or his own coronation—where he chose the throne name Khakaure,

Appearing Like the Souls of Re—before taking the helm, and beginning to steer the Two Lands in the direction it was already heading, in great part due to the assistance and support of the vizier. One of his first official acts was the renovation of a bypass canal around the first cataracts, which had been dug hundreds of years ago by Pharaoh Merenre. The original canal was cleared, broadened and deepened, and Joseph told her this was in order to facilitate the military campaigns the new king was planning in Kush—the southern wastelands inhabited by a barbaric people who had no concept of, much less any respect for, the rule of Maat.

"He intends to enslave the women and children, poison the wells, kill the men, and burn the fields. When he's finished with them, they will no longer dare to graze their herds or steer their boats anywhere near Pharaoh's specified border."

From what she had heard of Down Below, its inhabitants were more like hyenas than humans, so she could find no fault in Pharaoh desiring to protect his people from them. Joseph's tone when he informed her of these plans had been neutral, and she had not attempted to find out how he personally felt about them. She had learned that if he did not wish to share his feelings with her, there was no point asking him about them. By then they were back home in Iuno, so instead she went to see Manesseh, who shared all his thoughts openly and innocently with his mother. She prayed he would never outgrow this virtue.

Khakaure also lost no time in making Sithathoriunet one of his wives. Asenath was not surprised. She had long been privy to the princess' desire never to marry, and was glad the king had chosen to indulge his sister's desire to remain single and in the royal palace, where she resided in her old apartments, consort in name only. The lovely Neferthenut was the new pharaoh's true wife, and no one doubted there would be others. The king was still quite young and virile, and he towered over his subjects, not only because of his exalted position, but because he was literally much taller than most men.

Asenath began thinking about her tomb again in earnest. It was time she hired craftsmen and artists to begin working on it, but she could not do so until she talked to Joseph about his own tomb. Worried he might not wish to be buried in her family's section of the silent desert, she had not yet found the courage to broach the subject with him. She knew she should do so soon, but as the days and the weeks and the months passed, she kept failing to.

☼

When the following year the River again did not rise to even a fraction of its normal height, the pressing thought of her future death and burial were, paradoxically, pushed out of Asenath's mind as life was threatened by a shortage of food. Famine loomed over the Two Lands like a nightmare slowly solidifying into an inescapable reality as Pharaoh's children all cried out to him for food, and Khakaure said to them, "Go to Joseph, and do whatever he tells you." So Joseph opened up the storehouses and began distributing grain to the people of Kemet.

When her husband returned home in the evenings, Asenath gave silent thanks, and washed his hands and feet before embracing him. Then she followed him into their finely appointed dining room, poured the finest red wine into the silver cup she had given him as a birthday present, and together they enjoyed the delectable dishes prepared for them. Even before the famine, she had made it clear to their cook—who like all chefs delighted in lavish experimentation—that unless they were entertaining, the master was perfectly content with three appetizers, two main and side dishes, and a single dessert. However, if it had not been for their new Chief Steward, Khusebek—whose job was to help her manage all the intricate workings of the vizier's household—she doubted their chef would have curtailed his lavish impulses so assiduously. Khusebek possessed the invaluable skill of getting people to obey him by making it seem he was doing them a favor in the process, as a result of which they liked him even more, and were increasingly willing to do as he said.

Khusebek, who was twenty years old, was the son of a native Overseer and of a Hebrew slave. Before he came to them, he had served in her aunt's household. After her husband's death, Tarset had lost no time in making the handsome and intelligent slave her lover. As a wealthy widow, she had done as she pleased, until one night when, unable to sleep, she went for a walk in her garden, and stepped on a yellow scorpion. She could not have known at the time what color it was, or even what exactly she had trod on in the dark. Apparently, she had felt only a mild stinging sensation, for she did not immediately return to the house for a healing salve. Just before dawn, her servants found her lying near the pool, where she may have gone to cool the slight burning in her foot. Her physician reported that the swelling caused by the venom had spread very rapidly through her body, and fatally cut off her breath.

Listening to Sadeh tell her the story of Tarset's sudden death, pity for her aunt stirred in her gut, but did not quite manage to ascend to her heart as compassion. She was feeling angry on behalf of her beloved uncle, who had still been in the embalming house when his wife further dishonored him by not even waiting until he was buried before sleeping with another man.

Having now inherited all of her brother's property, cattle, servants and slaves, Sadeh had recommended Khusebek to her daughter. Asenath had told her husband about him, and after a brief conversation with the youth, Joseph lost no time in granting Khusebek his freedom before offering him the position of Chief Steward in his household.

☼

The next time Joseph traveled to Shedet, Asenath went with him, and not only because Queen Sithathoriunet had decreed the vizier was to be accompanied by his wife whenever he was in the capital. Always being close to Joseph felt as vital to the life, health and strength of her heart as drinking water and eating was to her body.

Alone in their cabin, her head resting on Joseph's chest and her eyes closed, she was lulled into a thoughtless peace by the tireless beating of his heart merging with subtle lapping of the River against the hull, and the almost subliminal whisper of oars sinking into and rising out of the water in perfect rhythm. Like a dragonfly skimming the water's surface, her awareness hovered between wakefulness and sleep. She knew the drumming sound all around her was her husband's pulse, but also that she was already dreaming when she felt herself floating as though in his blood, which was a deep red color at the center and nearly black around the edges. And shining in its darkness she saw stars. Overwhelmed by the awesome beauty of his blood welling up out of a fathomless darkness shimmering with stars, she woke up, but kept her eyes closed. She sensed Joseph had also fallen asleep, and the slow, deep rhythm of his breathing carried her smoothly back into the dream space. At first she could see nothing, but focusing her vision directly before her, she waited, and gradually the darkness was pervaded by a deep red color that brightened and shifted, until she was looking straight down into a silver cup filled to the brim with red wine illuminated by sunlight.

Addressing the dream space as she prayed to Elohim, but more casually, in a spirit of play, she said, "I would like to know what it feels like to be a falcon" careful not to say that she actually wanted to become a falcon. At once, she became aware of blue sky all around her, and sensed more than saw wings stretching out on either side of her—wings she felt growing longer and more powerful as she flew higher and higher in broadening circles. She heard the rushing of wind, and then something else—a high-pitched note she vaguely felt vibrating in her left ear. Far below her, a long blood-red cloud stretched just above the horizon, yet she could not see the sun either rising or setting. A bright, even light illuminated the dream scene, making it easy for her to spot a shape as slender as a serpent—but not undulating like one—moving slowly forward through the landscape directly below her.

Intrigued, she began descending, and soon discerned the figures of men and donkeys traveling through a land she did not recognize. Everywhere her dreaming eyes could see were green pastures flowing up into hills dotted with sheep. Vivid blue lakes were bordered by groves of golden date palms, and beyond them stretched barley fields ready for harvesting on either side of a river so distant, it shone like polished silver.

Continuing to glide downward, Asenath suddenly understood she was watching a group of Hebrew men on a long journey, even though only a handful of the donkeys they led were burdened with supplies. She counted ten men, and somehow she knew they were traveling west toward Kemet on the Horus Road.

Intensely curious, she landed on a rock, and the sensation of her bare feet making contact with the stone made her aware she was in her human form again, and also helped root her in the dream. She even felt a gentle breeze caressing her as she studied the faces of the passing men. She was close enough to them to hear the subtle swishing of their ankle-length robes, and the creaking of their donkeys' harnesses. When not a single one of the travelers turned his bearded face in her direction, her impression of being invisible to them was confirmed. The men looked weary, yet she also sensed their determined strength, the source of which was not merely the resilience instilled in them by decades of hard work. At the same time, she noted the interesting fact that although all her other senses were life-like, she could not smell anything, which was probably a good thing so near a caravan of unwashed men and animals.

Leaping lightly off the rock, she approached the travelers, conscious now of wearing a long white dress that was looser around her ankles than was currently fashionable. The garment wafting lightly around her legs, she did not feel herself so much walking as dancing as she fell effortlessly into stride beside one of the men. It was hard to tell, but beneath his graying beard he still looked presentable enough. His nose was straight and strong beneath thick black eyebrows feathered at the ends like a vulture's wings. His forehead was a little too tall, but curling strands of hair helped conceal this fact, and he had remarkable blue eyes. She wondered if it was because she was seeing his eyes in a dream that they glimmered with such luminous intensity.

"Who are you?" she asked him, and was disappointed yet not surprised when he did not react in any way to the sound of her voice. Nevertheless, she suddenly knew who he was. Who they all were!

She woke abruptly when the earth shook as her husband stirred beneath her.

Sitting up, she said urgently, "Joseph? Are you awake?"

"I am now."

"You are much more handsome than your older brothers!"

His eyes flew open. "What did you say?"

"I just saw ten Hebrew men traveling west on the Horus Road, and in the dream I knew who they were, and where they were headed. Joseph, your brothers are coming to Kemet!"

Chapter 18

Asenath got her first taste of what it might be like to encounter the man Joseph—not as her lover but as the vizier of all Kemet second in command only to Pharaoh—when he began interrogating her. Pinning her beneath a penetrating, almost suspicious stare, without raising his voice he demanded she tell him her dream again, and then a third time. At first she was pleased, but she soon had nothing new to offer him, and it worried her he kept insisting she try to remember more. Never before had he seemed skeptical about any of her dreams. On the contrary, he obviously enjoyed hearing about her dreams the way he relished diving into a pool after a hot and tiring day. The dream space could be compared to life-giving water with its soothing weightlessness and stimulating fluidity, events and scenes flowing into each other on fathomless currents of meaning, in which objects could feel solid yet also be insubstantial as reflections.

Her mind wandered into such musings as Joseph questioned her. Apparently, what made him doubt the veracity of her dream was the lush, life-filled landscape she had flown over. Only yesterday, scouts dispatched to the lands of the Retjenu had brought back reports of dry fields and fruitless trees everywhere. Joseph explained to her that his family lived in what was known in Kemet as Djahy, the southernmost lands of the Retjenu, and that the famine extended even farther north to Amurru, the kingdom of the Amorites.

“Perhaps as I flew like a falcon, I saw the land as it once looked, and as it will appear again,” she suggested. “But, as I told you, when I landed and resumed my human form, I saw only rocks and dirt, and distinctly noticed how dusty the traveler's feet were, as were the hems of their robes, as though no rain had fallen in a long time. The men looked very tired, but determined to walk faster than the despair nipping at their heels like the jackal of Anubis.”

Joseph responded with a brooding silence which lasted so long, her thoughts drifted to the subject of her children, always foremost in her mind. She was wondering if Manesseh and Ephraim would inherit their parents' gift for dreaming true when, in a completely different tone of voice, Joseph said, “Forgive me, Asenath. I believe you, I just... I just needed to be certain.”

“Do not ask me for forgiveness, Joseph.” She rose from the bed where she had been kneeling for far too long. “Ask God Almighty to forgive you for questioning the news he was so gracious to send you through this dream, for which I can take no more credit than a pigeon trained to deliver news strapped to its legs by a higher power. All I did was receive the message, and give it to you. I don't understand how I knew in the dream the men were your brothers, but I'm sure they were.”

Silently, he watched her pour them both cups of water, but as she handed one to him, he met her eyes as he took her free hand in his, "I have always been too proud, Asenath. Your humility makes you even more beautiful to me. Please believe me when I tell you that you don't look anything like a pigeon." He smiled.

She laughed. "No, but I did fly just like a falcon. I think I even heard like a falcon, for there was this strange high note vibrating in my left ear while-"

He interrupted her quietly, "One of my brothers has blue eyes."

"I know."

She was not surprised her dreaming soul had intuited it was important she go and walk beside this one particular man, and make note of the fact that his eyes were blue, because it was this detail which seemed to make it impossible for Joseph to dismiss her dream.

As she took the empty cup from her husband, he told her, "The famine has struck all the surrounding countries, and my father will have heard there is grain available here in Kemet. I don't need to be dreaming to imagine the scene in his tent when he called my brothers to him and said, 'Why are you standing around looking at one another?' I've heard there is grain in Kemet. Go down there, and buy enough grain to keep us alive. Otherwise we'll die!'"

"I like the sound of your father. He stares Maat in the face even when she is terrible to look at."

"The truth is not something my brothers honor above all else."

"Maybe we should step out on deck for a while," she suggested. "It would also be nice to have a picnic lunch on shore, since we're in no great hurry to reach Shedet."

"Oh but we are. We must arrive, and leave, with all haste, and then make our way, as fast as the current will take us, to Rowaty."

Of course. His brothers were on the Horus Road, and it was to Rowaty they would first go to buy grain. It struck her then, almost with the force of a physical blow, that these men would be stepping out of the dream space into her waking life, a fact that was, in this case, much more troubling than elating. They were not even here yet, but already she was jealous of them, for they were Joseph's blood, so they would always be closer to him than she was. Yet considering how badly his brothers had treated him, this reasoning made no sense. With an effort, she set the thought aside and said simply, "We must pick the boys up on the way."

"Of course." He slipped his arms around her waist from behind, so that she felt his warm breath against her cheek as he said, just as warmly, "I'm remembering the dreams I had before my brothers sold me into slavery, and your faith that they would come true, my Asenath."

"Surely you never doubted it yourself, Joseph." She turned to face him. "I wonder if your brothers will remember your dreams when they bow down before you, as God showed you they would."

☼

Queen Sithathoriunet almost perfunctorily expressed her regret the vizier and his wife would not be remaining long in the capital. Asenath had expected her friend to be more upset, and to try and convince her to stay behind when Joseph left. But the princess, she discovered, was much too involved with someone else now, not another lady who had become her favorite companion, but a man, a palace servant she had fallen in love with and was secretly—in the sense that only her most intimate attendants new about it—welcoming into her bed whenever possible.

Asenath suddenly understood the tension she sensed in the queen's handmaidens. She recognized only two of the women, for the rest had all married and left the court. At first, she thought the queen had surrounded herself with more mature companions, but she soon came to realize this new batch of women did not talk and laugh constantly and freely because they were afraid. The only one who chatted and giggled without apparent reservation was Sithathor's new favorite, whose job it was to inform the other ladies what the queen wished done, with the utmost discretion, of course. This included preparing the potions and creams necessary for preventing pregnancy, and coming up with viable excuses for keeping the special young servant as close as possible to the queen at all times. To this end, Sithathor had promoted him to Queen's Herald.

Asenath foundherself thanking God for her dream of Joseph's brothers—which meant their stay at court would be brief—as she eagerly anticipated the journey north. She was even looking forward to a delightfully dull life in Rowaty. She could scarcely imagine how Pharaoh would react if he ever discovered that his sister-wife was sleeping with a commoner behind his royal back. Sithathor had blithely assured her, “Oh, he won't care! We're married in name only, and he can't expect me never to taste life's greatest pleasure!” But Asenath—one of the quietly tense handmaidens surrounding the queen—was afraid her friend was seriously deluding herself. Sithathor's favorite diversion now was listening raptly to her harpist sing love songs, a dreamy smile painted on her face. The queen's lover was tall and broad of shoulders, but in Asenath's opinion he was not remotely worthy of such dangerous devotion.

“I do not believe the affair will last long,” Lady Amunet confided to her the day before she and Joseph were due to depart. “He is the third young man Sithathor has surrendered her heart to since she was crowned a queen. But if you ask me, the only man she has ever truly loved, and who will ever truly love her, was her father.”

In Asenath's eyes, Lady Amunet possessed the lovely countenance of Maat despite the fact that her features were exceptionally plain. “Being in love is not the same as loving, and truly being loved in return," she said sadly.

"Indeed."

"The princess should not have married her brother."

"No, she should not have," Amunet agreed. "At the time, however, it seemed to her the best option. She was confident her brother would let her do as she pleased, whereas a husband might have proved less indulgent, if only because he was less indifferent to her well being."

"Yes... It's very tempting to spoil my sons, but I realize this impulse springs not from how much I love them, but from how much I want them to love me even more than they already naturally do, because I fear losing all their attention once they're grown up. Some part of me is tempted to try and buy their undying devotion, which wouldn't work anyway, of course. How much I love my children is what gives me the strength not to overindulge them, and to understand proper discipline is a far more loving caress."

Amunet lowered her head and stared down at her hands where they rested formally on her knees. "Your sons are fortunate to have you as their mother."

"Lady, if I may ask, are you married? You speak with great discernment on the subject."

"I am a widow," she said, but her eyes were dry as she returned Asenath's candid gaze.

"Is that how you came to be here at court as handmaiden to a queen?" She did not wait for a reply. "If you are not at peace here, Amunet, I will plead with Sithathor to give you to me, for I would be delighted if you would consider joining my household. Conversing with an intelligent, sensible and sensitive woman is a pleasure I would love to get used to."

"I would be honored, Lady Asenath, and very pleased, to accept your gracious offer."

And so it was that Lady Amunet left Seshet as the newest member of the vizier's entourage. Sithathoriunet had been delighted to grant their request. Asenath suffered a twinge of guilt for removing the one solid source of good judgment in that particular wing of the royal palace. And she thought she understood now why she had felt such a chill in the cold shadow of Senwosret Shines as she passed Sithathor's future tomb. It was as if her friend's soul had flown away with her father, leaving behind only her body, outwardly doing its best to enjoy life's pleasures, while her heart tragically waited to move into the little stone house at the base of the pyramid in which forever slept its king. She sensed Sithathor was profoundly unhappy, and that no number of superficially passionate love affairs would be able to disguise this truth from anyone who truly knew and loved her.

As the ship made its way North, Asenath wondered if there was anything more she could have said, but Sithathor had always been proud and stubborn. She could only hope that, as time passed, the friend she had known, and still loved, would return to herself.

They remained for a restful week in Iuno before boarding the ship again and proceeding straight to Rowaty. As it turned out, she had Joseph all to herself again in their cabin, for their sons had been given their own boat, which followed closely behind theirs. It was a delight when Manesseh's voice occasionally carried across the water to them, his excitement flowing straight into the soft shells of her lovingly receptive ears as he yelled, “Oh look at that!” So far, she knew he had spotted a “humongous crocodile” a mother hippo and her “fat ugly babies” and a group of noisy baboons, one of whom had turned around and waggled his bare ass cheeks at him, a story he delighted in telling everyone.

While in Iuno, Joseph had hired two scribes who could speak the Hebrew language.

“My bothers will expect me to need an interpreter, Asenath,” he explained. “The governor of Kemet should not be able to speak the language of all those who come to him to buy grain.”

“Of course not,” she agreed absently, more interested in caressing his chest—smoothly shaved and rubbed down with expensive unguents every morning that left no greasy mark on her fingertips. “But don't you think they'll recognize you, their own brother?”

“It has been over twenty-two years since they last saw me, and I'm sure I've changed more than they have.”

“That's true! You were so skinny when I first saw you, and your beard hadn't grown in yet, although it was trying to. But now you are the most fashionable of men, Joseph. You have even grown bangs to shorten your forehead. In addition, of course, to being clean shaven, and bathing every day. And your eyes are even more striking framed by kohl and malachite." Bending over him, she kissed his mouth hungrily.

He pushed her away gently. "My brothers are all decent men, Asenath," he said, staring intently up at the ceiling—brightly painted with ducks flying over papyrus stalks growing out of water teeming with fish.

Hurt by his rejection of her amorous advances, she almost retorted, "Even though they sold you into slavery?" but she bit back the words, and after a moment said carefully, "Of course they are. Any man who believes in God Almighty is a decent man, even if he does not always behave as if he is. But I cannot believe Elohim will look favorably upon them if they do not in their hearts regret how they treated you."

His mood changing abruptly, he drew her down onto the bed beside him and rolled on top of her. "We shall see. Won't we, my kitten? I will play with them as a cat does with mice, and determine just what they are made of now!"

Some small part of her was a little frightened by the way he kissed her then, almost angrily, but most of her was thrilled.

Joseph further delighted her with the improvements he had ordered made to their half of the royal residence in Rowaty while they were away. The expanded garden boasted a greater variety of trees, shrubs and flowers, and a third pool had been dug for the children. The banquet hall had also been freshly painted, and more lamp stands added. Close to the palace, but not connected to it, was the official receiving hall, which had also been enhanced with extra lamp stands set on either side of the dais, so that the wooden throne's gold lion paws shone even more splendidly.

"You did not tell me you had ordered all these renovations, Joseph!" she accused him happily.

"I wanted to surprise you."

She was obliged, however, to wait until that night to properly express her gratitude, for they had only just arrived, and first she had to attend to the enjoyable task of helping their steward orchestrate the proper distribution of their possessions, which included thirty-three cases of wine, four smaller but even more valuable chests of unguents, dozens of flasks of scented oils, and hundreds of cakes of the finest incense, the latter a gift from Queen Sithathoriunet. Khusebek did not really need her assistance, but she loved everything that belonged to her and to Joseph so much, it was a pleasure to help ensure all their treasures were safely carried to their proper places. It deepened her contentment to assure herself that not one of the pleasures they enjoyed together—from the smallest and most modest to the largest and most extravagant—would be interfered with. The chests containing her dream papyri always traveled with her in their cabin, and were always the first items to be unloaded whenever they arrived at their destination. Joseph had suggested it might be safer to leave them in Iuno, "Just in case the ship sinks," he teased, but she could not imagine being parted from them. She felt the need to always be surrounded by her most memorable dreams, and to know she could take them out and read them whenever she wanted to. Her dreams were the bread and wine of her soul.

And yet, on this particular homecoming, Asenath was aware that by concentrating on bedding and spices and other domestic satisfactions, she was deliberately diverting her thoughts away from something else. Rowaty was more crowded than she had ever seen it, and the majority of the newcomers were foreigners. She had never approved of the temple of Set, and it made her uncomfortable that the streets around it swarmed with strangers who had no knowledge of Maat, but many of whom stopped to make offerings to the enemy of Osiris as if they recognized one of their own gods in him. It was obvious the famine was spreading far into alien lands she had no desire to visit, not even in her dreams. As she stood in the safety of the palace, helping Khusebek properly and securely store their possessions, she was forced to admit to herself that it was the mysterious health of her heart she was so anxious to secure and protect.

The day after their arrival, the vizier of the Two Lands began receiving petitioners, for only he had the authority to sell the grain Kemet still possessed in abundance by the grace of God, who had made his warning to Pharaoh understood through Joseph.

In the early afternoon—when it was too hot at this time of year to do anything except nap or wade in the pool—Asenath found herself too restless to do either. So she requested that Amunet accompany her to the official receiving hall, only a short litter ride from the palace. There they sat on gilded stools set against the wall parallel with the vizier, who was seated on his throne. His handsome and sternly regal profile was visible to them because of his elevated position, for scribes and officials stood around the dais, and they in turn were flanked by numerous servants. Petitioners entered the hall, and they did not leave until they had paid for the exact amount of grain they had requested.

Musing on the nature of dreams while Amunet stroked the tawny cat sleeping curled up on her lap, Asenath thought how disturbed she would be to see a cat with its whiskers clipped off. Whiskers were part of a cat's sensory perceptions, a way of perceiving and collecting information, especially at night in the dark. In that sense, dreams were similar to cat's whiskers, for dreams could be sources of hidden knowledge and information. Yet so many people never remembered their dreams, and made no effort to do so, which seemed as unnatural to her as a cat deliberately cutting off its own whiskers.

She had believed Amunet was too polite to inquire why they

spent up to three hours everyday watching the vizier execute his authority, but eventually she realized the lady was also curious about foreigners. Initially, they shared some quiet laughs—hidden behind their ostrich feather fans—as they remarked on the strange, sometimes outlandish clothing some of the Retjenu favored. They sat far enough from the petitioners to be spared any offensive odors, but the smell of desperation that clung to them seeped into their own emotions. By the end of the third day, their lighthearted banter had died away as they saw only men spending all the coin they possessed to feed themselves and their families. Many had traveled unimaginable distances with the strength of hope, for they had heard that in Kemet there was still plenty of food.

On the first occasion a group of Hebrew men entered the hall, Asenath's breath caught as her eyes were torn between them and her husband, who she noticed had sat forward slightly in his throne. But as the men drew nearer, he slumped back in his chair, and her own speeding pulse slowed in response to this signal the newcomers were not his brothers. Then, on the ninth day of the second week, a herald announced another party of petitioners, and her heart leaped in her breast when into the hall suddenly strode the ten men from her dream. She knew them at once even though they all looked considerably older, as if it had taken them years to arrive. Their deeply lined faces shocked her without truly surprising her, for she had long since noted the fact that people often appeared younger in dreams.

When they came close enough to the dais, soldiers halted their progress. Glancing at each other, the brothers hesitated only a moment before bowing to the vizier. Then they lowered themselves to their knees, and bracing themselves with their hands, put their faces to the floor.

Asenath immediately saw in his expression that Joseph had recognized his brothers, but just as he had told her he would do, he pretended not to know them. "Where are you from?" he asked them sternly.

Raising his head just enough to look up at the dais, the man she had focused on in her dream listened intently to the scribe translating the vizier's words before replying, "From the land of Canaan. We have come to buy grain."

Becoming aware of a growing pressure in her chest, Asenath let out the breath she had been holding. Nothing in the man's expression indicated he had recognized Joseph, who said harshly, "No, you are spies! You have come to see how vulnerable our land has become."

His blue eyes widening with shock as the scribe translated the vizier's words, the Hebrew spoke quickly, "No, my lord! Your servants have simply come to buy food. We are all brothers—members of the same family. We are honest men, sir! We are not spies!"

"Yes, you are!" Joseph insisted while his scribes and officials began whispering among themselves. Many seemed surprised, while others looked impressed by their master's powers of discernment.

"Sir, there are actually twelve of us. We, your servants, are all brothers, sons of a man living in the land of Canaan. Our youngest brother is back there with our father right now, and one of our brothers is no longer with us."

For a long moment, Joseph was silent, and when he spoke, his voice was deeper than normal, "As I said, you are spies! And this is how I will test your story. I swear by the life of Pharaoh that you will never leave Kemet unless your youngest brother comes here. One of you must go and fetch your brother. I will keep the rest of you in prison. Then we'll find out whether or not your story is true. By the life of Pharaoh, if it turns out that you do not have a younger brother, then I will know you are spies."

Asenath reminded herself these men had sold Joseph into slavery, for she was tempted to feel sorry for them as soldiers promptly yanked the stunned Hebrews to their feet, and hauled them off to prison.

During the three days Joseph's brothers were incarcerated, Asenath was with them in spirit, for her husband's brooding silence ruined both their appetites, and life's pleasures seemed no more available to them now than to the imprisoned men. She wondered how she could possibly have imagined that watching Joseph lord it over his brothers would be exciting. He had hinted to her that day on board ship that he might enjoy playing with his siblings as a cat does with mice, but she had never met a cat who suffered on behalf of the mice. She felt ashamed of herself now for not having better prepared herself, and her husband, for the pain this reunion would bring him. But whenever she asked him how he was feeling, he replied firmly, "I'm fine."

If he had not made the situation so intolerable for her, she was sure—or so she told herself—she would not have betrayed his confidence, which she did, by telling Amunet everything. The lady was much too discerning not to know something was wrong, and too skilled at extending sympathy, without asking too many questions, to resist confiding in. Amunet swore on Maat she would tell no one, and Asenath survived the three days by being able to complain to her friend about Joseph's behavior.

Amunet was again seated beside her in the receiving hall when, on the third day, after his brothers had been dragged out of prison and made to kneel before him, Joseph said to them through the interpreter, "I am a God-fearing man. If you do as I say, you will live. If you really are honest men, choose one of your brothers to remain in prison. The rest of you may go home with grain for your starving families. But you must bring your youngest brother back to me. This will prove that you are telling the truth, and you will not die."

To these terms, the ten men readily agreed, and the profound relief on their faces finally eased the pressure around Asenath's heart. After having seen them all in a dream, she could not help feeling almost a little fond of them, albeit reluctantly. She sensed they were reprimanding themselves for something, but because the interpreter did not bother to translate what the brothers spoke among themselves, she did not find out what they had said until Joseph told her later, apparently reciting their conversation to her word per word as though it had been burned into his memory: "'Clearly we are being punished because of what we did to Joseph long ago. We saw his anguish when he pleaded for his life, but we wouldn't listen. That's why we're in this trouble.' Then Reuben asked, 'Didn't I tell you not to sin against the boy? But you wouldn't listen. And now we have to answer for his blood'!"

She would not soon forget the sight of her beloved husband turning his back on his brothers as they spoke among themselves, unaware Joseph understood them. It was nearly impossible for her to remain seated as she saw the man she loved begin to weep in that silent, stoic way of his, his back held rigid as his eyes stubbornly blinked back tears. Quickly regaining his composure, Joseph once again faced the hall, and pointing at one of his brothers, ordered him tied up right before their eyes. He then stepped off the dais, and calling three servants to him, commanded them to fill the petitioners' sacks with grain, and also to provide them with supplies for their journey home. She later learned that he had already given these same servants instructions to secretly return each brother's payment at the top of his sack.

So the brothers loaded their donkeys with the grain, and once more set their feet to the Horus Road. She was glad to see them go even as she wished the painful matter could have been resolved once and for all. Instead, it was destined to drag on, because as soon as the brothers stopped for the night, and one of them opened his sack to get grain for his donkey, he would find his money in the top of his sack.

That evening, Joseph's expression was so still and distant, she felt him seeing, as though in a waking dream, the actual place where his brothers were camped as he murmured, "Then they will wonder, and say to each other, 'What has God done to us'?"

Chapter 19

A week after his brothers left Rowaty, Joseph decided they should return to Iuno. Asenath found out when Khusebek requested a meeting with her. She quickly wrapped up the game she had been playing with Manasseh, and received the steward in the fragrant shade of her garden pavilion. The news he brought was the best she had heard in a long time. Although she felt more than a little hurt Joseph had not informed her first—as he had always done before—her relief outweighed her concern at this sign the intimacy between them had suffered since his encounter with his brothers. Being physically reunited with his own flesh and blood had profoundly affected him, but because his brothers had not recognized him, the experience was incomplete, and should they never return, it would remain so, a possibility she refused to even contemplate.

She could not, however, stop herself from suffering with, and for, her husband. It did not help to resent him for putting them both in this position, for he had only himself to blame, really. It seemed to her he had treated the situation like a conscious dream, from which he had woken just as he was about to discover something of vital importance. In her opinion, he should have flown directly toward the goal. His brothers were not mere characters in his dream, and now that they had left—and discovered the incriminating money in their packs—she feared they would never willingly return to face the wrath of Kemet's vizier. They had, after all, sacrificed one of their brothers before.

Hesitantly, she said as much to her husband, but instead of remaining furious with his brothers, he became angry with her, which broke the dam of her self control. “Why should I have any faith these men will return?” she demanded. “They already betrayed their own blood once before! And if they don't return, do you intend to leave this one brother of yours in prison forever? If so, then you should at least tell him who you are, so he knows why he will never again see the sun!”

Bending over his wash basin, Joseph splashed water over his face three times, then brusquely dried himself before stating, with contrasting calm, “My faith is in God, and in my father.”

“And my faith is in God, and in you, Joseph!”

“Well, you have a funny way of showing it, Asenath!”

She did not feel she deserved that remark, and it still pained her—like a small but sharp thorn embedded in her domestic contentment, which every day sank a little deeper into her sense of well-being. It was difficult to give Khusebek her full attention as she again relived that scene with her husband.

“There are approximately two dozen jars of wine in the cellar that I believe will benefit from remaining here until such time as you return,” Khusebek was saying. “But there are fifteen jars I recommend you take with you to Iuno. Three are labeled *Year Five. Wine of excellent quality of the House of*

Unasankh of the Western River. Chief Vintner Thethi. Four are labeled-"

"Khusebek, you know more about wine than I do," she interrupted him with a sharpness she immediately regretted, and which further aggravated her unhappiness. She added more mildly, "Please pack the wines you think should be enjoyed sooner. We will make short work of them on the journey, I assure you!"

Holding a palette in one hand and a reed pen in the other, Khusebek boldly regarded her with undisguised sympathy.

Meeting his eyes, she silently encouraged him to express whatever was on his mind.

It came as a painful relief, like the popping of a blister she had been limping on for days, when he said, "The Master has confided in me, Lady" and looking back down at his palette, busied himself marking off certain items as he kindly gave her a moment to absorb his meaning.

Her thoughts were so full of conflicting and confusing emotions, it was a relief to suddenly be offered this living canal into which both her confidences, and Joseph's, might flow freely, which would help keep them united even when the gulf between their experiences made them feel as separate from each other as the two banks of the River.

Asenath suspected one important reason they left Rowaty

was because Joseph could not stand feeling that he was waiting for his brothers to return. His heart was, indeed, waiting, but at least his body could behave otherwise, and its daily needs could be satisfied even more pleasurably in the City of the Sun. Foreigners arriving in Kemet in search of grain would, for a time, be obliged to travel even farther south for their audience with the vizier.

When she asked Khusebek if he had any idea when her husband's brothers might be expected to return—should they do so at all—he shrugged and replied, "Only God knows."

She suspected Joseph had a better idea, but she had made the decision to stop worrying about the matter. It was enough they were back in Iuno, and planning to remain there for longer than they had in years. All, she told herself, was well. Her parents remained in excellent health, both her boys were thriving, her friendship with Amunet deepened with each passing day, and she was increasingly fond of Khusebek, who was now as much her friend as a servant. And most importantly of all, Joseph was behaving like himself again. It was as though he had confined the experience of seeing his brothers again to some corner of his heart, where it remained hidden away like the one brother he had left imprisoned in Rowaty. She knew the man was in good health for Joseph received regular reports from the prison warden.

She hoped, but failed, to conceive another child. Yet she was content, for they were already blessed with two beautiful sons, and there was no denying it was a relief to imagine that the danger and the pain of childbirth was safely behind her, for in less than two years she would be thirty years old. It scarcely seemed possible. It felt like only a moment ago that Joseph had lifted her onto his chariot, and driven them both to the ship waiting to launch them on their new life together.

Time was a mysterious, enchanted and dreadful thing. Time was like the River, which never stopped flowing into the future while never losing touch with its past, for they were one and the same in its life giving water. Some memories were like vividly colorful fish that regularly leaped into her mind, while others she only glimpsed in murky depths whenever a word or incident abruptly illuminated them. She was fortunate to have only three truly painful experiences in her memory basket—the long ago loss of Kyky, and the more recent deaths of her uncle and her dog.

They had been in Iuno for several weeks before Asenath decided it was high time she visit Potifer Setka's offering chapel.

Amunet accompanied her across the River, and the journey by litter into the western desert felt shorter as they busied themselves planning Manasseh's birthday party, determinedly celebrating life even as they made their slow way through the city of the dead. Amunet also helped her carry the generous offerings she had brought for Setka into his public offering chapel, then she retired so that Asenath could be alone with her uncle. Recalling their last dinner together—during which he had confided to her his fear of death—she left behind the wine, bread, beer and flowers she had brought him, and entered the small private room reserved for family members. All the walls around her were exquisitely carved and painted in neat rows consisting of miniature figures of men alternately herding rows of cattle, hauling nets heavy with fish onto boats, or bending at the waist as they harvested bundles of grain. These vibrant scenes of life's bountiful pleasures all led to Potifer Setka, who sat facing them, their lord and master.

Pausing, she admired a smiling young man carrying the entire haunch of a cow in his arms, part of one of the several long processions of male servants walking toward the deceased. It reminded her of how much her uncle had enjoyed how her chef had prepared the beef stew she served him, one of the last dishes they enjoyed together in this life. Joseph had been one of these nameless smiling young men once, a worker on Setka's large estate, which had actually been as prosperous as it was depicted in his tomb. The artist had been a skilled one, for even though the figures on the walls all wore identical smiles, each face was subtly unique.

The one scene in which Setka was shown with his wife—who was seated just behind him, her arms wrapped around his shoulders—was small, and hidden away in a corner. Its position made Asenath smile sadly, and then quickly turn away from it in a vain effort not to confront the questions she had been avoiding, but which were impossible to escape now as the silence of the ancient cemetery pressed insistently against her ears and heart.

Would Joseph desire an eternal home like hers? How would he feel if she had him depicted in her tomb so they could be together forever? Would they be together forever? Did Joseph's people have a special land promised to them by God on the other side of the River? She believed in Elohim now, and prayed to him, but if she chose to be buried in the style and spirit of a daughter of Re, would she be parted from her husband after death? Would the Ba birds of their souls fly away in different directions? She could not continue denying how much it disturbed her how little thought Joseph seemed to give to life after death. It was the only thing about him that truly felt foreign to her. Yet surely the God who took such personal care of his people on this side of the River would not abandon them when it was their time to journey into the land beyond the sunset.

She remembered then—as she had hundreds of times before—the dream she had had shortly before Joseph's release from prison, in which she encountered a man she had thought might be one of Joseph's brothers. She knew now he was not, and there was also no point in denying to herself any longer that this dream man—who had walked across water to her—was even more beautiful than her husband. Standing alone now in her uncle's stone tomb, questions welled up from the depths of her heart she mysteriously found the courage to ask in defiance of the remorseless stillness and silence around her, which implied that all questions had but one terrible answer. Could this man, whose eyes and smile she would never forget, have been Elohim—God revealing Himself to her, letting her see Him, and hear His voice, in a dream? If God spoke to some of Joseph's people when they were both awake and asleep, why was it not possible that, on rare and wondrous occasions, he also chose to speak to her? Yet Joseph had never said anything to her about his people seeing God, only that they sometimes heard his Voice. While this was amazing, she felt it was not enough. One day, she hoped to see the face of God, and since she could not conceive of a countenance more magnificent than that of the most beautiful man, she imagined Elohim would have to look, at least for her, much like the man in her dream.

Having lingered over the paintings and in her own thoughts for as long as possible, she finally went and stood before her uncle's statue house—an enclosed and inaccessible chamber in which Setka stood staring out at her through a narrow aperture in the wall. She knew from having listened to some of her mother's conversations with her brother that he had deliberately chosen to build himself an old-fashioned House of Eternity, for statue houses in tombs were generally no longer in use. If her uncle had once been as slender and fit as his life-size effigy, it must have been before she was born, and in his painted face she detected none of the self-indulgent softness of his living smile.

His statue's eyes gleamed as if with awareness, but in the polished black stones she saw no trace of the dread and hope with which his living eyes had shone the evening he sat across the table from her, staring straight into death's inconceivable face. Setka had always spoken of Joseph's God with respect, for he had been a direct beneficiary of His power, and she was glad now that her beloved uncle had been blessed with a taste of Elohim, if only through the food and wine his Hebrew slave helped provide him with in such pleasurable abundance.

"I love you uncle," she said, braced by the sound of her own voice which, ringing clear and strong in the small chapel, sounded a little like the Voice she sometimes heard in a dream just before she woke up. "We will see each other again one day on the other side of the River. I know we will. God will not abandon us!"

The peacefully smiling statue did not respond with words, but as it stared through her, she suffered the haunting impression that although everyone died alone, it was only together that they would be able to eternally remember having lived and loved. And there was only one place she could think of big enough to fit everyone in the world who had ever been born and would ever be born, a place that was no place and yet also every place that had ever been, was, and could be—God's heart.

After visiting her uncle's offering chapel, Asenath felt mysteriously richer, as if there she had received an invisible gift she opened with every heart beat. Her days glowed with such quiet joy, she no longer felt compelled to try and hold on to them, for they would never, she felt, really be lost but simply transform into even better days sustained by the love she felt for everyone in her life, and for life itself. It no longer saddened her to think of the future, when Manesseh and Ephraim would be grown men living their own lives, apart from hers. It would be a selfish desire on her part to arrest the adventure of their growth, which would always mysteriously be linked with hers. In the treasury of her memory—filled with moments as small and humble as faience beads—there were also many experiences akin to large golden pectorals set with heavy precious stones. One such was the evening when Ephraim, courageously bracing himself on his nurse's arm, managed to stand up straight and, for the first time, run to his mother, who caught him in her arms. His father walked into the room just in time to witness his youngest son's first triumphant steps, and the look in Joseph's eyes as he gazed at them both had helped seal that moment in her heart for eternity. All the demons of the underworld would never be able to wrest that memory from her. When they attempted to barr her way—demanding the incantations and prayers required for her soul to progress as set down in the *Book of Coming Forth By Day and Opening the Tomb*—she would simply call to mind those moments, and break effortlessly through all the supernatural challenges in her path. Just as her son had run to her, she felt her soul would run straight into Elohim's loving embrace. Or so she dared to hope.

In the dead of night, however, her courage was sometimes strained as she found it impossible not to think of Joseph's brother, the one imprisoned back in Rowaty who was, undoubtedly, waiting desperately for his brothers to return, and wake him from the nightmare of his captivity in a strange land. She did not doubt Joseph would eventually free him, one way or the other, yet she selfishly hoped it would not be too soon. It was wonderful living in her hometown. She was grateful to Pharaoh for keeping Joseph busy in Iuno, even if it meant her husband was sometimes late for dinner, or did not arrive at all. The king had enlisted the vizier's help in establishing a new administrative system that would extend throughout the Two Lands. From what Joseph told her, Pharaoh intended to create three divisions—a Waret in the North based in Iuno, a Waret in the South based in Waset, the town of Amun, and a third Waret even further south, at the head of the barren rocky land on either side of the River, where he was already building a series of forts within signaling distance of each other. These eight heavily fortified and manned fortresses would effectively deal with any incursions from the godless people of Kush, decimating their barbaric forces the father north they dared to march. Each Waret was to be administered by a council of senior officials, who in their turn would report to a vizier, all of whom would answer to Pharaoh. Behind high stone walls, the fortresses were populous towns, and in the largest one was located the southern region's administrative center.

Manasseh had heard about Pharaoh's forts from his tutor, and one afternoon he proudly told his parents he was going to become a general when he grew up so he could command one of them. “Each fort has a moat full of crocodiles, so you have to be very careful not to fall off the drawbridge into the water!” he informed them happily. “For my next lesson, Neferu is going to teach me how to draw a catapult!” Raising his skinny right arm, he flung the rock he was holding over the wall dividing one section of the garden from another.

Asenath said indulgently, “Be careful, my love. You don't want to accidentally hit one of the gardeners.”

Joseph smiled, but made no comment.

Recognizing the far away look in his eyes, Asenath did not ask him to share his thoughts with her. She suspected he was thinking of his family, and it was beginning to worry her that the future of her sons might turn out to be as mixed as their blood.

Leaving Iuno again was like reluctantly waking from a long and fully conscious dream. Asenath had known it would happen sooner than later, and she felt refreshed, even invigorated after more than a year free of travel. Nevertheless, departing from her hometown was akin to dragging herself out of a comfortable bed where she would have preferred to linger at least a little longer.

Their ships formed part of an even greater fleet, for Pharaoh and his vizier were sailing north together. She often missed the old king, the pharaoh she had grown up with who had gotten on well with all his Nomarchs, and who had been content to allow neighboring countries to do as they pleased as long as their presence in Kemet was motivated by friendly trade. His son and successor could not have proved more different. Perhaps because he was so tall, it was impossible for the current king not to look down at everyone else, and he seemed to be of the opinion that arrogance and inflexibility were the mental and emotional equivalents of physical height and strength. She could appreciate the safety of Kemet motivated and informed all his actions, but she also did not doubt that his virile restlessness was responsible for the pleasure he took in strengthening and growing the army with which he intended to penetrate, and force into submission, the southern lands as soon as his frontier fortresses were completed.

It was difficult for her to discern exactly how Joseph felt about Pharaoh. She knew her husband admired the king on many levels, and on the evenings they dined alone together, she enjoyed listening to him tell her about his day. At times, however, he seemed almost to be speaking to himself, unaware she was absorbing all he said. Like seeds he absently tossed her way, his words were sprouting in Asenath a greater appreciation for the complexity of the society into which she had been born, and whose strengths and pleasures she had always taken for granted. She began to understand that, by preparing for war, Pharaoh was also encouraging the growth of trade. Senwosret took a special interest in craftsmen, especially the royal sculptors, and had even set a trend—which initially shocked many people—by having himself portrayed looking just as he actually did rather than in an idealized fashion. The heavy black granite statues he had carved of himself were only as tall as he truly was, and their stone faces wore his customary stern and unsmiling expression.

The procession of ships and boats crowding the River were all bound for Rowaty, where Pharaoh would be erecting a personal temple to Osiris boasting a tall granite gate and a columned chapel. Asenath found this desire of his pleasing, for it would balance the presence of Set's temple in the city. The king undoubtedly had other motives for traveling north with his vizier to which she was not privy, and did not much care about, for it was Joseph's reasons that concerned her. If his brothers intended to return, it would have to be soon. They had failed to show up in Iuno, where officials had orders to immediately inform the vizier whenever Hebrew men arrived in the city hoping to buy grain.

With both Pharaoh and the vizier in residence, the palace in Rowaty, along with the surrounding buildings and villas, were as crowded as Re's beehives. The king, and the one wife he had brought with him, were naturally occupying the royal apartments. More than ever, Asenath was grateful for Amunet's presence in her life, for when they attended the young queen, her friend took it upon herself to keep the conversation going. She found herself thinking—as she studied the delicate features and wide black eyes of Senwosret's bride—that Neferthenut was a little afraid of her husband, who could easily have broken her wrist with one hand. In private, she and Amunet shared more than one laugh trying to picture how the king and his queen managed to come together as man and woman considering their great difference in height. It was almost like trying to imagine a bull mating with a cat.

It was this silly conversation the steward interrupted by suddenly appearing in the doorway of the house overlooking the shady pavilion where she and Amunet were sitting, and announcing breathlessly, as if he had run all the way there, "They have returned!"

Rising, Asenath commanded, "Fetch my litter!"

"The Master has already seen them. They have brought their younger brother with them, just as he instructed them to. They will be eating with him this noon. He ordered me to slaughter an animal, and prepare a big feast. Then he told me to take them into the palace, but his brothers were afraid to enter. I heard them whispering to each other, 'It's because of the money someone put in our sacks last time we were here! He plans to pretend we stole it! He'll seize us, make us slaves, and take our donkeys!' Then they approached me and said, 'Sir, we came to Kemet once before to buy food. But as we were returning home, we stopped for the night and opened our sacks, where we discovered that each man's money—the exact amount paid—was in the top of his sack! Here it is! We have brought the money back with us. We also have additional money to buy more food. We have no idea who put our money in our sacks'! But I said to them, 'Relax. Don't be afraid. Your God, the God of your father, must have put this treasure into your sacks. I know I received your payment.' After that, I went to the prison, and had the brother they left behind released, and brought him out to them. I then led them to the Master's private waiting room, and left them there. Now I'm on my way to fetch water for them to wash their feet with."

"Thank you, Khusebek! I will be quick!" Feeling a little sick with anxiety and excitement, she turned to Amunet. "I must know what is happening. Have my attendants pour me a bath while you lay out my finest dress and gems. I will return shortly."

"Yes, my Lady." Amunet followed her into the house, remaining in the bedroom while Asenath quickly procured a large wooden key from one of her chests, and hurried down the hall. She made several turns before coming to a narrow door. She ran into no one on her way, which meant Khusebek had already routed most of the servants to the kitchens. Pausing to take a deep and steadying breath, she inserted the key into the lock, and lifted it upward. When she heard the internal pins fall, she quickly pushed open the door, and entered a space as small as the statue house in her uncle's tomb.

Her pulse quickening at the sound of male voices, she silently closed and locked the door behind her before stepping over to the only illumination in the stuffy space. The light came from a tiny circular opening in the wall on her left. Slowly, she positioned her right eye over the hole.

In the much larger room beyond, Joseph's brothers were standing close together, alternately looking around them, and talking quietly. The man she had focused on in her dream, the one with the striking blue eyes, stood as if protectively beside the youngest member of the group, who she had never seen before. He was a handsome youth about twenty five years old, and he bore such a striking resemblance to Joseph, her heart stumbled over its swift beats like two feet instantly taking her back to the rooftop from which she and Kyky had secretly observed him. This man had to be Joseph's youngest brother, born of the same mother, Rachel, Jacob's most beloved wife. She stared in fascination at his face, partially concealed behind a short black beard. His eyes were arresting, a lighter brown than Joseph's, or perhaps they only appeared that way because he was looking around him, and as a consequence reflecting all the lamplight in the room. He was not smiling, and she did not blame him. The situation was too serious and strange, the outcome dangerously uncertain. And yet beneath his dusty white robe his shoulders appeared relaxed, as if he was more intrigued by this adventure than worried. Just by looking at him, she was certain his father doted on him, and probably spoiled him as he had Joseph.

The door to the room in which the men stood opened, and Khusebek walked in at the head of a procession of male servants carrying basins, pitchers of water, and clean linen towels.

"I have provided food for your donkeys," Khusebek informed the tense group. "And here is fresh water for you to wash your feet and hands. You will be dining with my Master at noon. I will return for you when it is time."

As soon as the door closed behind the steward, the brothers quickly did as he had instructed. Their faces grave, they removed their sandals, bathed their leathery feet and hands, and thoroughly dried them. Then they opened the packs they had brought with them, and rummaged in them for small items they quickly unwrapped, and held onto like protective talismans. It was not until the youngest among them looked down to admire what he was holding in his hands that she realized they had brought gifts with them.

Asenath was wondering if she should return to her room, and begin dressing for the feast, when the door to the room in which the men stood opened again, and Joseph strode in. The contrast between his smooth bare chest and beardless face, framed by two black wings of hair tucked neatly behind his ears, was even more striking in such close proximity to the travel soiled robes and untrimmed beards of his brothers, who all quickly, with a desperation tempered by pride, offered him the presents they had brought him. Khusebek, who had entered the room behind his master, collected the gifts, handing them over to servants waiting out in the hall, after which he closed the door behind him, leaving the vizier alone with his guests, who had all bowed low before him.

Joseph waited until they straightened up to face him before asking in a firm but civil voice, "How is your father, the old man you spoke about? Is he still alive?"

The man with the blue eyes replied, "Yes. Our father, your servant, is alive and well." And then they all bowed low again.

Staring at the newcomer, Joseph said, "Is this your youngest brother, the one you told me about? May God be gracious to you, my son." Then abruptly, he hurried from the room without excusing himself.

Understanding that her husband had been overcome with emotion, Asenath's first impulse was to follow him. But as she turned away from her peep hole, she heard a key thrust into the lock, and the door opened, admitting a refreshing gust of air into the stuffy space along with Joseph, who kicked the door shut behind him and, apparently blinded by tears, walked straight into her arms.

"It's all right!" she whispered. "It's all right!"

He did not inquire how she came to be there but simply clung to her as he wept silently, burying his face in her hair.

With her cheek pressed against his chest, the only sound in the world for her was the thudding of his heart as she felt it costing him all the control he possessed not to sob out loud. Every thought flowed out of her mind on his tears, which the soft depths of her hair helped absorb and wipe away.

Regaining control of himself, he pulled away from her gently but firmly. Still without saying a word, he stepped around her to the small table at the back of the room, on which sat a basin of water. Quickly, he washed and dried his face.

She whispered, "I love you!" afraid he might be angry with her for eavesdropping.

His response was to grip and squeeze her hand in passing. She did not put her eye back to the peephole, but she clearly heard it when he reentered the room beyond, and ordered in a loud voice, "Bring out the food!" at which point she hurried out of the secret room to make sure he was obeyed.

Chapter 20

Notice was never too short when a feast was concerned. The dining hall was full of guests—various important officials and scribes who worked closely with Joseph every day, accompanied by their wives. Asenath also spotted a handful of noblemen and ladies attached to Pharaoh's court she suspected had not been invited, but had simply wandered in curiously, confident they would be seated near the dais even if it meant other people had to be displaced. Entering the room from behind the dais with Amunet, Asenath heard no laughter, and few heads turned in their direction. She was disappointed when even Joseph did not glance her way, for she had taken great care with her appearance, hoping he would be proud to show off to his brothers the beautiful wife God had blessed him with. But no one seemed to notice her as, accompanied by her handmaiden, she took her place at a small table to the left of the vizier. Everyone was staring at the table of unclean Hebrews shockingly placed in the position of honor at the foot of the dais.

When a serving man filled her cup with wine, Asenath concentrated on drinking while Amunet remarked on the impressive variety of delicious dishes. But this was like no banquet ever before held in Kemet, for Joseph instructed the servants to fill the empty plates of his brothers with food from his own table, a public gesture of esteem that shocked everyone, including his wife. And he gave his youngest brother five times as much as he gave the others.

Fortunately, the wine flowed freely as always, and it was not long before she sensed the mood of their guests mellowing from appalled distaste to intrigued curiosity. Gradually, the presence of bearded foreigners became more of an entertaining mystery than an offense as people tried to guess who the strangers were, and why they were occupying seats of honor. She wondered how many guessed correctly—that these men were related by blood to Pharaoh's right hand man.

She felt it certainly worked in their favor that the youngest of the Hebrews—who the vizier clearly honored over all the others—comported himself with the smiling dignity of a visiting prince, breaking his bread with a patience that was positively elegant compared with the ravenous way his older brothers attacked their food. When he sampled certain dishes he particularly enjoyed, his smile reached all the way to his eyes, so that his delight became its own spice to Asenath as she observed him, her appreciation of the cuisine enhanced by his. He gave no indication of being surprised by the special treatment he was receiving from the vizier, and she was increasingly certain Jacob had spoiled him as much, or even more, than he had Joseph. His older brothers, on the other hand, were obviously disconcerted by the highly peculiar situation they found themselves in, and their fixed concentration on the food gave her the impression they feared this might be the last meal of their lives.

The more she studied the young Benjamin—for so she heard him addressed—the more Asenath felt herself dreaming while awake. The exemplary vintage Khusebek had provided for the feast had something to do with it, as did the implausible sight of a group of bearded Men of the Donkey occupying places of honor in a banquet hall of Kemet. This fact alone was reason enough to believe she was dreaming, but it was Benjamin who especially made her feel this way, for he gave the mysterious impression of already being somewhere else. Perhaps it was the wine, but he seemed to her like a bird that had surprisingly landed right in front of her, so that for a few heartbeats she enjoyed the pleasure of being so close to him. Until he turned his head, and spotting her presence, immediately flew away. So she felt the one time Benjamin looked up at her. He had not intended to look at her, she just happened to be near where his body had landed, and when he quickly looked away, she sensed that anything he might have thought about her had already flown from his mind because she was not of the chosen flock. Asenath distinctly felt that to Benjamin, she was simply a feature of the landscape, whereas he and his people were blessed by God's breath uplifting the beating wings of their hearts.

She turned her attention longingly to Joseph, and felt herself made human again when he picked up the silver wine cup she had given him for his birthday, raised it in her direction, and waited for her to follow suit so they could drink together.

☼

That evening, Joseph issued these instructions to his chief steward: "When my brothers are ready to leave tomorrow at dawn, fill each of their sacks with as much grain as they can carry, and put each man's money back into his sack. Then put my personal silver cup at the top of the youngest brother's sack, along with the money for his grain."

After Khusebek left, Asenath asked her husband, "Why are you giving them your silver cup, Joseph? That cup was a gift from me to you! I filled that cup with all my love for you, and now you are pouring it out, and giving your cup away as if it is merely just a cup?" The tears burning in her eyes overflowed their banks, and the pain in her heart was suddenly so great, she did not think she could survive it. Then she felt another much lesser pain when he gripped both her hands in his, and squeezed them so hard she winced.

"Once my brothers are on their way, after they have gone only a short distance and are barely out of the city," he explained quietly, "I will have Khusebek chase after them, and stop them. When he catches up with them, he will ask them, 'Why have you repaid my kindness with such evil? Why have you stolen my master's silver cup, which he uses to predict the future? What a wicked thing you have done'!"

She laughed. "To predict the future?"

"A future without love is no future at all, my Asenath."

The following morning, Khusebek caught up with Joseph's brothers after they had gone only a short way on the Horus Road, and spoke to them as he had been instructed. The steward then quickly returned to the palace to give his report to Joseph, who was in the garden perfuming his mouth with Asenath.

"When I accused them of stealing your silver cup, which you use to predict the future," Khusebek said, his tone carefully neutral beneath the amused gleam in his eyes, "they replied, 'What are you talking about? We are your servants and would never do such a thing! Didn't we return the money we found in our sacks? We brought it back all the way from the land of Canaan. Why would we steal silver or gold from your master's house? If you find his cup with any one of us, let that man die! And all the rest of us, my lord, will be your slaves!' To which I responded, 'That's fair, but only the one who stole the cup will be my slave. The rest of you may go free.' Then they all quickly took their sacks from the backs of their donkeys and opened them. I searched your brothers' sacks, from the oldest to the youngest, just as you had instructed, and found the cup in Benjamin's sack, where I had put it. When they saw this, they tore their clothing in despair. I left them reloading their donkeys, and returned to the city straight away."

"Thank you, Khusebek." Rising, Joseph offered Asenath his hand. "I expect they will be arriving soon. Take them to the receiving hall where I'm scheduled to meet this morning with craftsmen working on Pharaoh's temple to Osiris."

After Khusebek had bowed and departed—the grin that possessed his face as he turned away revealing how much he was enjoying himself at the expense of his fellow countrymen —Asenath declared, "I'm coming with you, Joseph."

"Of course you are," he retorted, and slapped her backside with his right hand as if to send her running ahead of him. On that occasion, the playful gesture proved almost painful, which alerted her to how tense he was feeling.

Kemet's supreme vizier was seated in his gilded throne on the dais when his brothers arrived, and promptly fell to the floor before him.

"What have you done?" Joseph's angry voice echoed through the hall, which instantly grew as silent as it was breathtakingly hot. "Don't you know that a man like me can predict the future?"

Sitting alone in her usual place against the wall, Asenath hid a smile behind her fan.

Communicating through the interpreter, the brother named Judah answered desperately, "Oh, my lord, what can we say to you? How can we explain this? How can we prove our innocence? God is punishing us for our sins. My lord, we have all returned to be your slaves—all of us, not just our brother who had your cup in his sack."

His hands tightly gripping the golden paws of his throne,

Joseph waited until the interpreter had finished speaking before he said, "No. I would never do such a thing! Only the man who stole the cup will be my slave. The rest of you may go back to your father in peace."

The interpreter was still translating Joseph's response when Judah dared to gain his feet and took a step forward. "Please, my lord, let your servant say just one word to you. Please, do not be angry with me, even though you are as powerful as Pharaoh himself. My lord, previously you asked us, your servants, 'Do you have a father or a brother?' And we responded, 'Yes, my lord, we have a father who is an old man, and his youngest son is a child of his old age. His full brother is dead, and he alone is left of his mother's children, and his father loves him very much.'

He paused so the interpreter could convey his words to Joseph, and as he did so, Asenath sensed her husband's growing impatience with this delay.

"And you said to us, my lord," Judah went on, 'Bring him here so I can see him with my own eyes.' But we said to you, 'My lord, the boy cannot leave his father, for his father would die.' But you told us, 'Unless your youngest brother comes with you, you will never see my face again.' So we returned to your servant, our father, and told him what you had said. Later, when he said, 'Go back again and buy us more food,' we replied, 'We can't go unless you let our youngest brother go with us. We'll never get to see the man's face unless our youngest brother is with us.' Then my father said to us, 'As you know, my wife had two sons, and one of them went away and never returned. Doubtless he was torn to pieces by some wild animal. I have never seen him since. Now if you take his brother away from me, and any harm comes to him, you will send this grieving, white-haired man to his grave.'

"So now, my lord, I cannot go back to my father without the boy. Our father's life is bound up in the boy's life. If he sees the boy is not with us, our father will die. We, your servants, will indeed be responsible for sending that grieving, white-haired man to his grave. My lord, I guaranteed to my father that I would take care of the boy. I told him, 'If I don't bring him back to you, I will bear the blame forever.' So please, my lord, let me stay here as a slave instead of the boy, and let the boy return with his brothers. For how can I return to my father if the boy is not with me? I couldn't bear to see the anguish this would cause my father!"

Rising and looking around him at all the scribes, craftsmen and officials, and finally directly down at the royal interpreter, Joseph commanded, "Out! All of you!"

For a heartbeat, no one moved, but then as if suddenly seeing a lion where only a moment ago had sat a pampered cat, they all hurried from the hall.

With only her eyes visible over her fan, Asenath remained motionless as a lioness hidden in the underbrush. She had long hungered for this day, which was all about the power of blood.

She did not need to understand the words to experience the moment when Joseph told his brothers who he was, after which he broke down and wept, a universal language. He sobbed so loudly, she was sure all the men waiting outside the hall could hear him, and did not doubt word of the vizier's breakdown would swiftly reach Pharaoh. Meanwhile, Joseph's brothers simply stood staring at him, as if they had been struck dead by the lightning bolt of this revelation and become statues in a shared tomb.

☼

Khusebek had been one of the men waiting just outside the hall when Joseph revealed his identity to his brothers, and though he was a Hebrew, Hathor had seen fit to endow him with large ears as sharp as a dog's, while Thoth had chosen to gift him with an exceptional memory, so that he was later able to describe to Asenath all she had seen but not understood with words. “Your husband said to his brothers, 'I am Joseph!' But his brothers were speechless! They were stunned to realize Joseph was standing right there in front of them. 'Please, come closer,' he said to them. So they came closer. And he told them again, 'I am Joseph, your brother, whom you sold into slavery in Kemet. But don’t be upset, and don’t be angry with yourselves for selling me to this place. It was God who sent me here ahead of you to preserve your lives. This famine, which has ravaged the land for two years, will last five more years, and there will be neither plowing nor harvesting. God has sent me ahead of you to keep you and your families alive, and to preserve many survivors. So it was God who sent me here, not you! And He is the one who made me an adviser to Pharaoh—the manager of his entire palace and the governor of all Kemet.

"'Now hurry back to my father and tell him, 'This is what your son Joseph says: God has made me master over all the land of Kemet. So come down to me immediately! You can live in the region of Rowaty, where you can be near me with all your children and grandchildren, your flocks and herds, and everything you own. I will take care of you here, for there are still five years of famine ahead of us. Otherwise you, your household, and all your animals will starve. Look! You can see for yourselves, and so can my brother Benjamin, that I really am Joseph! Go tell my father of my honored position here in Kemet. Describe for him everything you have seen, and then bring my father here quickly'."

Khusebek fell silent, but she knew the rest. Weeping with joy, Joseph had embraced Benjamin, and Benjamin had hugged him back fiercely. Then Joseph had kissed each of his brothers, and wept over them. After that, they all began talking freely with him, at which point she had thought it best to slip away unseen. Stiff from sitting for so long, her legs were also weak with relief that it was finally all over—the truth had been exposed and Maat was smiling down upon all of them. But knowing now what Joseph had told his brothers to do, anxiety and jealousy began floating like oils over the clear deep water of relief that had washed over her in the receiving hall watching the man she loved at long last remove the thorn lodged so painfully in his heart. She now realized, however, that in the future, she would be sharing Joseph's heart not just with their sons but with his entire family, to whom she was the only one not related by blood.

The news had indeed quickly reached Pharaoh that Joseph's brothers had arrived. The foreigners the vizier had honored at his feast yesterday had been observed leaving the city early that morning, heading east on the Horus road, but were then later seen returning, and this fact—coupled with Joseph's emotional breakdown in the receiving hall—left no one in doubt as to their identity.

From Joseph, Asenath learned what Pharaoh had said to him when he summoned him, "Tell your brothers, 'This is what you must do: Load your pack animals, and hurry back to the land of Canaan. Then get your father and all of your families, and return here to me. I will give you the very best land in Kemet, and you will eat from the best that the land produces. Then tell your brothers, 'Take wagons from the land of Kemet to carry your little children and your wives, and bring your father here. Don't worry about your personal belongings, for the best of all the land of Kemet is yours'."

The following day, Joseph provided his brothers with wagons, as Pharaoh had commanded, and gave them supplies for the journey. He also gave each of them new clothes, but to Benjamin he gave five changes of clothes and three-hundred pieces of silver. He sent his father ten male donkeys loaded with the finest products of Kemet, and ten female donkeys loaded with grain and bread and other supplies he would need on his journey. So Joseph sent his brothers off, and as they left, he called after them, “Don’t quarrel about all this along the way!”

Chapter 21

Her eyes closed and her head resting on Joseph's chest, Asenath listened to his breathing slowing and deepening, until she felt herself drifting off with him, her awareness riding the gentle rhythm through dark yet wondrous depths she knew had the potential to become dream scenes she might be able to step into...

Fully waking a short time later, she rolled over, and sank into a restless slumber. In the morning, she remembered only a handful of vaguely stressful dreams.

With Pharaoh's consent, they remained in Rowaty, where Joseph supervised the construction of the king's new temple, in addition to performing his other duties. Having no idea how long it would take his brothers to reach their home and collect their father, all their wives, sons, daughters and possessions before setting off again—probably many months—Asenath resigned herself to waiting, glad for this final quiet time alone with her husband. It was much more unsettling than exciting preparing for an inundation of relatives she could not imagine immersing herself in on a daily basis.

She sensed Joseph was aware of her unease, yet though he spoke no words of reassurance to her, his expressive eyes let her know he perceived the conflicting emotions flowing beneath her loving smile, and his lingering kisses went a long way to making her feel everything would be just fine. Perhaps his silence on the subject was wise, and he was acting like a good ship's captain steering well clear of the sandbanks of her doubts and fears. Of all the people in the world, she felt only Joseph could truly plumb the depths of her heart, and when they were lying together in bed, it was impossible to believe anything, or anyone, could ever come between them.

And then one blessedly cool afternoon, much sooner than she would have thought possible, Joseph's brother, Judah, arrived at the palace. Jacob had sent him ahead to get directions. Considering that his sons had already made the journey twice, she guessed Jacob had actually wished to send word to Joseph that he was on his way.

Several days later, a scout dispatched by the vizier reported that a large caravan of Hebrews had been spotted less than half a day's walk from the city. Joseph immediately prepared his chariot, and traveled to meet his father. Asenath watched him go, and remained standing on the palace steps even after his tall body was obscured by a cloud of dust. She was remembering the morning—which still felt like only yesterday—when she had ridden beside him in his chariot to the ship that set them on the course of their life together. That same ship had brought her here, to this moment. She turned back toward the palace feeling more alone than she ever had before.

That same night, however, in the blessed privacy of their bed, Joseph's arms holding her close, she forgot that chilling sense of isolation as he described to her how he had leaped off his chariot, and run to embrace his father. He told her how he had wept, and when he finally let go of his father, how Jacob had said to him, "'Now I am ready to die, since I have seen your face again and know you are still alive'."

Supervised by Khusebek, the palace servants prepared rooms for Jacob and Benjamin, and Benjamin's wives and children. The other Hebrew men, with their wives and children—all looking extremely tired where they sat huddled together on the wagons Pharaoh had provided for them—were settled with their personal belongings in small one-story houses Joseph had ordered constructed on the western end of the existing city, adjacent to verdant grazing grounds into which all their livestock was herded.

So it was that Jacob and his entire family came to Kemet, sons and grandsons, daughters and granddaughters—all his descendants.

The rising sun was gilding the tops of the tallest date palms when Asenath met a man God had spoken to. The flowerbeds were still in shadow, and her bare feet were cold on the stone walkway as—clutching her cloak tensely around her—she approached the two tall figures. Joseph and his father were framed by the pavilion beneath with they stood facing each other, deep in a conversation even the birds seemed to respect, for the hushed silence around her remained dream like. And, in truth, it was a dream to be approaching a man who not only believed in God, but who knew, beyond any doubt, God truly existed, for Elohim had personally spoken to him, as well as to his father and his mother.

Walking slowly and silently, she wondered if Joseph had told his father about her dreams, and that she also believed God had spoken to her when she was mysteriously awake in her sleep. She fervently hoped he had, for she would not dare bring the subject up herself. It would seem presumptuous, as was approaching them now without their knowledge. But she had been too excited and impatient to wait to be formally introduced to Jacob later that morning along with her sons, during which an adult conversation about God and dreams would not have been possible. She could also wait no longer to see herself in Jacob's eyes. She was afraid she might feel as she had when Benjamin looked at her—like both a threat and a non-entity. Not only was she a female, she was a daughter of Re, and it was a well known fact the women of the Retjenu did not possess as many rights under the law as the women of Kemet.

The two men were so engrossed in each other, she was less than a body's length away from them before Joseph sensed her presence, and Jacob followed his gaze.

Her fists already clenched over her heart to keep her cloak around her, she inclined her head respectfully. Then she met

Jacob's eyes and said, "Like running feet, my heart would not let me stay in bed this morning, for it could scarcely wait for the joy of meeting my husband's father, and wishing him—as well as all his loved ones—life, health and strength in their new home." She inclined her head again, and her heart pounded several times beneath her hands before she dared look up again.

Jacob was staring down at his own bare feet, one of his arms supported by Joseph, who was helping him step slowly down off the pavilion.

When he was standing before her, the patriarch extended both his hands with the palms facing upward. "Daughter," he said. His low voice was gravely with age, yet there was a smooth force in its depths that reminded her of how huge blocks of stone are moved across wet sand.

"Father!" Relief rang in her voice as she placed her hands in his.

He smiled down at her. His thin mouth was framed by a beard that in the soft morning light appeared smoother, finer and whiter than the most expensive mist linen. It hung down over his chest far more richly than the brown tunic beneath it, from the sleeves of which emerged wrists nearly as thin as hers. But his hands were large, and their grip firm. "My son was just singing your praises, Asenath. I understand you are also a dreamer."

"Yes, father, I am."

"And the daughter of the high priest of Re."

"Yes, but but when I was still a child, Joseph told me about Elohim, and I came to believe in Him." She glanced at her husband for support, but he was looking at Jacob. "It is to God Almighty I pray, and I feel He truly listens to me."

Jacob released her hands. "Then I will also share with you the dream I just told my son, the dream I had on my way here to Kemet."

"Please sit down, father," Joseph urged, and gently taking the old man's arm again, led him back up the steps into the pavilion, where he helped him sit down before he himself perched on an adjoining stool.

Following the men, Asenath chose to kneel before them, her heart as warm in her chest now as the morning was cold against her flesh.

Jacob's eyes—small, black and bright as a bird's in a fine nest of wrinkles decades in the making—stared over her head as he spoke. "When we came to Beersheba," he said, "I offered sacrifices to the God of my father, Isaac, and during the night, God spoke to me in a vision.

"'Jacob! Jacob!' he called.

"'Here I am,' I replied.

"'I am God, the God of your father,' the voice said. 'Do not be afraid to go down to Kemet, for there I will make your family into a great nation. I will go with you down to Kemet, and I will bring you back again. You will die in Kemet, but Joseph will be with you to close your eyes'."

When he stopped speaking, Asenath exhaled the breath she would have been happy to hold for much longer. It was not surprising Joseph would outlive his father, and Jacob had indeed arrived safely in Kemet with all his people, who she did not doubt would flourish here in the Two Lands once the late pharaoh's dreams were fulfilled, and the famine ended. What she did not want to understand was what God had meant when he said to Jacob, "And I will bring you back again." But it was clear enough. Jacob would die here, but his people—by then greatly increased in numbers and strength—would one day leave Kemet and return to their own land, the land promised them by God, who would personally lead them there.

Abruptly, she wished she had stayed in bed. Hearing God's words before breakfast was not necessarily good for the appetite. She felt weak and helpless as she wondered just how long the Hebrews would remain in Kemet, for whenever they left, Joseph would go with them. Kneeling there, she knew all this would happen, and that she was not only powerless to prevent it, it was wrong to want to. For it was the will of God Almighty, who she had come to believe in and to trust even more than she did her own heart. It seemed that her beloved Two Lands were only the breasts destined to nourish God's people, until the time came for them to lead a life of their own elsewhere. She could only pray, as she did now fervently, a great many years would pass before God fulfilled His promise, and that by then she would be dead. Because she knew—as surely as she knew Joseph was taking her hand now to help her rise, and then letting go of it so he could walk beside his father —that she would never leave her homeland.

☼

For the rest of the day, Asenath—already aware of her husband's intention—entertained herself helping Khusebek arrange the evening's celebratory feast at which Joseph, standing before them all holding the silver cup she had given him, said to his brothers, "I will go to Pharaoh and tell him, 'My brothers, and my father's entire family, have come to me from the land of Canaan. These men are shepherds, and they raise livestock. They have brought with them their flocks and herds and everything they own'."

Shortly afterward, he said privately to Jacob and his sons, who were all sitting at tables on the dais with him, "When Pharaoh calls for you, and asks you about your occupation, you must tell him, 'We, your servants, have raised livestock all our lives, as our ancestors have always done.' When you tell him this, he will let you live here in the region of Rowaty, for the people of Kemet despise shepherds."

A week later, Asenath once again found herself onboard the vizier's ship with Joseph. Manesseh and Ephraim—who would be dropped off in Iuno with their grandparents—were following them on their own boat, behind which sailed another ship containing five of Joseph's brothers, as well as his father,

Jacob. They were bound south for the royal capital to be officially presented to Pharaoh.

Alone with Joseph in the ship's cabin, their naked bodies rocking together, she was temporarily able to forget all about God's promise to Jacob. She could not remember ever being so desperately hungry for Joseph's flesh. Merely caressing him was not enough. She longed to feel every part of him against her. She had to kiss him, and lick him, and even scratch him, running her nails down the length of his back in a frenzy of lust worthy of Sekhmet the lioness.

"That hurts!" he protested, his breath hot in her ear as he rolled over onto his injured back, so that she was now on top of him. But this only exposed his chest to her fierce hunger.

"I love you!" she cried, her tone accusing. "I love you!"

"Do you?" He trapped both her wrists in his hands. "Then why are you trying to skin me alive?"

Not knowing the answer, she struggled to break free of his hold.

"Asenath..."

"Let go of me!"

"No. Not until you tell me what's wrong."

She said flatly, "I love you too much" and ceased struggling.

"Come here..." He drew her down into his arms.

Sekhmet at once transformed into a kitten as she curled up against him, and thinking out loud murmured, "Passion is of the blood, but love flows from the heart."

"And it is death to separate them," he caressed her hair as he spoke, "for blood flows through the heart."

"The priests of Anubis drain the body of all its blood, but the heart—the center of all intelligence and feeling—is left in the body. In the afterlife, we will have our heart to love with and to think with, but how can we experience passion without our blood?"

He replied lightly "We aren't mummies yet."

"So you intend to be mummified, and buried in a House of Eternity?"

"Yes."

For a profoundly sweet moment, she was at last free to anticipate their adjoining tombs.

"Mummification is the best way," he went on, "to ensure something remains of me when God comes to lead my people out of Kemet. God will bring them back to the land He solemnly promised to give to Abraham, to Isaac, and to my father, Jacob. When I am an old man, I will make the sons of my people swear an oath. I will tell them, 'When God comes to help you and lead you back, you must take my bones with you'."

Asenath rolled away from him onto her back feeling as desolate as if she was already lying in her own lonely tomb in the desert, where at night all her dead ears would hear would be the howling of hungry jackals.

Joseph soon fell asleep, but it did not matter, for there was nothing more to be said. Even if they were buried in adjoining Houses of Eternity, he would still be leaving her one day. It did not help to tell herself she was being silly, behaving like a child confusing her two favorite dolls with the people they represented, for only their bodies would be lying in the tombs, not their souls. It also did not help to tell herself that her husband understood this, and had no idea how much he had hurt her by telling her he had every intention of abandoning her here, in the country of her birth, while he left for the land God had promised his people.

"But not to me," she whispered. "Not to me."

☼

Asenath was in one of the royal palace's private receiving rooms—sitting beside Queen Sithathor, who was enthroned just behind and to the left of Pharaoh—when Joseph told the king, "My father and my brothers have arrived from the land of Canaan. They have come with all their flocks and herds and possessions, and are staying in the region of Rowaty."

Just returned from fishing in the lake, Senwosret sat relaxed in his chair, his legs outstretched, the hard lines of his face softened somewhat by the lingering rosy kiss of sunlight reflected off water. But now he sat up a little as he studied the row of Hebrew men standing behind Joseph, all of whom wore new robes and were clean shaven. "What is your occupation?" he asked them.

Judah replied, “We, your servants, are shepherds, just like our ancestors. We have come to live here in Kemet for a while, for there is no pasture for our flocks in Canaan. The famine is very severe there.”

Relaxing in his throne again, Pharaoh said to Joseph, “Now that your father and brothers have joined you here, choose any place in the entire land of Kemet for them to live. Give them the best land of Kemet. Let them live in the region of Rowaty. And if any of them have special skills, put them in charge of my livestock as well.”

Sithathor whispered in her ear, “He is always thinking of himself.”

Joseph bowed to Pharaoh. Then striding to the door, he opened it, led in his father, and presented him to Pharaoh. Jacob had not shaved, but a quick glance at the king's face told Asenath he shared her admiration of the old man's beard, which in the generous lamplight shone regal as a banner proclaiming the mysterious strength and wisdom of his great age.

Raising his right hand, Jacob silently blessed Pharaoh.

“How old are you?” Senwosret asked him curiously.

“I have traveled this earth for one-hundred and thirty hard years,” Jacob replied. “But my life has been short compared to the lives of my ancestors.”

Sithathor whispered in her ear again, “One-hundred and thirty?! My brother will definitely want to know his secret!”

But only moments later the audience ended, and Asenath

soon found herself alone again with her old friend. The queen dismissed her attendants, and curling up on her favorite couch, gestured for Asenath to do the same on the couch opposite her as she said, “I'm sorry I haven't written you in so long, honey. I simply didn't have anything new to report. I continue struggling to stay out of the deep gulf of darkness!”

Asenath had no idea what to say. Her friend had apparently suffered some rude awakening from her dreamy, dangerous love affairs, and now felt trapped in the sterile reality of her circumstances. For most women, her exalted position as a queen was itself a dream come true, but for her it was a nightmare of loneliness.

Gazing down at her hands, her head slightly cocked as if she did not quite recognize them, Sithathor confessed quietly, “Sometimes, I feel the darkness encroaching all around me, as if it were more hungry than I am myself. And waiting as long as it can, it will swallow me whole without me even knowing. But despite suspicions of lurking oblivion, pressing on one moment to the next is how this phantom of my self has sewn the 'hem of this address. That is to say, I'm just clearing my throat here. A-hem! Get it?” She smiled sadly.

“Yes, I get it. Very clever words for a phantom, my queen.”

“Yes. Just imagine what I'll be capable of when I become a shining Akh, possessed of all the powers of my Ka. I promise I'll send my Ba bird into your dreams with many messages for you from the beyond, which will arrive in a heart beat!”

“You look perfectly healthy to me, my queen.”

“Stop calling me that!” Sighing, she began playing with one of her bracelets. “I'm still just Sithathor to you, please.”

“Of course you are, but you are also a queen, and fortunate enough to know you will be buried under the protective wing of your beloved father's pyramid, surrounded by the rest of your family, near the home in which you all lived and loved, and not in some lonely little tomb all by yourself!”

“Honey?!” As lithely as a cat, Sithathor uncurled herself off her couch and came to sit beside her. “What's this all about? What's wrong? Are you crying? Talk to me, sweetie.”

By the time she returned to her own rooms, Asenath felt much better for having shared, as best she could, many of the thoughts and feelings which had flowed through her heart ever since Joseph's brothers first arrived in Rowaty in search of grain to feed themselves and their starving families. And it seemed to her that Sithathor was also in better spirits after listening to her in compassionate silence, and speaking only to ask questions that would help her better understand what her friend was going through. Mysteriously, offering sympathy and comfort to someone else seemed the best way to bestow it upon oneself.

Chapter 22

Before leaving his court, Jacob blessed Pharaoh again. Then it was back on board the ships for the journey north to the city Asenath had resigned herself would be her permanent home. They stopped in Iuno only long enough to pick up Manasseh and Ephraim.

As soon as they reached Rowaty, Joseph provided food for his father and his brothers in amounts appropriate to the number of their dependents, including the smallest children, and acquired a generous amount of property for them. He gave the choicest land nearest the palace to Jacob, and to Benjamin and his wives.

That year, the famine became so severe, all the food had that had been stored up by individuals was used up, and throughout Kemet, people began to starve.

Joseph sold the grain he had stockpiled in silos throughout the Two Lands to Pharaoh's subjects, as well as to growing crowds of foreigners. The Horus Road was now heavily patrolled by the king's soldiers, and a temporary camp had sprung up outside Rowaty's city gates to prevent starving Retjenu from overcrowding the streets.

Asenath suspected the royal treasury buildings would soon need to be expanded. It seemed to her that Joseph was collecting all the money in Kemet, and the surrounding lands.

Pharaoh also came to Rowaty, with a large contingent of his militia. Instead of grain, Kemet was growing an army. Stiff ranks of soldiers were now as common a sight as sensually swaying fields of grain had once been. Senwosret led the way in his chariot while his troops, sending up choking clouds of dust, effortlessly carved a path between people walking wearily west as they marched energetically east.

Not long afterward, word reached them that Pharaoh had captured and plundered the town of Sekmem. Upon his return, Senwosret had a long conference with the vizier, after which Joseph met with dozens of foreign dignitaries who were now destitute, and forced to put their lives in his hands. Asenath remembered what Sithathor had whispered in her ear about her brother, "He is always thinking of himself." With his enemies weakened by the famine only Kemet had prepared for, it was easy for Pharaoh to take by force what wealth his enemies still possessed, leaving them no choice but to do as Joseph ordered them to, and bring him all their livestock as payment for food. In exchange for their horses, their flocks of sheep and goats, their herds of cattle, and donkeys, Joseph provided them with food for another year.

The following year was even worse. Asenath and Amunet were in the receiving hall when a group of men from the southern city of Djeba in Kemet said to Joseph, "We cannot hide the truth from you, my lord. Our money is gone, and all our livestock and cattle are yours. We have nothing left to give but our bodies and our land. Why should we die before your very eyes? Buy us, and our land, in exchange for food. We offer our land and ourselves as slaves for Pharaoh. Just give us grain so we may live and not die, and so the land does not become empty and desolate."

So Joseph bought all the land of Kemet for Pharaoh. Men sold him their fields because the famine was so severe, and soon all the land belonged to the king. The only land Joseph did not buy was the land belonging to the priests, who received an allotment of food directly from Pharaoh, so they did not need to sell their land.

Then Joseph issued a proclamation to the people, "Today I have bought you and your land for Pharaoh. I will provide you with seed so you can plant the fields, then, when you harvest it, one-fifth of your crop will belong to Pharaoh. You may keep the remaining four-fifths as seed for your fields, and as food for you, your households, and your little ones."

This proclamation was followed by a decree that, from that day forward, Pharaoh would receive one-fifth of all the crops grown on his land. Only the land belonging to the priests was not given to the king.

Asenath saw less of Joseph than ever before. When he was not occupied with his official duties, he was personally seeing to it that his brothers and their families were all settling comfortably in their new homes. She spent most of her time waiting—waiting for her husband to come home; waiting for the River to begin rising again; and waiting, in vain, for the sisters, wives and daughters of Joseph's brothers to pay her the respect due to her as the wife of the man who had saved all their lives. It severely injured her pride—and put her in a serious bad temper which began affecting her overall mood—that she could not include the honorific, "Daughter of the High Priest of Re" to her self-esteem when thinking about why she had every right to be upset that not one Hebrew woman had come to see her. They all seemed completely uninterested in meeting, much less getting to know, the lady married to the most powerful of Jacob's sons.

"Certainly they can't expect me to go to them!" she complained to Amunet when they were, once again, dining alone together. "And why do so many Hebrew men have more wives even than Pharaoh? Thank God Joseph is not like them, at least not in that respect. Yet even he does not seem aware that I am being insulted. Or do you think Hebrew women are simply shy? Perhaps they feel unworthy to cross my threshold?"

"I doubt it, my lady. It is much more likely they would feel contaminated if they crossed your threshold."

"Contaminated?!" She stared at Amunet incredulously. "*They* are the ones who would be required to wash themselves before I even considered letting them into my home!"

"I suspect they find it shocking the women of Kemet do not conceal their bodies from the eyes of all but their husbands. I have spoken to Khusebek about this, and he told me, reluctantly, that transparent and formfitting mist linen dresses, not to mention the fashion of exposing one breast, can incite lust in men, and tempt them away from their marriage beds, which is why Hebrew women cover themselves more modestly."

"Well, they must not be very confident of their husbands' devotion!" For a moment, Asenath felt better, because she had never been afraid Joseph would be tempted away from her, not even by the most beautiful of women wearing nothing except her jewels. But the next moment, she felt insulted again, and even angrier, for Hebrew women seemed to be implying the women of Kemet all dressed like prostitutes.

"I'm even more glad now that Joseph has adopted many of the ways of Kemet," she declared, "where most men are happy with one wife they truly love, and whose children do not grow up jealous of each other because their father favors one of their mothers over all the others. From now on, I will think no more of these Hebrew women than they do of me!"

"Joseph has sent scribes to their village to begin teaching the male children our language," Amunet informed her neutrally.

"I care not! Let us change the subject, for this one no longer interests me!"

"Yes, my lady."

"I desire to relax, Amunet. Please fetch my masseuse."

"At once, my lady."

Lying on her stomach, one cheek resting on her folded arms,

scented oils soothing her hot, dry skin as an occasional breath of wind helped cool her anger, Asenath tried to forget about the Hebrews. Instead, she found herself remembering—as vividly as a recurring waking dream—the morning Jacob had met Manasseh and Ephraim. As they appeared on the garden path, Jacob had looked over at the two boys and asked Joseph, "Are these your sons?"

"Yes," Joseph told him, "these are the sons God has given me here in Kemet."

And Jacob said, "Now I am claiming as my own sons these two boys of yours, Ephraim and Manasseh, who were born here in the land of Kemet before I arrived. They will be my sons, just as Reuben and Simeon are. But any children born to you in the future will be your own, and they will inherit land within the territories of their brothers Ephraim and Manasseh. I never thought I would see your face again, but now God has let me see your children, too!"

As the moon swelled and waned, so did Asenath's moods—bright and brimming with contentment when Joseph was home, as dark and sharp in his absence as the waning crescent. More and more, she suffered the impression that the land of Kemet and her own body were one and the same. She was not much surprised when a full year passed without the River rising again, and without any sign of life-nourishing blood flowing from between the banks of her thighs, which were not, she was forced to admit to herself, as slender and firm as they had once been. She had not expected to have more children, but it still came as a blow to know for certain she would never be able to surprise Joseph with another son. Although he had sounded perfectly satisfied and proud when he told his father, "These are the sons God has given me here in Kemet" she wondered now if there was more to this statement than she had realized. Did her husband hope there was a chance God would give him more children in another land?

Hours, days and weeks of tormented speculation followed as she wondered if Joseph would decide to take a second wife. If he did, she would undoubtedly be a lovely young fertile Hebrew woman who would be able to accompany him when God led his people out of Kemet. It was useless to remind herself this scenario made no sense, for God had promised Jacob that his people would flourish in Kemet, and they had only just arrived. The fear might be mostly imaginary, but the distress it caused her was real enough.

One afternoon, Joseph returned home unexpectedly. He announced his presence by diving into the pool where she was swimming, and frightening her half to death as, for a few heart stopping seconds, she feared a crocodile had had gotten past the gardeners. The low level of the River for so many consecutive years meant that animals and reptiles were hungrier than they had ever been in living memory, and those that did not perish were wandering far from their usual hunting grounds in search of food. Fortunately, however, it was not a crocodile's sharp jaws that caught her ankles, but her husband's strong hands as he yanked her to him, and weightlessly embraced her beneath the water before pulling her with him to the surface.

"The reports are in!" he declared, shaking water out of his hair like a dog as she delicately rubbed her eyes with the backs of her hands like a cat. "This year the River will rise again, and I will begin building our house!"

"But we are free to live here in the palace, Joseph."

"I know." Reaching down into the water, he gripped the backs of her thighs and lifted them up around his hips, forcing her to slip her arms around his neck. "But I want us to have a home of our own, Asenath. The famine will end, and the work Pharaoh's father created for me will be finished. I will then be able to do as I please, and it will please me to live in my own home, closer to my people."

Her heart—which had taken flight with joy at the thought that he would no longer be traveling up and down the River but would always be home with her—sank like a bird fatally struck by a stone.

"The palace has many rooms, but they are small," he pointed out after pausing to kiss her. "Our house will have only the rooms we need, but they will be larger and airier, and all will open onto a garden I will let you design, so that it as pleasing to your heart as possible."

Not dead after all, her heart fluttered in her chest, but though she tried to spread the wings of pleasure and contentment to share in her husband's soaring excitement, she found she could not. Still, she smiled, making an effort to raise her spirits with her lips, but the moisture in her eyes was suddenly hot. It was a relief when she saw Manasseh running eagerly toward the pool, and the conversation was drowned by his huge splash.

The River did indeed overflow that year, and the rejoicing in Rowaty lasted for many days. After livestock was herded together into higher and drier pastures, groups of celebrants launched reed boats that bobbed gently on the rising waters. At night, the lamp-lit party boats seen from the shore evoked great fireflies as they skimmed swiftly over the water on the current. Asenath was not as happy as everyone else. She could not forget she would soon be living even closer to foreign women who did not truly respect her. She was compelled to confess to Joseph how hurt and insulted she was by the fact that none of his brothers' sisters, wives or daughters had come to visit her. They were dining alone in their garden pavilion, and she had drunk more wine than usual, when she finally poured her feelings out to him. "I see no reason why you can't believe in God Almighty and also treat your women better," she said angrily. "Here in Kemet, if a wife is mistreated by her husband, she can declare the union forfeit."

"Are you feeling mistreated by me, Asenath?" Joseph's voice was quietly sober.

Lowering her own voice, she quickly replied, "No, of course not. My uncle was your master, but now I am your slave,

Joseph, for I love you so much, and so naturally I want your family to love me, just as I desire to love them."

"You are not my slave, Asenath, you are a free woman. And you know I love you."

What he failed to say resonated with a disturbing violence in the gentle darkness. "Joseph, I feel... I feel we must both be freed from the past we share..."

He had been staring down into his silver cup, but now he looked up. "What do you mean?"

Listening to the echo of her own words—which had flowed from her as words sometimes did in a conscious dream without her thinking about them first—she admitted, "I don't know. But just because I believe in Elohim doesn't mean I don't also love my country and my people, and desire they be respected by your people. I would, at least, like for them to believe that God Almighty sometimes speaks to me, a daughter of Re, in my dreams."

"You know I believe it."

"And that is why God made you the savior of your people, Joseph. If it were not for you, they would all have starved to death!"

After a moment's reflection, during which he seemed to consult the dregs in his silver cup, he said, "It is love which fed them, God's love for His creation. And our love, Asenath. Your innocent child's love for me even when I was a slave, and my reluctant fondness for you, which bloomed into love even when

I hated all you stood for."

"Forgive me," she begged softly. "I do not mean to complain, not on such a night as this, when we are together and two more dreams have come true. For everything has come to pass just as God told Pharaoh it would in his dreams."

The jubilant songs of frogs prevented the silence that stretched between them from feeling awkward as her thoughts drifted off to another subject.

"You know I have been corresponding with my father for some time now," she began, keeping her tone lightly conversational. "We have been discussing my eternal home. He has closely supervised its construction for me, and it will soon be ready for the painters. It is time for me to think about the scenes with which I will decorate it."

"I would think," Joseph said, rising abruptly and offering her his hand, "you would be more excited about decorating our new home, the one in which we will live together for many years to come."

"Of course I'm excited about that as well." She was glad of his support as her head spun from too much wine and intense emotion. "But you are also working on your tomb here in Rowaty, Joseph, so far away from mine, and I've been thinking... Maybe we can each paint a door in our tombs, a magical door. My door will open onto your house of eternity, and your door will open into mine..."

"You've had too much wine," he accused mildly, stroking her

hair. “But that's not a bad idea, actually. You are the greatest treasure in all Kemet, my Asenath.”

Chapter 23

Asenath wrote in her most recent dream papyrus:

Standing on the rooftop terrace of a stone temple as tall as the greatest pyramid, I'm looking through an open archway, beyond which Queen Sithathoriunet is seated close to the waist high wall, blue sky beyond her. Another indistinct shadowy figure is seated on her left. When I see her, my heart ignites with joy. The sister of my heart meets my eyes and smiles, but for some reason, I find this strange. Somehow, I know I am watching her from the future, so she shouldn't be aware of me observing her. By being conscious of each other, we are changing what already happened.

What occurs next is totally magical… Looking away from me, and staring straight ahead of her, Sithathor raises her right hand before her, her palm facing up toward the sky, and her index finger touching the ball of her thumb. She blows out her breath, and suddenly a bright golden star is shining in the spot where her fingertips are touching—a star from which shoots a ray of light that lances outward in a long narrow pyramid shape. At the same time, I hear a sound so loud, I almost seem to lose my dream hearing for an instant. And then she is gone! But she doesn't simply disappear. In her place remains a slender pillar of some incomprehensible force.

Turning to a man I have sensed standing behind me all this time, I say something to him about what just happened, and when I look back outside, I am overjoyed to see Sithathor sitting there again, smiling at me! Since this is a visual record of some kind—like a temple painting come to life except that it was already completely alive—the scene replays itself. Sithathor performs the same magical gesture, but this time when the pillar of force appears resoundingly where she is sitting, I discern vertical lines of color within its gray-black darkness. I comment on these lines to the presence behind me, and ask him if he saw them as well. He says he did not, and we discuss how Sithathor performed this feat. He tells me she was aware of the man to her left who raised a silver sword, and that even though she wasn't looking toward the sword, she sensed when it moved, and timed her gesture exactly with its motion.

It is all so incredible, I am not upset that Sithathor has apparently vanished.

Delighted as she was with this intriguing dream, it also worried Aseath, for she had not received a letter from her friend in a long time. So she was therefore devastated but not surprised when approximately three weeks later, word reached Rowaty by royal messenger that the princess and queen, daughter and wife of kings, Sithathoriunet, Daughter of Hathor of Iunet, had gone to her Ka.

There was no question of not attending the funeral, but when Joseph offered to go with her, Asenath heard herself saying, "You need not bother. I would be happier if you stayed here to make sure the gardeners follow my instructions, and that the correct tiles are placed in each of the pools. I know you're tired of traveling up and down the River, and-"

"Asenath," he interrupted her, "if you don't want me to go with you, just say so."

"I didn't say I don't want you to go with me, Joseph, I just thought you might like to stay home for a change."

"I would," he admitted, holding her at arms length as he studied her expression. "But are you sure you wouldn't rather I come with you?"

She gave him a reassuring smile and, shrugging her arms free, reached up to caress the soft black ringlets framing his face. "The only thing I'm sure of is that I love you, and I always will. And yet, I must admit, I preferred it when your hair was straight, and you wore it tucked back behind your ears. But your new robe is very nice. It reminds me of the one I saw you wearing in my first dream of you, although that dream robe was, of course, much more splendid, woven of such indescribably beautiful colors!"

She took her time packing, enjoying the oddly stimulating anxiety of planning her first journey alone. She was glad not to be taking the vizier's ship. She would have missed Joseph far too much if she had found herself alone in the cabin they had always shared. It was Amunet who accompanied her on a much smaller but well appointed boat, where they spent most of their time on deck beneath an open pavilion enjoying the changing scenery. Her emotions remained contentedly below the surface of her thoughts, except for when an especially delicious memory presented itself to her like a fish leaping out of her innermost depths into the sunshine of her mind. The journey felt well balanced and pleasing to Maat, for she was not looking forward to the funeral in Shedet, but she was happily anticipating returning home to her loved ones in Rowaty, the city she had been forced to accept as her home. Her sons were growing up faster than she could fathom, becoming their own persons and paying less attention to her, the woman who was just their mother and had always been there and—they were still young enough to believe—always would be. And between these two destinations was the center and the heart of her journey's imaginary scale—a visit to the house where she had been born, and where she would once again be the only child in residence. She was selfishly looking forward to having her parents all to herself again for a few days, without Manasseh and Ephraim hogging all their grandparents' attention.

It was very strange arriving in the capital without Joseph, where she could also not look forward to seeing Sithathor as soon as she washed and changed. It was only then that her friend's death fully hit her. Asenath realized she had expected her sadness to be lifted as soon as she reached the royal palace where Sithathor had always lived and, until now, never failed to be. Like a dog whose litter mate had died, she had hoped to find solace from her grief when she returned to the location where she and her best friend had lived and played together. What happened was the opposite—her loss struck her like a physical blow, and a sudden weight of regret that they had grown apart in the last few years forced her into bed the moment she reached her rooms. Amunet was left to supervise the unpacking, and to dispatching polite messages of greeting to the remaining queens and other important persons. Pharaoh was expected back in the capital any day now, fresh from yet another victory in Kush.

All the next day, Asenath felt as tired and depressed as she had before going to bed the night before. She had not slept well, and it was only the desire for fresh air on the rooftop that gave her the strength to rise, and call for her attendants. She had revived only slightly when she stepped outside, and breathed deeply of the North Wind, which seemed to blow more freely here than in Rowaty even though she was farther south. Before her was the sunrise, and behind her the blinding slopes of Senwosret Shines, the pyramid beneath which the sister of her heart would soon be sleeping. Apparently, Sithathor had forgotten that she had once told Asenath she wanted one of her poems inscribed on her heart scarab. Or perhaps she had not forgotten, but just changed her mind. There was so much about her friend she would never know.

Three days after the burial ceremony, on her last night in the palace, when the feasts honoring the late queen's immortal Ka were finally over, Asenath had another vivid dream she recorded in her papyrus once she was on board her ship en route to the City of the Sun:

> I dreamed I was sitting in a darkened room on a couch, and Sithathoriunet was sitting on my right. Joseph was somewhere behind the couch. Beside me, Sithathor was talking, smiling and relaxed, as we both held cups of red wine. As I sat there happily with her, it dawned on me very gently, coming as no major surprise, that she was visiting me, and was really there with me. I was seeing her quite clearly, and it felt perfectly natural to be sitting there with her. I found myself leaning closer to her, gazing at her profile and thinking, *Sithathor is here! She's visiting me*!
>
> I remember her talking about books she had read, or parts of books, and of how occasionally she came across a passage or a sentence that strongly resonated with her, and in which the author had succeeded in saying something very wise, something she could tell, without a doubt, was the truth. She seemed to be referring not only to great writers, but to writers who otherwise were not very good and yet who, a handful of times, "mined gold" from the dross of their otherwise unremarkable works, and those moments were what mattered.
>
> Smiling, Sithathor then turned to face me, and as we

gazed at each other, sitting even closer together, she said, "I want you to kiss me."

I was a little frightened of her then, and told her so. Her expression was affectionate yet detached, kind and yet also challenging. Her face was that of my friend, and yet also a stranger's face. I wanted to kiss her because I love her, so I leaned toward her lips, which were parted slightly. I was wary of the darkness I could see between them, more than a little afraid of what I was opening myself up to. But the kiss was brief, not the long scary affair I had been nervously anticipating.

"We will meet again," she said.

Glancing down at the space between our bodies, I had a very lucid thought. "Can you give me a dream sign?" I asked her. "Something I'll recognize in other dreams, so I'll know it's you? You don't really look like Sithathor anymore..."

No longer smiling, she sat up straight, and raking her right hand across her chest in a diagonal downward motion, stated firmly, "Sithathor is dead."

I woke abruptly in the dream (a false awakening) and whimpered, "Joseph!" He immediately got out of bed, and came to see what was wrong, but I murmured, "No, no!" intensely disturbed now as I had not been before. He lit a lamp, and as he slipped into bed with me, I told him that I had just dreamed with Sithathor. Then I woke for real.

☼

As soon as they reached Iuno, Asenath sent word to Joseph in Rowaty that she would be remaining in her old home longer than expected. She simply could not abide the thought of getting back on the boat. She had felt dizzy and nauseous the entire way there, and more than three weeks passed before she regained her equilibrium. It took her appetite even longer to recover. For a time, she was able to eat only fruit softened in milk accompanied by boiled vegetables, before graduating to bread with a little red wine and a few slices of roast fowl. One pleasing side effect of her indisposition was that she lost much of the weight she had gained over the years. Her body was now nearly as slender as it had been on the day she and Joseph first slept in each other's arms. She was looking forward to undressing for him again.

Being indisposed in her old home was oddly wonderful. With her mother fussing over her, she felt like a child again. She enjoyed her parents' concern a lot more, of course, once she began feeling better, and could properly relish being pampered. Amunet—and her faithful old servants, Ana and Ipy—always enjoyed their stay in the high priest's coolly palatial yet also warmly welcoming home. Although she missed Joseph terribly, it was no hardship for Asenath to prolong their stay in the City of the Sun. Her old nurse had gone to her Ka three years ago, but her husband was still living in the little house Aneski had been so proud of. Asenath was very glad she had visited them there.

Walking in her old garden one day, feeling marvelously content with everything, she wondered at this strong feeling of peace, and understood she felt perfectly healthy again. It was time to go home! But first she would enjoy one last stroll through her childhood Pleasure House, so rich with the bittersweet scent of memories her soul relished inhaling.

As she followed the central path, her eyes lingered here and there on flowers just beginning to bloom. Their colorful petals were so purely luminous, the sun seemed to be shining exclusively down upon each one. Struck by the fact that not a single flowerbed was in shadow, she looked up to check the position of the sun in the sky, and suddenly saw Kyky standing before her wearing an excited smile.

"Kyky!" she cried. "What are you doing here?"

"Waiting!"

"Waiting for what, Kyky?"

"For the Sun to be born!"

Asenath was about to remark that the sun was already in the sky, and always had been, but looking up she could not locate the solar disc, which should have been at its zenith. "I'm dreaming!" she exclaimed.

Her smile deepening, Kyky turned and began running down the garden path, which now extended for as far as Asenath could see, and was bordered by rows of immensely tall date palms. As she hurried after her childhood friend, green palm branches fell across her path. Surprised when she felt their sharp edges cutting into her feet, she looked down and saw that she was leaving a trail of blood behind her. She had never felt pain in a dream before, but she could not stop to think about that now. She had to keep up with Kyky!

Abruptly, she found herself crouching beside her friend on a white rooftop similar to the one from which they had watched a slave auction so long ago, only it was much larger—the rooftop of a palace or a temple. Directly beneath them, a broad flight of stone steps led up to a grand entrance portico, where stood a group of men clad in long white robes with bands of color around the sleeves and hem, except for the central figure, who wore a crow-black tunic beneath a large hat resembling a square version of pharaoh's double crown. He was facing a man in a red robe who stood apart from all the others, his arms bound behind his back... Joseph?!

"This can't be," she said out loud to Kyky, who had become a little girl again, her face streaked with dirt as she stared intently at the tableau below them.

No, the man was not Joseph, but she was sure she had seen him before. His black beard was clean and trimmed, his shoulder-length black hair waved gently down to his shoulders, and his seamless red robe fell to his ankles. He was not Joseph, and yet he was the man she loved. That was why, when she first saw him, he had looked like Joseph to her, because she loved him! Then she understood it was the other way around—she loved Joseph because he resembled this man, the one she truly loved, had always loved, and would love forever! She did not comprehend how this could be, but there was no denying how she felt.

She became aware then that the darkness below her was a writhing, living mass of people, and abruptly understood that she was watching some sort of judgment. She could see her beloved as if she was standing right beside him, yet her dream body was also somehow observing the scene from a rooftop. The crowd was roaring with what sounded like hatred. How was it possible they wanted to kill her beloved?! Her dream eyes were fixed on his face, where she saw every emotion she had ever experienced intensified to the point where it thrust straight through her heart into her soul... Strength and kindness, righteous anger and sorrow, resolution and resignation, determination and anxiety, patience and sternness, passion and tenderness, hope and despair... Feelings passed like weather fronts over the world of his features.

Suddenly, she heard a high-pitched ringing sound in one of her ears and, looking up, saw a great falcon soaring over the scene. But it was no ordinary bird, for between its massive wings she perceived a man's slender body. Then, with a colossal rumble of thunder, everything went black.

This sometimes happened in a conscious dream, all she had to do was remain relaxed and wait for her visuals to return. She would not wake up! If she lost this dream, she would lose the man she loved above all things, and the mere thought was inconceivable, so she kept her awareness focused directly ahead of her. Gradually, inexorably, the darkness lightened and she discerned, a mere breath away, the silhouette of a man's profile looking downward. Then she heard again that powerfully ominous rumble of thunder as it began to rain... but it was not rain... it was blood dripping heavily from the man's forehead...

She lost all visuals again for an instant before a full fledged dream scene appeared around her—a scene from her worst nightmare. She was standing waist high in the River, and both horizons were a darkly flaming red as if the sun, sliced in half, was setting both in the east and the west. And yet, though the day was dead, night did not descend. The crimson water frothed violently around her, but crocodiles had no trouble gliding toward her as she struggled desperately to fly away, raising her arms and willing herself to ascend into the wounded sky. But she seemed to be standing knee-deep in mud, and could not manage to uproot herself from the spot as, on the shore closest to her, she saw the hippopotamus goddess standing erect on her hind legs, the crocodile god Sobek draped over one of her shoulders. Dreadful as the sight was, it also reassured her, for she had been taught that Tawaret protects the soul in the supernatural womb of the burial chamber, where one form of life is destroyed so another may be born. Yet the terrifyingly real looking crocodiles were almost upon her, and when the one nearest her opened its jaws wide as it sank beneath the water, she screamed, "Elohim!" as a pain such as she had never known penetrated her like a thousand knives all wielded by vicious demons. “Oh God, save me! Please!”

The scene vanished, and her awareness floated in a soft white light for a few moments before she opened her eyes, and found herself lying on her back in bed.

Joseph was bending over her, tears dampening and flattening the curls of hair falling forward over his cheeks as he whispered, “My love!”

“Joseph? What are you doing here? And why are you crying? What has happened?”

“Do not leave me, Asenath. It is too soon! You are too young!”

“Leave you? I was only sleeping, and having the most amazing, fully conscious dream!” But even as she spoke, a serpent of dread slithered between her heartbeats as she became aware of a profoundly disturbing sound, an utterly hopeless sound—the sound of her mother weeping.

“Am I dying, Joseph? If so, I'm not afraid...” Praying to see again the man whose blood was the rain and the River, and whose power had saved her from the demons swimming in its drowning torrent—she closed her eyes while in her mind crying, “Elohim!”

The white light of the sun shone directly into her eyes, but she did not need to blink and look away. Experiencing the sensation of hot sand between her toes, she glanced behind her, and saw the open entrance to her tomb, which was nearly finished. Then she looked back up at the solar disc. Light poured from its bottom edge, and as it touched the sand transformed into a man wearing a brilliant white robe. The only shadows were his hair and the beard framing his mouth as it spoke her name, "Asenath."

She took a joyful step toward him, but something yanked her back toward the tomb, and suddenly she was lying in bed again.

"Let me go!" she begged. "He's waiting for me!"

"Who is waiting for you, my darling?" It was her mother, looking shockingly old, bending over her now.

"God! And He is so absolutely beautiful!"

"Is he?" A spark of hope flashed in Sadeh's bleak eyes. "What does God look like?"

"To me he looks like Joseph, and yet infinitely more handsome! I love Joseph so much because he reminds me of God. But I can never love anyone as much as I love God. I know that now, and He's waiting for me. He's standing just outside my tomb, mother. I have to go..."

Sobbing, Sadeh stood up, and Asenath saw her father leaning back against a wall motionless as a toppled statue. His handsome features, thinned by age, were sharpened now by grief to such an extent that she seemed to glimpse Re-Horakhty himself—a man with a hawk's face.

Filled with an invulnerable sense of well being, Asenath said to her parents, "Thank you for my life! We will see each other again! I will be waiting for you in the palace of the other world!"

Joseph quickly sat down beside her again.

"I love you!" she told him, sensing the dream of her life was about to end, and that she could do nothing to hold onto it. She was about to wake up forever. "Please tell our sons that I'll try to watch over them in their dreams. And ask them to please remember me, their mother, who was born a daughter of Re, but who now loves Elohim with all her heart, as I know you are teaching them to do, my beautiful brother."

"I will!" he promised, and kissed her.

The feel of his warm lips pressed against hers followed Asenath to a shore of the River, and a place she recognized, for she had seen it in a dream before she became Joseph's bride—the dream in which a man resembling her husband walked across the water to her. And he was still here, as if he had been waiting for her all this time! Joyfully returning his smile, she knew who He was now, and like a fish thrown back into the water, her heart, stilled by death, sprang to life again.

Offering her His hand, He said in a kind but firm Voice, "Follow me."

To learn more about the author, please visit:

Lucid Dreams and the Holy Spirit

Maria Isabel Pita was born in Havana, Cuba. Her family moved to the U.S. when she was eight months old, and she grew up in Fairfax, Virginia. Reading, writing and history have been her abiding passions ever since she can remember. In college, she majored in World History, minored in English Literature and Cultural Anthropology, and since then has traveled extensively. Maria is the author of the non-fiction *Lucid Dreams and the Holy Spirit,* and of the historical epic set in ancient Egypt, *Truth is the Soul of the Sun—A Biographical Novel of Hatshepsut-Maatkare*, the female Pharaoh, also available as a six-book series beginning with *Daughter of Re*. A member of the International Association For the Study of Dreams, and a regular contributor to the *Lucid Dreaming Experience,* Maria invites comments and questions on her Blog: *Lucid Living Lucid Dreaming*